ANOTHER COUNTRY

Karel Schoeman was born in the Orange Free State, South Africa, with which he has had close connections throughout his life, and which has formed the subject of several of his books, including *Another Country*. After living abroad for many years – most notably in Amsterdam, Glasgow and Ireland – he is now once more resident in South Africa.

He has published a number of novels in Afrikaans since 1965, and is regarded as one of southern Africa's foremost contemporary writers. He is also the author of travel books and television scripts, as well as translations, most notably from Dutch, German and Irish, important documentation on the Orange Free State, and, most recently, a study of the early life of Oliver Schreiner.

One of his previous novels, *Promised Land*, was published in English in 1978; it received excellent reviews and a number of prizes, and is now being made into a film.

ANOTHER COUNTRY

KAREL SCHOEMAN

Translated from the Afrikaans by
David Schalkwyk

PICADOR

First published 1991 by Sinclair-Stevenson Limited

This edition published 1994 by Picador
a division of Pan Macmillan Publishers Limited
Cavaye Place London SW10 9PG
and Basingstoke

Associated companies throughout the world

ISBN 0 330 32763 1

1 3 5 7 9 8 6 4 2

A CIP catalogue record for this book is available from
the British Library

Typeset by Rowlands Phototypesetting Limited, Bury St. Edmunds
Printed and bound in Great Britain by
Cox & Wyman Ltd, Reading, Berkshire

1

WHEN THE journey ended, he did not even know it: he was not conscious of the fact that they had arrived, and that the seemingly endless clattering and lurching, creaking, swaying and shaking of the coach had abated. There had been the unceasing movement of the carriage and the drumming of the horses' hooves, the cramped space in which he and his fellow passengers had been crammed together, the uncomfortable seat, the hand-luggage squeezed into every corner and cranny; there had been the heat, the glare of the sun on the lowered blinds, and the dust which surrounded them in a fine cloud, penetrating everything and settling in a white powder over people and baggage. How many days had it taken? Ten days, the driver had promised at the beginning of the expedition, but somewhere along the way he had lost count, and he did not know whether the promise had been kept or not.

They had struggled up the rises, clattered through the shallow waters of the drifts or over the rocky beds of dry streams, leaving the trees and green pastures of the coast behind and penetrating ever more deeply inland. They had ascended the heights of the great plateaus, observing no further signs of civilisation except white houses isolated among their trees, as unreal as mirages in the distance. The blinds flapped and fluttered and shook loose, the glare of the sun blinded him; the heat of the long days became increasingly unbearable as his fever increased, and the fine, sifting dust aggravated his cough: he fumbled in his waistcoat pocket for the box of pills with numb fingers, unable to grasp it. He drifted in and out of sleep or lost consciousness momentarily, dreamt restlessly, and awoke, always to find himself back in the same swaying, creaking coach, on the same bleached plain, under the same implacable sun. 'Look,' the man next to him said, and leant forward to push the flapping blind aside and to look outside, 'look, there's a vulture.' Already delirious from the fever and half-dazed,

1

he looked out and saw through the haze of dust, churned up by the wheels of the coach, only the expanse of the veld, the metallic dome of the sky. 'Do you see?' the man beside him asked impatiently. 'Look, there!' His finger pointed at the sky, indicating a speck in the distance: the bird floated motionlessly on extended wings, searching, waiting. He closed his eyes once again, but the image remained as a symbol of this alien land: the broad veld over which the bird of prey glides on outstretched wings, etched silently against the sky, waiting for its quarry.

The other passengers were chiefly men travelling on their own, in checked suits and with ostentatious watch chains, who smoked cigars and spoke amongst themselves about the diamond industry, commerce and the latest news from England: it had become clear to them shortly after their departure that he was ill. Consequently they had tried to avoid or ignore him, uncomfortable in his presence with their rude good health and their loud self-confidence. There were a few other younger men, shop assistants or clerks, who had silently listened to the conversation of the others and obligingly laughed at their jokes, and two young girls on their way home from boarding school, but they too paid no attention to him. The only fellow passengers who did take any notice of him were the middle-aged Jewish couple who were returning from a family visit to Germany, with their travelling-rugs, fans, cushions and picnic basket, fully armed against the discomfort of the long journey, and the English teacher – early on the journey he had woken from his restless, delirious slumbers to see her leaning over towards him to offer him her flask of smelling salts, her eyes fixed somewhat worriedly on his face. The Jewish woman had insisted that he take one of their cushions behind his head, and her husband leant forward laboriously to adjust it for him, grunting in the packed, lurching carriage. At the stopping places it was this couple who took pity on him, helping him out of the coach and making sure that a place was made for him at the table, and that he was given something to eat. He could, however, not eat the food at the inns and the farm houses: he noticed the Jewish woman and the teacher talking softly to each other and looking in his direction. On one occasion, he remembered later, the man had sat next to him with a bowl of soup and had tried to feed him with a spoon, like a child – 'Come,' he had said kindly, 'come, you must eat something.' He had been conscious of the man's small hairy hands and his gold rings; he'd turned his head from the greasy soup. That must have been towards the end of the journey. Later – was it minutes or days later? – the man had tried to

2

dribble brandy into his mouth from a small flask. 'Come on, take heart,' he had said, 'just one more day and we'll be home.'

Days and hours, however, meant nothing to him any more: fever and delirium had taken over. Shuddering, jarring and jolting in the lurching carriage, with its flapping blinds, its cramped space into which they were all crammed, hot, clammy and unwashed, exhausted and stiff, he felt the long journey would never end. White with dust, full of the mingled stench of sweat, eau de Cologne, smelling salts and brandy, their coach seemed trapped on that dead plain under that high sun. They were going home, he thought to himself in one of his last moments of clarity; but he was being carried further and further, more and more deeply, into an alien country.

The motion had ceased; the fever and confusion had ebbed, leaving him weak and exhausted. He opened his eyes to the light, and lay for a long time looking at the patterns, trying to decipher them, before he realised that they were marks on the white wall of the room in which he found himself. The wall he could recognise, and slowly he began to explore the whole room, finding a chair and a wardrobe, and then he discovered a door, half-open, with a black woman on the threshold. She was staring at him from under the scarf which was bound low over her eyes. Motionless they gazed at each other, and then she turned as if to flee, and he heard the padding of her bare feet on the mud floor.

Time passed; he slept and woke up again, saw the white wall and the door and a woman standing there, a white woman wearing an apron, her hair done up in a tight bun, who observed him with suspicion and then approached the bed hesitantly, the apron held up slightly before her as protection. What she was saying he could not understand, her words both strange and familiar, and it took some time for him to realise that she was speaking Dutch with a strong German accent. 'Are you awake?' she asked, scared, and he nodded, but that was all that he was capable of, and he drifted back into unconsciousness.

The patterns on the wall had changed when he looked at them again, because now a candle burned on the bedside table, casting shadows on the uneven plaster. A stocky, bearded man with glasses stood beside him, putting something back into a leather case. 'So,' he remarked, 'you have returned to the land of the living. How do you feel?'

3

'Weak,' he answered, his voice apparently too soft to be heard. The doctor – for the man appeared to be a doctor – merely muttered to himself.

'You were ill, very ill. What prompted you to set out on a journey in your condition? You ought to be at home, in the care of your own doctor, not roaming about here in the wilds of Africa.' He expected no answer, however, and, casting a quick glance over the bed, he took up his case and prepared to leave. 'You must try to get better, it will take some time – milk, if you feel like some, soup, a drop of brandy if you need it. I have told Frau Schröder, she will see to it.' Then he thought of something else and approached the bed again. 'Do you have any money?' he asked. 'Can you pay for these things?'

He ought to take exception to the man's bluntness, he thought, but not now. 'I have money,' he said, and something in his tone nevertheless made his displeasure apparent.

'I need to know,' said the doctor. 'Otherwise we will have to make arrangements.' He had his top hat and his case in his hand. 'I'll be going now. Frau Schröder will call me if necessary.'

He gathered his strength to try to formulate one more question before the man disappeared. 'Where am I?' he asked.

The doctor turned and looked at him. 'You're in Bloemfontein,' he said, 'you've arrived. Bloemfontein was your destination, wasn't it? When somebody with a lung complaint boards a passenger coach they're inevitably coming here – we are used to taking the dead and dying off the coach; you are not the first person to be carried unconscious into this hotel. But it doesn't seem to me that you intend to join the corpses, even though I believed at first that you didn't stand much of a chance.' He showed a trace of a smile, and his eyes were not unfriendly behind his gold-rimmed glasses, in spite of his brusque manner. He made a vague gesture of farewell in the direction of the bed with the hat that he held in his hand, and left.

Days passed; night and day succeeded one another. From time to time he heard voices in the distance – random phrases or incomprehensible sentences somewhere on the other side of a courtyard or at the end of a long passage, or confused men's voices and laughter, a door slamming, the sound of breaking glass. He discovered from Frau Schröder that he had been carried unconscious from the coach into a hotel, and when she discovered that he could speak German she stayed for longer periods in the sick-room, even if she kept her distance from the bed and retained her suspicion of the stranger who had been brought in to die under her roof. Once he heard the sound of a men's

4

choir, accompanied by a piano: it was the German Lieder group which gathered there every month, she informed him, and he drifted between sleep and wakefulness to those distant, well-known folk songs full of memories, lulled by the discovery that what had been left behind was not as distant as he had thought.

But then again the land surprised him with the heavy roar of thunder and the clatter of hail on the corrugated iron roof of his room: a thunder storm, Frau Schröder said, tugging nervously at her apron. They had had a good summer, Doctor Krause told him on his next visit, it had rained well, but the hail had damaged the fruit trees. He discovered that his room looked out on to a narrow passage and a wall; daylight reached it dimly and indistinctly, and news of the world outside came to him indirectly, tidings from afar which had to be carried by messengers. He heard the call of voices in a foreign language and the shuffling of the servants' bare feet on the clay floor; a black man came to empty the slop-pail from time to time, hesitant before the sick stranger, smiling whenever he was greeted. This country is indeed alien, he realised; seas and continents separated him from all that was familiar, in spite of all appearances.

One day, on a chair opposite his bed, waiting patiently for him to wake up, he found Herr Hirsch, the merchant who had cared for him on the never-ending journey to this place, and who now smiled genially at him. 'I have come to visit the sick,' he cried. 'You may well ask why I have waited so long, but our good doctor has not considered you ready for such exertion up to now. Consequently I have had to be content with enquiring from him as to your daily progress. Nevertheless, I have not forgotten you, and my dear wife also sends you greetings and wishes you a rapid recovery – and, something of greater practical value. . . .' He jumped up and grasped a basket which lay to one side on the floor. 'Peaches from our own garden, late peaches – Free State peaches, of the best in the world – and a bottle of Moët: Doctor Krause assures me that it is exactly what you need to put you back on your feet, and, at the same time, despite your less happy arrival in Bloemfontein, to make you feel that you are welcome among us.' Beaming with health, with wellbeing, with goodwill he sat opposite the bed, legs apart and hands on his knees, a smile on his bearded face; the signet rings, the watch chain, and the tiepins glinted in the dim light of the room. 'And if you should require anything else in which we could be of service during this short period of discomfort until you have sufficiently recuperated – if, for example, you should wish to write letters. . . . There are friends in the Netherlands, perhaps, who

5

need to be informed of your arrival, business connections. . . .' He sat there expectantly, eager to be of service.

After the long period of silence, the long withdrawal, he once more had to involve himself in conversation; out of this silent territory bridges led back to the other bank, to the world of other people, of letters and messages, gestures and obligations. He had to return, but lay considering the move for a while, with Hirsch sitting opposite the bed, smiling at him encouragingly. 'No,' he said at last. 'No, thank you very much, there is no-one who needs to be contacted.'

For a moment Hirsch looked at him more intently, as if, behind the smile, he was busy considering, summing up and passing judgement, but when he spoke again his voice was as easy and his tone as carefree as before. 'If there are any other arrangements with which I could help – I know that you are a stranger in a strange country, and if I who live and work here – as I have done for nearly thirty years – and who have contacts and acquaintances, could be of service with anything. . . .'

Back across the bridge to the old, familiar bank, to the well-known country, to life that had in his absence continued its uninterrupted course. 'I can draw bills of exchange at a local bank,' Versluis began, but Hirsch cut him off with a rapid, dismissive gesture.

'When you are back on your feet I will introduce you to our bank manager. In the meantime, do not be concerned, everybody here trusts you.' There was another moment of silence, and then he leapt up. 'But I propose that we start at once with the cure; why wait?' He was already easing off the wire around the champagne cork, making rapid movements with his small, hairy hands. 'I will just drink one glass with you – to your health; then I must get back to my shop. But there will be all the more left in the bottle to help you while away the afternoon in the sick-room.' The cork shot out, champagne foamed and was caught with a napkin from the basket. 'It is of course not quite the condition one would prefer it to be in, but it has come a long way – from Europe by ship, and then to us by ox wagon, and you know yourself how long and tiring that journey is. I must also concede that it is not as well-chilled as it would have been in Europe, but I hope you will take into account that it is now mid-summer and that ice is an unheard-of luxury here in Bloemfontein. You will simply have to accept our good intentions and make concessions for Africa.' Two flutes appeared from the basket and the wine was poured out foaming; a glass was pressed into his hand. 'To your speedy recovery,' Hirsch

6

said, nodding at him with a smile, his own glass raised. 'And to a long and pleasant stay with us.'

They drank: Hirsch tasted the wine, considered it, and then wiped his moustache carefully with a handkerchief. 'I repeat, you merely have to give the word if there is anything that could make life more pleasant in your unfamiliar circumstances – it will be a great pleasure for me to open an account for you, and to obtain from elsewhere anything we do not have in stock. A single line, a note sent with one of the servants. . . .'

Versluis felt himself already beginning to grow dizzy from the warm, foaming champagne after going so long without drinking. He felt firm ground under his feet, and the perimeters of the world that he had left behind so long ago were becoming dimly visible to him once more. 'Perhaps . . .' he began slowly, and at once the little man stopped and leant over the bed in an attempt to hear what he had to say, and to help. 'If you would be so kind – my shaving equipment and other washing utensils are in my valise, and some clean linen. Perhaps you would. . . .'

Hirsch was already on his knees beside the case. 'With the greatest of pleasure; you should have spoken before – I should have thought of it myself.' He undid the catch of the valise, and while he spoke he busied himself with the articles that he withdrew from it, placing them in the wardrobe or chest of drawers with rapid, precise movements, as skilful as a valet. 'The rest of your luggage will of course follow by transport wagon; it takes longer, but it will be here by the time you are up, and then we'll attend to it and restore some order to your life after the disruption of the journey and this troublesome sick-bed.' Books, a writing-case, and a travelling alarm clock were placed on the bedside cabinet; containers for collars and cuff links; toilet bottles; a razor and shaving soap; a shaving mug and strop; clothes brushes; handkerchiefs; gloves; ties; shirts and underclothes, all packed so long ago, were taken out. And without interrupting the fluency of the conversation for a moment, Hirsch considered each object with a quick, discriminating glance, made an appraisal, and finally approved of the grand total: the small, hairy hands with their glittering signet rings lightly stroked each article of clothing or utensil as they packed it away, full of appreciation for the quality of the linen or silk, the value of the silver, leather or crystal.

'On the other hand I feel that I really ought to try to reassure you about the country in which you now find yourself. My dear friend, possibly you think that you have made your way to the outskirts of

7

civilisation, and after the exhausting journey that you have had to endure to get here, that would be entirely understandable; but I can assure you that that is not the case. Of course we lack many of the comforts and refinements that in Europe are taken for granted, and we are confronted by many problems that would be completely alien to you, such as droughts and dust storms, hail storms, beasts of prey and locusts, and the extreme isolation in which we live of necessity. But we are not entirely beyond the bounds of civilisation, we manage to keep Europe alive here in the heart of Africa. We can get champagne here – I don't have to try to convince you of that any longer – together with the best wines from France and Germany, and for special occasions our good friend Frau Schröder can prepare an excellent meal in celebration. We have a reading room where one may peruse the finest periodicals from Europe, a lending library, and a literary society, and some of our ladies have formed a reading club to study the great masters of world literature. We have a choral society and give excellent concerts, and if your taste is for something lighter, there are balls that last till dawn with women as elegant as any that you will find in Europe. You can play croquet here, and tennis; we have a gymnastics club, you can ride, and each year we have races that attract people from all over the country. And finally, if I may be personal, when you have recovered a little, you will be very welcome in our home; my own carriage is at your disposal for exploratory ventures into the district, and my wife and I would regard it as an honour to accompany you.'

The valise had been unpacked: his small, bearded face beamed as he stood at the end of the bed. 'But I must be tiring you,' he said. 'You want to rest and recover your strength, and I must return to my affairs – the shop was run by the clerk for long enough while we were abroad, and it is personal supervision that ensures the profits, is it not? I'll put the bottle on the cabinet beside you, within reach, so that you can finish it at leisure. And with that I'll leave you to the care of the good Frau Schröder and our capable Doctor Krause. My friend, I bid you farewell for now.'

He quickly re-filled the glass on the bedside cabinet before he left; on the threshold he turned with a raised hand and a wink, and then he was gone, the fall of his quick footsteps becoming silent down the passage. Exhausted by the visit and volubility of the visitor, Versluis lay back on the pillows without reaching for the glass of champagne beside him. It must be late afternoon, he thought, reminded for the first time that life was progressing outside this room where the light reached him only indirectly, reflected off the wall outside his window, and where he had unthinkingly come to accept the succession of lamp-light and candlelight, daylight and darkness. The usual duskiness of the room was deepening and the silence thickened around him like swirling water. Somewhere a man called; somewhere a door slammed and glasses tinkled. Beyond this enchanted circle of dusk and silence in which he was trapped, life carried on; the afternoon sun shone on the streets and squares of the city which he had not yet seen and which he could not even picture; walls reflected the full brightness of the sunlight and retained the heat of summer; in the orchards the peaches were ripening; Hirsch was back in his shop talking to customers and clerks.

The water rose, grey chilliness surrounded him, the bedclothes engulfed him. A sudden, inexplicable panic gripped him, and with a strength he had not thought himself capable of he flung the blankets from the bed so violently that the champagne glass was knocked from its cabinet and smashed against the floor; he swung his feet over the edge of the bed and tried to stand up. The single violent gesture was all that he could manage, however: exhausted by the effort he remained seated there, breathless and in a cold sweat, and he had to hold on to the edge of the mattress with both hands to stop himself from falling, to force himself not to lose consciousness, embroiled in a battle with body and spirit while an eternity passed.

He opened his eyes and saw the room in which the dusk of the late afternoon was deepening; he saw with a particular revulsion the thin white legs that protruded from his nightshirt and the shards on the floor at his feet, together with the damp marks where the champagne had spilled. He wanted to *live*, he thought with a last surge of energy, as exhausted as a bather after a battle with the surf; and then he collapsed backwards on to the bed.

Frau Schröders's hesitance and distrust gradually abated – with a corresponding change in the attention paid to him: without his asking for them, more pillows were brought in, and the candle in his room was silently replaced with a paraffin lamp. At first he assumed that it was because he had begun speaking German to her, but gradually he realised that it was rather the ivory brushes and toilet bottles with silver tops on the chest of drawers that had evoked this increasing friendliness. She came to his room more often, remaining there to talk or to offer some service, reassured about his ability to pay for it; she was an angular woman with her hair done up in a bun, and with a flush of excitement on her high cheekbones whenever she engaged him in conversation. Perhaps when he felt a little better, she suggested, he would like to change rooms? At the moment nothing else was available, but she had a fine, spacious single room looking out on to the street. And with a wooden floor, she added, as a final enticement. But that would be later, when he had a bit more strength and could cope with the move.

Doctor Krause droned into his beard as if humming some unrecognisable refrain, and examined Versluis. Frowning, he listened to his patient's heart, tapped his chest and back, and then continued with his indistinct muttering while he packed his instruments into his case. 'It seems that nothing can stop you,' he remarked. 'You have decided to get better, no matter what the medical profession has decreed.'

Versluis smiled to himself. 'If I had wanted to die, I could have done so in the Netherlands, Doctor. It would not have been necessary to undertake such a long journey.'

'Was it your doctor in the Netherlands who advised you to come here?'

'They advised me to move to a better climate. It was my own choice to come to Africa.'

Krause remained standing in thought, his hat in one hand and case in the other, as if he could hardly spare the time to stay and talk. 'So I see that you attach no value to doctors and their advice. Oh well, perhaps you are right, it has apparently paid off in your case. You must have been pretty far gone when you left the Netherlands – you were as close to dead as they come when they carried you out of the coach – but you were determined to live and here you are, still lying before me today. At the moment there is nothing more that I can do for you. Carry on with the diagnosis and treatment yourself – as a matter of fact, I believe that such things are to a certain degree within the patient's own control: only to a certain degree, mind you; after that you no longer have any choice, but that is another matter, about which we may be able to talk later. Anyway, you won't see me again, unless you send for me.' He was already on his way out of the room, as abrupt as always, without any farewell, as if he had suddenly thought of other, more important matters which commanded his complete attention. 'You will now have to decide what to do with your life, since it has been restored to you so unexpectedly,' he added, and was gone.

He wished to continue living where he had left off, Versluis thought: he wished to get up, he said to Frau Schröder, who flushed with excitement across her high cheekbones as she told the servant to bring an armchair to the room and to call the barman – a young German with rolled up shirtsleeves and an apron who was summoned to help from behind the bar counter. He looked around the room suspiciously, uncomfortable in the presence of illness and weakness with his fine young figure and brawny arms.

Versluis discovered that he was weaker than he had thought. He had hardly raised himself from the bed before his legs folded beneath him and he began to fall, so that he had to clutch like a drowning man at the barman, who caught him and half carried, half dragged him to the chair. With humiliating clarity he became aware of the impotence of his body, his gasping for breath after this tiny effort, the crumpled nightshirt that had not been changed in all the time that he had been ill, and the stench of his unwashed body; and at the same time he became conscious of the young man's lack of comprehension and his indifference to the weakness of the invalid, probably mixed with contempt for such helplessness.

Exhausted he fell into the armchair that had been placed for him, overwhelmed by a fit of coughing, while the barman stood self-consciously with his hands at his sides, waiting for further instructions. All he could do, however, was nod in thanks, and the young man turned around and went back to his bar. This was merely the first step, Versluis reminded himself as he sat doubled over after the bout of coughing had subsided, head on his knees, and then slowly raised himself to carry on. He needed to shave he said to Frau Schröder, who was still fussing eagerly about the room, his voice so weak that she could not even make out what he was saying. No, he would not like any tea, he assured her, just hot water and his shaving things; he was impatient with every objection and attempt at delay which hampered his return to life. She still shook her head. He was still too weak she assured him, he would not even be able to hold a razor, but when she noticed how much her resistance upset him, she gave in. She undertook to send for Gustav once more, and it was indeed the young barman who returned with water and a towel and mechanically began to sharpen the razor without a word or a glance at Versluis. Accustomed as he was to being shaved by a valet or barber, Versluis nevertheless felt uncomfortable about the service rendered to him slowly, carefully, and a little clumsily, by this silent young stranger, with his tongue clenched between his teeth in concentration, its point just visible between his lips; once again he was aware of the man's lack of interest in what he was doing and his suppressed scorn for the sickly middle-aged visitor whose toilet he had to take care of; once again he

11

was aware of Gustav's physical presence with his youth and his strength, the white, muscular arms under the rolled-up sleeves, the thick neck and the low forehead over which the hair had been carefully combed in waves. Feeling humiliated by the awareness of his own helplessness in comparison, Versluis could, however, think of nothing to say and at last it had become impossible to start a conversation. They maintained an uncomfortable silence in the silent room until Gustav finally stepped back, razor in hand, his task completed.

'I must change into something else,' Versluis then said with difficulty. 'There is a clean nightshirt in the wardrobe. If you would be so kind. . . .'

Gustav fetched it: mechanically and apathetically Versluis was helped to pull the old nightshirt over his head, and he let it fall on to his lap in order to cover his nakedness while he was assisted into the clean one. He would actually also have liked to have washed, he realised, uncomfortably aware of the stickiness and dirtiness of his own body, but he could not ask the other man to perform this intimate service, even if he were not too exhausted to attempt to say anything more. The dirty nightshirt remained in a heap on the floor; Gustav removed the dish of shaving water, and not long after that Frau Schröder entered with a tray. 'I have made you some tea,' she informed him more cheerfully than usual. 'Did Gustav give you a good shave? He is in a hurry this afternoon. There is a dance in town this evening and my husband has said he could go, he will look after the bar himself.' She giggled at the prospect of the entertainment in which she would have no share herself, and bent down to pick up the nightshirt. 'I'll fetch you some clean linen; just a moment.' She had already begun to strip the bed. He had returned from the dead, Versluis thought to himself, the cerements discarded. Frau Schröder bundled the soiled nightgown, crumpled sheets and pillowcases together: he was once again being recognised and accepted as a human being, his features recognisable to all; he had revealed himself as a traveller with a pigskin toilet case and little flasks with silver tops, as a man who could give orders and pay for whatever he consumed. He had become himself again.

The distinction between day and night became apparent once more, between patterns of light and dark and nuances of dusk and shadow: he recognised a growth and diminution in the intensity of the light reflected from the wall outside the window of his room, and variations in the succeeding days became discernible. On Saturdays there was an increased rowdiness from the bar, to which Gustav and Herr Schröder

12

had to devote their full attention, with the result that Frau Schröder managed the hotel on her own and was not to be seen. Sunday, on the other hand, was a day of sudden silence, noticeable even in the isolation of that back room, with the distant tolling of bells in the morning and, later on, Hirsch's smiling face which appeared around the corner of the bedroom door.

'So, up yet?' he asked. 'I heard the news and came to see if it was indeed possible, but it is – congratulations, I rejoice in your good fortune.' He stepped from behind the door and entered the room, a basket in his hand. 'All of my Christian friends have betaken themselves to church, and since no opportunity exists for the handful of Hebrews that we have here to celebrate our religion, on either Saturday or Sunday, I have decided to devote myself to the visitation of the sick: something which is also pleasing in the eyes of God, as we were taught as children. But I do not offer only my company – *voilà!*' He had put the basket down on a chair and now removed the napkin which covered it. 'From my wife, with her best wishes, a dish of chicken soup which may help to stir your appetite. And from our garden, a humble posy, just to show you that we are not without such delights, even if we do live here at the edge of the desert – a pledge, my friend, such as Noah's dove brought to him in the ark.' He glanced quickly round the room and put the posy into the ewer on the washstand – 'Until the good Frau Schröder is able to arrange it for you. And finally, I have brought you a few newspapers, copies of local dailies from the past few weeks, although I don't know if you'll be interested in what they contain. As far as news from abroad goes it will of course be old news, the news, to tell the truth, that travelled with us on the ship, and the South African reports will probably not be of much interest to you. Sir Barkly, President Burgers, Sekhukhune, Cetshwayo – what would these names mean to a newcomer in our midst? But if you'll allow me. . . .' The basket had already been placed on the ground and a chair drawn closer. 'A few general pieces, a synoptic article, a letter from a reader concerning some or other interesting topic – if it will not be too tiring, I'd be happy to read to you for an hour or so.'

He sat down and took out a pair of gold spectacles, opened a newspaper and, with his back to the window, spread it out to catch the dimly reflected daylight. His delivery was fluent and lively, even if he read Dutch and English with the same heavy German accent, and he clearly enjoyed giving this little performance. From time to time he would interrupt the presentation with a remark or observation of some sort, an explanatory or contextualising comment on the form of

13

administration in the Cape Colony or the political and financial problems of the Transvaal, or an explanation of an allusion to local conditions or of an English word which Versluis may not have understood, and then he would look up from the newspaper and observe Versluis with the same quick discernment with which he estimated the quality of linen, silver and leather. He expected no reply, however: he sat there relaxed, one leg placed across the other, the newspaper spread out widely before him to catch the daylight, and after an hour he folded it up in as relaxed and easy a manner and got up.

'I hope that I have afforded you a little diversion without tiring you too much, and to have effected some degree of contact between you and the outside world. I hope that it will not be too long before you are able to explore it for yourself, and I would even venture the hope that our next meeting may possibly take place in our own house. In the meantime I can only repeat what I have already said, if you should happen to be in need of anything, I am entirely at your service. *Au revoir*.' And he was gone. The stack of newspapers and the tureen of soup that he had brought remained on the bedside cabinet, and on the washstand the flowers were a bright show of colour; the scent of eau de Cologne that surrounded him lingered for a long time in the close, slightly musty hotel room.

Frau Schröder, buttoned up stiffly in her black Sunday dress, brought in a vase and put the flowers into it with abrupt, clumsy gestures. 'Indeed,' she remarked, 'if you have you own well, it is easy to keep a garden – particularly if you have time for such things. Of course they have enough water to soak the garden all day, those Hirsches – he has clerks to whom he can entrust the shop if they feel like going away, he has blacks to do all the work, their house is full of servants, his wife never lifts a finger except occasionally to make a little soup or a pie.' Her disapproval was clear, and it was equally apparent that she had no time for such trivialities as gardening. But then her face softened for a moment as she stood with the vase in her hands. 'They do have a beautiful garden,' she conceded, 'a flower garden and fruit trees. You should see it.'

The flowers remained there for a long time, bright, formal zinnias and marigolds. At the first signs of fading, Frau Schröder made a show of removing them, but he stopped her: so that every time she came back into the room she would glance disapprovingly at the dying flowers, but he kept them on the cabinet for as long as the colour could be seen in the petals.

Apathetically Versluis paged through the papers that Hirsch had left behind, looking at the columns of advertisements; the announcements of auctions and insolvencies; the death and marriage columns; the notices of cricket matches, horse-races and concerts; the names of places totally strange to him and of people whom he could not at all place: the first, sketchy topography of an unknown country waiting to be explored, shadowy indications of streams, hills and towns.

The land waited, the withered flowers on his bedside cabinet were merely an indication of gardens, orchards, plantations and parks which he had not yet seen, a reminder of the existence of a new and strange life out there, like the sounds that reached him from time to time along the corridor, voices, laughter or the banging of a door.

Joseph the black servant could fetch water for him from the well, Frau Schröder said, whereupon the man dragged a hip bath into the room and carried the water to him in buckets slung from a yoke, shuffling with his bare feet across the clay floor. Smiling and willing even though they both were, it was only with difficulty that they made themselves understood, the formal Dutch of the foreigner and the broken idiom of the servant being equally unintelligible to each.

He was reluctant to ask for any assistance and in fact wanted none: he undressed, and with small, careful movements he began to wash himself while holding on to a chair with one hand. The process was a laborious one, and he lay back exhausted in the armchair when Joseph returned to throw out the dirty water, but he had succeeded. From then on he had the man bring him water every day, and he also began to shave himself, even though at first his hands had hardly the strength to hold the razor. Day by day he could mark his progress, and he noticed that the weakness and the attacks of fever, the bouts of coughing and the shortness of breath were diminishing. He began to dress himself, even though at first he merely remained sitting in his shirtsleeves and slippers, without any energy for the battle with his collar, tie and shoes. One of these days he'd be able to come to the dining room for his meals, Frau Schröder observed encouragingly.

The few books that he had packed for his journey lay on the cabinet beside him, but he still found it difficult to concentrate on the words, so he finally took up the papers which Hirsch had left him once again, paged through them, read whatever article happened to catch his attention, and gradually became acquainted with such names of places or people that appeared regularly: the names of holders of office, of firms and shops, of attorneys, auctioneers and agents. Strange words which he encountered in the English or Dutch reports became so

15

familiar that in time he was able to gauge their meanings from the context. I have recovered he thought, when one day he succeeded at last in pulling on and tying up his boots. He would get up and visit the dining room, he would explore the hotel, would go out and see the town for the first time. He would see to his affairs, and perhaps look for alternative accommodation. The flowers that remained, wilted on the washstand, he had Joseph throw out.

He had dressed himself and was still standing beside his chair, his hand resting on the back, when there was a knock at the door. It was not the knock of Frau Schröder or Joseph; Hirsch would not have waited outside for an answer, and Doctor Krause, while he still called, had hardly taken the trouble to knock before entering. It must therefore be a stranger, and when he had called out and the man had entered, Versluis recognised him as a clergyman even before he had said a word, something in his bearing and manner as unmistakable as his white tie and slightly dusty black suit.

The visitor remained standing in the centre of the room. 'I hope I am not disturbing you,' he began, leaving the sentence unfinished, as if he would have preferred Versluis to take over and continue the conversation. He *is* a clergyman, Versluis observed again, conscious of his palpable subservience, his almost too-eager friendliness. He was nevertheless still inexperienced, a young man with a narrow, lively face and poorly cut hair which stood up about his head in untidy tufts; his suit was not merely dusty but also slightly worn, his shoes shapeless, and, standing like that in the middle of the room, he gave an impression of uncertainty. 'I am Pastor Scheffler of the Lutheran Church,' he then continued, confirming all Versluis's own conclusions. 'I must apologise for turning up here so uninvited, so unannounced, but Mr Hirsch asked me to call on you. Dominee Radloff of the Dutch congregation is on sick leave, and the church services are being conducted by a visiting minister, so at the moment there is no-one to look after the Dutch congregation in Bloemfontein.'

It struck Versluis that he had not been required to be sociable for some time, and it was with some effort that he prepared himself to talk to this unexpected guest. 'That is very kind of Mr Hirsch,' he said, 'and of you, too. Won't you be seated?'

The clergyman looked about him hesitantly as if he felt that he would rather not commit himself to staying, and then he drew up the upright chair which he found in the corner. 'We naturally heard of your arrival, it is a small community and everything that happens soon becomes common knowledge, but I knew that you were being cared for by Doctor Krause, and that he would inform me if I were needed. Have you recovered completely?'

'As you can see I am up and about again. I still feel weak, but I am entirely active – it was just a passing indisposition, exhaustion after the long journey. . . .' But then his voice died away. He realised that he was no longer accustomed to long conversations, and he was already beginning to feel tired.

'In the last few years we have been getting many invalids from other parts here in Bloemfontein, especially from abroad, and there have often been surprising instances of recovery, especially in the case of chest and lung complaints.' The pastor looked at his hands, the tips of the fingers pressed firmly together. 'In a number of cases,' he affirmed pensively. 'Our climate can perform miracles, it seems.'

'Or Providence, Pastor,' Versluis added drily, realising too late that such sarcasm was out of place; the clergyman, however, accepted the rebuke meekly.

'Yes, of course,' he agreed after a moment, still concentrating on the tips of his fingers. 'But I am sorry; I didn't wish to come here prematurely, so I waited until I heard that you had begun to recover a little. Nevertheless, I am sorry to have left you to your fate in this way. . . .' As he spoke he became confused, caught up in his own words. 'I mean, it couldn't have been pleasant for you to lie in this room on your own. It must be lonely for you, here in a strange city, a strange country. . . .'

He would like this young man to deliver the last of his platitudes and leave, Versluis thought, but at the same time he realised that it would not be easy to end this visit. 'I have actually grown completely accustomed to this room, Pastor, simple as it may be, and the loneliness hasn't bothered me. I am accustomed to being alone; it's not something that I find a problem.'

At these words the young man looked up quickly, as if Versluis had said something that had caught his attention. 'Are you fond of loneliness?' he asked, 'Do you like being alone?' The brightness of his gaze was disturbing, and however innocent the question, Versluis could not help drawing back slightly from such presumption, bothered by this sudden interest and the directness of his visitor's response.

'I have learnt to occupy myself usefully and pleasantly,' he answered dismissively at last. 'I have brought some books with me, and Mr Hirsch has been kind enough to supply me with a few newspapers.'

'I noticed your books,' the clergyman said. 'May I look? Do you mind?' But without waiting for permission he put out his hand to the

17

books that lay on the little table beside Versluis, his bony wrist exposed for a moment beneath the cuff, and picked them up with a kind of eagerness, his head bent low over the pages as if he were afraid that a word would escape him. 'You read Latin?' he asked. 'For me they were unfortunately just school subjects, Latin and Greek; I never really became involved in them. All I know is that I am missing something, a lack. . . .'

'I have always found Virgil a great solace,' Versluis said. 'My Virgil and my Montaigne always accompany me, to be read on journeys or at night when I lie awake.'

'I have a small library myself,' the clergyman said, with more enthusiasm than he had shown in the conversation so far; 'books that I received from my father, and some that I brought back from Germany after studying there, but there is so little time for reading, there is never enough time. When I get a chance I try to read a little Italian,' he added. 'As best I can, with the help of a dictionary.'

He was still looking at the books in his hands; he examined the title pages, paged quickly through them and caressed the worn bindings, and when he had finished his examination he did not put them down, but remained sitting with the little pile in his hand as if he had forgotten to give them back to Versluis.

For a while they sat opposite each other in silence. 'I assume that you are not a member of the Lutheran Church,' the clergyman finally began hesitantly.

'I am not a member of any church,' Versluis answered carefully, lest the words should sound too sharp, although he suspected that he would be able to bring the visit to its desired end in this way. 'I did not mention it to Mr Hirsch; in any case I did not think it necessary, otherwise he would certainly not have troubled you on my behalf.'

The young man looked at the books on his lap, his head slightly aslant, as if he needed first to consider the answer, but without any sign of surprise at this information. 'It is perhaps difficult for us to realise how strange the Christian world must seem to our Jewish friends,' he said slowly at last – 'Mr Hirsch undoubtedly assumed that for you as a non-Jew, I could, also as a non-Jew, be of obvious assistance.'

'Mr Hirsch's intentions were no doubt good. Indeed, I have received nothing but kindness from Mr Hirsch and his wife, both on the journey here and since I have been indisposed.'

'These tiny differences and distinctions and nuances are important only to us,' the clergyman continued thoughtfully, as though he had not heard Versluis's last remark. 'To an outsider it would surely be unintelligible for the two of us really to have nothing to say to each other, or that there should be nothing that I could do for you.' He emerged from his musing. 'Mr and Mrs Hirsch are noted throughout the Free State for their charity,' he said. 'For their active charity. By which, I could add, they unfortunately surpass many of us Christians.' He dutifully added the final sentence and continued to stroke the worn covers of Versluis's books. Then he put them back on to the little table, slowly and unwillingly as if it bothered him to let them leave his hands unread. The visit had ended, Versluis thought with relief; but the visitor made no move to get up and, sitting on the edge of his chair, he again looked at Versluis with that questioning, almost pleading gaze, his deep blue eyes fixed upon the other man with a disturbing frankness. If he had been searching for some final words of comfort or upliftment he did not find them; possibly he sought encouragement for himself, a young clergyman doubtless not long ordained, sitting on the edge of the chair in his slightly worn, black suit and dusty, thick-soled shoes. Perhaps in this uncomfortable situation he was the one who needed guidance, Versluis reflected with some surprise, this uncomfortable young man whose hair stood up in tufts about his head, subverting the seriousness of his office and his dark suit.

'I'm sorry,' the pastor then began suddenly. 'I would like to do something for you, however small. I'm sorry that I can offer you nothing that you might need.'

The spontaneity and the simplicity of this confession was so surprising that Versluis could not immediately find the appropriate words, the proper gesture with which to respond to it: the visitor was an unpredictable and even disconcerting young man, nothing in whose experience had prepared him for a social occasion of this kind he thought. Then the clergyman smiled and passed his hand with an impatient gesture through his hair, so that it stuck up even more untidily. The narrow, serious face brightened, and he was no longer a man of the cloth on his rounds but a young man unable to deal with this situation, aware of his own clumsiness but without any desire to hide it. 'I am not very good at this kind of thing,' he said with a smile, 'not even when I know what people want and they make things easy for me.'

'I'm sorry if I don't make things easy for you,' said Versluis, 'but I can assure you that I neither want nor expect anything from you. You need not reproach yourself.'

19

'But that's not what I mean; I don't necessarily want to read to you from the Bible or pray with you, not if you have no need for that sort of thing. I would like to be of service in some or other way because you are on your own here, a stranger in a strange country, in this hotel room. . . .'

A tactless young man who hadn't sufficient experience of life to cope with his own good intentions, Versluis reflected wearily, and again he wished that the visitor would get up and leave. 'I appreciate your kindness,' he said, but the pastor was not listening to what he was saying.

'I studied in Germany,' he said suddenly, as if this were an answer to some unasked question, an explanation upon an implied reproach. 'I was born here, in this country; my father came here as a missionary, but my parents sent me back to Germany to complete my education, and I later also received my training as a minister there.' His face became serious once more as he thought about it, a young minister of a small, struggling congregation – underpaid, inexperienced and uncomfortable – sitting on the edge of the kitchen chair before this stranger whom he had visited out of a sense of duty. 'I grew up here, but I am sometimes aware of how strange this country must seem to someone who comes from elsewhere, like you. I don't just mean the countryside –' His seriousness caused him to stammer slightly once again as he searched for the words with which to express his thoughts; '– rather the whole way of life, the whole course of events here in Africa.' He stared pensively at the floor. 'When I came back I did missionary work in Bethany at first, that's the mission station where I grew up, where I know people and speak their language. But two years ago a European congregation was established here in Bloem-fontein, and I was transferred here, the people here needed me more than those at the mission station.'

Why did this young man consider it necessary to furnish all this unsolicited information? Versluis wondered; why was he pouring out all these particulars as if he has been waiting all along for an opportunity to share them with someone? He had himself not given the slightest indication that he wished to hear all this, yet the young man continued without any encouragement.

'I became committed to the needs of my native congregation,' he said. 'The demands of Europeans and the expectations that they have of me are still strange to me, I have never been able to adapt myself wholly to them. I'm afraid there are many things which I ought to know, but which I still need to learn.' The plainness of his meaning was as disarming as the bright gaze of the blue eyes which still rested on Versluis.

'At least you have the benefit of your European education to fall back on,' Versluis remarked, without knowing precisely what he was saying, while he leant back in his chair. But the clergyman shook his head.

'No,' he said, 'it doesn't help me, that is exactly what I am trying to explain, that's precisely the problem. This is no longer Africa, but nor is it Europe any more. There are too many different worlds existing side by side, and finally there is no single world in which one feels at home or in which one knows how to conduct oneself; that is what I wish to apologise for now. I either know too much or too little, never enough and never the right things; there is no hope for me.' He shook his head ruefully and smiled, and then he bent down and felt under his chair for his hat which he had put down on the ground. 'But be that as it may, if you ever feel the need to talk, or if there is anything else with which I could help you. . . .' He got up, hat in his hand, he looked about the room and searched for words with which to say farewell. 'You presumably intend to remain here with us for a while yet.'

'I came here to recover from an illness,' said Versluis, 'and I suppose that I'll be here for some months. I have no firm plans.'

'Then we'll probably be seeing each other again – it's a small community, as I have said before. And if there is ever anything. . . . The parsonage is next to the church, just across the bridge, to the left as you go up the hill, anyone will be able to direct you.' He glanced around, looked at his hat, hesitated, and still did not leave.

Versluis could only bow his head in acknowledgement and get up himself, going through the motions of politeness which he had almost forgotten in his weeks of illness and isolation. 'It has been very kind of you,' he said, and then, in his weakened condition, he had to support himself on the back of his chair to remain standing.

'The arrival of a visitor is always a great event,' the clergyman remarked as if he had not heard. 'We are no longer as completely isolated as we were a few years ago. The discovery of diamonds has brought many people here into the interior, and in the past year or two there have also been many invalids from elsewhere who have come, like yourself, in search of health. It is nonetheless a small community, an isolated community, very dependent on its random contacts with the outside world. The arrival of every mailcoach, of every passenger-coach is a great event for us. To us every visitor is a welcome guest.'

21

Why was this man prolonging his visit? Versluis wondered impatiently; why did he keep on talking when he could in all propriety say farewell and go? He was much weaker than he had thought, and felt himself tiring as he remained standing – facing the clergyman who still lingered with his hat in his hand. The visitor, however, remained oblivious of this fact. 'If I may ask,' he added somewhat embarrassed, 'you didn't perhaps bring some magazines or newspapers with you from Europe?'

Versluis lowered himself once more on to his chair, without trying to explain or excuse his action. 'I'm sorry, Pastor, but I left such reading matter of that kind as I had with me behind on the ship. I did not think there would be any purpose in bringing it with me.'

The young man bowed his head. 'I was merely asking out of interest. One no longer has much opportunity to see such things, and one wants to remain in touch, or at least to maintain a modicum of contact, one doesn't want to perish entirely. . . .' Again he glanced about the room as if his attention had been diverted, and he did not finish the sentence completely: something remained unexpressed as his eyes roamed across the hairbrushes, the clothes-brushes, and the toilet-flasks without taking them in. Finally he laughed lightly. 'Sometimes one feels that one is in the process of dying of something.' He added, half to himself, 'Without being able to say precisely what it is.'

'How long were you in Germany?' Versluis asked when the clergyman went no further, closing his eyes as he leant back in his chair.

The question appeared to surprise him. 'In Germany? Oh, six years – really not that long when considered as part of a man's life, but I nevertheless find that I sometimes yearn for it, or at least that there are things in Germany that I miss. And strangely enough, when I was there, it was Africa that I longed for.' He smiled to himself at the memory, and then it appeared to strike him that he had stayed long enough. 'I won't keep you any longer,' he said. 'I have perhaps taken up enough of your time.' His hand was extended in a gesture of farewell. 'But if there happens to be anything – even if you were to need something to read. . . . My library is small, but it is at your disposal, you are always welcome. . . .' Once again he cast that quick, absent-minded look about the room, then he nodded and without further ado hurried out.

After the clergyman's visit Versluis remained seated in the chair and waited for the worst of his tiredness to abate: the young man had left so suddenly that he had not even had the time to get up. It was good to be left alone once again in the stillness of the dusky, close little hotel room, he thought, although he gradually became beset by a sense of disquiet. He had not undertaken the long journey for this – the empty room, the regular peal of the bell, the patter of rain on the windows, the tap of ivy. These were things that he had left behind. The bare winter garden and the rain-soaked trees. In this land it was summer: they had sailed to meet the sun, and across the equator they had entered a new world: they had appeared on deck in summer clothes and with fans in the cool shade of canvas awnings they had tried to obtain some relief from the growing heat. The shuffling of the servants' feet over the clay floor and the sound of their voices outside in the passage; the servile vowels of a strange language: these were signs that he had set foot upon a new land, that he had embarked upon a new life.

He stood up and moved through the room, he opened the door which the clergyman had closed behind him, and remained standing there for a moment, leaning on the door knob. The passage stretched blindingly to the door through which the midday sun fell, sharply reflected off the mud floor and whitewashed walls, and slowly, almost light-headedly, he walked through the dizzying light into the day at the other end – to the courtyard from which the glare of the sun rose up at him and from which he could hear the sounds of daily life. Hesitant, exploratory, supported by the wall, he edged towards the heat and brilliance of the summer day.

To him Bloemfontein was a name about which he had made no assumptions and concerning which he had harboured no expectations: a city to which he had betaken himself in blind faith from the other side of the world, the destination of the coach on which he had reserved himself a seat, the final goal of his journey.

It gradually took on a reality for him as a town of dust and heat and long, straight streets; of black watercarriers and of dogs and slow, irregular traffic; of narrow strips of shade along the buildings where people sat on the stoeps or stood in doorways in their shirtsleeves to stare at him. And every time he went into the streets Versluis was aware of the detached curiosity that he aroused: a tall, thin, middle-aged man in the clothes which he had brought with him from Europe; with a hobble in his gait, so that he had to put his full weight on his cane instead of carrying it lightly in his hand, slightly unsteady on his feet when he was overcome by dizziness from the heat; a stranger who could immediately be recognised as such in this tiny community. Across the empty stretch of the market square he walked from the hotel to the bank, blinded by the white glare of the daylight that rose up at him. Regular streets extended on all sides of him towards a low white church or to the white tower of a public building, or they ended in emptiness, in nothing; and above him the sky was a wide, undisturbed dome filled with a glare and heat that hurt his head and his eyes. He soon learnt to avoid the heat of the day and to go out in the cool of the early morning or late afternoon in order to see to such simple business as he needed to settle, or for quiet walks, supported by his walking stick – unhurried sight-seeing trips during which he occasionally stopped, leaning on his cane, to look about him or to catch his breath.

Shops with scales in front of their doors and wares stacked on the stoeps: trunks, buckets, saddles, zinc baths, blankets, and boots tied up in bundles; auctioneers' offices, and the shiny brass plates of attorneys or the bank. Uneven streets of stone and gravel, and dust that rose and remained suspended in a fine white haze after the rider or vehicle had passed; white walls that reflected the light and brick walls amongst willow trees, peach and fig orchards, dry-stone walls behind which gardens lay concealed and houses that sheltered in the shade of wide verandahs and creepers. A street made its way up a hill in the shade of bluegum trees, to the top where the battlements of a fort were outlined, the white-and-orange of the national flag bright against the sky – this marked the end of the town, and at the top he turned and saw it all laid out before him: a few regular streets around a market square, with the white tower of the government building and the silver roofs and chimneys of the houses amongst the bluegums, willows and fruit trees. About him lay the veld, all around an emptiness swept far out towards the distant hills and a few even more distant mountains etched dimly against the horizon. Even the sounds of the town – the shouts, the hammering, the tinny peal of a bell – had died away below him: silence and space and solitude surrounded the little community with its brave show of trees and smoking chimneys, its fluttering white-and-orange flags on the flagstaffs, its schools and churches and all its trivial activities, its business, the offloading of wagons and fetching of water from the communal wells.

In the languid silence of the day a single vehicle, a hooded cart or a spring wagon, would pass by, with a clink of harness and the thud of horses' hoofs; and one day, from a victoria with a black driver on the box, Doctor Krause raised his cane in silent greeting, and remained for a long while leaning out around the hood to inspect Versluis across the increasing distance between them. Women crossed the streets under the protection of their parasols, holding up their dresses with one hand to stop them from dragging in the dust; men stood talking together, formally dressed in dark clothes in the heat of the day, and broke off their conversations to stare as he passed. He overheard fragments of conversation in English, and the inscriptions on shops windows and name plates were also in English; in the streets children called to each other in a language in which he sometimes recognised Dutch words, and blacks spoke the same mutilated Dutch that Joseph from the hotel used. In the dining room where he was now taking his meals at the long table with the other hotel guests, the general conversation was in English, with the occasional German thrown in, and authentic German dishes were served under Frau Schröder's watchful eye by German waiters. In the lounge there were dog-eared issues of week-old English newspapers from the Cape, and month-old periodicals from England and Germany.

The kind of life that he found in Africa was much like the one that he had left behind in Europe, Versluis thought to himself as he leant on his walking stick to rest in the shade of some willow trees, or when he returned gratefully to the accustomed gloom of his room. It was in any case a reasonably convincing imitation at the furthest reaches of the world, beneath a more relentless sun and alien stars, upon such dismal and desolate plains, and in the first days of his acquaintanceship with his environment he could not suppress a certain feeling of disappointment. Was this why he had embarked on his long journey, to find in an alien world a reflection of his own familiar one, only without the comforts and refinements to which he was accustomed?

The heat, the dust, the blinding light, the sweat which ran beneath the rim of his hat down his forehead and made his clothes cling to his body, the English which he could not always follow easily and the crude Dutch which frequently irritated him: all kept breaking into the more familiar pattern as disturbing reminders of Africa. In the mornings he would open his eyes to find his view stopped by the bleak off-white wall, and for a moment he would not know where he was: hearing the servants outside speaking to each other in their own language and the shuffling of their feet over the clay floor, he would experience a moment of disorientation and panic, conscious of the strangeness of this situation, and then it would come to him once more that he was in Africa.

The dust, the heat and the glare of the day overwhelmed him whenever he went outside; the narrow leaves and dry red berries of the pepper trees quivered lightly in the heat. The square in front of the hotel was filled with ox-wagons for the morning market, and as he moved among the people he saw pumpkins stacked on the tables and corn-cobs in bags, dishes of butter and eggs, a dead buck with its neck broken and a pool of dried blood that had formed on the ground under its mouth. Wagons brought goods from the country, and as he walked past the slow, swaying teams with their wide horns he heard the cries of encouragement or censure from their drivers; he saw farmers conversing together in little groups, and the silent farmers' wives with their faces concealed behind the pokes of their bonnets; he saw barefoot black children wrapped in a fragment of blanket, and in the shade of a shop wall a black woman lay motionless on the ground suckling the baby on her lap.

Unpleasantly taken aback Versluis turned away from this unsavoury sight, and then realised that it was obscene to no-one else. I am in a foreign country, he thought. I am indeed in a different land. And in his gloomy, viewless room, into which he withdrew again, still easily exhausted by the crush and the noise, he retained the slight thrill of excitement that this observation called up, as suddenly and inexplicably as the aversion which it had evoked the previous day.

In the cool of evening he often climbed the ridge against which the town lay, attracted by the height and the distant views that it afforded him, even if he found the incline tiring and often needed to stop and catch his breath; past the last houses, past the little monument on the brow of the hill, with the fort on one side and the cemetery on the other, the tombstones hidden from the eye by a stone wall, he could sit resting on a rock without being unpleasantly conscious of the closeness of the graves, his back to the town that he had left behind. Here he could gaze out over the wide panorama to the south. It still disturbed him as it had the first time, although he would not himself have been able to account for his uneasiness. The emptiness extended as far as the horizon – either greyish-brown or a dull gold in the changing light, or turning grey in the haziness of the evening – beneath a sky from which the colours of the sunset flamed with a growing light. Only from the deck of a ship on the open sea, after the last bit of land had vanished below the horizon, had he seen any desolation like that of the plain across which he now gazed. He saw an empty expanse waiting for something to happen, a surface that had never been described, unmarked by any house, tree or sign of life.

The land disappeared into the gloom as he looked at it; the hills to the west were etched black against the sky. He had not yet grown accustomed to the sudden darkness of Africa, nor to its intensity, and it seemed wiser to return to the hotel while the last of the fading light was strong enough to show him the way back. In any case he knew that it was not sensible for him to linger outside in the night air, but as he stood up he remained looking out over the dark land, at the blaze of the sky. This was another country, he realised again; it was a new domain, and its emptiness held immense promise, its darkness was charged with mystery.

He sent Joseph to Hirsch with a note of formal thanks, folded double, and an acknowledgement arrived within a half an hour, informing him in a firm, rapid hand that they would pick him up for a short sight-seeing tour on Wednesday afternoon at five o'clock. And at the appointed time a landau drew up in front of the hotel with a coloured coachman on the box and the Hirsches inside; the carriage had scarcely drawn to a halt before Hirsch had leapt out and rapidly approached Versluis to enquire after his health, congratulate him on his recovery, and convey him to the vehicle where Mrs Hirsch awaited him with a smile. Talking all the while, Hirsch had appraised him with a single quick glance, determining with approval the cut of his jacket, the quality of his gloves and the authenticity of the gold band on his cane; it was an appraisal so automatic and inconspicuous that Versluis could not take umbrage, and had the jacket been of poorer quality, or the gloves of stuffed cotton, the couple's geniality would presumably not have been affected. They insisted that he get in beside Mrs Hirsch, while Hirsch himself would ride at the back. Should they not put up the hood for him; was the sun troublesome? They would ride through the Kloof, where it was shady now, and the afternoon was already growing cooler. They had thought that he might enjoy a short ride outside the town, so that he could see something of the surroundings – it would surely not tire him? Amien would drive carefully. Amien always drove carefully, Mrs Hirsch added as a light warning: he had never had an accident – 'in five years, not so, Amien?' Hirsch called to the driver. 'Or has it been six already? We brought him with us from Cape Town when we returned from our last visit to Europe, we brought a landau there and came back to Bloemfontein in it.'

'But never again!' cried Mrs Hirsch, laughing under her parasol.

'No,' her husband assented, 'a month on the road in an overloaded vehicle! After that even the passenger coach from Port Elizabeth is not that bad. But in any case, we fortunately kept Amien on after that episode, and he has been with us ever since.'

27

'He is a Malay,' Mrs Hirsch, who was sitting beside Versluis, confided, and leant over slightly towards him. 'He is not one of the local people.'

The man on the box sat very upright in the shelter of his wide, funnel-shaped hat, whip in hand, and showed no sign that he had heard, nor any inclination to answer Hirsch's question.

They left the town and rode across the veld with the shadow of the landau beside them in the light of the setting sun: a misshapen vehicle on elongated wheels drawn by horses with long, extended legs. In the direction in which they were heading the hills lay half in shadow and the road fed into the cool gap between them, beside hillsides covered with little bushes and small, distorted trees which Versluis was unable to identify, and which released a pungent, wild scent into the late-afternoon air. Once again he was aware of a fleeting sense of strangeness, before he was forced to shift his attention from the landscape to his hosts. Hirsch was as good-humoured as Versluis had come to expect from his visits, and he talked casually and gaily about everything as it occurred to him, so easily and amusingly that his conversation became neither tedious, nor his person obtrusive; while his wife continually interrupted him with exclamations, interjections and her merry, cooing laugh. She was no longer young and the smoothly-gathered hair beneath her hat was beginning to show a good deal of grey, but she had the carefree, round face and the liveliness of a young girl excited by the outing, her husband's conversation and their guests's company. From time to time she leant across to Versluis to whisper something, as if the remark were meant solely for him and however trivial her words, the gesture was clearly intended to be a sign of confidentiality and trust – to make him feel that his company was appreciated and that some words were for his ears only. On the swaying suspension of the landau the tassels of her parasol bobbed rhythmically together, the flowers on her hat and the ribbons which bound them vibrated lightly, and the gold earrings danced in her ears. Radiant, she leant back in the seat; in the folds of her mauve dress replete with bows and frills, a reticule, a flask of perfume and a lace handkerchief were gathered on her lap in one plump hand, while the other held the ivory handle of her tasselled parasol.

Together the couple talked of the town and its inhabitants; of the country, its customs and its climate; of their own lives, their family and their recent journey abroad, apparently quite content to enlighten their guest in this way without expecting anything in return – not even that he contribute to the conversation – and without giving the

28

slightest indication that they wanted him to provide any information about himself in exchange. Inviting him, driving out with him and affording him some sort of diversion appeared to be quite sufficient for them. He thus abandoned himself to the rocking of the well-sprung vehicle – for the coachman did drive carefully along the stony track which ran through the hills – and to the stream of anecdotes which gushed from the Hirsches as they laughed and gesticulated and interrupted and put each other right.

They had begun to talk about Hamburg and Kassel and Hanover, about family visits and meeting people again after many years in the alien country, about the changes that they had seen during their stay in Germany and the adaptation that had been necessary both on their arrival in Europe and their return to Africa. Had he ever been to Hamburg? Mrs Hirsch enquired, leaning slightly towards him once again to ask the question, so that he caught the scent of her eau de Cologne, mingled with the dust and the strange, pungent smell of the local bushes and shrubs. Did he know Sonnenschein, the jeweller in the Jugfernstieg? Her cousin was married to Julius Sonnenschein. Then her husband began talking of the six weeks that they had stayed in Hamburg, about art galleries, concerts and restaurants.

The road left the pass through which they had driven and now skirted the long, low rise that lay to one side of them. They were still in shadow, for among the hills the light was obscured from them, but in the distance the land still lay stretched out in the sunlight – slightly hazy as the day drew to an end, the drabness of the plains softened to a dusty gold and the few mountains on the distant horizon to the east an almost unreal blue, their usually clear outlines almost totally erased. After the gloomy confinement of the Kloof the sudden revelation of this expanse bathed in light was all the more dramatic; blinded by the lustre of the sunlight and light-headed before that spaciousness, Versluis forgot for a moment his courteous duty to attend to his hosts' conversation, but they took no notice. Hirsch engaged in a humorous account of their experiences with the cab-drivers, while his wife offered additional details. They considered the landscape which extended before them unworthy of their attention: they took it for granted, this space which surrounded and held in its setting the tiny, familiar reality of their lives, but which neither touched nor influenced it in any way.

Then skirting the mountain, they returned to the town, rocking on the suspension of the landau, and with the coloured coachman erect and motionless on the box. They had considered a visit to Berlin, the Hirsches remarked, the city had of course changed a great deal in the previous few years, since the establishment of the empire, but they had nonetheless decided against it in the end. He had been to Berlin as a young man in '44, Hirsch said, just before he had come out to Africa. Her husband had taken her to Paris for their honeymoon, his wife added. Whoever had thought of going to Prussia in those days? As a matter of fact they had spoken French almost as often as German, although she had forgotten a great deal during the years in Africa.

The day had hardly begun to soften before there was also a change in colour: the sun, unseen behind the hill along which they rode, was disappearing below the horizon and the light fell in a deeper glow across the plain, while the shadows through which the road carried them grew more intense and the sky lighter and more rarified. The colour changed from moment to moment: it deepened, lingered briefly across the veld, and already it had begun to die away; the earth havered between dark and daylight and then toppled into dusk. 'We chose our time well,' Hirsch said approvingly as he opened his pocket watch. 'We fitted the journey in precisely. The Free State may not have very much to offer by way of landscapes, but we have managed to let you see something of our surroundings.'

'You'll be eating with us tonight,' his wife informed Versluis, as if it had already been arranged long beforehand, and she thrust the vial of perfume and the handkerchief back into her reticule. 'We won't bother you – you'll be able to relax. You can sit in the garden if you like.'

'The grapes are just beginning to ripen,' her husband added, and the conversation passed almost imperceptibly into a discussion between the two of them of domestic affairs, their guest forgotten for a while.

Versluis leant back against the upholstery of the vehicle and gazed at the changing colours of the landscape which had for incomprehensible reasons begun to fascinate him so. He was tired after the long journey, and would have preferred to have gone back to his hotel room, but he could not properly refuse the invitation. Besides it did not matter much, for the conversation was undemanding, and so he allowed himself to be carried along by the hospitality with which the Hirsches had embraced him, as if it were entirely natural for them to shower their benevolence in this way upon a total stranger.

They returned to the town where the dirt roads which meandered across the veld met in a small knot of streets, houses and trees: children stood at garden gates; a man sat on a stoep; two black women crossed the square with buckets balanced on their heads. And they were back. The vehicle stopped in front of a low, unpretentious white house which had been built directly adjoining the street. A servant appeared to open the door and help them out. He should sit in the garden where it was cool, Mrs Hirsch called out before disappearing into the gloom of the house, from where Versluis could hear her calling gaily to servants or children. He should come and sit in the garden and enjoy the cool, Hirsch repeated and led him inside.

In the half-dark he could distinguish nothing, but he suddenly became aware of life and movement surrounding him in the series of interlinking rooms which he was unable to discern: of voices and footsteps, laughter, of someone singing and playing the piano before the closing of a door dampened the sound, the creaking of floorboards, the clicking of high heels and the rustle of dresses.

'The garden isn't looking bad this year,' Hirsch said. 'Although it's about time we had some good rain. Water is what one needs in this country, and fortunately it's been years since we've had a bad drought.'

'The children have turned the house upside down again today,' his wife, who had gone to return her reticule to her room and had also come outside, added with a smile. 'You mustn't take any notice of them.'

'But it is nevertheless an old garden,' her husband continued, 'an established garden – almost thirty years old, that's a long time in this country. I began at once; while they were still erecting the house I had planted the trees and the orchard. It makes all the difference.' He remained staring across the garden for long time, hands behind his back. 'But, I'll go and open the wine for tonight meanwhile,' he added, and disappeared without another word into the house.

'Another half an hour, and then we can eat,' his wife called after him.

After the motion and activity of the afternoon it was suddenly quiet, with Hirsch's lively monologue suspended for the first time and the bustle of the young people in the house muffled by the shutting of the door: Versluis stood in silence with his hostess on the high stoep, looking out over the garden. On the uncovered stoep there were canvas chairs and pot plants, partly sheltered by a pergola, and nearby stood syringa trees and a few formal flowerbeds, but the largest part of the garden was taken up by vegetables and an orchard where the shadows of evening were beginning to grow amongst the trees.

As he saw her for the first time without a hat, Mrs Hirsch seemed younger than ever to Versluis; she stood beside him on the stoep with the little gold earrings that danced whenever she moved her head, and smoothing down the folds of her dress with a gentle, preoccupied gesture. She had enjoyed the afternoon's outing with the light-heartedness and exuberance of a schoolgirl, but it was over and she was back in the serenity of her home. Her children were laughing and singing in another room, her husband had gone to fetch wine for the meal, her servants were busy in the kitchen, her flowerbeds had been watered, and the whole of her little world was once again under her watch and her control, while she herself felt content in the tranquillity of the evening.

'It's a beautiful time of day,' she said pensively, only half addressing the words to her companion. 'Everything is always so severe in this country, the heat and the storms in summer and the frost and snow in winter, the droughts – there are so seldom moments like this. Very early in the morning perhaps, at dawn, when the dew is still on the ground, and then at this time of the evening – particularly at this time of the evening, I have always thought.' Lost in thought, as if she had forgotten completely about Versluis's presence, she descended the steps that led to the garden, her dress held up with one hand, and then she turned around suddenly and smiled at him, her attention focused completely upon him once more. 'Shall we take a walk in the garden while it's still light?' she asked. 'Or would you prefer to rest after the journey?'

The Hirsches' continual concern about his possible exhaustion irritated him, however well-intentioned it might be, as if they doubted his recovery. 'I would love to take a walk with you,' he thus said, and followed her into the twilight of the garden.

'My husband takes no interest in flowers,' Mrs Hirsch said, and gave an understanding laugh. 'Trees he'll plant, and fruit trees, but it's the vegetable garden that interests him. Virtually our whole garden is given over to vegetables. And what's more, he has conjured it out of absolutely nothing, Mr Versluis. When we were first married – when I first came here – there was nothing – bare veld from our back door to Thaba Nchu, with only a few small trees that looked as if they would never take root. All day, all day long a black man walked back and forth from here to the well with buckets of water to water them, and that was all the work he had to do. I never thought that I would be able to sit in the shade of our own trees, or walk under our own vine. Just look how fine the grapes are this year.'

'It must have been difficult for you to adapt to this place,' Versluis said.

'Difficult!' she cried in confirmation, and again laughed her carefree maiden's laugh. 'Each day I would weep and long for Germany. This country seemed to be an enemy my husband had taken on with his garden and buckets of water, but without the prospect of any victory. For me it was like an inimical being that did not want us here and which did everything in its power to drive us away.' Again she laughed, and pressed her handkerchief to her lips. 'It sounds very funny now, but I was extremely unhappy during those first few years.'

'And yet your husband won the battle in the end.'

'Yes,' said Mrs Hirsch, and for a moment she was silent. They walked under the pergola, covered in vines and extending along the entire depth of the garden, with thick stems that coiled around the supports, and above their heads bunches of grapes ripened in a dense canopy of leaves and matted tendrils. 'Yes,' she repeated, 'he won in the end, or at least achieved a provisional victory, not so?' The tidy beds of vegetables were on one side, cultivated, raked and weeded; on the other side lay a small dam, lines of peach trees, and an outhouse, overgrown with honeysuckle. 'Until we have another hail storm or a drought and everything is ruined – then I recall how scared I used to be of this country, and I realise that it is all merely a ceasefire.'

They had reached the end of the garden and remained for a moment in the shadow of the trees, of which only the outlines were now visible, drawn against the evening sky. The house lay at a distance behind them; the lamps had since been lit, so that the windows glowed with a golden lustre, dimmed from time to time as someone passed in front of the light. They turned around in silence and walked back, and as they walked Mrs Hirsch put her hand on Versluis's arm for support. 'At first I felt very homesick,' she recollected. 'But I had friends, the children were born, the shop became established, and now I am at home here – yet whenever we've been to Germany I am always pleased to be back home. Oh well, I say this, but still, but still. . . . One remains aware of the fact that this land really does not want us. It suffers us for a while.'

She had grown quiet, her liveliness of the afternoon gone, and it became difficult to maintain the conversation, to ask questions and expect answers, and perhaps also to exchange ideas. Only now did he find how tired he really was, and he almost stumbled over the uneven ground. 'How many children do you have?' he asked.

'There are eight still alive.' From the house came the laughter and the exuberant cries of young girls. 'Joseph the oldest is married already, he looks after the shop in Kroonstad, and Louis is being trained by his uncle in Colesberg, but the others are all still at home. The girls are growing up so fast. . . .' She leant on his arm a bit more heavily

33

as they ascended the stairs to the stoep, and smiled at the gay sounds coming from within. 'They've half the town in there tonight, the young Krauses and the Bloem girls and the Becks and the Pages – half of them ought to be in bed already. Children, children!' she called, and carried him along with her into the house filled with the hazy glow of paraffin lamps and dancing shadows and boisterous young people who were hardly able to contain themselves in the presence of the stranger. 'Bertha, come and let me introduce you to Mr Versluis, and you too, Adelaide – who else is here? Jeannie, look at your hair, what will your mother say? Shouldn't you all be going home? Or are you staying for supper?' As radiant as a girl she moved amongst the young people, tying a ribbon here, combing someone's hair there, chiding and laughing and allowing herself to be teased. Some of the older girls, her daughters it appeared, came forward to greet Versluis with a German curtsey and began to introduce him to their friends, but then Hirsch arrived with the wine, and a whole entourage of black women carried dishes in from the kitchen, and he was caught up by the company and carried along to the dining room.

The brief conversation with his hostess in the tranquillity of the garden had been an exceptional interlude, Versluis realised, a departure from the usual course of life in this family and in this house, which was now resumed with redoubled gaiety. Hirsch drew out a chair from the end of the table next to himself and his wife and offered hock or claret, and Mrs Hirsch oversaw the further seating of the guests, keeping one eye on the servants, to whom she issued orders through the door; the young people called gaily to each other at the table, and the conversation darted to and fro without interruption, with no fewer than three or four people talking at once, but they still managed to follow all the other conversations as well. Most of the young people spoke English, with the interjection of an odd German or Dutch phrase, and Versluis found it difficult to follow what they were saying amidst the commotion and the noise; the room full of people was stifling, the paraffin lamps aggravated the heat of the evening and their transparent white shades blinded him. More soup? Mrs Hirsch enquired attentively. Wasn't he hungry? Couldn't she perhaps make him an omelette? Hirsch filled his glass, full of laughter at the children's jokes, with a reddening face, his napkin tucked into his waistcoat. He must try a peach, they came from their own orchard – where had the fruit-knives gone? Mrs Hirsch rang for the servants and was once again on her feet, dishing-up spoon in her hand, scrutinising the table to see whose plate was empty. A fruit-knife and finger-bowl were brought for Versluis, and he tried to cut himself off from the astonishing din which surrounded him, concentrating on the peach that he was peeling while its juice ran down his fingers. It was some time before he became aware that young Bertha Hirsch, who sat beside him, was speaking to him, but in the general hubbub he could not hear what she was saying, and even when she leant over to him he could only understand the formal schoolgirl Dutch that she spoke, apparently out of politeness to the guest, with great effort. She was asking something about the Netherlands, and her sister, who sat next to her, leant across to hear his answer too; with clammy fingers he raised his glass to drink some more wine, and he was overwhelmed by a kind of panic at the bubbling gaiety of the company, at the young, radiant faces, the gleaming locks of the girls who inclined their heads towards him, with golden earrings which danced like their mother's.

It was a relief when the meal finally ended and everyone got up with a shuffling of feet and scraping of chairs. Servants came to clear the table, the younger children were sent home or to bed, and the older ones withdrew to an adjoining room where they gathered around the piano, while Versluis was led out by his host and hostess to the stoep at the back of the house where coffee was served to them. The darkness of night was complete: the garden had become indiscernible, an impenetrable terrain filled with the calls of nocturnal creatures.

'A beautiful evening,' Hirsch said languidly. 'Our evenings are always fine, no matter how hot the day has been. Can you see the Southern Cross?'

'It's not too chilly for you?' his wife enquired. 'Aren't you afraid you might catch cold? We can fetch you a rug if you like.'

Versluis declined, however, and lay back in the canvas chair with his coffee cup in his hand and looked at the stars that Hirsch pointed out to him. Up to then he had avoided the evening air and so had not seen the night sky since his arrival, and as he gazed up at it from the easy chair, the richness of the agglutinated starlight overwhelmed him for a moment.

'Schubert,' Hirsch remarked to himself as he strolled calmly up and down the stoep. In the house a duo was being played. 'Life is good; life is very good indeed. Don't you agree, my friend?'

His wife had momentarily resumed her serenity, she had arranged the folds of her dress about her, rearranged the coffee things on the table in front of her, and then clasped her hands on her lap. 'Yes,' she said in quiet affirmation.

Life is good, Versluis, too, reflected and shut his eyes to the brilliant

35

dome of the heavens. He thought of his room at the hotel, in which he would have to feel his way to the candle and matches on the bedside cabinet; he thought of the house that he had left behind, blinds over the windows, furniture under dust covers and the chandeliers enshrouded in the reception rooms, that empty, dark house that he might not see again for a long time. Perhaps never again, he thought, and suddenly opened his eyes and sat upright in the low chair.

Mrs Hirsch, who thought that he was looking for a place to put his empty cup, leant forward to take it from him, while her husband continued talking. 'In any case we hope that we have made you feel at home here,' he said, 'and that you will also be at home amongst us, both in the town and also especially in this house. And if you decide to extend your stay and wish to get away from hotel life you are very welcome to settle in here with us.'

'Extremely welcome,' his wife confirmed. 'With the two boys out of the house, we have more than enough room.'

He thanked them for the offer, surprised by their kindness and aware of their sincerity, even if he clearly realised that he would never be able to take advantage of the offer. There was no room for him in that full, lively house.

The young people inside were singing and playing the piano, mostly English songs which he did not know, but occasionally also more familiar German folk songs which Mrs Hirsch, seated behind the coffee table, accompanied in a clear voice. Hirsch strode up and down the stoep with measured steps, apparently unable to stand still or to control himself to any greater extent.

Versluis got up: he had to go, he said, it was really time for him to go now, he did not think it wise to expose himself any further to the night air, and besides, the long day. . . . But not without accompaniment, Hirsch assured him, despite the beauty of the stars, it was a dark night without the moon. They would send a servant along with a lantern, and besides the Page girls were also going home, they lived just across the square, right next to the hotel. He was thus further detained while the girls were called and got themselves ready, the servant sent for and a basket of peaches packed for him to take along. He must come again, the Hirsches called to him from the front door, he would be welcome at any time; he should come and have Sunday lunch with them some day.

The two girls who accompanied him were friendly but shy, and he allowed them to walk ahead, giggling and whispering to one another. The night was utterly dark and the town deserted, the lights were out in most of the houses: in the light of the swinging lantern he could make out only the girls' light dresses and the high heels of their shoes under them as they ran across the market square to their house. It was only at the hotel that lights still shone, and the bar and billiard room were filled with voices and noise and smoke. With one hand against the passage wall he had to grope his way through the dark to the door of his room.

He had already got to know the minor events that punctuated the course of the days in the town: the half-day on Wednesday and the day of rest on Sunday; the morning market; the cattle sale on Saturday mornings with its lowing herds and wagons in the square in front of the hotel; the coming of the mailcoach, announced by a distant bugle-call; and the regular arrival and departure of the passenger coaches which always caused a brief stir in the town, with strange people travelling between the Diamond Fields and the Colony, inhabitants returning from visits to other towns or abroad, awaited by crowds of friends, and the occasional disembarking stranger whose luggage had to be off-loaded. In the lobby and on the hotel stoep the trunks, suitcases and baskets of those who were leaving were already piled up long beforehand, while the doors of the vacated rooms stood open and servants had begun to strip the beds.

'Oh, Mr Versluis,' Frau Schröder called upon meeting him in the passage, and excitedly beckoned him closer. Since Versluis's recovery she appeared to have to come to a satisfactory estimation of his social and financial position, and her conduct towards him had altered accordingly, it now took the form of a certain subservience, combined with the self-consciousness which coloured her high cheekbones. 'Please come and look,' she now called, as if she had some surprise which she wished to share with him, and led him to a narrow room at the side of the building. He saw a steel bed with a stained coir mattress, a wardrobe and a washstand on which there were a few damp towels; a window covered by a limp curtain offered a view on to the street and across the fruit trees of the distant houses on the other side.

'Mr Griessel stayed here,' Frau Schröder said, 'he was in town for a long time. He had some business with the attorney. And today a gentleman from Kimberley is expected; he reserved a room for himself a long time ago, but he won't stay long, no more than a week, then he'll be off to Queenstown, and then I'll keep the room for you.'

Versluis surveyed the room without any enthusiasm, and although it was clear that he did not share her own sense of satisfaction with the offer, his silence was enough for Frau Schröder – who responded with a small, automatic curtsey, one of a series of inculcated gestures of servility from her distant European past which his presence had recalled, and, relieved, she hurried to the kitchen. Versluis was free to proceed, and he went outside.

He needed to see an attorney to discuss some arrangements which had been neglected in his hasty departure from the Netherlands, and he remained standing for a moment amongst the piles of baggage, the idle men with their hands in their pockets and the scattered black onlookers who awaited the arrival of the coach, even though it was clear that it would be some hours before it arrived. The morning market was over, and in the middle of the square a calf stood motionless, chewing the cud and watching him as he approached with its head slung low. It made no move to get out of the way, so that he was forced to walk around the animal. If so much were not familiar, the things that were alien would not be so irritating by being unexpected, he thought to himself in the middle of that dusty square, holding his cane in his hand. Finally one was no doubt grateful to discover so many things here in the heart of Africa that had survived the transplantation from Europe, but the process had occurred too half-heartedly: the hock and moselle were not chilled, and when his fine holland shirts had come back that morning their buttons had been torn off by the washerwoman and they had been pressed with a careless hand.

At the well in front of the market building the town's servants had crowded together and they were now calling to each other while they waited their turn with buckets and vessels: the water had overflowed and all around the earth was trampled into a mire. On a stoep in front of a shop a man sat, leaning back in the shade, his chair balanced on its two back legs and his feet on a bale, chewing tobacco and spitting it heedlessly on to the ground in front of him; on the corner near the attorney's office a dead dog lay in the street, surrounded by a buzz of flies, while none of the few pedestrians took any notice of it. The country was weird, Versluis thought to himself, and he sought the narrow strips of shade along the buildings, for the heat was already becoming severe; the familiar had been transfigured, like well-known objects on a riverbed, perceived through the wash of clear water, or else seen from a distance, quivering in a haze of summer heat.

The clerk in the front office looked at him questioningly, thought for a moment and shuffled out to make enquiries. Nothing happened: a wall clock ticked, a horse-cart went by, and the sunlight fell obliquely across the floor, so that the office boy got up after a while to draw the blind further.

The clerk returned apathetically to announce with a certain flicker of interest that Mr Helmond would see him, and Versluis got up too eagerly, so that he dropped his hat and his cane; but he had picked them up before the young man was able to make any half-hearted gesture to do it for him. He was beginning to feel annoyed, he realised, irritated by the heat of the day and the tardiness with which everything was done in this country, and he felt his irritation grow when, on his entry, the attorney glanced up from behind his desk with the same apathetic indifference and made no move to rise in greeting. Only after Versluis had introduced himself did the man get up and shake his hand, but then he resumed his place behind the desk and fiddled distractedly with an ivory ruler, as if he were observing, pondering and digesting the matter without, however, wishing to divulge the outcome. Being a Netherlander he had been recommended to Versluis at the hotel, and it was clear from his accent that he must be one by birth, and he showed no reaction to meeting a fellow-countryman in a foreign land, nor did he display any sign of interest in the arrival of a client; he toyed with the ruler in an attitude of near-boredom while Versluis tried to contain his annoyance as best he could and explained the purpose of his visit: he spoke of the arrangements which had been made from the Netherlands with people and institutions in Cape Town and Port Elizabeth and the changes that had to be introduced now that he had provisionally decided to stay in Bloemfontein. 'Meester Helmond,' he had addressed the man in passing.

'We do not use that title in Africa,' the man quickly put him right, and tried unsuccessfully to balance the ruler on the tips of his fingers.

Versluis remained silent and waited, conscious of the constriction of his collar, the pinching shoes, and the sweat that in the heat had begun to form on his forehead and which he continuously and fruitlessly dabbed with his handkerchief.

The attorney did not look up. 'It can't happen that quickly,' he finally remarked.

'It is surely not that complicated a matter.'

'Perhaps not, but one can't get a letter to Cape Town overnight. It goes on the cart to Worcester and by train to Cape Town, or in the coach to Port Elizabeth and then it continues by sea; it takes time. You are in Africa now,' he added in the same, half-sneering manner with which he had earlier corrected Versluis's form of address.

The man's accent and his behaviour were not those of an entirely well-bred person, and the lack of courtesy which he palpably revealed towards his visitor was in its own way as annoying to Versluis as Frau Schröder's servile politeness. 'Would you in any case see what you can do?' he asked coolly, and got up. 'I'll leave the relevant documents with you for the moment.' He again pressed the handkerchief to his forehead. The attorney examined the ruler, considered, nodded, and rose slowly to end the meeting without committing himself to any further action.

The clerk had disappeared from the front office, the empty room was gloomy behind the drawn blind, and on the stoep the office boy stood gazing at the dead dog. 'It's Mr Goddard's bull terrier,' he informed Versluis. 'Mr Stephens's boy ran over it with the buggy. Mr Goddard is going to be really mad when he finds out.'

Versluis did not feel any need to go into the matter, and he averted his eyes from the stiff, bloody jaws around which the bluebottles buzzed. The black people were still crowded around the well in the middle of the square and the solitary calf still stood pensively between him and the hotel. He should not let himself be put out by this irritation, he thought, rather he should go back to his room and calm down before attempting to make any further arrangements about his accommodation. As time passed he would get to know this land and its customs and find a pattern in the wearisome series of events that kept imposing themselves upon him. Somewhere in all this jumble, amongst all the confused impressions and discordant reactions – the oppression of a well-lined jacket and starched collar in the heat, the incompetence of the washerwomen, the unchilled wine, the dead dog – somewhere there lurked something that he would find if he waited and watched for long enough.

A number of the old hotel guests had left on the passenger coach and new ones had arrived, and for a while everything in the hotel was disrupted; doors were banged, bells were rung and people called for water in which to wash themselves; trunks were carried to and fro and Frau Schröder trotted nervously after the servants, supervising and giving orders. In the lobby an unknown woman in a red-and-green tartan dress sat on a trunk, and children ran screaming around a corner directly into Versluis; in the lounge men talked loudly in English. That night, in the room next to his, which had been empty up to then, Versluis heard muffled sounds of movement, a faint cough, a jingling and clink of a glass, and these discreet sounds annoyed him, for he had grown accustomed to his isolation in the back room of the hotel to which, on his arrival as an unconscious stranger, he had been carried to die.

The restlessness and the bustle which had accompanied the wave of new guests continued the following day, and the meals in the dining room became exasperating for Versluis, caught as he was at the long table between clerks and commercial travellers with their conversations in English which he could follow only with difficulty: about somebody's new horse, about a future cricket match or concert, about the diamond trade, the political developments in Transvaal or the price of cattle or grain – issues in which he had no part or interest. It can't go on like this, he thought; somehow he would have to make other arrangements about his accommodation. He left the table even before the meal had ended.

In the back yard which he had to cross to reach his room he came across Frau Schröder, so put out that she forgot to greet him with her usual compliments. 'It's the English lady in the back room,' she declared before he could say anything. 'She went out this morning to do some shopping, she came back because she wasn't feeling well, and now she has fainted, right in the middle of the passage. She arrived only yesterday and already today she needs the doctor, she doesn't know a soul in this country to help her, and naturally we are the ones who have to do everything.' She walked away with quick little steps, her dress flapping about her legs, and for a moment Versluis wondered whether she had expressed similar sentiments on the day that he had been brought there.

The tranquillity which had been the single advantage of that simple room had now been lost, and all afternoon Versluis was conscious of sounds in the adjoining room: the creaking of the bed, the clinking of a glass, the opening and shutting of the door, and the same light, nervous coughing that he had already heard occasionally during the night. The ceilings in the rooms were no more than unbleached linen stretched between the walls, he realised, and every sound from next door was clearly audible to him. Later in the afternoon he heard Doctor Krause's familiar grumble, the words themselves inaudible, and he was overwhelmed by panic at the thought that the doctor might decide to drop in on him; but it seemed that Doctor Krause had forgotten about him, and his voice faded away along the passage again.

After that Versluis could no longer relax, and that evening the privacy of his room was irreparably disturbed by his constant awareness

41

of his unknown neighbour, her suppressed cough, her timid movements and other more intimate sounds which disconcerted him even more. Even after everything had fallen silent, enveloped by the darkness of the night, he found that he still lay waiting for a fresh sound from beyond the wall, and that he was roused immediately by every creak of the bed, each smothered cough, until he finally lit the candle beside the bed and, getting up, he went to look for the laudanum in the medicine cabinet which he had not opened since his arrival. Even after he had taken it his sleep was still restless, full of imaginary noises, imaginary people at the door of his room, and a strange murmuring and rustling around his bed.

The following day Versluis fled from his room and sought refuge in the lounge, the only public room in the hotel besides the billiard room and the bar. Two of the arrivals of a few days earlier were already sitting there, hats perched on the back of their heads, waiting for someone who was coming to fetch them; they whistled through their teeth and struck up aimless conversations full of nicknames and professional jargon. The old crumpled Cape newspapers on the table offered no news of any interest to him and the European dailies were still those that had arrived with him, filled with the events of a few months earlier, and as he glanced through them Versluis was at once conscious, with renewed clarity, of his alienation in an another country, an alien part of the world. Europe and his familiar life were so far away that a whole range of developments could occur there over a period of weeks or even months without his being touched by or even aware of them.

He spent the morning in the lounge with a growing sense of discomfort and injury, but after lunch he returned to his room to lie down during the heat of the day. He remained restless at first, but the drowsy stillness of the afternoon had also enveloped the room next door and muffled any sound which came from it. He fell asleep on his bed in the close, gloomy room and was already in a deep slumber when he was roused by the clatter of something falling over and the tinkling of a handbell. It had come from the next room he realised while he remained sitting on the edge of the bed in the position to which his startled awakening had brought him, and he heard the sound of bare feet on the clay floor, the scuttling of servants, and Frau Schröder's firm and more determined tread. Still half-drugged by sleep and with movements that trembled with alarm, he put on his shoes and jacket and brushed his hair in front of the mirror while the coming and going continued in the next room, and when he looked out of the doorway he could just see Frau Schröder disappearing down the end

42

of the corridor and called her back. For how long was it going to continue like this? he asked indignantly. Was there really no other room available for him in the hotel? She stood nodding affirmatively in a half-automatic response while he spoke, without giving her full attention to what he was saying, while her own sense of indignation possessed her. No, it was completely impossible, she assented, it couldn't carry on in this way, but unfortunately there was absolutely nothing else at present, she hadn't even a double room to offer him. She spoke impatiently and was already hurrying on. 'But don't worry, Mr Versluis,' she added from a distance, 'it won't last long,' and she nodded reassuringly.

There was thus nothing that he could do about it, and the sense of acclimatisation that he had gradually begun to feel, despite the inadequacies of the room, the hotel, and the country, was lost; the reassurance which he had slowly begun to experience about this environment as it had grown familiar to him, had been destroyed with one blow by the unexpected encroachment made upon it by this unknown woman and her illness, her relapses and crises. He had no specific, detailed knowledge of these things, but even the general indications were disturbing enough – the creaking of the bed, the coughing, the insistent ringing of the bell, and the footsteps and voices in the corridor.

That night Versluis took a dose of laudanum before he went to bed, and, after a moment's consideration, he increased the usual amount so that he would fall asleep quickly; he was woken up once again during the night, however. It was not the usual sporadic coughing that came from the next room, but a fit that refused to abate: he did not know for how long it had been going on before it had wrenched him from his drugged sleep, but as he lay in bed listening, in a clammy sweat, it carried on almost despairingly, as if the unknown woman had long since lost all strength and now merely let herself be dragged on by the spasmodic contractions of her lungs. He lay motionless in the dark with his eyes shut and heard the sounds like smothered cries or violent sobs, still half-asleep and half-awake, in the hope that if he did not move he would once more be overcome by sleep; but at last, trembling, he sprang up and felt for the matches and the candlestick on the cabinet beside him. He failed to find them, however, and he scrambled about in the dark with a sudden rush of anguish, found his pocket watch, his handkerchief, the glass of water, and suspected that he had knocked the matches on to the floor. His nightshirt clung coldly to his back, drenched in sweat; the dark was like a wall before his eyes, unbroken by the faintest reflection, its immense presence pressed down upon him as he groped on his knees along the mud floor beside the bed, and in the next room the noise continued as if the woman would finally, in a fit of coughing, choke in her own saliva or blood. He should probably do something, he thought confusedly, something had to be done to silence that terrible noise. But he could not appear in her room in his nightclothes, candle in hand. And where would he go to look for help in the corridors and locked doors of the hotel if no-one else woke up?

Then, with a final smothered sob or cry the coughing ceased, and the silence that followed was even more threatening than the sounds of suffocation that had preceded it. Kneeling on the floor in his nightshirt, Versluis waited in the dark for it to be resumed, but no further sound came from the next room, not a sigh or groan, not a creak from the bed. He finally raised himself and got back into bed, as exhausted as if he had himself suffered that fit of coughing, but it was a long time before his drugged sleepiness returned, for at every instant he expected to be startled by some noise or other. Perhaps he had imagined it all, he thought, feeling himself sinking into sleep; perhaps it had been some nightmare called up by the laudanum and the closeness of that room. The woman will go away, he thought, or be sent away to look for another refuge, and he would be free to enjoy his isolation without further disturbance. Frau Schröder had indeed said that it wouldn't last for long, he recalled even as the clarity of his thoughts was beginning to fade; and he realised too late that that was not necessarily what she had meant by those words.

The greyish light reflected through the window indicated that it was morning, and Joseph brought in his coffee, followed by the jug of hot water and his polished boots. The usual distant morning sounds of the hotel penetrated to his room: the back yard being swept; Schröder shouting at a servant; and next door he heard occasional footsteps, a door being opened and closed with the sound of low voices, and finally also the brusque tone of the doctor, but he paid no attention to them. While he shaved and dressed, calmly and methodically following the routine which he had established for himself since his recovery, knotting his tie, checking his watch, brushing down his jacket, he came to a decision: to leave that hotel that very day and to look for somewhere else to stay, without waiting for the room which Frau Schröder had promised him. He had already cut himself off from any further developments in the next room.

He thus left the hotel after breakfast carrying his hat and cane, and he hesitated on the stoep. There were two other hotels in the town which he had occasionally come across during his perambulations, but he knew nothing about them, and in any case they were probably just as full of visitors. Then, of course, he recalled as he donned his hat and stepped into the market square, where the morning market had as usual initiated a certain degree of activity, there was the Hirsches' clearly sincere offer of hospitality. He considered it for a moment, that large house full of young people, life and bustle, and rejected the idea. Who else could he approach – Frau Schröder? The reproving attorney? And then he remembered the confused young German pastor who had visited him one afternoon during his recuperation, full of good intentions and offers of help, and whom he had not given a thought since. He enquired after the Lutheran church from one of the men lounging on the hotel stoep, whereupon the man removed his pipe from his mouth and explained at length. It turned out to be the little church with the pitched roof just across the stream which he had already passed on his walks up to the rise on which the fort stood, and the simple, low house lurking next door behind its verandah appeared to be the parsonage. Both buildings were new, and apart from the plants on the stoep and the wilting hollyhocks in the flowerbeds, there was no garden; the odd trees that had been planted there were still tied to supports to keep them upright. Without any shelter other than the verandah, the house looked out from the hill across the trees and scattered houses of the town and the desolation of the veld which surrounded it.

A servant wearing a white apron appeared from the gloom of the house when he knocked on the door and, without a word, left him waiting there while she disappeared with his visiting card. So that he found himself hesitating on the stoep, between the gloom of the hall and the bleached, sun-drenched morning, when Pastor Scheffler himself threw open the glass doors on the verandah and hurried out, doing up the buttons of his jacket as if the visit had surprised him in his shirtsleeves. 'Sir . . . Mr Versluis, this really is a surprise; I'm pleased to see you, so pleased. . . .' He came up to Versluis, bemused but full of warmth, and stretched out his hand. 'Come in, come to my study,' he added, and whilst talking he led his visitor inside through the glass doors. There were bookcases against the walls, a desk covered in papers, a few framed pictures, a settee and a small cast-iron stove; the windows held no curtains, just a blind which had been drawn so that the morning sun fell across floorboards which had been scrubbed white. It was an inhospitable, slightly poky room, the room of a

45

student or an ascetic; or in any case of someone who did not care much for comfort, Versluis realised as he sat down in one of the uncomfortable armchairs that the clergyman had indicated while having seated himself at the other end of the room.

'I heard about your recovery,' he said, 'and I have even seen you passing my window on one or two occasions – I should have gone out, and yet I didn't, you must please excuse me. The good intentions were there, but there was also, as I have said before, the fear that I might be imposing.'

'Sometimes, towards late afternoon, I walk a short distance up the hill for the sake of the view,' Versluis said, and searched his pockets for his handkerchief. 'I was not at all aware that it was your church.'

'I had hoped that I might even find you in my congregation one Sunday, even if it were merely out of curiosity. Yes, I know, you did say that you were not a member of any Church, but that doesn't exclude curiosity, does it?' He smiled at the question, with that innocent, disarming boy's grin which made it impossible for one to be offended by what he said. 'Naturally I have no right whatever to expect something like that from you, and yet, last Sunday in particular – I preached about the necessity, or not, of faith, following Romans, and I tried to say something intelligent about it; I had imagined that my ideas might possibly interest someone like you, even if you aren't a churchgoer. I put a lot of effort into that sermon.'

'I trust that there will be an opportunity to listen to one of your sermons in the future,' Versluis remarked politely, and found the handkerchief he had been looking for in his inside pocket.

'But I fear that my motives were not entirely pure,' the clergyman continued with some resignation; 'or at least, not pure enough – I saw myself as an orator and not as a someone in the service of the Word, and so I was punished for my arrogance, because as a result the majority of the congregation didn't understand what I was trying to say, and one or two were even offended. But I would have appreciated your comments, coming from a sympathetic outsider. As well as your criticism.'

Versluis pressed the handkerchief against his face and forehead, refreshed by the scent of the eau de Cologne with which he had sprinkled it. 'As soon as I feel stronger, I'll be happy to take the opportunity to listen to you one Sunday,' he said without thinking about what he was saying. 'At present I'm afraid that my health is still. . . .' He touched his lips with the handkerchief. The walk up the hill in the heat of the morning had been too demanding, he realised, and the same thought had presumably occurred to the clergyman, for he sprang up quickly.

'I'm sorry, I have been inconsiderate, I should offer you something. Tea? Or a glass of water perhaps?' he added, and looked hesitantly at Versluis.

'Thank you, nothing,' he said, just in time to catch the young man at the door. 'I can't stay long, I merely came to ask your advice.'

Surprised, the clergyman remained standing in the centre of the room, and Versluis was again aware of the shoes with their thick, curling soles, the worn jacket, and the poorly trimmed hair which resisted any treatment with a brush. The white cuffs of his shirt had begun to wear along the edges, he saw, and there were ink marks on his fingers. He must get out of there, Versluis thought, and without thinking he raised himself from the chair, his handkerchief still in his hand, and the clergyman moved automatically towards him as if he feared that he would stumble or fall.

'If there is any way in which I can be of service. . . .' he began.

'I still tire very quickly,' Versluis mumbled in apology for this sudden, unexplained gesture. 'You must please excuse me for taking up your time.'

The clergyman merely shrugged his shoulders a little ruefully. 'I had begun to work on next Sunday's sermon; if one waits until Saturday something unforeseen always happens. But it's not urgent. In fact it's not even very important.' But Versluis did not wait for him to finish: speaking rather hurriedly, because he was not feeling well, and moreover because he desperately wanted to get out of that room, he explained that he was looking for alternative accommodation, and he noticed with relief that the clergyman understood without expecting any further explanation.

'We would naturally have been delighted to have offered you shelter under our roof,' he said, 'it would have been a pleasure and a privilege, but unfortunately we have no spare bedrooms in the parsonage – when we do happen to have visitors we have to put them up here in the study.' The possibility of being offered the settee in that spartan room was as alarming to Versluis as the prospect of the Hirsches' house with its hordes of exuberant young people, but luckily Scheffler was himself aware of the impracticality of the idea. 'We must find something more suitable for you, since it is to be hoped that you will remain amongst us for a long time yet. There are of course boarding houses, private people who rent rooms, but these are usually for single men who work here, they're not for you.' He stared thoughtfully at the horsehair settee while he weighed up the possibilities. 'Mrs Van der Vliet perhaps,' he then remarked to himself. 'She doesn't rent rooms, but she frequently takes in guests, some eminent people from the Cape and from abroad have stayed with her. She is moreover a Dutch lady, a widow – her husband was secretary of the Volksraad. . . .' He grinned with delight at Versluis, his satisfaction at the solution he had come to radiantly visible. 'Would you like to go and speak to her? Or should I make enquiries? Then I can arrange for a letter to be sent to the hotel – tomorrow morning, will that do?'

Versluis pressed the handkerchief containing the eau de Cologne to his face, conscious of the oppressive heat of the summer morning and of his own weakness. He hadn't slept well, he thought to himself; of course, how could he not feel unwell after such a restless night? He must get away from the hotel, he thought, and shut his eyes. 'If it could rather happen . . .' he began. 'I should, if it is at all possible, like to move today.'

The clergyman was only too pleased, even eager, to help. He would go that very morning, he would send the servant with a letter to the hotel before lunch, he promised, and if Mrs Van der Vliet was unable to help, he would find another solution. He stood thinking for a moment and then shook his head. 'No, Mrs Van der Vliet is the best prospect, we'll arrange something for you. She lives just around the corner, next to the spruit – we'll virtually be neighbours. And I hope that we'll see you often if you come and live so close by; not in the church, you need feel under no obligation as far as that's concerned, that was not what I meant, but if you ever felt like some company, or, as I said, if there is anything in my library which interests you. . . .' He did not complete the sentence: he passed one hand across a row of books on a shelf, coyly but with affection. Versluis looked politely at the rows of books along the wall, and he allowed his eyes to pass disinterestedly over German theology collections and exegeses, punctuated by the odd devotional book. He had already turned away with a word of thanks when he realised that the shelves which Scheffler was indicating to him contained mostly literature: Goethe, Schiller and Lessing in collected volumes, and single volumes of other writers and poets; Leist, Holderlin and Morike, and he remained there to inspect them more closely. There were also a number of newer works of history and science he saw, and it surprised him to discover on a lower, less prominent shelf the names of Darwin and Strauss.

Scheffler, however, had already continued talking, as if he felt that he had perhaps already given up too much: it would be a pleasure, he assured Versluis, it was no trouble at all, anything he could do. . . . He spoke too loudly and too emphatically, caught uncertainly between the proper formalities which one observed towards a stranger and his own inclination towards openness and familiarity. The house remained silent and even the servant gave no further indication of her presence.

The intensity of the sun on the gravel street blinded him – he fled through the glare of the morning to the hotel and installed himself once again in the lounge with a writing pad and a book, ordered a glass of soda water, and gradually relaxed. There was no-one else in the room that morning and the servants had finished working there; the voices and footsteps which travelled along the corridor did not bother him, and even when he looked up to see Doctor Krause stepping slowly and gravely on to the verandah in his black frock coat, bag in hand, the sight did not frighten him. He had recovered and no longer needed the doctor's care, and whatever else happened in that hotel had nothing to do with him, for he sat waiting for the message that would assure him of release and a speedy departure. Nor did the developments in the room next to his touch him in any way, he thought to himself with a certain degree of satisfaction, and took up his ivory paper knife to cut the pages of a new book: he would not be woken and kept awake that night. He would have set up his life elsewhere in a more satisfactory manner, and even that dispersed, moribund, dusty little town took on a friendlier and more welcoming appearance at the prospect.

A team of oxen went past to the cries of the team-leader; a woman crossed the square leading a little girl by the hand, her white parasol carefully slanted against the sun which had reached its zenith. In the slightly dancing light reflected from the dust of the square and in the gathering heat of the day all movement became more languid, and Versluis, feeling himself affected by this listlessness, leant back in the chair and stared out of the window, the paper knife left between the pages of the book at the place where he had interrupted his task.

At the hotel a black man had begun to carry cases of empty bottles from the bar to a hand-cart which had been dragged in front of the stoep. He progressed slowly and sporadically, in the way that all work seemed to be done in this country, with long, inexplicable interruptions, and intervals taken up by conversations with those who happened to be passing by. Those loitering around the stoep – some of them were men who needed to do business at the post office or the magistrate's office next door, some visitors to the bar and there were others for whom life consisted entirely of hanging around this place with hands in their pockets – these loiterers watched the activity, knocked out their pipes and from time to time would converse pensively.

The appearance of the barman Gustav from the hotel prompted the servant to resume his work, and Gustav paced up and down the stoep in the apron which he always wore, his shirtsleeves rolled up as usual almost as far as his shoulders. He was conscious as he stood laughing in the sunshine of his authority in the eyes of the black man – of the appreciation with which the idle men greeted his jokes, and of his youth and strength and powerful white arms. The book on his lap with the paper knife between the pages, Versluis looked out from the gloom of the lounge at the cluster of people in front of the hotel who represented the only sign of life in the whole wide panorama across the square and the town, and then forgot about them again, lulled by the sound of their voices in the quiet.

A sudden outcry roused him from his slumbers so that, bewildered, he had no idea of what had happened. Outside he saw Gustav, with some or other bellowed imprecation, deliver a blow to the black man's head. The man tottered for a moment on the step of the verandah, toppled, and fell backwards into the dust with the case that he was carrying, so that the bottles scattered in all directions and the onlookers burst out laughing. 'Hurry up, hurry up, hurry up!' Gustav shouted, standing on the stoep with his hands on his sides and looking down at the man. The servant slowly picked himself up, his clothes white with the dust from his fall, and wiped the blood from his mouth and nose with his hand. Then when Gustav growled something at him, he bent down and began to collect the scattered bottles while Gustav resumed his promenade along the stoep and his conversation with the grinning group of whites.

Versluis rose and walked to the bell at the other end of the room to ring for the waiter and, frowning and thoughtful, he remained standing in front of the wall mirror. That was unnecessary, he thought to himself, and then it dawned on him that he had been upset by the minor show of violence, and that his heart was beating rapidly and irregularly. He ordered another flask of soda water, and wondered for a moment whether he ought to take a little valerian, but then he heard the hand-cart being pulled away and Gustav whistling along the passage on his way back to the bar. What kind of half-civilised country was this, he thought indignantly, in which dead dogs lay around in the streets and one man could wilfully assault another in public while the bystanders laughed? The paper knife had fallen; he bent down to pick it up, and then had to sit still for a moment until the sudden dizziness had passed. He would have liked blinds and curtains to subdue this harsh light, he wished for a tranquil room in which an armchair stood ready and the clock ticked away with a hardly discernible sound; he was longing for the safe and familiar world at the other end of the globe, he thought to himself as he sat and waited for the waiter to bring his soda water.

Deliverance, however, was near at hand, as had been promised: during lunch a letter was brought to him at the table and, opening it the instant he rose, he learnt from the clergyman that Mrs Van der Vliet would be happy to see him later that afternoon.

Relieved, he remained standing in the passage with the letter in his hand and decided to return to his room in order to rest before the appointment. He was a trifle hesitant at first, still expecting some further disturbance from the room next door, but there all was still – the whole isolated rear section of the hotel was as undisturbed as he had come to know it in the early days of his stay, and so he relaxed; he removed his shoes, his jacket and tie and stretched himself out on the bed.

On waking up, surprised by the protracted tranquillity and the fact that he had slept so deeply and for so long, he rang for coffee and for water with which to wash himself, then threw his sweat-drenched shirt and handkerchief on to the floor in a corner for Joseph to pick up, had his shoes repolished, and stepped into the late afternoon with renewed hope.

It was a large, low house just the other side of the spruit, on a piece of ground which ran down to the willows and the pools of water made by the stream. The formal front garden was swept clean and raked neatly, its shrubs and flowers arranged in immaculate ranks; the steps to the stoep had been scrubbed white and spotless sash curtains covered the windows behind the verandah; through the front door, open as was customary in this country, he was greeted by the gleam of polished floors and the scent of furniture polish. As he put his hand out to the gleaming door knocker, Versluis realised that this was indeed the refuge that he longed for.

In the house a floorboard creaked, groaning beneath the weight of a heavy, shuffling footstep, and from the gloom a middle-aged woman in black approached him.

'Mrs Van der Vliet?' he enquired, but she nodded and replied even before he had finished speaking. 'Mr Versluis,' she declared, her hand small, soft and without life in his. 'Come in.'

51

In the drawing room into which she led him, Versluis could see nothing in the gloom behind the sash curtains and the heavy, suspended drapes, but heard only the rustle of a dress somewhere in the dark. Gradually, however, the details of the room grew visible to him – armchairs, little ornamental tables, footstools, and pot plants rose one by one from the murkiness of the ocean. And then he saw Mrs Van der Vliet, who with a wave of her chubby hand indicated him to sit down before lowering herself with a sigh on to a chair.

'I believe that Pastor Scheffler has explained my position to you,' he began tentatively.

'Yes,' she assented with a nod.

'I have been staying in a hotel since my arrival, and I have not found it entirely satisfactory.'

'Yes,' Mrs Van der Vliet replied once again, but with greater emphasis, as if she wished to indicate her understanding and sympathy, but without committing herself any further.

'I am thus looking for alternative accommodation,' he continued and waited for a further response, but she remained silent, her hands clasped. 'Pastor Scheffler had thought that it might be possible for you. . . .' Confronted by that silence he hesitated, however. 'He thought that you might be prepared to assist me.'

He waited for her to reply. But she sat opposite him like the sculpture of a lonely widow, motionless in her wide black dress, a heavy brooch at her throat, and on her head a bonnet with trailing lappets that had been carefully arranged over her shoulders, until he began to wonder whether she had heard him.

'I do not rent rooms,' she said finally, with a clarity and emphasis which removed any possible doubt. 'I do not run a boarding house.' Once again she paused to let the words sink in, and in the long silence that followed Versluis wondered whether it was now expected of him to apologise for the mistake and leave. Outside in the street a black woman called out as she passed by, and in the distance another replied. 'It is not necessary for me to concern myself with such things in order to make a living. My husband ensured that it would not be necessary.'

With these words she turned her head and raised her eyes, and Versluis followed her gaze to see a life-size portrait of a man with a drooping moustache and slightly bulging eyes hanging on the wall above her chair, its frame draped in heavy crepe. They gazed at it in silence for a few seconds.

'He came to Africa in '51,' Mrs Van der Vliet said. 'We met each other in Cape Town and were married there. We came to the Free

52

State together.' With a small white hand she smoothed out the folds of her mourning-dress. 'They had him come out here from the Netherlands on the recommendation of Professor Lauts to teach in the government school.'

'A very useful occupation,' Versluis remarked politely, but she did not hear him.

'That was still during the time of the English,' she continued. 'When the Dutch took over here he became Secretary of the Volksraad, for he was an educated man, and that he remained for eleven years.' Again he felt constrained to utter a few polite remarks, but she continued once more as if he had not spoken. 'He served under all four of the Presidents,' she said with emphasis. 'He died in harness.'

There was nothing that Versluis could add; there was nothing for him to do but remain silent for a moment with the widow.

'It has been twelve years since he died,' Mrs Van der Vliet resumed, 'but in those twelve years there has not been a single day on which I have wanted for anything, just as when he was still alive – widow as I am in a strange country with no children or relatives. Not a single day,' she repeated emphatically, as if she wished to dispel every last vestige of doubt about the subject. There was obviously no point in remaining, Versluis thought, and he reached for his hat which he had placed beside his chair.

'Indeed, Pastor Scheffler did tell me about your problems,' Mrs Van der Vliet began suddenly, as if the movement had recalled her from her reverie, even though her face was still turned away in the direction of her husband's portrait. 'Pastor Scheffler is aware that I have a large house and that in the past my husband often put up visitors from the Netherlands. And that was not all, Mr Versluis, he was also always ready to help any of his countrymen who found themselves in need here in South Africa. I am myself no less willing to offer hospitality to visitors from the Netherlands and to help them where I can, even if it is only in memory of him and of my parents who also came from the Netherlands.'

He had not yet picked up the hat when she had begun to speak, and so he remained seated, frozen in that posture, to hear her out. She spoke Dutch, better Dutch than he had heard from most people in this country, with a fluency and grammatical correctness which indicated that it must be her mother tongue rather than a second language; but at the same time it was not the Dutch of an inhabitant of the Netherlands. There was a hardly discernable weakness in the vowels and a slight impurity of intonation, slight errors in the gender of

53

words, small shifts of meaning, and a general absence of idioms which imparted a weird lack of colour to her speech. Without fully listening to what she was saying to him, he began to concentrate on her usage in an effort to place her.

'I keep no boarding house,' she assured him once again. 'I do not rent out rooms. But if it is question of helping someone, and if there happens to be a fellow Netherlander who needs my help, then I am always willing to render such assistance as it is in my power to give.'

As if she had been waiting outside for her cue, a servant now entered with coffee on a tray, the spotless white of her headcloth and apron distinct in the duskiness of the room.

'I continue to serve coffee in my house,' Mrs Van der Vliet said while the tray was being proffered to Versluis, 'not tea as most people here in Bloemfontein now serve. An authentic Dutch cup of coffee.' With folded arms she watched him as he drank it, weak and milky like all the coffee that he had had in that country, but he hastened to proffer the compliment which she clearly expected, and she nodded in modest satisfaction as she received it.

'At the moment I have Miss Pronk staying with me,' she continued when Versluis had put down his empty cup. 'She is from Almelo, she's to be married in a month to Helmond who works in Mr Voigt's office, then they'll be going to Aliwal North; he's going to begin a practice there. A very respectable young lady, her father is head of the gymnasium in Almelo. And in the outside room at the back I have young Polderman, he is an assistant clerk in Mr Fichardt's shop, and Du Toit. Du Toit is not Dutch, he comes from the Cape, but he is an entirely decent young man, and Polderman did ask if he could move in with him, since they are close friends. But the large room at the back is available,' she said thoughtfully. 'Come along,' she decided, and rose to the rustle of her dress, 'come, I'll show you.'

He followed the rustling of her dress, the creaking of floorboards beneath her slow footstep along the still deeper gloom of the passage. 'My father was born in Amsterdam,' he heard her voice ahead of him. 'He came to the Cape to teach at the Tot Nut van 't Algemeen School. You must have heard of it. My mother came from Hoofddorp.' This was important information which she was conveying to him, Versluis realised as he followed her: confidential particulars were being offered and he was himself being drawn into a more intimate inner circle.

'I live in Delft myself,' he began on the assumption that a corresponding gesture was expected from him, but Mrs Van der Vliet flung open a door, and he was permitted to enter the room offered to him: he had been accepted.

The white cover on the double bed which stood high under the bedclothes and piled-up pillows greeted him with a faint glimmer; on the washstand an ewer and basin caught the light, together with the whiteness of the towels on the stand nearby; the mirrors of the wardrobe and dressing-table reflected the oblique light that reached them from the lowered blinds in surfaces of empty silver. The large, formal room awaited his approval and acceptance, as did Mrs Van der Vliet herself where she had remained standing with her hand on the door knob.

'It seems very pleasant,' Versluis said. 'It is extremely pleasant,' he quickly corrected himself when he realised that this response was not enough to satisfy her silent expectation.

'Wooden floors, as you can see,' Mrs Van der Vliet informed him; 'all of the rooms in my house have wooden floors. And it looks out over the orchard and the spruit. In winter you will have sun in the room all day.'

'I don't think that I'll need to stay in Bloemfontein that long,' Versluis said. 'I am here on a fairly short visit.' But even these words, he realised, might seem to disparage the proffered hospitality, and he broke off quickly. 'But if you would indeed be so kind as to offer me your hospitality for the short time that I need to remain here. . . .'

'It is also very quiet,' she continued, as if he had not spoken. 'I will not allow any rowdiness: Polderman and Du Toit know that.'

'I am pleased to hear that. In fact I have not been able to sleep at all well for the last few nights.'

'Pastor Scheffler said that you have been ill?' she asked with sudden interest.

'I was indisposed when I arrived here, the journey was a bit tiring for me, and the climate too, it appears, so soon after the winter cold in the Netherlands. But happily I have recovered almost completely,' he quickly added in case she should have second thoughts; but Mrs Van der Vliet merely shook her head in sympathy.

'There are many invalids coming to Bloemfontein at present,' she remarked. 'And what would the pitiful Mrs Schröder know about looking after them? Besides, she has more than enough other things to keep her occupied, her husband never leaves the bar. But there has always been a great deal of disease here in Bloemfontein,' she added as she led him back down the passage. 'Whooping cough and croup and measles amongst the children – we buried three children ourselves,

55

all of our children in fact. I laid out their little corpses with my own hands, all three of them. And diphtheria and dysentery. My husband died of dysentery. He came home one evening after the Raad had sat till late complaining that he felt tired, and a week later he was dead.'

Should he offer his condolences? Versluis wondered, although before he could find the appropriately neutral but polite words Mrs Van der Vliet had stopped in the hall and turned to him with a sudden businesslike and resolute manner which he had hardly expected from her. 'I ask twenty pounds a month,' she informed him. 'Including three meals, coffee in the mornings, washing and ironing, and a bath once a week. If you wish to bath more often we will arrange for water to be fetched especially for you.'

It was considerably more than he was paying at the moment at the hotel, but under the circumstances that was no consideration for Versluis, and he bowed slightly to express his agreement; but Mrs Van der Vliet had walked on ahead of him, as if she wished to forget as quickly as possible the painful subject which she had been forced by the circumstances to raise. 'Here is the dining room,' she indicated with a wave of her small white hand. 'This is the back porch. It also gets sun in winter; you will be able to sit here in the sun and be entirely protected.'

He would not be there for winter, Versluis thought once again, but he refrained from expressing this and went outside. The long vegetable garden stretched immaculately to the willows of the spruit, the beds cultivated, raked and free of all weeds, with peach and fig trees in rows on each side.

'It's nice to have the spruit at the bottom of the garden,' he remarked.

'It smells,' Mrs Van der Vliet said disparagingly, and returned indoors. 'When can I expect you, Mr Versluis?'

'I would like to move in tonight if that would not be inconvenient for you.'

She nodded without any sign of surprise, as if it went without saying that he would be eager to transfer himself to her house. 'I will tell the servants to prepare the room for you,' she said, although it was not at all clear to him what more could be done to it. 'I'll expect you in an hour or two.' When he left, she accompanied him and remained standing on the top step of the front stoep while he took his leave. 'Mrs Schröder does what she can,' she remarked without any apparent prompting. 'I believe that there are visitors who are entirely satisfied with the hotel.' Unconvinced, she shook her head at the thought.

He returned to the hotel, and without resting first he began to pack – too hurriedly, he soon realised when the shortness of breath, the palpitations and dizziness returned, and he had to sit for a while on the edge of the bed to recover. He was still sitting there when Frau Schröder's anxious face appeared around the door in answer to the message he had sent her via Joseph.

'Oh yes, Frau Schröder,' he said, and he had to think for a moment to recall why he wanted to speak to her, for the sudden illness had driven all other thoughts from his head. It was the time of day when she was busy in the kitchen and, standing nervously before him, she was impatient to return. 'Frau Schröder, I must ask you to be so kind as to draw up my account. Unfortunately I have to leave the hotel, I have made other arrangements. . . .' She looked at him with alarm, and he felt a surge of impatience as he sat on the edge of the bed, his heart beating in agitation: how would he ever recover if he never got any rest, if it was not even possible for him to sleep soundly at night? 'That has simply become too much for me,' he then blurted out, more sharply than was seemly, and gestured towards the next room. It was clear that Frau Schröder understood. The patches of colour appeared on her high cheekbones, her hands fumbled with her apron, and instinctively she made her usual servile and apologetic curtsey. 'I'm sorry,' she muttered, 'it's a pity, I understand. Perhaps – but there is nothing, I have no other room, three gentlemen from Kimberley arrived this afternoon and we had to turn them away.' She felt the need to stay and offer her apologies, she felt obliged to be in the kitchen, and at the same time her eyes passed rapidly over the room as if she were contemplating how fast she could have it tidied and whether she could manage to get three people into it. 'But I understand,' she repeated. 'The account, yes of course – I'll send it to you.' In the midst of her hasty departure she stopped for a moment. 'All those sick people come here,' she declared, 'all of them are offloaded here, there is no-one to care for them, they come here to die, and once they are dead there is not even enough money to bury them. One even has to fight with the attorneys to have the accounts paid. We are not a hospital!' she cried out angrily from the corridor. 'We are not a charity!' To anyone listening in the room next door her words must have been clearly audible, and he wondered whether his unknown neighbour understood German.

When Frau Schröder had left he resumed his packing, but more slowly now; he counted out the money demanded of him without checking the account, arranged with Joseph to have his baggage taken to Mrs Van der Vliet, and left the familiar room for the last time while Joseph preceded him down the passage with a candle. Night had already begun to fall and the bar was noisy: there were loud voices in the billiard room and the clatter of cutlery came from the dining room; only the room next to his remained silent, no sign of light visible beneath the door.

From the kitchen Frau Schröder swooped quickly upon him to bid him farewell. She was sorry, she said again; she understood, she said. But he had been satisfied with everything, she hoped. She followed him outside along the passage, still seeking a last word of approval and endorsement before saying goodbye and hurrying back to the kitchen.

He was free, Versluis thought, and with an almost physical sensation of relief he left the hotel. It was already dusk, and the roofs of the low buildings around the square were visible only where they were etched against the darkening light, their windows illuminated by the glow of candles and lamps now being lit. It was just light enough for him to be able to make his way across the expanse of the market square, but not light enough to see clearly where he was going, and he stumbled over the uneven ground, nearly fell, and then stopped for a moment, his forehead cold with sweat. He waited for a while on that deserted square while the darkness deepened around him, and he noticed the evening star blazing radiantly above him, incandescent above the low houses of the town. The day had been too tiring and upsetting, but he forced himself onwards, leaning heavily on his cane, past the houses with their glowing windows, past the dark gardens from which the dogs barked at him, and groped his way across the narrow footbridge across the spruit. He could not arrive at Mrs Van der Vliet's in that condition, he thought, and wondered at the same time how he would be able to withstand the exhausting process of introductions and a meal with strangers; when he arrived, however, there was no need to find words of apology or explanation. On meeting him in the hall Mrs Van der Vliet lit the lamp, gave him a look of appraisal as he stood in the doorway, and nodded, as if his appearance fulfilled all her expectations. 'You will want to go to bed,' she informed him firmly. 'You ought not to be outside at this time, the night air is not good for chest complaints.' Nor did Versluis protest, aware only of lamplight and shadows sliding through the large, high rooms of the house, of bedclothes being turned back, baggage being carried in. He got undressed without paying much attention to folding and putting away his clothes; he lay in the high white bed in his new room and the servant brought him tea and bread on a tray. The white counterpane, the tea things, the large napkin and the woman's apron and headcloth gleamed before his eyes in the lamplight; the room ebbed into shadow, and darkness gathered in the corners, almost drowning Mrs Van der Vliet as she stood in the doorway in her black mourning-dress to overlook the servant's activities. Why had she made tea for him when that very afternoon she had prided herself on the fact that in her house coffee was always served? he wondered incoherently. Slowly she nodded in his direction, encouraging, approving, kindly, as if quite satisfied with the course of events and the installation of an ailing stranger in her guest room; and then she withdrew into the dark.

A new life had begun, Versluis realised with a feeling of wellbeing, or at least a clearly defined new phase of his sojourn in Africa, in a cool, quiet house with high rooms where everything went its course in almost complete silence: a life of large beds and down pillows, of white tablecloths, starched napkins and clean towels; a house which smelt of beeswax and turpentine, and in which lowered blinds subdued the glare of the afternoon sun and lighted lamps were carried in when dusk began to fall.

Slowly he began to reconnoitre, still weak and unsteady on his feet; gradually he settled in and calmed down. Furthermore, the baggage that had been carried from the coast by the transport riders also arrived at this time: the great gleaming black cabin-trunks which had been packed and locked months earlier in the Netherlands, bound with rope and sealed with lead, were carried into his room, and as he threw open the lids and bent over their contents he recalled the sombre, low, late-autumn sky in Holland when they had been carried to the cab by the porter: how they had glistened in the rain, how the horses had stood waiting in the drizzle with low-slung heads. The floorboards in the passage creaked, and he heard the rustle of a dress: Mrs Van der Vliet appeared in the doorway to enquire whether he had anything to be washed. Phlegmatic and composed, she returned from time to time to make further enquiries, implacable in her desire to be of service; each time she would convey another bundle of clothes under her arm to be washed, pressed, or brushed out, and she sent a servant to fetch his shoes. In the spacious wardrobe his suits hung in a row, while his other belongings were arranged in the drawers: his shirts, underclothes and socks, his woollens and linen, his nightshirts, handkerchiefs and ties, his gloves – from the folds of tissue paper there appeared all the items of clothing that Pompe had folded and packed for him with such care, concerned that nothing which might come in useful in the strange country should be forgotten. He brought out his toilet set, the shaving kit with its strop; the containers of collars, studs and cufflinks; the writing-case which was intended for use at sea; the travelling-rug; the hip-flask; the scarf which had been brought to protect him from the sun and the parasol which he had not used yet; the fan; the books; all the effects which had been transported into the interior with so much effort and at such cost, now to be unpacked at last in this moribund, dusty little town: clothes made or purchased in the Netherlands, books written in strange languages, the scent of eau de Cologne and of sandalwood soap. A new life had begun for him; or, he reminded himself, a new phase of his life had been initiated in this remote terrain – the invisible bridge spanning the gulf had been crossed, and the road extended once more before him through a landscape which was often surprisingly familiar.

Those living in the house ate together at a long table in the dining room. In the passage a middle-aged man in slippers shuffled up to Versluis: 'Van der Vliet,' he said, proffering his hand, and gave no further explanation of who he was. Mrs Van der Vliet presided over the table and Versluis was ceremoniously seated at her right hand and introduced to the others: Miss Pronk, the bride-to-be from Almelo, with almost colourless blue eyes and pale eyelashes which she fluttered as she flung her head back to set curls, ribbons and earrings dancing, and the two clerks whom Mrs Van der Vliet had already mentioned to Versluis – young men with plastered-down hair and stiff collars who paid less attention to the introductions than to the food being carried in from the kitchen by an entourage of servants. The middle-aged man had shuffled in and taken his place at the bottom of the table without anybody paying any attention to him.

With a regal hand Mrs Van der Vliet dished up for everyone and passed the plates on as if they constituted alms provided out of her manifold charity. 'Good Dutch food,' she remarked to Versluis, and it was indeed a stodgy, nourishing winter meal, *petit bourgeois* Dutch cuisine which had been parodied with African ingredients and served in the blazing heat of summer, much too heavy and hot for a day such as this; but he smiled and commented appreciatively, trying to eat as much of it as he could. The two young men divided their attention between their food and Miss Pronk, enthusiastically passing the bread, salt and jugs of water, while she in turn fluttered affectedly in her ribbons, curls and earrings and laughed at all their jokes. The conversation at the table remained disjointed above the scrape of knives and forks and the buzzing of flies behind the lace curtains, but in time a political debate developed between the two clerks. It was Polderman, a friendly, lively man with reddish hair and a snub nose, who, being Dutch, displayed the most self-confidence, and turned to Versluis to ask his opinion about events in the Transvaal and to make worldly-wise remarks about possible intervention by France, Germany and Portugal; but it was not clear to Versluis what he was talking about, so the young man enjoyed showing off his knowledge before the others. While beside him Du Toit concentrated on his food, busily plying his knife and fork, and looked up only occasionally from his plate.

'On his visit to Europe President Burgers was received in the Netherlands with a great deal of enthusiasm,' Polderman assured the group, who showed no noticeable signs of interest. 'I saw it myself in the Dutch papers, my uncle sent me the clippings. That cannot be insignificant; don't you think so, Mr Versluis?'

'I recall in '59,' the middle-aged man interjected from his place at the bottom of the table, as if he had been waiting for just such an occasion, 'that was when I had just arrived in the Free State, it was of course still in the time of President Boshof, or at least just after he had retired – I remember Grey was still Governor of the Cape. Sir George Grey,' he explained to Versluis, since he was the only one at the table who was paying any attention to this tale. 'He was here on a visit in '61, '61 or '60, I remember it well, when I was still working for the Treasury. . . .' Then he became aware of Mrs Van der Vliet's gaze fixed upon him and his voice died away, although no-one else noticed it. Du Toit, who had emptied and pushed aside his plate, had begun a lively conversation with Polderman across the table about Cape politics, and Mrs Van der Vliet was attending to the servants who had come to remove the empty dishes.

'There is semolina,' she informed Versluis as if this were an exceptional treat.

'Semolina pudding, delicious!' Miss Pronk exclaimed and clapped her hands ecstatically.

'We obtain the currant juice from Holland,' said Mrs Van der Vliet, and the two clerks shifted their attention to the young lady as, with tiny cries of delight, she poured currant juice on to her pudding.

'But he always said,' Van der Vliet's voice suddenly sounded across the table, 'like President Brand after him – indeed, in that respect there was no difference in their respective views, they followed the same policy. . . .' But no-one paid any attention to him; nobody even heard him.

Dinner was eaten early, as was apparently the custom in this country. Then the servants came to clear the table while Mrs Van der Vliet installed herself behind the coffee pot and handed out cups of coffee which had been diluted still further by the addition of large quantities of hot milk. At the bottom of the table Van der Vliet had begun to lay out cards for a game of patience, while Miss Pronk coquettishly moved to drape herself over his chair and looked on. Helmond, her fiancé, arrived and nodded dismissively to Versluis, but either out of shyness or boredom the engaged couple hardly paid any attention to each other, until finally Helmond collared young Polderman and they strolled up and down the stoep in the cool of the evening, smoking cigars and thrashing out the events in the Transvaal. Versluis had come to sit on the stoep, and from there he listened to their vehement discussion. Helmond ignored him, and it was Polderman who made some attempt to include him in their conversation, and informed him of the merits of President Burgers, the backwardness of the Transvaal and the unreliability of Britain, lamenting somewhat this stranger's ignorance of matters which, in his view, had stirred up the whole of South Africa. Helmond stood staring absently across the garden, drawing on his cigar, but when the sounds of his fiancée's gaiety filtered through to them a little too loudly from the dining room where she had remained with Du Toit, he frowned, threw the cigar end away, and returned inside. This was followed by Mrs Van der Vliet who came out to upbraid Versluis for sitting outside in the night air, and they all went back indoors.

Night had already begun to fall: it grew dark so quickly here, Versluis realised again as he remained for a moment in front of the dining room window, staring out at the shadowy garden: each time he was surprised anew by the suddenness of nightfall. The servants had already brought the lamps, silently on bare feet, and the young people made preparations to play a game of *pandoer* with Van der Vliet. Mrs Van der Vliet watched the group around the table for a moment, and then rose to unlock the sideboard and produce a decanter of gin, bitters and some glasses. She poured some for each of the younger men, and finally, after a moment's consideration, and with a palpably less generous hand, some for Van der Vliet, who had been staring at her in silent expectation since the appearance of the decanter, the cards forgotten in his hand.

62

Versluis had gone to fetch a book and Mrs Van der Vliet produced some crochet work. Du Toit, who had not taken part in the game of cards, followed it detachedly for a while, yawned, sipped his gin reluctantly, and finally announced that he had better go to bed, although the players hardly noticed his departure in their growing excitement with the game – their cries, jokes and laughter becoming increasingly boisterous. Van der Vliet beamed in a haze of cigar smoke at the end of the table and turned his head from one of his fellow players to another lest he miss anything; he coughed over his cigar, dealt the cards with eager, abrupt gestures, and from time to time he would wipe one eye which had begun to water.

Strange nocturnal creatures called outside in the dark and moths beat their wings urgently against the lampshades; Mrs Van der Vliet's crochet needles flashed in the light. The exuberant Dutch voices rang out to Dutch gin and cigars, and as the players became more involved in their game they increasingly lost their later accretions – the English expressions, the local vocabulary and idoms, the alien, flattened vowels. Versluis wavered as he sat listening to them, tottered and regained his balance for a moment on the subtle boundary which divided the two worlds, like a disc balancing precariously on its edge without toppling to one side or the other; he listened to the sound of Dutch voices in a room whose windows were open to an African summer's evening and its strange nocturnal calls.

He had brought out his travelling-desk and spread out its contents: his last letters to the Netherlands had been written on the boat and mailed on his arrival in South Africa, before he had attempted the journey into the interior and fallen ill, and it was time he wrote home again. The aunts would be surprised at not having heard from him for so long, and would be enquiring about mail ships from Africa; the Van Meerdervoorts would appreciate a few lines, as would the Lohmanns, and he needed to inform Pompe of certain things which should be packed and sent on.

The stationery lay ready for him – the writing paper and the envelopes, the little crystal ink pots and the blotting paper, the different coloured wax, the wax-lights – and with a sense of satisfaction he arranged a sheet of paper and dipped his quill into the ink to begin writing. On the floorboards outside his door the bare feet of the servants moved with barely a sound and he heard their subdued voices as they talked to each other; beyond the hazy film of the short blinds the town lay stretched out in the blinding reflection of the midday sun. The paper waited. What should he say? What could he say? he pondered, and he did not know how to begin.

The clock would be ticking in the silent house in which the aunts sat bowed over their crocheting, the flames of the little fire flickering behind the firescreen. What could he write that they would want to hear, for Aunt Dorethee to read out aloud? He imagined all sounds dying away in that undisturbed and imperturbable room: the drone of his aunt's voice, the crinkle of the sheet of writing paper as she folded it, the rustle of their dresses and the crackle of the fire in the hearth. What should he write to the Van Meerdervoorts? The calash riding ahead to fetch them for their afternoon drive or visit, the black woodwork of the vehicle gleaming in the drizzle, and the servant spreading a rug across their knees against the winter cold. The fire would be laid and the lamps burning; candles would be lit on the long table, and after dinner the guests might play cards or someone would take a seat at the piano. What could he write to them that they could share with mutual friends, news from Africa to be conveyed over the hot-house flowers on the table between the passages or over the fans of their cards? Or to Pompe, alone in the basement of the deserted house where dust covers now shrouded the furniture, shuffling up the stairs when the postman rang the front door bell with a letter containing strange postage stamps, the address on the envelope spattered with rain?

He wavered while the ink dried on the pen, and then he dipped it into the well once again and, still hesitantly, he resumed his efforts to reach out to the distant world which he had left behind. He had arrived safely he stated, after a long and exhausting journey by coach, and pondered before continuing. He had been a trifle indisposed on arrival he wrote; he had recovered from this slight illness – for he needed to explain why he had not written sooner. Bloemfontein, where he was now staying, was the capital of the country, but it was really no more than a town, situated unexpectedly on these plains with its Dutch name, and the heat of summer was tiring, making it inadvisable to go out during the day. He was, however, fortunate enough to be accommodated in a Dutch household, and since his arrival here he had had contact with virtually only Dutch and German people, so that the worst of the alienation to be expected from such an interlude had been moderated. Slowly and deliberately he drew the sweeping figures of his g's and f's, elegantly crossed the t's. His health had already improved as a result of the dry climate, he added to reassure the aunts; and with that he knew that he had said everything.

Of what more could he tell them? Mrs Van der Vliet's abraded vowels and the Dutch coffee which she served with such obvious pride; the German pastor, born here but homesick for Germany? How could this possibly interest the aunts in their distant sitting room, or the Van Meerdervoorts and their guests at their dining room or card tables? He searched his memory and allowed his gaze to pass over images recalled from the past few weeks. The barefoot servants; the bathwater that had to be carried by bucket from the well – would they find these things amusing? The primitive toilet facilities, the outhouses hidden at the bottom of the long gardens. The black man with blood on his face, or the dead dog with its rigid jaws? Unthinkable, he thought absently to himself as he pushed the bizarre images aside, and stared out of the window at the summer afternoon. This glare, this pulsating bleached expanse filled with heat and light and dust – should he try to describe it to them?

The rain streams down from a sky which hangs low over the gables and chimneys, it stirs through the bare trees. The canals are turbulent, the railings of the bridges glimmer, the vehicle gleams in the rain as it waits in front of the door, his trunks glint as they are carried out, gleaming black in the rain. He put the pen down. The trunks that had been carefully packed by Pompe and removed from the house under his watchful eye had been unpacked here and Mrs Van der Vliet had sent the gardener to fetch and store them in an outside room. Why had it remained with him, he wondered, that memory of his luggage being carried outside on an autumn day in Delft and loaded on to the waiting coach? In some way it was as if that single, arbitrary image of the black trunks with their ropes and lead seals encapsulated for him everything about the transfer, perfectly expressed his alienation, emphasised the inexorability of his parting, and sealed his departure with complete finality.

There was a knock at the door: coffee was served a servant informed him, and he realised that Mrs Van der Vliet was waiting for him in the sitting room, but he nevertheless stayed at the desk on his lap. There was really nothing to write to those that had been left behind, he realised in a flash of disturbing clarity, although he would not have been able to explain the logic of this awareness. There was no road, there was no path along which a message could reach them across this distance.

He wiped his hand across his forehead, both surprised and upset by this inexplicable insight. He had sat too intently and for too long over this letter, hence his strange thoughts, and slowly and methodically he tidied his writing materials before joining Mrs Van der Vliet for coffee. Yet, he realised in that moment of unexpected clarity that had been granted him, he would have liked to find words to represent the white glare of this afternoon heat for them. He would like to find words for the desolation of the surrounding veld, and for the feelings of disquiet and excitement that it aroused in him. But were there words, he wondered; did he have the language which was needed for such reports?

Even if words could be found he thought as he hastily drew on his jacket, the aunts would only be able to respond to them without any understanding, perhaps even with a degree of disquiet; the Van Meerdervoorts would not understand, the good Pompe even less. The letters he had begun he would end, seal and send off, and those who received them would probably not realise that they had been left unfinished.

Mrs Van der Vliet emerged from the gloom of the passage to inform him that there was a visitor for him, coyly, as if it were some kind of surprise, but there was only Pastor Scheffler waiting for him in the hallway, unrecognisable for a moment as he stood silhouetted against the light of the street outside.

'I came for only a moment,' he assured Versluis in his usual way – sincere, hurried and nervous – even before Versluis could complete his conventional words of welcome. 'I have already told Mrs Van der Vliet that I can unfortunately not stay for coffee. I'm on my way to the Misses Zastron, they are expecting me, and I fear that I am already late, but as I was passing I felt that I had at least to come and ask how you are.'

Mrs Van der Vliet had again withdrawn to the room where she spent her afternoons in silence beneath the portrait of her late husband, a footstool at her feet. The conversation in the hall was clearly audible to her, and in the circumstances Versluis could hardly do anything but express his satisfaction with his present accommodation, even if he had wanted to do otherwise, but it was clear to him that this was not what interested the clergyman.

'I am pleased,' Scheffler said thoughtfully, 'I am pleased to have been of service to you,' and he was already moving towards the drawing room to bid Mrs Van der Vliet farewell. With her hands clasped on her lap, her dress spread out to cover the footstool, she imparted further messages to be conveyed to the Misses Zastron and Mrs Brand, while he went out to the stoep and then suddenly paused on the steps. 'The real reason for my visit,' he said to Versluis – 'that is to say, not that I didn't want to find out how you were, but the reason why I dropped in so hastily this afternoon in particular. . . .' He hesitated, as if uncertain of the way in which his next suggestion would be received. 'There are a number of us here, German-speaking people, and the women in particular, who have started a reading cycle and get together once a month to read a little German, and I wondered . . . that is, Mrs Hirsch suggested that I ask you if you wouldn't perhaps like to attend our next meeting. And, if this is not asking too much,' he added hastily, 'if you would be so kind as to read something for us.' He looked up expectantly at Versluis from the steps where he had remained standing, his hat in his hand, and grinned. 'We would appreciate it greatly,' he said. 'I know that Mrs Hirsch would. And so would I.'

It would be churlish to decline this friendly invitation, Versluis knew, and besides, since his arrival in Bloemfontein he had been nowhere with the exception of that single visit to the Hirsches' house: it was time for him to begin to participate in the town's social life, and a meeting of the German reading circle promised to be a relatively intimate and not too demanding occasion. 'It would be a pleasure for me to try to read something for you,' he said, and the clergyman beamed.

'I knew you wouldn't let us down,' he said; 'at least, it unfortunately sounds very presumptuous, but I trusted that you would be willing to help. Would it be in order if I came to fetch you – on Wednesday afternoon at four o'clock?' He had already turned away, on his way to his appointment. 'You do have some books from which to select? I'm afraid our taste is not particularly refined, and you may also find us a little old-fashioned. If I could send over a few books to help with your choice. . . .' Still talking, he walked backwards down the steps while Versluis remained on the stoep and then, donning his hat, he suddenly looked up and smiled once more with that trusting, candid schoolboy grin which lit up his serious countenance. 'I hope that the invitation is more attractive than one to a church service or a sermon,' he added, and was gone.

The servant had brought the coffee, and Versluis joined Mrs Van der Vliet, seated behind the tray. 'The Germans are very active in Bloemfontein,' she remarked, without any attempt to conceal the fact that she had overheard their conversation. 'They have their club and the reading circle and the choral society, and they hold a large ball every year on the Kaiser's birthday; the President always attends – but of course, his wife's family is German. There have always been so many Germans in the city, Doctor Krause and Doctor Kellner. And Mr Fichardt, and the Baumanns and the Hirsches and Mr Leviseur – half of the shopkeepers. And Mathey,' she added derisively as she sipped her coffee. 'Naturally, I am not given to visiting the Matheys myself,' she added, as if she wished to remove any possible misapprehension on the subject. 'Even though I am sure that his wife is a good soul and deserves our sympathy.'

Versluis was uncertain whether to take her eloquent silence as a sign that he should enquire further about the Matheys; but as he grew to know her better it became clear that her conversations usually took the form of definite opinions, unsolicited, and furthermore expressed without any evident reference to the immediate context. 'It's another matter as far as the Dutch are concerned,' she continued. 'In the old days, when my husband was still alive, it was different.' She paid homage to his memory by nodding slightly in the direction of her husband's portrait without finding it necessary to look directly at the familiar image. 'Mr Groenendal was still here and Mr Spruijt, the Secretary of State; and Advocate Hamelberg and Meester Smellekamp and Magistrate Van Soelen – how many evenings they gathered in our home, a confirmed group of Netherlanders! My husband always had fine tobacco and cigars in the house.' She shook her head sadly as she recited the litany of their names to him, and then reached for the coffee pot to pour herself another cup. He observed for the first time that the heavy brooch at her neck contained locks of hair, and reflected whether they might have belonged to her deceased husband. 'And Mr Heijligers from the newspaper,' she remembered. 'But who is left? Even Mrs Smellekamp has left for the Cape with her children. He always ordered his cigars directly from Holland,' she added somewhat passionately while she surveyed the past to the rhythmical stirring of her coffee spoon. 'And we used to order tinned cauliflower and endives from Holland, together with *spekulaas* and *pepernote* for St Nicholas. But the young people show no interest in these things any longer. They don't even speak Dutch any more. It's the Germans who celebrate Christmas in their own way now, and found choral societies and celebrate their Kaiser's birthday.'

'Most people I have met so far have been German,' Versluis remarked when her thoughtful silence allowed him to contribute to this conversation over the coffee cups.

'At least they are still able to speak Dutch, or in any case they try.

The others, the English, don't even take the trouble, they expect everybody to speak their language. But I have nothing against Germans, no matter what may be said about them. Since Pastor Scheffler has been here, I have even been to the occasional service in the church.'

There was again a short pause: this disclosure had been important to her, and she expected an appropriate acknowledgement. It was, however, unclear to Versluis which stance he was being expected to admire or endorse, and he considered it unwise to venture on a comparison of the Lutheran and Reformed Churches to which the conversation seemed to allude. He thus merely remarked: 'Pastor Scheffler seems to be rather young to have to lead a congregation.'

Mrs Van der Vliet was busy smoothing down the folds of her mourning-dress with a small, well-manicured white hand, as if their proper arrangement was in itself a token of piety towards the deceased. Finally the folds of the dress, with its shiny, stiff black frills and ribbons, had been arranged to her satisfaction: she clasped her hands again and cast a quick, practised glance at the tray, the carpet, and the room to ensure that everything was in order. Apparently it was, and she sighed softly and then considered his remark. 'Of course my husband and I always attended the Dutch church,' she informed him, 'although in my opinion Dominee Radloff is not what Dominee Van der Wall was – a clergyman of the old school, Mr Versluis, who was not afraid to express his opinion.' For a moment it seemed that she might elaborate on this subject, but she thought better of it. 'Pastor Winter used to be at the Lutheran church, in the early days, when the parish had just been founded, but then he went over to the Dutch church and served there; although one asks oneself where the difference really lies, and whether it matters that much. Then Pastor Scheffler came from Bethany and, as I said, I attended a few of their services. In any case, it's just around the corner, within easy reach.' Once again there was a pregnant pause, and Versluis sensed a number of branches in this conversation that she could choose to follow – expositions regarding her health, further particulars about palpitations and anxiety, something that he had already heard – but she rejected all these possibilities. 'Not that I really feel at home there, Mr Versluis,' she continued; 'as you no doubt will understand,' and she leant forward slightly. 'Those crosses,' she confided. 'And the altar. They're contrary to scripture. But finally, it was Mother's church,' she conceded and leant back in her chair, 'and there are differences of opinion about all these matters.'

Versluis waited, detached, for what might follow, conscious of the fact that the detours which Mrs Van der Vliet took in her circuitous monologues were employed to contribute to the effect of the final judgement for which her listeners were being prepared. She once again quickly smoothed the folds of her dress, touched the brooch with the plaited locks of hair and then put her hand to her own hair beneath the lace bonnet with its black ribbons.

'Of course, Pastor Winter was himself the son of a missionary,' she said thoughtfully. 'In fact both of them come from Bethany, both he and Pastor Scheffler; they grew up there together.' She fell silent; she pondered; she rejected something. 'It's not that he does not preach with conviction,' she then continued, 'but then even if one does know that the Lutheran Church is not really reformed. . . . There are people in his congregation who have their misgivings about him, Mr Versluis, despite the fact that he hasn't been here long.'

The conversation had once again reached a point at which he was expected to respond. 'He has always been particularly kind to me,' was his contribution.

'He is indeed a very fine young man, nobody will gainsay that; and perhaps he is too good. Too much goodness turns to folly, as we know, Mr Versluis. But then, what sort of life has he had, what kind of upbringing is it to grow up on a missionary station amongst the blacks? And then, after that, in Germany – where the churches are no longer what they used to be and where doctrine is being attacked every day, according to the newspapers.' Once again she leant over towards him to emphasise the confidentiality of her remarks. 'Bloemfontein is a small community, even if there are so many Germans in the town, too small to support a clergyman adequately. And then there is his sister who is a constant problem for him, and indeed I believe that his wife is not very well.' She shook her head gravely without adding anything to help him make sense of these incoherent allusions. 'What kind of a life is it for a young man?' she asked rhetorically, and leant back with her arms folded as if she had no choice but to expect the worst of the situation. But then the servant arrived to collect the tray and the cups, and Mrs Van der Vliet withdrew in silent meditation, and the coffee hour with its measured sociability had come to an end. Versluis took his leave and returned to his room; for a brief moment he stood in the hall and looked out at the garden and the street beyond the verandah, and suddenly he was reminded of that clumsy figure in black, backing down the steps of the stoep with his hat in his hand, vanishing into the glare of the day.

70

He felt at home in this large, cool, well cared-for house: he had already settled into it. The two clerks went to work early and after a surge of chattering and bustling about, Miss Pronk left in the shelter of her parasol to do some shopping or visit her friends – sometimes she came back for lunch and sat loudly recounting her adventures, but just as often she did not. A floorboard creaked, a dress rustled in the dusky gloom of the house, and Versluis would hear the low sound of Mrs Van der Vliet's voice, so subdued that he could not discern the words. The creaking floor, the rustle of the dress, the admonitory voice were interwoven with the tranquillity of the morning, and in time he stopped noticing her constant movements to and fro in the house to supervise the servants and issue instructions. He was grateful for the silence and the orderliness of the house where nothing threatened or encroached upon him, where nothing disturbed him except at most the timid knock of a servant returning the ironing or announcing that coffee was served.

In this period moreover, after he had moved into Mrs Van der Vliet's house, the town's inhabitants began to make initial overtures towards him: visitor's cards were left by people whom he did not know, and one by one the members of Bloemfontein's small, Dutch community arrived in person, singly or with their spouses, to meet him: the State Attorney, the Auditor General, the head of the boys' school, the local attorneys and a few members of the Volksraad – some came for lunch, some for afternoon coffee, and others at night after dinner. These visits were so stiff and formal that it was clear to Versluis that they had been organised beforehand by Mrs Van der Vliet. Coffee and *sandgebak* would be served, gin and a box of cigars brought out, and the conversation, which was initially devoted to accepted small talk, would soon find its proper level: they spoke about the Netherlands, about Zutphen and Twello, Utrecht and Arnhem, while the country they inhabited was mentioned only in passing – in the course of tales about their arrival, or in reference to fellow-Dutchmen who had settled there. 'Africa', they would say, from some distant perspective, an area that had grown familiar to them over the years, but which remained outlandish in its institutions and customs. It was to Scheveningen or Haarlemmerhout that the talk would return: the shops, coffee houses and reading rooms of the Netherlands; its mailcoaches, barges and rail service; the education system of this country would be examined and be found wanting; the level of Dutch newspapers and sermons unsatisfactory; and amongst themselves the women would lament the unavailability of endives, chicory and purslane. Occasionally Miss

71

Pronk would join the company, coquettish towards the men and fluttering her eyelashes while she listened, sometimes joined by her fiancé or Polderman, and in this small circle of visitors there grew the fellowship which binds exiles in a strange land. At other times Van der Vliet would also shuffle up in his slippers, to stand nodding and smiling at the edge of the conversation, but Mrs van der Vliet took no notice of him – it was as if she did not see him standing there outside the circle of the lamplight, and although the visitors would greet him when he appeared, they had little choice but to follow the example of their hostess. Finally he would move off, and they heard the sound of his slippers dying away outside on the dark stoep.

When the conversation had been going for some time, and a sufficient degree of conviviality had been generated, Mrs Van der Vliet would rise with a great jingle of keys and produce the decanter of gin from the sideboard. The paraffin lamps cast their heat and their oily fumes into the still night air, and the blue haze from the men's cigars hung more densely in the room as their companionship increased. They spoke of the English-speaking inhabitants of Bloemfontein – shopkeepers, teachers and clerks – of their arrogance and complacency and their strange eating and other habits; they complained of their refusal to learn Dutch or laughed at their clumsy attempts to speak it; shook their heads at the Papist tendencies of the Anglican Church and its growing influence within the community, and hinted darkly at abuses which, if they did not exist already, were almost certainly brooding in the bishop's palace. Mrs Van der Vliet passed the decanter around once more, radiant at the conviviality of such a genuinely Dutch evening, as she was later to represent it to Versluis. They grew more and more at home as the evening progressed, talking about fellow-inhabitants and other acquaintances, about present and past scandals and rumours, about cheating, fraud and bankruptcy, with tongues that were beginning to slur – as far as the men in the company were concerned – and reddening faces. Passionately they aired their grievances and lamented the injustices which they had always been forced to bear, until gradually the last trace of resignation or acquiescence vanished and they complained freely about the country in which they found themselves exiled and the people amongst whom they lived as strangers. Versluis was already accepted as a member of the inner circle from whom no secrets need be kept – or perhaps his presence was simply forgotten as they talked amongst themselves. The country with its distances, its heat and dust, where there was a dearth of good sermons or newspapers, endives, *witloof*, or purlane; the land in which

all labour was carried out half-heartedly and left unfinished; of carelessness, indifference, procrastination and neglect; and the people, as
degenerate as the language they spoke – round and round these subjects
the conversation revolved in the glow of the lamps and the haze of cigar
smoke, until the women began to yawn behind their handkerchiefs and
cast surreptitious glances at the clock. With less and less inhibition
they expounded on the backwardness of the local farmers, and illus-
trated their criticism with suitable anecdotes. What the country needed
was a few hundred hard-working Dutch farmers who knew how to
put a hand to the plough, a dozen or two Dutch teachers, and
the assistance of Dutch capital. Africa was good for nothing, they
concluded, nor could anything be made of it given its droughts, its
hailstorms and its locusts. The gin did a final round; the cigars
crumbled into fine, silvery ash, and only the haze of smoke still hung
suspended around the lamps; a final, longing glance was cast across
time and space: to Rotterdam and Amsterdam, to Beveland and
Terschelling, pale beneath their winter skies and hardly visible in the
mist. Then the guests rose to leave, the men loud and slightly unsteady
on their feet, and their goodnight calls rang down the dark streets,
beneath the brilliant African stars.

Initially Mrs Van der Vliet tried to prevent Versluis from going out
in the late afternoon or coming back after sunset, but as he kept
on forgetting her warnings and ignoring her admonitions – it was
unnecessary for her to be concerned about him, he informed her
politely but firmly; he had recovered completely – she merely shook
her head in dark foreboding whenever he went to sit on the stoep after
dinner in the evenings to enjoy the cool night air. They ate so early
that it was always still light: Mrs Van der Vliet would be in the house,
the servants busy in the kitchen; from across the gardens and orchards
of the town there would come the occasional sound of a voice or of
dogs barking, but in the bright toneless light of the dusk no-one was
visible, and even the brilliance of Miss Pronk's dress would have
vanished among the peach trees where she had gone for a walk with
her fiancé. Tonight Versluis had intended to page through the poetry
collections that Scheffler had sent over and to select a few poems for
reading aloud, but he was unable to concentrate on the words for very
long; both the language and imagery seemed equally alien against the
backdrop of this summer's evening with its radiant heat and growing
drought, and he felt a degree of irritation at the way in which the

clergyman had dragged him into this predicament and at the way in which he had allowed it to happen. What were these people doing with Klopstock and Herder? he wondered. What place was there for Storm or Meyer in this country? He shut the book and put it aside.

Restless, impatient and bored he rose and walked down the steps of the stoep into the garden – it was getting dry and the air was oppressive; it was the heat that made him feel as if he had a fever again tonight, he thought, and tried to put it out of his mind. The earth was parched under his feet, the day's heat rose up towards him, and even in the dusk the air seemed to scorch his forehead. He recalled being on the beach at Egmond, as he remained standing in the centre of one of the straight little garden paths, raked and swept clean; he turned around as if in search of something: on the beach of the North Sea at Egmond he had as a youth years before walked alone one breathless winter afternoon along the unbroken shore, among the dunes and the grey sea, beneath a depressed sky. When had that been? he wondered to himself thinking of it now, of the unstirring cold and the emptiness of the beach on which he had been alone.

Van der Vliet came shuffling out from behind the quince hedge and nodded a friendly greeting, as if he were a trifle uncertain whether his presence was welcome or not. 'Bit of dry weather,' he remarked. 'We need rain; it's been some time since we had a shower.'

Versluis tore himself way from the unexpected memory in order to speak to the man. 'It's an exemplary garden you have here,' he said politely.

Van der Vliet stood nodding with his hands on his hips as he looked out over the beds. 'This is my kingdom,' he agreed, 'just as the house and the chicken-runs are my wife's domain, and one could say that I rule with a firm hand. But then firmness is essential if one is to create and maintain order here.'

The formal, slightly florid reply was the more surprising since Versluis had never heard Van der Vliet express an opinion or take part in a conversation, and his random attempts to do so were usually ignored by those around him; he remained on the periphery of the circle, nodding in a friendly way, and finally disappeared again without anyone noticing his departure. Here in the vegetable garden, however, he stood with his hands on his hips and gazed over his empire like a little Napoleon.

'It is clear that you know a great deal about gardening,' Versluis said, but Van der Vliet simply chuckled quietly to himself.

'Oh no,' he said, 'no, not at all, as a boy I didn't even help the gardeners. Latin and Greek, those were my forte. I was the best student in classical languages at the gymnasium. Haarlem,' he added by way of explanation, and regarded Versluis with a watery eye. He had lost his usual shyness, as if he felt at ease only here amongst his beds, dignified in a waistcoat and shirtsleeves, and wearing his slippers as usual. 'After that I read law – in Leiden, I studied in Leiden.' Once again he laughed with that low chuckle. 'I have no background in gardening or agriculture.'

'Did you practise in the Netherlands?' Versluis enquired, but Versluis's attention had wandered.

'Oh no, no,' he said absently. 'I came to Africa. Nor did I manage to complete my studies,' he added after some thought, as if he were compelled to make this confession in the interests of both courtesy and honesty.

Up to then Versluis had paid scant attention to Van der Vliet or his unexplained position in the house, but from the confidence with which he spoke here and his meticulous Dutch, it began to appear that he came from a better class than Mrs Van der Vliet or the Dutch visitors who gathered there for gin and cigars. It struck Versluis that his last question had been tactless; the silence became a bit uncomfortable.

'Have you lived here for long?' he asked.

'In Africa, you mean? Or in the Free State? But it doesn't really matter what you mean exactly, it comes to the same thing. An eternity, Mr Versluis, an eternity – so long that I can no longer calculate the exact time in years.' He turned around, hands on his hips, and they wandered slowly among the raked and cultivated flowerbeds. 'I travelled with the transport riders from the coast, in ox-wagons – it took two months to get here from Port Elizabeth. Now there are passenger coaches, and trains too, they tell me, at least for part of the way; but I wouldn't know, I have never been back since I first came here across the Orange River.' The dusk had begun to fade, and as usual the tempering of colour, the softening of outlines cast a fleeting delicacy over the harshness of the land. Children called from beyond the trees as they played, dogs barked from plot to plot in the distance; above them the sky changed colour. 'We lived off venison and black coffee,' Van der Vliet said; 'the men shot game every day, right there on the way, from the wagons, it was so plentiful. I was young, I enjoyed it – I thought that everything was possible in this land where everything was new and unspoilt. I believed that it was simply waiting to be taken.' He laughed softly to himself and, suddenly conscious of the

75

fact that his eye was watering, he took out his handkerchief to wipe it. 'Bloemfontein was merely a handful of buildings beside the spruit, the wildebeests wandered amongst the houses and at night one heard wolves and wild dogs howling in the koppies. A tiny, dead, moribund little town – but that is precisely what was so exciting, so challenging, I would say. Nothing has ever happened here; in other words, everything could still happen.'

The light was growing dim through the branches of the fruit trees at the end of the garden. Could he still discern the brilliance of Miss Pronk's dress gleaming for a moment in that gathering dusk, could he hear a suppressed laugh beyond the trees? Versluis was not sure. He had also walked with Mrs Hirsch in this way in the dusk while she had talked of Africa, he remembered, and he remembered too the journey around the mountain and the wide panorama, with the Malay coachman straight and still on the box. He had not seen the Hirsches since then.

'Yes,' Van der Vliet said, half to himself. 'We laid out gardens here, we planted trees – Bloemfontein has become quite a neat little town, all things considered, don't you think? We have churches, schools, shops – theatre. . . . We have fought with this land, and it almost looks as if we might be winning.' He looked at Versluis questioningly. 'Almost. Or are you not convinced?'

Mrs Van der Vliet had appeared on the stoep at the back of the house, her black dress hardly more than a shadow against the growing darkness, although Van der Vliet, looking out over the garden, did not see her. 'I have begun to dream about Haarlem again,' he remarked half to himself. 'I dream that I am a child again, and that I am running across the Grote Markt and down Koning Street.' He looked up; he saw the motionless figure of the woman in the semi-dark under the verandah. 'Oh well,' he said, 'it was all so long ago. I must not keep you any longer.' Without another word he shuffled down the path in his slippers.

Mrs Van der Vliet stood motionless while Versluis walked slowly back to the house and took up the books that he had left on the stoep. 'Are you sitting by yourself here in the dark?' she asked disapprovingly, although only half of her attention was focused on him.

'I came out here after dinner to do some reading,' he said. 'I have to prepare something for the reading circle.'

She leant over the balustrade of the stoep as if she were trying to see whether Van der Vliet was still visible, but she could not discern anything and came back to him. It was not clear to him whether she was concerned or relieved about the old man's disappearance. 'Oh, the reading circle,' she said in a tone which left no doubt as to her feelings about literature. 'Mrs Hirsch and Mrs Baumann and all the other ladies who don't have enough to do. I remain here to keep an eye on what is happening in my own house,' she informed him, and swept majestically back into the house with a rustling of skirts. He heard her chastising the servants inside where they were busy lighting the lamps and taking them to the rooms.

During his stay in the house Versluis had assumed that Van der Vliet was some or other relative of the deceased paterfamilias, who had been taken in and whose presence was consequently tolerated, but during the conversation that evening he had said something about his wife. Was he perhaps Mrs Van der Vliet's husband, Versluis thought with astonishment, successor to the Secretary to the Volksraad who gazed at the world from behind glass in the drawing room? This possibility had never occurred to him before.

The earth was ashen; the day was dissolving in a flush of rose and gold which glowed ever more deeply and faintly, and the evening star had appeared in the west. In the house the gleam of the lamps was visible behind the blinds of the bedrooms where they had been placed. From where he stood on the stoep he again heard that distant laugh where Miss Pronk had gone walking with her fiancé in the orchard, now invisible in the dark.

Pastor Scheffler came to fetch Versluis as he had promised; he carried a large cotton umbrella which he held carefully above his head to protect him from the sun, and from time to time he would take his companion's arm to assist him across the unpaved street. The gathering was to take place at the English convent school which lay some distance outside the town against the ridge behind the government buildings, its brick walls and green garden standing out clearly against the emptiness which extended westwards from there. Talking all the time, the clergyman helped him across the largest rocks and ditches in these unchartered outskirts where there was hardly a footpath to be seen through the veld.

Hollyhocks, rambling roses and stocks bloomed against the brick walls of the school where young trees were already beginning to cast a tentative shade, and in one of the classrooms a number of women had gathered to have tea while they waited: cups clinked, dresses rustled and voices buzzed in a mixture of English and German, while

77

sepia-tinted Raphael and Botticelli prints gazed down at them from the walls and the scent of an English garden wafted in through the open windows.

A woman in a rustling bright purple gown approached Versluis and, with eyes still accustomed to the bright sunlight outside, he did not recognise her at once as Mrs Hirsch. She greeted him gaily and seized him in order to introduce him into the small circle of the Bloemfontein community. 'We have not forgotten you,' she whispered to him with her head nearly touching his, the garnets in her earrings flashing to and fro; 'I keep telling my husband that we should invite you to dinner, or send you another basket of fruit – the grapes are particularly fine at the moment. But then he told me that you have moved in with Mrs Van der Vliet; she has assumed responsibility for you, and so we had better keep our distance!' She tapped his arm playfully with her fan and laughed with her carefree young girl's laugh at her joke, the import of which he did not quite grasp, and then led him into the room to be introduced to everyone. The ladies and adolescent girls of the town had gathered there that afternoon, and the room was filled with the ample folds, pleats, ribbons, frills and trains of their fashionable gowns, and with the flowers and ribbons of their hats. They were delighted to meet him, each one assured him, they had heard so much about him and had looked forward so much to making his acquaintance, and in their artless geniality there was nothing to suggest that these were merely the platitudes of courtesy. What was the state of his health now? they enquired with concern. Had he recovered completely?

From the maelstrom of colourful dresses Scheffler suddenly appeared before him in his dusty black suit, a cup of tea in his hand. 'May I introduce you to my sister?' he asked, and from the chair near the window where she was reclining, her feet resting on a low stool, a young woman in grey half rose and smilingly offered her hand to him without saying a word.

Cups clinked down, chairs were shifted, and Scheffler cleared his throat and glanced down at a piece of paper which he had produced from his pocket. They were ready to begin, and Versluis fled from the eddying whirl of dresses, trains and bustles to take a seat in a chair at the edge of the group, close to the window where the clergyman's sister had remained sitting.

Scheffler spoke of the power of poetry and about the Romantic poets, offering facts which he had obviously collated from an encyclopaedia, but he presented them with great enthusiasm, so much so that he sometimes stumbled over his words or became ensnared in his long, uncompleted sentences. This was followed by readings by some of the young women and teenage girls, with lowered eyes and a great deal of blushing, who read so softly that they were virtually inaudible. Versluis leant his head back against the frame of the window behind him, conscious of the scent of the flowers in the garden outside. The attention of the others was focused on the readings, their backs turned to him; of Scheffler's sister sitting slightly to one side of him he could discern only her unfashionable grey dress, her averted head, and the narrow white hand lying motionless on her lap as she listened. What had Mrs Van der Vliet once said in passing about Scheffler's sister? He tried to recall.

The earnest young woman in blue who stood reading to them, her head bowed over the book she held, had lost her place: she broke off and blushed while her friends suppressed their giggles behind their handkerchiefs. By turning his head slightly, Versluis discovered, he could see the garden outside without his lack of attention becoming too apparent to the company. The beds were filled with a profusion of English flowers, and beyond them and the stone wall which surrounded the garden, the open veld stretched out towards the west, its flatness broken only by the occasional lone hill on the horizon. In the background the land waited he thought absently, a silent witness to this tiny world in which young women were educated, where bells marked the convent routine, where people had come together that afternoon to read poetry.

His attention was drawn back to the room in which he was sitting: Scheffler's sister had turned around and was staring at him with a clear and direct interest which surprised him in a woman, but then he noticed that the others were also looking at him, for it was his turn to read, so he rose quickly and took his place before them. They listened sympathetically, although it was apparent to him that the poetry did not mean much to them, and it had indeed become clear to him earlier that afternoon that he had aimed too high with his selection. He looked up for a moment and saw his audience gathered before him in their fashionable afternoon dresses. Miss Scheffler, seated some way off near the window with her feet on a stool, was leaning slightly forward and still looked at him with the same clear, direct gaze, her chin supported on her clasped hands; outside he saw the English garden and the convent building with its Gothic windows; he saw the wide expanse of the veld. The poetry was dead on his lips he realised, the words flagged and died as he pronounced them; his reading was even more wooden than that of the girls; why had he allowed himself to be dragged into this situation?

He completed the reading as best he could, however, and closed the book. The poems read that afternoon would now be discussed, Pastor Scheffler informed them, so Versluis had to remain sitting there in the middle of the circle. It now became clear to him that no-one was really very interested: Scheffler was the only one who was trying to generate any discussion and Mrs Hirsch contributed with the automatic eagerness of a born hostess, a quality which had undoubtedly revived countless flagging gatherings. A sporadic discussion ensued, a few people spoke at once, remarks became confused and died away in silence; the young girls giggled helplessly to each other at jokes that no-one else shared, and only Miss Scheffler in the corner near the window, in her sober grey dress amongst the bright gowns and ornate haberdashery, leant forward as if awaiting something, as if she expected something to come out of this gathering. The discussion drifted away from poetry, took a direction of its own, and grew much more lively: they spoke about one of the sisters in the community who was ill; about the fête to be held at the school and about another planned for the other girls' school in the town; about the drought and its effect on their gardens; all at the same time and with a liveliness that they had not shown till then. The meeting had come to an end and they began to rise, pushing their chairs back and gathering into little chattering groups. One by one they came up to Versluis to thank him and to express the hope that they would see him again and be able to receive him in their own homes, palpably relieved to be on home ground again now that they had fulfilled their obligations towards literature. Only the clergyman's sister did not rise to join the others, but retained the aloofness which she had shown during the reading by staying seated at the window in her unfashionable dark dress and the strange, equally unfashionable bonnet, reminiscent of the uniform of some German religious order.

In rustling purple Mrs Hirsch bore down upon Versluis through the folds and trains of the brightly coloured gowns which opened like a sea before her: her carriage was coming to collect her, she said, and Mr Versluis was welcome to accompany her; no, she insisted; she was going to take Miss Scheffler back in any case and her daughters were going to walk back with the Baumann girls. It had been pre-arranged with Scheffler, and, with his cotton umbrella in his hand, he too appeared to thank Versluis for his contribution. The ladies took their leave and, still talking amongst themselves, they began to depart. Carriages arrived to fetch them or else they walked back to town along the footpath, dresses held up out of the dust and parasols opened against the afternoon sun. Only the three who were to ride back together remained with the clergyman, who had stayed to talk to Mrs Hirsch, and, as if this were the sign for which she had been waiting, Miss Scheffler produced two sticks from behind her chair, raised herself with them, and moved heavily towards them, shifting her weight from one stick to the other.

Versluis had been unaware that she was a cripple, and his initial reaction was one of discomfort: nothing in her appearance – the narrow, lively face like her brother's, the fine features – had prepared him for this grotesque locomotion, nor did it square with anything else that he had been able to perceive in her. Mrs Hirsch gabbled on unperturbed, obviously entirely accustomed to this scene, but he found it repulsive and he tried to avert his eyes from the young woman hobbling laboriously towards him across the classroom on her clattering sticks. It was improper for her to expose herself in this way to a stranger, he thought to himself while he tried as coherently as possible to maintain a conversation with the others: someone might have had the good taste to spare him this unnecessary spectacle.

The Hirsches' landau stood outside, the Malay coachman on the box. Pastor Scheffler had propped his umbrella against a chair and had taken his sister's arm to help her outside, and from somewhere in the garden Mrs Hirsch had commandeered a servant to assist them, but Versluis turned away to avoid having to see her being hoisted into the carriage, unwilling to become involved in any way. He turned and looked at the garden where bees buzzed amongst the flowers, at the young trees, the sudden luxuries of scent and colour, and then became aware of the fact that a woman had approached him unawares and was now standing beside him. 'I merely wished to enquire,' she began; 'you must excuse me for coming upon you in this way, but I happened to see you from my window and I simply wanted to ask, have you recovered completely? I have often thought of you, we have all been so concerned about you, and I specifically asked Doctor Krause when he was here a while ago. . . .'

He turned but did not recognise her; blinded by the brilliance of the flowers, at first all he could see was a shape silhouetted before him against the light, but then gradually he was able to discern the striped yellow dress and finally also the person's features. Who was this young woman who stood staring at him so expectantly? he wondered. The freckles, the reddish-brown hair, the whole attitude of concern were familiar, and then he recognised the English teacher who had sat

81

opposite him in the coach which had brought him to this place, and suddenly the horror of that journey returned: the shaking and pitching, the heat and dust, the pain and confusion into which he had kept submerging without any hold to steady his groping hands, and the acridity of the smelling salts which she had proffered with the same concerned expression as the one she now displayed.

He started; he stammered something, confused and upset, while she listened with intense interest. Miss Scheffler had been installed in the carriage, semi-prone on the bench behind the coachman; Mrs Hirsch had got in; the clergyman had left. He had to go, he said to the teacher, thank you very much; yes, very much better; yes, a very pleasant town. So attractive with its willows and orchards, she informed him, following a few paces behind him as he walked towards the landau. And everyone at the school was so friendly, such a fine spirit of co-operation. He really ought to come to one of the chapel services, she called to him, but he had already climbed up into the carriage, and so it was sufficient merely to raise his hat to her as if he had not heard the invitation.

The landau began to move, swaying on its suspension over the uneven terrain between the school and the town. That was the new teacher who had travelled with them from Port Elizabeth, said Mrs Hirsch, sitting straight up under her tasselled parasol; she should invite her to tea one day, such a pleasant young woman, and in fact the girls at the school all liked her. 'I recall how concerned she was about you on the way here, Mr Versluis,' she added.

She had indeed been concerned about him, yet Versluis took no pleasure in the fact that she had appeared in the garden like an angel of death to remind him of his illness. Why should the woman feel herself obliged to impose herself on him, completely uninvited, merely because they had once, weeks earlier, fortuitously sat opposite one another in a coach?

And the gatherings of the reading circle were always so nice, Mrs Hirsch chattered gaily. Mr Versluis had chosen particularly affecting poems to read to them. Did Miss Scheffler not agree?

From where she reclined on the bench opposite them, her fine profile turned towards them as she listened to their conversation, Miss Scheffler now turned her head, thought for a moment, and then nodded with a smile that suddenly lit up her serious face. In her staid grey dress with its wide sleeves and that old-fashioned bonnet tied loosely under her chin with ribbons, she did give the impression of being a deaconess or woman belonging to some order, even of a nun,

82

Versluis thought. Was there a Lutheran sisterhood in the town in addition to the Anglican and Catholic orders about which Mrs Van der Vliet made such suspicious pronouncements, or was this just the expression of an idiosyncratic taste in clothes?

She was just going to fetch the ribbons from Mrs Prince, Mrs Hirsch suddenly cried in the middle of a sentence: she had promised to select them herself, so that she would have a choice, it wouldn't take a minute. At her command the carriage stopped outside a house at the edge of the town, and with an unexpected agility she had bounded down the steps, the skirts of her dress lifted in one hand and the parasol in another, and had reached the garden gate before Versluis was able to make any move to assist her, so that he was left alone with the German pastor's deformed, nunnish sister and the silent Malay coachman on the box above, whose back was turned to them. He ought to say something, start a conversation, Versluis thought, and had begun to clear his throat when Miss Scheffler turned her head to look at him once again with her brother's unflinching gaze. Such directness disconcerted him, much more in a woman than in a man; although he was already becoming accustomed to the ways in which the well-known forms of courtesy were liable to be abandoned without warning in this country – in favour of unexpected displays of familiarity or obtrusiveness which the locals seemed to find perfectly acceptable – and he had noticed in the Hirsch girls and their friends a degree of boisterousness and rowdiness, a disconcerting lack of modesty which was not confined only to them. The questioning, enquiring gaze which Miss Scheffler now fixed upon him was in its own way no less out of place.

'The sun must be very hot for you,' she then remarked, oblivious of his response to her.

'No,' he said; 'no, not particularly.' The late afternoon sun had already begun its descent, its light entangled in the branches of the pepper and bluegum trees; he had put on his hat, but she had no parasol to shade her as they sat waiting in the carriage outside the house, nor did she show a desire for any protection.

'I have never been away myself, but I have always – perhaps I am mistaken – I have always believed that everything is much more intense here with us than it is with you in Europe. That at least is the impression that I have from books, and from the stories of visitors and people who come from Europe, like my parents, for instance. But also from the ways in which they respond to Africa, or at least the things to which they respond - the heat, the thunderstorms, the dust storms.

This open space,' she then added and looked away for a moment, behind them. The last of the houses, the last gardens ended westwards from that spot: the Government offices thrust their tower against the emptiness, and behind that the convent school gathered together its buildings and small trees around itself. Versluis observed the bare, dusty plain, crisscrossed by ditches and stony tracks; the vulture hanging motionless in the air; and as he saw the English teacher standing before him with her angular shoulders, her implacable concern, he felt the shaking of the carriage in a haze of white dust and the anguish with which he had kept slipping away into unconsciousness.

Miss Scheffler's eyes were still fixed upon him. The people here were tiresome he thought in sudden irritation, still upset by his memories and their associations, with their excessive hospitality, their unsolicited intrusions, their inquisitiveness and their rash attempts at intimacy, their need for approval – he had learnt by now that in their eyes distances in that country had to be the greatest, the heat the most exhausting, droughts the most scorching. If they could claim nothing else for their forsaken outpost, it had at least to be this.

'These things upset many people,' Miss Scheffler remarked appositely and clasped her hands on her lap. 'I grew up with them, they're all familiar to me of course, but I can imagine that they might be disconcerting for someone who came from outside.'

'They do require a certain amount of adjustment from a European,' he conceded.

'But do you not also find something here. . . .' She hesitated while she searched for the right word. 'Something worthwhile? Something that makes the long journey worthwhile?'

Health, Versluis thought to himself. Why else had he come here, what else did this land have that could interest him? He removed his hat, then pressed his handkerchief lightly to his forehead. 'The unfamiliarity of a strange country may in itself be interesting,' he said.

'But also oppressive after a while.'

This woman made him feel uneasy, Versluis thought, and as he replaced his hat and put his handkerchief back into an inside pocket, he cast a sidelong glance at the garden, the verandah, and the house to see if there was no sign of Mrs Hirsch. He had been mistaken to attribute Miss Scheffler's initial silence to shyness: she had merely been reconnoitring for a moment, and once that had been completed, she had addressed the stranger without the slightest hesitation or self-consciousness; she had regarded him with that bright, direct gaze and had said what had occurred to her, without any attempt at the polite small talk that might have befitted the occasion. He looked up and saw the coachman with his wide-brimmed hat sitting motionless on the box above them. Could the man hear them? he wondered. And how much could he understand? Unconcerned, however, Miss Scheffler continued talking from where she lay on the bench of the carriage. 'And yet,' she said with sudden enthusiasm, carried away by the thought of fresh possibilities, 'yet it must be exciting to be able to make such comparisons: to be able to say Europe was yesterday, Africa today; yesterday I was there, now I am here. To have all that, and then to chose for yourself. Myself, I have never been abroad, I have never even left the Free State, this country is all I know except what I have learnt from books and the tales of others.'

Yes indeed, Versluis reflected, remaining aloof in his corner of the landau, since it had become quite clear that in her flights of fancy she expected no contribution from him; yes, she was like her brother, not only in her narrow, alert face, that guileless look, or the sudden smile, but also in her mannerisms – their unpredictability being even greater than that of the other people in this unpredictable country, their openness even more palpable. Without hesitation or reserve they opened themselves to one, gave themselves over to strangers, and it never occurred to them that such confidence might be misplaced or embarrassing.

'But on the other hand,' she continued thoughtfully, 'perhaps it is better not to be confused by having too much to compare and not to feel compelled to make a choice. For August, for instance, it was not at all easy to adapt after being away for so long.' It took some time before Versluis realised that she must be referring to her brother, the pastor. 'It was actually too long; long enough to lose something without receiving anything in return which might have compensated for the loss.' Again she looked back at the motionless bluegums, at the drabness of the veld, the emptiness, softened by a gradual tempering of the sunlight. 'We all live in two worlds,' she then remarked, as if the idea which she wished to convey to him were the result of years of thought. 'Where do we really belong? Do you perhaps know?'

From the corner of his eye Versluis could see a movement among the plants which covered the verandah of the house; above the low drone of the afternoon, the rustle of leaves, the stamping of the waiting horses in the dust, he could hear the sound of voices. Mrs Hirsch was returning he thought with a degree of relief.

'It means a great deal to August to have met you,' Miss Scheffler remarked casually. 'He speaks very appreciatively of his conversation with you.'

Appreciatively? Versluis thought with surprise, forgetting to listen for the approaching footsteps and women's voices. Their brief meeting in the hotel room, the even shorter conversation at the parsonage, the few hurried sentences in Mrs Van der Vliet's hallway – how could these have been in any way meaningful, or have called for appreciation? 'You are too kind,' he said with some embarrassment. 'I hardly. . . .'

She leant slightly towards him, now also aware of the approaching women and the end of their conversation. 'You are not merely somebody from abroad, it's not just that. He feels that he can talk to you, and that is important. It's not easy for him,' she added in a quick, low voice; 'in his position as a clergyman. . . .' But with a rustle of gowns and of voices, Mrs Hirsch and Mrs Prince had reached the carriage. Introductions were made and greetings and questions passed to and fro: Mr Versluis must come and visit, Mrs Prince insisted, he should come around one afternoon for croquet; he should come for tea on Thursday afternoon, Mr Justice Buchanan and his wife would be there, and perhaps the Reitzes too. . . . He replied, thanked her, evaded the invitations, until finally Mrs Hirsch got in and the carriage began to move, leaving Mrs Prince calling after it. Such a hospitable person, Mrs Hirsch assured them from under the tassels of her parasol. But they would themselves like to entertain Mr Versluis once more, she added. They had given him time to recuperate, they had neglected him for long enough now. He was to dine with them on Sunday afternoon she charged, as the landau stopped in front of Mrs Van der Vliet's house, in a tone which permitted no evasion, and he could do nothing but accept the invitation and bid the woman farewell. 'We would also be very pleased to have you with us, Mr Versluis,' Miss Scheffler said as she offered her hand to him, recumbent on the bench in her grey dress. 'I know that in saying that I speak for my brother and sister-in-law.'

The landau continued on its way; he looked up and as he approached the house he noticed a slight movement of the lace curtain in the drawing room. He had just enough time to prepare for Mrs Van der Vliet's early supper, he realised. While he washed and changed his clothes he continued to think of Miss Scheffler's final words as she had sat alone with him in the carriage, and he could see her brother before him: the dusty black suit, the inadequately cut hair, the sudden boyish grin, his enthusiasm. How could *his* presence or company possibly mean anything to a young clergyman living in the heart of Africa? he wondered. Or could the loneliness be that great, he pondered as he stood in front of the mirror; was the despair that intense?

It was already time for dinner: the sound of the gong, the footsteps of the servants carrying bread and milk and butter along the passage to the dining room, and the lively voices of Polderman and Du Toit, together, all signalled this fact, and Versluis left his room to join them at the table. Mrs Van der Vliet had already installed herself at the head of the table where she maintained an emphatic silence which declared that she wanted further information but was not prepared to demean herself by asking any questions, or else that she felt herself to have been slighted, offended, or aggrieved in some way or another. Her husband – if he was indeed her husband – coughed nervously and looked around the table from countenance to countenance. She would remain silent Versluis knew from experience, until she had discovered from him everything she wanted to know about the afternoon reading without asking a single direct question, or even showing the slightest apparent interest in the matter. And so he occupied his place of honour at her right hand with some reluctance, for after such a tiring day he had no desire for an officious conversation.

When Mrs Van der Vliet spoke, however, it appeared that other, more significant events, which had diverted her attention from his outing, had occurred. 'There is a Dutch gentlemen in the Bloemfontein Hotel,' she declared with the deepest sense of indignation.

This information was received with complete indifference by her fellow diners. 'Yes,' Polderman said unsuspectingly, 'he arrived last Thursday on the passenger coach from Algoa Bay,' and he proceeded to cut himself some cheese, unaware of the indignant stare which she had fixed upon him.

'He's from Meppel or somewhere around there,' Polderman said with a mouth full of bread. 'His name's Gelmers. Chest problems, like the rest of that bunch. This place is turning into a sanatorium.' Then he stopped, suddenly aware of Versluis's presence, and coloured while Du Toit concealed his delight at his friend's embarrassment behind his napkin.

'Surely you mean that this place is turning into a cemetery,' Miss Pronk added, oblivious of everything, and with a sudden, half-automatic gesture she put her hand to her curls, then to the brooch at her throat and the ribbons that adorned her little body. 'I heard today from the Krauses that that English girl at the hotel has also given up the ghost.'

The annoyance with which Mrs Van der Vliet put down the bread knife signalled that this piece of news was not known to her, and she forgot for a moment about her enquiries after the unknown Dutchman. 'After all the trouble she caused everyone,' she declared in disgust. 'The doctor will never see that account paid.'

'Pastor Scheffler visited on her, even though she was apparently Presbyterian, and he's going to conduct the funeral service, although I don't know who'll go. Naturally she knew nobody in Africa; she was from Scotland, from Dundee or some such place. Is there such a place?' she wanted to know, and her pale blue eyes slid for a moment over Versluis at the other side of the table, but without waiting for an answer.

'She once came into the shop to buy some ribbon,' Du Toit added, with unusual loquacity.

'Ribbon? What on earth would she want ribbon for?' Mrs Van der Vliet enquired witheringly, and in the face of her incredulous countenance he withdrew into his customary silence.

'It appears that she simply wasted away,' Miss Pronk babbled on while trying to extract a gherkin from the pickle jar. 'The Krauses say their father told them that she'd simply coughed away her lungs.'

'But of course you knew her, Mr Versluis,' it suddenly dawned on Mrs Van der Vliet. 'You arrived here together.'

'No,' he said quickly, 'no, I did not know the lady.'

'But she was in the hotel with you.'

'Yes, I remember, she was already ill when you came here to us,' Miss Pronk said. 'Did you know her? Did you ever speak to her?' She regarded him enquiringly through her bulging, pale blue eyes and colourless eyelashes.

In panic Versluis pushed away his plate and cup. 'I know nothing about this woman,' he said, and realised that his voice had been too sharp, even though this had had no marked effect on Miss Pronk. 'I did not become acquainted with the other people in the hotel.'

The expressionless, bulging eyes remained fixed upon him, but then she turned away and shrugged her shoulders. 'A wispy little woman with red hair,' Polderman added. 'One could look right through her.'

'I saw her in church one Sunday,' Du Toit announced eagerly, as if this would assure him of the others' attention.

'I also saw her in church,' Miss Pronk said, 'although I didn't know who she was. She sat right at the back, in a funny, meagre little dress, as if she didn't have enough material. Made of tartan, too,' she added as an afterthought. 'Green and red. Certainly not something I would like to wear.'

'To die completely alone in a foreign country, without a soul to care for her!' Mrs Van der Vliet announced with palpable delight as she put two spoons of sugar into her coffee and stirred, her former indignation entirely forgotten. 'Without a loved one or an acquaintance to look after her, and not a penny to her name to comfort her in the last days of her life.'

'Mrs Schröder wouldn't have kept her in the hotel for so long if she'd had no money at all.' Polderman remarked soberly. 'She's been known to turn dying people out into the streets.' But Mrs Van der Vliet merely sipped her sweet, milky coffee and pondered silently to herself the process of decline and death.

Versluis felt something bitter, like retched blood, rise in his gorge and fill his mouth, and he struggled to swallow it behind his napkin. He had forgotten the discomforts of the journey and of life in the hotel in that spacious, well-run house, and the memories of his illness had been almost totally eradicated: he had forgotten the helpless coughing that had gone on and on as if, alone and in darkness, life itself were being hacked out. He did not wish to be reminded of that; he did not want to think of it! He almost cried out in anguish. While at the same time an image came to him of the young woman whom he had seen in passing in the foyer of the hotel, sitting on a suitcase, waiting, a small case on her lap, and to whom he had given no further thought. Had that been her?

He did not wish to think about it, however, he repeated aghast to himself, crumpling up his napkin while the conversation babbled on around the table, with Polderman cutting himself more cheese and Van der Vliet, unsolicited, filling Miss Pronk's glass with water. All the bridesmaids had been there that afternoon she told them, and Hannchen's dress was nearly finished; they had pinned it on her and she had looked ever so pretty. The bouts of coughing in the dark had been bad enough, and he had no desire to put a face to them or to give them a personal identity.

Mrs Van der Vliet looked at him sharply. 'I'm not feeling very well,' he mumbled in apology for his behaviour. 'It's the sun . . . If you would excuse me. . . .' He had already risen, supporting himself on the edge of the table.

Clearly in the eyes of Mrs Van der Vliet, present illness superseded any case of settled death: she had been sitting pensively at the head of the table without paying much attention to Miss Pronk's plans for her approaching wedding, but now her empty cup was pushed aside, together with the memories of deathbeds and early graves which she had begun to recall, and she rose from her chair with a rustle of skirts. 'But of course,' she said, 'all this gadding about in the blazing sun, and in an open carriage too in the midday heat. . . .' She beamed with pleasure at not only being able to display her disapproval of Versluis's outdoor activities, but also at this opportunity to resume control of his life. He should go to bed at once, she urged; she would have some tea sent to his room. . . . Grateful to be able to flee the conversation at the table, Versluis retired without protesting, and the young people, glancing up for a moment to bid him goodnight, gave him no further thought. The death and funeral of the stranger already forgotten, Miss Pronk sat telling Polderman who their groom's men were to be.

It was a relief for Versluis to reach the safety of his room and to be able to withdraw into bed. A cold sweat still clung to his forehead, his hands shook, his heart beat uncontrollably, and there was still something like hot blood in his throat – what was it about this unhappy day that had upset him so? he wondered as he leant back against the pillows and drew the spotless sheets over himself. Mrs Van der Vliet brought him a glass of water and a flask of valerian, she also sent some tea with a servant and called for a light and a fan. Were his feet not cold? she returned to ask. Or perhaps a hot compress against the abdomen, would that not have a soothing effect?

He was pleased when he was finally able to extricate himself from her attentiveness and put out the candle next to the bed, even though it was still early evening, for he was tired and wanted to sleep; but sleep, when it came, was broken and restless, and there were still far too many muffled noises in the house which constantly woke him up: Miss Pronk's giggling and her high heels; the voices of Polderman and Du Toit on the stoep on their way to their room; their calls to each other in the garden on their way to the privy. But the house finally settled down as the last door was shut, the final candle put out. He groped through the dark, he coursed his way like a swimmer through the gathered night. Something brushed his hand, a wing beat lightly at his cheek, and he recoiled in terror from this peril – a bat, a bird – rising with beating wings before him; his arm covered his face to prevent any further attack. But then he saw, as it hung suspended for a moment before him, that it was no bird – but a thin, hovering woman in a striped dress which resembled some multicoloured yellow

90

plumage, her shoulders angular as wings. Her hands were clasped as she stood before him, her eyes upon his face, and as he backed away into the surrounding dark to avoid her he knew that this was the unknown young woman in the adjoining room, her blood oozing from her mouth in a stream that soaked into and saturated the night.

He awoke to another, more familiar darkness, and with a shaking hand he lit the candle at the bedside to see the crumpled, tangled sheets and the hollow pillows drenched in sweat. Why this disquiet and menace in the tranquil course of life that he had begun to create for himself in this house? he wondered. What had upset him so much? But he could find nothing in the events of the previous few days that might elucidate this disquiet, no single image that passed through his memory offered an explanation. The bright convent garden enclosed by its surrounding wall, the English teacher in her striped dress among the flowerbeds, Miss Scheffler's eager outpourings and the questioning gaze of Miss Pronk's pale blue eyes – why should the congruency of all these coincidental events have so disrupted his day and disturbed his rest? And the reeking face he thought suddenly as he put the candle out once more: the rigid neck, the poorly made tartan dress, glimpsed weeks earlier in passing in a dimly lit hotel lobby and immediately forgotten – what were these? Even this thought, this image, he pushed firmly and quickly aside and pressed the handkerchief sprinkled with eau de Cologne to his face, his temples, and his wrists. It helped the dizziness that he felt; but the alarm would not be expelled.

The day was oppressively hot, the sky veiled in a dull grey, so that the light was washed out and colourless. In such intense heat every sound was subdued and people were listless; in the garden flowers wilted in their dusty beds and the leaves hung motionless on the trees.

'Perhaps it will rain today,' remarked Mrs Van der Vliet while they were taking their afternoon coffee together in the drawing room. 'But then, perhaps not.' She sighed. 'Indeed, drought is no pleasant thing, Mr Versluis. One works one's fingers to the bone, day in and day out, only to see everything for which you have laboured fade before your eyes in a few weeks as if it had never existed.' She shook her head despairingly, as if it were she who in the heat carried the buckets to and fro in the garden all day long.

The sudden, shrill sound of a church bell broke the tranquil silence in which they were sitting, so unexpectedly that it startled Versluis. 'It's the funeral,' Mrs Van der Vliet said, and then withdrew from speech, as if the mere sounds of the knell from beyond the neighbouring gardens imposed a duty to be silent upon them. So Versluis left her and, casting a glance through the open front door, he observed in the harsh afternoon light a group of men in black moving towards the German church. Was that tinny peal going to continue all afternoon? he asked impatiently. Even in his room he could not escape it and so, irritable and hypersensitive as he had been all day, he picked up his panama hat and cane and took himself outdoors. He would of course not be able to escape from that ringing anywhere in the town, but at least he felt a sense of release at being able to get away from the house and walk down the street, away from the pealing bell and the little church with its steeply raked roof – where the coffin now stood before the pulpit and a few inhabitants of the town were gathered in their black suits to mourn the passing of the deceased stranger. He knew that the entourage would struggled up the incline to the cemetery, so he walked quickly in the opposite direction, to the edge of the town, towards the little Catholic chapel and the convent school and the Dutch girls' school on the ridge. The day had become gloomy with the accumulation of leaden clouds, but the late afternoon had brought some cool relief from the heat.

Versluis had heard that beyond the small, humble Presidency lay the fountain and the dam, although he had never been there himself. Perhaps now was an opportune moment to seek some refreshment in the form of water and foliage he thought; though when he reached the fountain, making his way with difficulty across the stepping stones and ditches of the spruit, there was nothing but weeds, trampled mud, and a tank from which the water dripped despondently.

Without purpose, he continued walking towards the west where the sky was still visible as a small strip of light beneath the clouds, behind the Presidency, between the town and the surrounding veld. A horse neighed, men called to each other, and the tall, dry grass rustled as a restless breeze sprang up. The call of voices, laughter and the splashing of water led him onward, until finally he climbed the steep bank and found the dam before him – its wide, muddy brown surface rippled by the wind. At the other end, against the bank where the water was deepest, a group of young men were bathing, the white of their naked bodies indistinct through the drooping willow branches, but clearly silhouetted under the leaden sky against the earth-brown banks and muddy water. He had been led there by their loud cries. With averted eyes, Versluis followed the footpath which continued along the bank. Water splashed, voices called, a few young boys dumped one another laughingly under the water, oblivious of him walking by. The instant he looked up as he passed them, supported on his cane over the uneven path, he recognised Gustav from the hotel with his broad pale body, his heavy, solid hips and thighs, standing with his legs apart at the edge of the water, and smiling down at the others. He did not recognise Versluis, or else he simply had not seen him, secure in the strength of the muscular body that he was so casually displaying. For an instant Versluis remembered the way in which the man had shaved him while he had been ill – the round white arms, the point of his tongue just visible between his lips as he concentrated – and, conscious of the fact that he was intruding on their fun, a thin, middle-aged man in a summer suit, propped on his cane, he walked past quickly while the cries, the laughter, and the splashing continued and the wind rippled across the wide expanse of water.

He left the dam wall the moment he found a path that led away from it and carried on walking across the empty veld, across which the wind was now blowing more strongly; he walked in a wide arc around the town, which was hidden from him by the ridge against which it had been built. Only the fort was outlined high up against the sky. He was aware that he had ventured further than ever before on his walks, for until now he had always turned back at the limits of the built-up area and had remained in touch with the houses, the gardens, the small signs of civilisation, while he gazed out across the expanse of the surrounding veld. This afternoon was the first time that he had left the beaten track. Where he now stumbled onwards there were no longer even any signs of a footpath, through dry grass, over patches of uneven ground, fissures and rocks. The shrill sound of the church bell could no longer be heard here, or it might even have stopped ringing, so he could probably return safely to the town. This thought had hardly struck him when he realised that what lay ahead of him in the distance between him and the town was the cemetery, and beyond the surrounding wall he could see a mill of people in black among the tombstones. It occurred to him that the funeral procession had just arrived, and in sudden panic he turned out again into the veld, stumbling through the grass, the little bushes plucking at his trouser legs and grass seed clinging to his clothes. The sky had become ominous and the wind gusted more strongly, bits of paper were blown past him, whirling up into the sky before being blown against the bushes, and he had to cling to his hat to stop it being blown off. Even for someone as unfamiliar with the signs of this country as he was, it was clear that bad weather was approaching but it was too late to turn

93

back and, already breathless from this exhausting effort, he hurried along behind the fort in an effort to reach the town.

It became apparent to Versluis that he had turned towards the black quarter, but there was nothing he could do about that. Dust rose, pieces of paper whirled past, corrugated iron clanged, a broken bucket rolled along the ground like an old newspaper. He had heard people talking about this area, or rather, he had heard them complaining about it, but to him it had been no more than a remote corner of the town over which a thick haze of smoke hung in the evenings and from which the silence was disturbed by the continuous barking of dogs, punctuated by shouting and drunken cries. It was obviously unwise for him to pass through here, but rain was on its way – the first drops were already being whipped against his face, and he was struggling to fasten his jacket with one hand while holding on to his hat with the other, and as far as possible maintaining a grip on the cane. The people that he could see were all running for shelter with fluttering blankets or hides blowing up around them. Dust was being driven into the air, smoke eddied from the dilapidated grass huts and mud houses that were scattered against the ridge on which the fort stood, and suddenly there was a flash of lightning from the dark skies and rain poured down with a violence that he had not foreseen.

It became apparent to Versluis that he would not reach the shelter of the town. It was useless even to try, for he would be drenched before he could go another hundred yards, but he had no alternative. There was no tree to be seen, and the sunken huts and rickety dwellings of wood and corrugated iron that he could see about him could not be considered places of shelter. Then the shabby little structures disappeared behind driving curtains of rain and he could not even see his path forward – the dusty ground at his feet was transformed in an instant into a mass of slippery red clay and water rushing down the hill. His shoes were soaked, his clothes clung to his body, his eyes were blinded by the violence of the downpour; forked lightning streaked down to illuminate the area briefly in a bluish glow, and then the pelting rain obscured everything once more. He clutched his panama hat and his walking stick with its gold band, astonished at the violence that had broken about him. He groped blindly ahead without being sure of the direction in which he was moving, without even any clear knowledge of what he was doing, and then slid out across the slippery mud and, in a fall that seemed to last forever, he crashed on to his knees, unable to control any of his movements. Kneeling in the rain and in the clay he tried to raise himself on his cane, but all force

94

seemed to have deserted him, and he appeared to be watching these events from a distance, hardly conscious of the elements which had been unleashed around him.

The rain abated, the roaring stopped, the afternoon brightened, and in the gleam of the scattered light he noticed someone moving in his direction under the shelter of a large umbrella. Given the weird circumstances in which he had so unexpectedly landed, he was surprised to recognise the Hirsches' Malay coachman stepping towards him on his clogs through streams and pools of water, as careful and dignified as a long-legged bird. The man had never taken any notice of him, but now he was bending over Versluis beneath the shelter of the umbrella – silent, questioning – and he placed a hand beneath Versluis's elbow as if he wished to help but did not know whether such help was either required or welcome.

The two of them looked at one another while the rain drizzled more softly around them and the water ran down the hill, and then they heard a cry and saw another man, wearing a slit sack around his head and shoulders, running towards them with arms waving and puddles splashing about him. Versluis could not hear what he was shouting, but the Malay withdrew and disappeared with his umbrella into the rain, while he found himself being held and helped up in the careful grasp of Joseph, the black servant from the hotel.

He was no longer able to take in what was happening to him, but allowed himself to be led by the black man to one of the nearby huts and taken inside. Blinded by the semi-darkness indoors, he could only vaguely discern a chair being brought and dusted off with a cloth so that he could sit down; along with a battered enamel basin of water and a towel, spotlessly white and completely threadbare, offered to him so that he could wash his mud-smeared hands; and Joseph kneeling before him in an attempt to wipe the clay from his trousers. He was, however, unable to understand what the man was saying to him, the mutilated African Dutch that he spoke being rendered even more incomprehensible by his strange intonation, and it dawned on him only gradually that the servant was speaking of the appearance of the Malay coachman with disapproval or even abhorrence, and that he was cautioning Versluis about him. More than this he could not make out, however: he mumbled a few words of acknowledgement, and the black man nodded in radiant pleasure, despite the fact that he understood just as little of Versluis's Dutch.

He sat on the rickety kitchen chair that had been provided for him, his clothes drenched and covered in mud, and listened to the sounds outside – the clatter of raindrops on corrugated iron and the dripping of water through a leaking roof – conscious of the smell of human bodies, smoke and mustiness in that unfathomable darkness. After a while he also became aware of the black people squatting across the room near the opening of the entrance, lit up briefly from time to time by flashes of lightning, their eyes gleaming in their dark faces, their bodies shrouded in shapeless rags – a woman with a headcloth tied low over her eyes, an old man, and children. He could not distinguish them clearly and the darkness of the hut, or house, and the alien feeling that pervaded it overwhelmed him. What was he doing here? he wondered. How had he got here, far from the home in which the maid used to come to put coal on the fire and draw the curtains against the dusk, where Pompe laid out his nightclothes on the bed? Oceans reached out; a chasm lay before his feet; dizzying expanses filled with darkness surrounded him; every beacon and landmark seemed lost. He shut his eyes against the slight giddiness which overcame him, conscious of his exhaustion after all the day's difficulties; but there was nothing to be done except to sit there and wait.

The rain murmured, water dripped: a scraggy dog appeared from the depths of the hut and began to sniff at his shoes, but it was startled by a cry from Joseph and disappeared, tail between its legs, into the rain. The afternoon was clearing and it was possible to see into the distance once more, the scattered huts and shelters of mouldering grass and rusty corrugated iron resurfaced; people reappeared, moving hesitantly among the puddles and mud. Versluis rose, half without thinking: he should go, he thought, and there was a stirring among the black people who had kept away from him out of shyness or respect. Joseph called upon him to wait while they talked and gabbled away in their own language in the dark interior, from which Joseph then appeared carrying a dilapidated remnant of an umbrella, its spokes bent askew by the wind, and with hardly any covering. The master should take it he insisted, and he would accompany the master to his house he assured Versluis, beaming benevolently. Nor did it matter to Versluis any longer: tired, overwhelmed, stupefied by this unusual and exhausting afternoon, he made no move to protest but merely spoke a few words of thanks to the black in whose home he had taken shelter. He could see the silent faces and the flashing eyes in the semi-darkness: could they understand what he was saying? he wondered. But without waiting for a reply he took himself outside, out into the brightly rinsed daylight, all the more wholesome after the stuffiness of the ill-smelling native hut.

Among the little houses and huts people were busy reclaiming their possessions from the flood, wringing out cloths and rags and bailing out their homes. Even in the white section of town with its straight streets and more decorous homes, people were stepping carefully through the mud, slush and puddles, but he paid no attention to them, giving no thought to the spectacle that he must have presented in his wet, soiled suit, struggling, cane in hand, with great effort through the clinging clay of the streets, shadowed a few paces behind by his black companion bearing the cast-off umbrella. The clouds began to clear and before them the sun suddenly broke through to overwhelm the flooded landscape in light; the heavens were bathed in gold while the town, with its silver pools of water, its glistening trees and shrubs, its gleaming iron roofs, was suffused with a single radiance – the impassable reality of clay and mud, of seething ditches and flooded gutters, magically transformed into an unacceptable beauty.

Blinded by this radiance before his eyes, by the wide glare that surrounded him, struggling, staggering, stumbling, Versluis at last reached the house where Mrs Van der Vliet was standing on the stoep as if she were peering out across the deck of an ark, and she greeted him with a cry of amazement as, like a drowned man, he was washed up at her feet.

He retained sufficient presence of mind to grope in his pocket for a coin and press it into Joseph's hand, conscious from the man's dumb amazement and Mrs Van der Vliet's indignant cry that it was much more than was customary, and then he bid him farewell with a wave of his hand and allowed Mrs Van der Vliet to take off his shoes, caked with clay, and lead him down the passage to his room.

Nothing happened. His suit was cleaned and pressed, his shoes were scraped clean and polished, and his clothes no longer bore any signs of their adventure. Mrs Van der Vliet allowed him to remain in bed, ordering hot flasks and warm drinks to be taken to him and considering anxiously whether or not to call the doctor, but no such concern was necessary. A strained knee and a grazed hand, which brought Mrs Van der Vliet rushing in with iodine, were the only visible results of his expedition, accompanied by exhaustion; neither the drenching nor the injuries had left any lasting scars. He had become invulnerable Versluis thought with amusement as he recalled the anxious way in which Pompe had wrapped him up in coats and scarves and accompanied

97

him with shawls and umbrellas from front door to cab. He had withstood a test and had emerged unscathed.

A new person in a new world he thought to himself when Mrs Van der Vliet finally consented to his getting up and installed him in a cane chair on the back stoep. The brown, faded landscape that he had known since his arrival, still in the glare of the heat, had been rinsed clean and now gleamed in a fresh green that decked the fruit trees and gardens. Nurtured by the sun under an azure sky, the earth breathed a fecund aroma; and in the garden Van der Vliet, with a tattered straw hat on his head, busied himself all day, giving his assistants instructions and supervising their activities.

Versluis sat on the stoep, drowsy in the heat which was no longer oppressive, listening to the distant voice of the old man. And to the song of the birds in the trees and the chatter of finches in the willows along the spruit at the bottom of the garden where the muddy waters now churned high up along the banks; to the cries of children somewhere and the voices of servants; to the sound of a piano in a nearby house where someone was practising scales, and indoors, behind him, to the coming and going of Miss Pronk and her friends who had come to visit her today; to the clatter of their heels and the rustle of their skirts; to the suppressed giggles and cries and whispers as they busied themselves trying on the bridesmaids' dresses. All these noises flowed together into a low murmur which suffused the day, and in which the individual sounds could no longer be distinguished; they grew to a single sound like the far-off buzzing of bees in the heat, and permeated the atmosphere of the summer's day like the scent of sublimated fertility and saturation that now rose from the rich red earth.

2

O N SUNDAY afternoon Versluis went to dine as arranged with the Hirsch family: Mrs Van der Vliet received this information formally, maintaining a polite silence which indicated that she did not regard the desertion of her own table favourably, and that in time he would deeply regret such disloyalty.

When he saw the churchgoers returning home from the Lutheran church and the Anglican cathedral, Versluis made his way to the Hirsches' house, along streets where the wheels and hooves continued to churn the soft clay into mud and where it was difficult to avoid the pools and puddles left by the storm – past gardens in which the scent of flowers now hung heavily in the sunshine, their beds filled with colour, past garden walls and verandahs covered in a luxuriance of creepers, and along the footbridge across the spruit where the storm-waters still churned muddily.

Even as he climbed up the verandah steps to the Hirsches' open front door, he could hear the noise and bustle that filled the house, as if it had been going on uninterrupted since his previous visit. Young people darted across the passage and through the folding doors which linked the rooms, servants moved to and fro, children gambolled about with a puppy, and Hirsch emerged from the bustle and came towards him with his hand extended. 'Welcome!' he called. 'You're just in time, we've already opened the wine. We haven't seen you for a long time, much too long. Not that we had forgotten about you, but – I'm sure you understand. We do not wish to tread on the worthy Mrs Van der Vliet's toes, do we now?' He drew Versluis closer by the arm, and added the final words with a wink.

Children surrounded him to say hello. 'Lieutenant Michell brought us a puppy!' one of the younger girls called excitedly and disappeared into her crowd of playmates.

'Let me introduce you to our other guests,' said Hirsch. 'This is Lieutenant Michell from the Cape.'

'Michell of the 24th,' announced a slim and very erect young man.

'Codrington, of the Royal Artillery,' added a companion even more erect and slim, and they bowed simultaneously.

He should have remembered how exhausting the hospitality of his previous visit had been, Versluis thought, and not have ventured from Mrs Van der Vliet's sober table and heavy Sunday lunch, but it was too late now to extricate himself in any way from this gathering. A glass of wine was pressed into his hand. 'Do you know this country well?' Michell, standing beside Versluis, asked formally – but the pack of screaming children rushed between them and carried Codrington away with it through the open verandah doors and out into the garden behind the house; a wild charge of flying plaits, ribbons and pinafores propelled down the garden path.

Only Michell remained behind, a little discomfited. 'We're on our way to the Transvaal. Are you acquainted with those parts?'

'I have never been further than Bloemfontein,' Versluis said. 'I have only just arrived in South Africa.'

'Oh, so you're a foreigner? Funny place this, such a new country. One never knows who belongs here and who doesn't.'

'The children enjoy playing with Captain Codrington as much as with the puppy,' Hirsch said with a laugh. 'You mustn't allow them to become a nuisance.'

The glass doors and the tall sash windows at the back of the house were open, and from the dim room they looked out at the brilliant green of the garden where the dresses and pinafores of the dancing girls flashed through the trees and their gay, ragged cries carried back and forth in the sunshine.

'Peculiar country,' Michell remarked to himself over his glass of wine. 'There was a drought when we came up here, we could hardly get any feed for the horses, and now look at everything.'

'Oh, our land is not that bad, my friend,' Hirsch cried excitedly. 'It can also be a paradise.'

'But only for a while,' the officer remarked and gazed unmoved at the luxuriant green of the garden.

Versluis sipped his wine and was just about to compliment Hirsch on its quality when he was interrupted. 'Our missing guest,' Hirsch said. 'Mr Versluis, may I introduce you to a fellow countryman? He has been amongst us for a week already, and proposed to stay for an unlimited time, so how could I fail to introduce the two of you? Mr

Gelmers, from the Netherlands – do come in, come and get a glass of wine.'

The stranger had entered from the garden, perhaps from the privy, and now hesitated on the threshold of the verandah door, a dark figure against the light outside.

'Gelmers,' he said, and added in English, with a pronounced accent. 'My pleasure. Pleased to meet you.'

His palm was hot and sweaty and his grip slack, his voice high-pitched, nasal and slightly breathless. Versluis bowed and said a few words, but the man made no reply, nor did Michell take it upon himself to say anything, so that as usual it was up to Hirsch to break the silence with some or other remark. But at that moment his wife also appeared from somewhere behind the house. On seeing her guests she pulled off the delicate little lace apron which she was wearing and, throwing it behind a chair, smoothed back her hair with a rapid gesture. Versluis was caught up in the effusiveness of her welcome and her enquiries concerning his health; Gelmers and Michell were collared to carry cushions out to the back stoep so that they could sit outside after dinner; servants appeared with laden trays and put the food on the table, and everything returned to its usual bustle and stir, with Mrs Hirsch smiling and unruffled in the centre, completely in control of the situation.

'But did you enjoy our little literary afternoon, Mr Versluis?' she asked, her attention turned wholly towards him once more. 'The level may have seemed extremely basic to an erudite man such as yourself – but at least we are trying, we are trying. Even here in the heart of Africa we are keeping the torch of civilisation alight. A little Weimar in Bloemfontein!' She burst into a gay laugh at the thought. 'Just as long as you weren't bored. You must come again next month, and Mr Gelmers too. Mr Gelmers, are you also interested in literature? I mean, in German literature? In poetry?'

Gelmers, who was on his way to the stoep with an armful of cushions, dragging a rug behind him, stood still for a moment. 'German has never interested me,' he said bluntly.

'What about French then? English? We have regular little literary gatherings.' But Gelmers was already on his way to the stoep; he tripped over the rug and nearly fell. 'We are not complete barbarians, Lieutenant. Or do such things not interest a soldier?'

'I never set out on a journey without my Tacitus,' said Michell. But Mrs Hirsch had already darted away to put the servants, who were setting the table, right. 'Are you acquainted with Tacitus, Mr. . . .' It

101

was clear that he was unsure of Versluis's surname, or perhaps he found it difficult to pronounce.

'I prefer poetry myself – I, on the other hand, always take Virgil along when I travel.'

'Oh, Tacitus is superb, simply superb! When you have bivouacked out on the veld, and you're sitting on your camping stool in the midst of that emptiness, reading by the light of the camp fire, you don't feel that you are entirely in a wilderness. Somewhere there are still things that mean something, secure forms and prescribed rules.' He stood there, very erect, pronouncing these words with conviction, even with a degree of vehemence.

'We can take our seats, gentlemen!' called Hirsch. The young people stormed into the house once again, with Codrington in their midst.

'Mr Versluis, you're sitting next to me,' said Mrs Hirsch and, placing her hand on his arm, she led him through the crush. 'Even if we do not achieve much,' she continued above the noise, 'there are some exceptional people here in Bloemfontein – you'll come to see that, I hope you will, if you haven't done so already.' He drew out her chair for her, but she remained standing pensively beside the table for a moment without noticing it. 'In the beginning, when I was still very strange and lonely in this country, that was a consolation,' she said. 'The fact that there were people to whom I could talk. Not many, oh no, there are never many of them, just one here, one there – once in a while someone like that appears in your life, if you are fortunate.' Those seated at the table shifted chairs back and forth; the children called to each other across the table; Hirsch indicated to the other guests where they should sit, and Gelmers squeezed past Versluis to take the place beside him. 'One needs other people,' said Mrs Hirsch, oblivious of the uproar. 'Even if there are only one or two; you must have somebody you can talk to. And I myself have always been extremely fortunate as far as that's concerned, Mr Versluis; even here.'

Dishes covered the table, roast chickens and pies beneath crusts of gleaming, golden pastry; steaming bowls of vegetables; one of the boys fetched more wine and the decanters were passed around the table. Hirsch sharpened the knife to carve the chickens, asked Michell about India and involved Versluis in the conversation with a question about the Dutch colonies in the East. Michell began expanding somewhat enthusiastically about his hunting adventures in the Punjab, implying that the small game that Africa had offered so far could not be compared to such exotic splendours. 'Mr Versluis, some breast?'

Mrs Hirsch asked. 'Or a little pie? Mr Gelmers, what can I give you?' Versluis leant back a little in his chair so that she could speak to his neighbour, aware even from his own limited knowledge. of the language that Gelmers's English was poor, despite the confidence with which he spoke it. Then he shifted his attention to the conversation at the head of the table once more, while the Dutchman turned to the young people lower down. From time to time Versluis could hear that slightly too high-pitched, slightly over-excited voice at the edge of their gaiety, but then it would carry on without him. Gelmers took no notice whatsoever of Versluis, making no attempt to engage him in any conversation, while Versluis remained conscious of the man's yellow check suit and the odour of sweat that clung to it. Why did he find it so repulsive? he wondered as he leant back for a moment, as overwhelmed as he had been on his previous visit by the clamour of this exuberant household. In this climate, where every movement was an effort, all clothes were suffused with sweat and even he was often uncomfortably conscious of his own lack of cleanliness, no matter how often he washed or changed. It was more probably the cheap, loud suit that irritated him he thought, and the man's high-pitched voice beside him. Never again, he thought to himself as Hirsch carved second helpings and the girls at the end of the table chattered about Miss Pronk's approaching wedding. One of them − the oldest and prettiest of the Hirsch girls − dared to lean over and solicit some further information from Versluis which he was, however, unable to provide. One of the young men made a disrespectful remark about Mrs Van der Vliet and they all burst out laughing, and Mrs Hirsch admonished them with a gesture of her small white hand, although she did so with a smile. 'They're just playing the fool,' she said in extenuation, nodding towards Versluis. 'Mrs Van der Vliet can be difficult at times, a little too strict on the young people, you know, and they can sometimes be extremely disrespectful, even though they don't mean to be. The boarders from the College always go there to steal fruit. . . .'

'Old Van der Vliet doesn't mind,' one of the boys cried. 'She's the only one who complains.'

'A little more respect, Julius,' chided his father. Gelmers sat amongst them in silence, unable to follow their allusions and excluded from the general laughter. He should probably make some remark to this unattractive young man, Versluis thought, and turned a little reluctantly towards his neighbour; the man was, however, not looking in his direction, his head still turned towards the young people and their banter. Versluis looked at the check suit, unsuitable for summer, and at the square hands which rested on the table, with their unmanicured, chewed fingernails. An unkempt young man, he thought, wondering whether any approach from him was desired or even desirable.

'But there are not at all as many Dutch people in the Free State as we had expected,' said Lieutenant Michell. 'We have met almost no-one but English-speaking people.'

'Almost everyone in the town can speak English,' Hirsch said. 'Most of them come from England in any case.'

'The visitors too,' his wife added, dishing up more food. 'Almost everyone who comes from the Diamond Fields is English. And so are most of the invalids that we get from abroad. Captain Codrington, a little more pie?'

'An English doctor has given a paper in which he recommends Bloemfontein for lung complaints in particular,' her husband said. 'Our city is world-famous – no coach arrives without bringing visitors from England.' Gelmers's head turned from side to side, he followed the conversation from mouth to mouth, as if he were finding their English difficult to understand. He could at least have had his suit cleaned and pressed, Versluis reflected, uncomfortably conscious of the young man's shoulder rubbing against his own as the company sat squashed around the table.

'Only last week a young English woman died here,' one of the Hirsch daughters remarked to Codrington. 'It was terribly sad. We sent flowers to the funeral.'

'We came across the funeral procession as we rode into the town. We were riding fast that afternoon, because we could see that there was a storm on its way.'

Versluis shifted his attention back to the talk at the head of the table, where Michell was telling them about their visit to the President. 'But he spoke extremely good English,' he added. 'In fact, so did the Chief Justice.'

'They are both from the Cape,' Hirsch said. 'Our older generation of civil servants were mainly Dutchmen, but nowadays we import them from the Boland.'

'How did you like your first real thunderstorm, Mr Versluis?' Mrs Hirsch asked. 'It *was* the first one, wasn't it? It was so welcome after the drought, but they can be frightening if you're not accustomed to them. I recall how scared I used to be myself.'

'The Bishop was talking of founding a hospital here,' one of the older boys at the far end of the table informed Codrington. 'People are always dying in hotels and backrooms. They come here only to die.'

'Then the best thing is simply not to die!' Gelmers cried with forced joviality, a trifle too eagerly, as if he had been waiting for this moment to rejoin the conversation, and he laughed too loudly at his attempt at a joke.

Versluis turned away towards his hostess on his left. 'I had not expected the storm at all, or at least, I had not expected it to be so violent. I had in fact taken a stroll that afternoon.'

She laughed her merry laugh, which rang clearly above the confusion of voices that surrounded them. 'Oh, we all have to learn, Mr Versluis; you will learn to take care yet. One can never trust Africa.' She looked rapidly round the table, checking that all the plates were still full, judging the amounts remaining in the dishes, and beckoned to the servants. 'But did you get wet?'

'I was caught in the veld by the storm, without any shelter nearby,' he said, leaning slightly towards her in an effort to make himself heard above her husband's conversation with Michell.

'Someone dies in this town every week,' one of the girls said. 'It's not at all pleasant.'

'Your coachman came to my assistance,' he added a little more loudly.

'Amien?' she asked in surprise. 'But where was this?'

'In the coloured quarter.'

'Oh, he was probably visiting some of his friends. There is a handful of Cape people living there with whom he has some contact.'

'But one of the hotel servants appeared and chased him away, almost as if he did not want the man to touch me.'

'Oh, the blacks are scared of Amien,' Mrs Hirsch said, amused. 'The Malays say he is a carrier.' But then she dropped the subject, her attention diverted by the servants who were looking enquiringly around the door, and she beckoned them closer.

'Do you mean that he suffers from some kind of disease?' Versluis enquired uncomprehendingly, but she did not hear him. The young people burst out laughing at something that one of them had said, and beside him Gelmers's laugh again sounded too loudly. His question was lost in the din.

'Have you met our President yet, Mr Versluis?' Hirsch asked, leaning across the table. In all the talk that ebbed and flowed around him, the ragged sentences in their passage around the table, Versluis was unable to hear the question, and Hirsch was forced to repeat it.

'No,' he said, in some confusion. 'No, I'm afraid that I have neglected my social duty. I haven't been out much since I arrived in Bloemfontein.'

'But you must meet him, really – it's your loss, if I may say so. Besides, he will be only too pleased to get the chance to speak to a visitor from the Netherlands.'

'I should not want to impose myself upon such a busy man,' he said defensively, and Michell laughed from across the table.

'I do not believe that the head of a rural republic such as this could often be overloaded with work,' he remarked flippantly.

'But I can assure you that you are mistaken, my friend,' Hirsch said rather sharply. 'The Diamond Fields question has required his full attention for some years now. Basutoland has been an abiding source of trouble, it has always been, even though it has now crept under the wind of the Cape Colony – our little state may seem peaceful to you, but we are being threatened on all sides.' He forcefully opposed this disparaging judgement of the country, as if he had been directly touched by it. 'And the politics that England is now pursuing with regard to our neighbours in the North, if I may say so. . . .'

'Come, come, Mr Hirsch,' Michell said, smiling, 'you don't mean to say that you are bothered by what happens to the Transvaal?' Hirsch drew sufficient breath for a weighty answer, and the conversation had turned to politics.

'Have you managed to become acquainted with many people in Bloemfontein, Mr Versluis?' enquired Mrs Hirsch beside him. The dishes had been cleared from the table and now a crystal bowl of dessert was placed before her, covered in whipped cream, gleaming with cherries and angelica, saturated with liqueur, from which she began to dish.

'A number of people have called or left their cards, but I haven't been out much yet. As a matter of fact, my visit to the reading circle was my first outing of that sort.'

'I hope that there will be many more,' she said genially, busy filling the dessert bowls. 'Do you mind passing them to me? Mrs Prince is really exceptionally hospitable, I know that she extended her invitation to you in all sincerity.' Whipped cream spilt from the over-full bowls; she cried out, laughed, and grabbed for a spoon, a napkin, to wipe it up. 'Miss Scheffler is also a dear woman,' she suddenly remarked. 'A very dear woman,' she repeated, forgetting the dishing-up for a moment as she emphasised this judgement amidst the stack of dessert bowls and the cloying aroma of liqueur that saturated the trifle. 'She is an exceptional woman,' she said after some thought. 'She does not belong here, she will never fulfil herself here. Is there any place in this country for someone with promise? What kind of possibility exists for any kind of development? Everything is still too new, too impoverished. But on the other hand, would there be greater opportunities for her in Europe?' She pondered the question with a frown, shrugged her shoulders and continued dishing the dessert. He handed the bowl which she passed him on to Gelmers, and for a second that young man's fingers touched his, so that Versluis quickly drew back, remembering the square hand that had rested beside him on the table, its chewed nails.

'But the Transvaal is surely not South Africa,' Michell said. 'From what I've heard of it, it has always been poor, backward and divided, scarcely half-civilised – President Burgers's attempts to drag it into the modern world have failed miserably. As an inhabitant of a prosperous little state can you conceivably be concerned about what happens on the other side of the Vaal?'

Hirsch thoughtfully sipped his wine, his attention diverted from the conversation for a moment while he savoured it. The young people roared, with Gelmers's high-pitched laugh clearly audible amongst them. Mrs Hirsch passed down the bowls of dessert, and the servants in their bare feet shuffled endlessly around the table.

'When I came to this country,' Hirsch began deliberately, 'as long as thirty years ago, such an attitude may still have been possible, but not now at the end of the Seventies. Then civilisation virtually ended at Grahamstown: Colesberg was an outpost, Bloemfontein no more than a garrison, and the Transorange was hardly more than a wilderness where bushmen still hunted wild animals – and farmers – with bows and arrows. What happened in the Colony, we hardly knew; we relied on couriers and transport riders, and news often reached us weeks later – from the Transvaal we sometimes had reports of explorers and hunters returning from the interior, but what happened there did not concern us. But today. . . .' He pushed his dessert aside, untouched; from the end of the table the young people were already beginning to send their bowls back to be refilled. 'There are towns, churches, schools throughout the Free State and deep into the Transvaal; the telegraph has just reached us, and no doubt the railway will be on its way within the next few years. The discovery of diamonds off-loaded the whole world on to our doorstep; and the Diamond Fields question has dragged us willy-nilly into international politics. It's no longer just developments in our immediate vicinity that involve us, but everything that happens in this part of the world. No single part of this region can remain unaffected by the developments in another.'

Mrs Hirsch cast a kindly, smiling look upon her husband. 'Can I tempt you with nothing else, Mr Versluis? A little compote, perhaps?'

With only half his attention Versluis tried to decline all further offerings as politely as he could, while with the other half he listened to the exposition that Hirsch was giving to his English guests as he leaned back comfortably with his glass in his hand, his face red from the food, the wine and the heat. 'Up to now everything that has happened in this part of the continent has occurred largely by chance,' the host continued, 'but in the last ten or twenty years signs of purpose have begun to appear. For the first time we are becoming aware of the fact that we belong to Africa and that we must accept responsibility for what is happening in Africa.' Michell listened, even Codrington and a few of the young people in the rumbustious group at the end of the table were now leaning forward to hear, although Gelmers still tried to joke with the uninterested girl beside him.

Only Mrs Hirsch's attention remained fixed on greater matters, sweeping the table in search of bowls that needed filling. 'Mr Gelmers, another helping for you?' she called, but the young man did not hear her. 'Mr Versluis, you disappoint me. You wouldn't dare refuse if you were at Mrs Van der Vliet's.' The girls, bored by the conversation, overheard her remark and giggled, and among the young men too there was a stirring, their attention wandering once more. Gelmers jerked round rapidly, as if he suspected that the laughter might be directed at him. 'Don't worry, I'm merely teasing you, Mr Versluis,' Mrs Hirsch added with a smile, dishing-up spoon in her hand. 'You won't tell her, will you? We all know what a fine person she is. Mr Gelmers, you haven't met Mrs Van der Vliet yet, have you?'

'I've not had the pleasure yet,' Gelmers replied stiffly.

'Then I'm sure Mr Versluis will be kind enough to introduce you to her some day. She is a prominent inhabitant of our town, one of the pillars of the community.' No matter how hard she tried to look serious, however, she did not quite succeed, and had to bite her lip to stop herself laughing – as mischievous as one of her own daughters, who were in turn as delightful as she was.

'Dominee Radloff is afraid of her,' said one of the smaller boys in a deep, solemn voice, and everyone burst out laughing. Mrs Hirsch put a handkerchief to her mouth. Gelmers sat uncomprehendingly in their midst, looking from one face to another.

The laughter recalled Hirsch's attention from the conversation concerning Britain's involvement in South Africa in which he and the two officers had become so embroiled and, ignorant of the reference, he smiled broadly. 'Has everyone finished?' he enquired. 'Has everybody had enough? My dear, gentlemen – shall we have coffee on the stoep?'

There was a general clatter and sound of chairs, feet and voices; they all rose simultaneously and left the table in a single turbulent wave which broke out in laughter, banter, cries and chatter over the back stoep, with the barking of the puppy in its midst, and washed up along the garden paths. Versluis allowed himself to be led by Mrs Hirsch who was babbling along happily at his side. He was carried along by the wave, bobbing on the voices and cries and bits of conversation that churned around him, overwhelmed by the rustle of gathered skirts, trains and wrestling boys. Hirsch offered cigars, asked if anyone would like a liqueur; his wife organised the children, the servants and the coffee. The children clamoured for bonbons – laughing, teasing and threatening they pressed around her and rendered all further conversation impossible with their cries.

What was he doing in the midst of all this? Versluis wondered once again as he stood in the shade of the house, looking down from the high stoep at Mrs Hirsch who was surrounded by the rumbustious children, while Michell and Codrington laughingly looked on. It struck him in a flash of insight that he did not belong there, a guest invited into that jovial circle, a spectator who could have no share in that uncomprehending gaiety, and with a rapid movement he turned towards the house, away from the people. But where was he going? he wondered. He could not simply abandon the gathering he chided himself, and he remained where he was, noticing in the doorway which led to the dining room, the young Dutchman in the crumpled checked suit who he had been jettisoned by the exultant wave.

He would have to speak to the young man, Versluis reflected without any enthusiasm: since the two of them had been accidentally washed up together there at the edge of the group he could hardly avoid some sort of elementary gesture of goodwill. Full of reluctance, he hesitated for a moment, and then raised his voice in order to be heard above the chatter and laughter.

'Have you been in Bloemfontein long?' he enquired, realising at once that he had spoken too loudly, for Gelmers appeared to have been startled, unprepared for this advance, and had recoiled slightly.

'I arrived a week ago,' he said at last with palpable reluctance.

'And do you propose to stay long?'

'I don't know, I haven't thought about it. I'll see.'

No indeed, Versluis thought to himself, definitely not a particularly pleasant or even acceptable young person. The suspicions aroused by the forced laughter; the loud, checked suit; the chewed nails: all now confirmed by the peasant Dutch, his evasive eyes and his obvious reluctance to talk.

'You will soon feel at home here, I am sure,' he remarked, and searched for an excuse to disengage himself from his companion. 'There is quite a large colony of Dutch people in Bloemfontein.'

'I'm not interested in Hollanders,' Gelmers replied bluntly, but before Versluis could decide whether this remark was intended to be offensive, Hirsch had approached them with a stack of cigar boxes.

'I must apologise to you bachelors for dragging you along here,' he laughingly called above the din. 'But they are not all our children. Half of Jagersfontein and Fauresmith seem to have come to visit this weekend.'

Gelmers moved rapidly away, as if he wished to escape before it was too late, turning towards the young people in the garden, but as nobody took any notice of him he turned back to the house with one hand held out in front of him; only then Mrs Hirsch looked up from amongst the young people and, seeing him excluded, she detached herself from the group and went up to him with the spontaneous, natural friendliness that marked the whole family. He should help her pass around the coffee cups, she called. The children ought to go and play in the garden and not be a nuisance; the girls could come and help; Michell and Codrington should come and have some coffee. The children laughed and bantered, and without paying much attention to her instructions they formed fresh, flowing patterns on the stoep and among the flowerbeds, while the servants brought the coffee.

'It must all be rather tiring for you,' said Hirsch without listening to Versluis's polite denials. He laughed quietly to himself at the sight of all this bustle. 'Oh, it can all be a bit too much for one sometimes, I concede that – there are problems. It takes years of money and effort and sorrow to see a child through life and out of the house, to see your sons established in the business world and your daughters married. But it is worth it, I can assure you of that.'

He approached Michell and Codrington with the cigars; Mrs Hirsch listened with a smile to Gelmers's explanations while she kept an eye on the servants. Versluis stood by himself in the shade next to the wall of the house, and as he watched the carefree people before him he was suddenly overcome by a sense of loneliness and fear on that bright afternoon – the fear that he felt whenever he looked out from the edge

110

of the town, protected by the last houses and gardens, at the vast expanse of the veld. This was loneliness, he realised for a moment. This was longing. And without being absolutely conscious of what he was doing, he turned away as he had seen Gelmers turn a few minutes earlier on that stoep, and wondered to himself what form of escape, what kind of refuge there could be for him. But already Hirsch was handing him a cognac, Mrs Hirsch wished to pour him some coffee, and he had to stay, caught in his panic amongst these kindly people.

'They also invited Mr Gelmers,' he remarked at the table that evening in the course of the report which had been awaited in silence rather than demanded outright. 'He is the young Dutchman who arrived last week.' Mrs Van der Vliet inclined her head in a gesture which could have expressed either acceptance or rejection of this information. 'He says that he does not know yet how long he will be staying in Bloemfontein.' But her continued silence made it clear that it was not necessary for him to enlarge any further on the new arrival, so he dropped the subject with relief.

'We must ask him to join us for a game of billiards at the hotel,' said Polderman. 'What about Wednesday evening, Du Toit?'

'Our little circle of Netherlanders is beginning to grow once again,' Van der Vliet declared enthusiastically, but as usual nobody took up the subject, and he withdrew once more, pressing his handkerchief to his weeping eye. Miss Pronk was moody, perhaps because of some disagreement with her fiancé or some trouble with the bridesmaids; Mrs Van der Vliet sat passively at the head of the table, a daunting image in black crowned by her tired bonnet, silently pondering her own dark thoughts. As the scraping of knives and the clatter of cups fell silent, the only sound at the table was that of the moths fluttering against the lamps.

When Versluis went to sit on the stoep at the back of the house after supper, the sweetness of the saturated earth and its plants rose up to him – of the climbing roses in front of the verandah, the honeysuckle over the pagoda. He leant back in the cane chair with his book unread on his lap and gazed at the deepening shadows in the garden, the softening of the light, the changing colours of the sky; he heard the lowing of cattle returning from their pastures outside the town, together with the distant sounds of nightfall, clinking and cries from other houses.

Polderman had come to stand next to him on the stoep. 'If we were

111

in the Netherlands now,' he said, 'we'd be able to play tennis until ten o'clock.'

'If we were in the Netherlands now,' Versluis remarked, 'it would have been dark by five o'clock.'

The young man did not reply at once. 'Yes,' he said, 'it's winter isn't it? One forgets.'

Helmond the attorney had appeared as usual after supper to visit his fiancée, and he now paced back and forth along the path in front of the verandah smoking a cigar, but he did not look up at the house or at them, as if he were there purely by chance.

'Have you been in Africa long?' Versluis asked when the young man remained standing next to him and made no move to go to speak to the lawyer.

'Almost five years,' Polderman said absently as he gazed out over the garden. 'One will probably never go back, eh? To come here is simple enough, but to go back and carry on with your life there, that's another matter.'

'I hope not,' Versluis answered lightly, but Polderman was not listening, for Miss Pronk had come outside. Her heels clicked across the wooden floor of the stoep, her dress rustled about her, and the scent of tuberoses surrounded her. She paid no attention to the grinning Polderman or to her fiancé waiting in the garden, but remained standing for a moment beside Versluis's chair and smoothed down the ribbons and pleats that clung to her figure with a self-conscious vivaciousness that made it quite apparent that the performance was intended for the two younger men.

'Poor thing, Mr Versluis, always with a book!' she cried. 'One day your eyes will stick to the pages.'

'And if I happen to enjoy reading?' he enquired, but she did not hear him above her incessant chatter.

'Wait until my wedding, Mr Versluis, then you won't have a chance to sit and read. We'll have you dancing!' she called back at him as she went down the verandah steps.

A rather brazen young woman, Versluis thought to himself as he watched her join her fiancé without making any attempt to greet him, merely shrugging her shoulders impatiently in reply to something that he asked her as they walked away.

'One can't really go back completely, can one?' Polderman said after a while. 'Once you have gone – I mean, you've gone, not so? It's over.'

'Are you planning to pledge your future to Africa, then?' Versluis asked.

112

The young man gazed at the engaged couple – his genial, smiling face with its snub nose darkened for a moment and his thoughts appeared to be elsewhere – until they disappeared amongst the fruit trees and not even the brilliance of Miss Pronk's dress could be distinguished in the gathering dusk any longer.

'If one were in Amsterdam now,' said Polderman, 'in Kalver Street or on the Nieuwendijk. . . .'

'I don't know Amsterdam very well,' said Versluis, recalling for a moment scenes filled with the masts of ships, church bells, the clatter of a cab over the cobbles of the Dam: strange, unreal images against the glow of the sunset that they were now observing. How old would Polderman be? he wondered. Twenty-three, four? And how young he must have been when he arrived here. He wanted to say something, to ask the young man more, but Polderman had already turned away from him and was now leaning over the balustrade of the verandah as if he were still trying to discern something amongst the blur of the trees. Then they heard from far down in the orchard, above the sounds of the nocturnal creatures, Miss Pronk's low, sensual laugh.

'Polderman!' Du Toit called from within the house. 'Polderman, where are you? How about it, are we going across to the hotel tonight?'

'No, I'm not going, you go on your own,' Polderman called back brusquely, and then he turned and walked away abruptly without even taking leave of Versluis. Du Toit appeared on the threshold, looked about enquiringly, and disappeared once more.

No light remained: in the sky the evening star glimmered. Versluis rose and went inside, found the lamp on the table in his room and the candlestick on the bedside cabinet; he prepared himself slowly for the night, folded his clothes, put shoe-forms into his footwear, wound up his pocket watch and put it on the cabinet. The smooth sheets had been turned back. From beyond the window there came no further sound but the calls of the night.

Bloemfontein's entire small Dutch community was involved in the marriage of Helmond and Miss Pronk, and as the appointed date drew nearer the house was taken over by the married women of the town and their daughters, who filled it with lively conversation conducted in various degrees of broken Dutch and English as they darted from room to room.

The bridesmaids came to have their dresses fitted and to admire each other's appearance with cries of rapture: dresses and veils filled every

113

room, wreaths and artificial flowers lay strewn in every unexpected place, and little bits of ribbon and thread clung to everything. The bare feet of the servants padded continuously over the floor as they fetched and carried, tidied up or were called to steam, press or iron yet another object. The fearful silence in which they usually worked was infected by the prevailing excitement; they now whispered to each other and from time to time giggled behind their hands. Mrs Van der Vliet sailed through the house like a ship, dignified and serene in her black dress amongst the sprightly girls, nor did she consider apologising for this unprecedented disruption of both peace and routine. 'At least we won't be losing Miss Pronk entirely, Mr Versluis,' she informed him in passing, as if he wanted reassurance on this point. 'She and her husband will happily be staying here with us for a while.'

There was no longer any place in the house where he could sit undisturbed, and when he withdrew into his own room a young woman knocked at the door to ask if he could lend her a pair of nail scissors. Even the afternoon coffee was served half an hour late and was brought to his room by a servant who had clearly forgotten about him entirely.

Irritated by the disorder and the noise, Versluis finally took his hat and cane and left the house. Since he had moved in there his walks had become more infrequent and his outings took him no further than the small business centre around the market square, or at most to a house of one of the members of the tiny Dutch community whom he had got to know at Mrs Van der Vliet's: Doctor Brill of the College, the Bloems, or the Van Andels. He had become lazy he thought to himself as he stood at the gate smoothing down his gloves. Or was it really only laziness? Perhaps it was rather an unwillingness to leave his settled existence in the house and be confronted by a terrain which he could not always deal with or assimilate easily – unwillingness and possibly a degree of aversion, perhaps also something like fear. He frowned at the thought and hesitated about the direction that he should take. To the west? The east? Why fear, exactly, and what for? The houses lay peacefully in their gardens behind the long shadows of the trees – smoke was beginning to curl from the chimneys, and far away some children were playing in the street. What was there to be afraid of in this bright world? he wondered, and shook off the ridiculous thought. He turned down to the left, with the late afternoon sun behind him: he would go up the hill again he thought, and from the top, near the cemetery, he would look out across the wide panorama

114

to the south which had so enthralled him at the beginning, but which he had not visited for some time.

He walked down the middle of the street, which as usual was almost deserted – there was the odd child, the odd watercarrier, and here and there a dog sleeping in the shade of a tree – and then he marked at the far end, beyond the boys' school, a figure in black coming towards him like a mirror image. One which he recognised even at that distance as Pastor Scheffler. Scheffler had, however, not seen him: hands behind his back he strode along deep in thought, with the sun in his eyes, and it was only when he saw the shadow on the ground in front of him that he was aware of an approaching person and shielded his eyes with both hands to see whom it might be. His joy and surprise when he recognised Versluis were palpably sincere, though Versluis himself discovered that he greeted this unexpected encounter with mixed feelings. Up to now he had regarded the clergyman as a strange and somewhat disturbing young man whom he preferred to keep at a distance, but this afternoon he was rather relieved to meet a familiar face, and so he stayed to exchange pleasantries about his health, the weather and the literary gathering at the convent.

'I decided to take a walk before dinner,' he said when these topics had been exhausted.

'I never have time for walking any more,' Scheffler said. 'I was once an avid walker – in Bethany, for instance, the mission station where we grew up, I used to walk for miles through the veld.' He half turned as he spoke and looked across his shoulder to where the veld receded flatly at the end of the street, as if he wanted to reassure himself that it still existed and was still waiting for him. 'One is always on the go, and amongst all one's usual obligations there are always ones that you don't expect. This afternoon, for instance – I've just come from the jail, the son of one the members of my father's congregation has been locked up here, and I had to go and see if I could do anything for him.' They walked together up the incline while he talked, the clergyman on his way to his church and parsonage, and Versluis up to the top of the hill, to the cemetery and the panorama over the veld.

'It's such a steep road,' Scheffler said, aggrieved. 'It's really completely impractical as a road to the cemetery. It's not feasible to struggled up here with a funeral carriage and a coffin, and burials are becoming increasingly frequent as our town gets bigger.'

The last burial had been that of the young Scottish woman who had died in the hotel Versluis remembered, hearing once again the pealing bell from which he had fled that afternoon; the horses had drawn the

115

funeral carriage up the steep incline, that they themselves were now climbing, followed by a handful of mourners – clergymen, representatives of the town's Scottish community and a few curious hangers-on. They had collected money amongst themselves to pay for the funeral, Miss Pronk had informed them at the table.

He remained standing, supported by his cane. The road up the hill was very steep, and perhaps he had been unwise to attempt it. It stretched darkly ahead of him, shaded by the bluegums on either side. The cemetery was at the top of the hill, beyond it lay the wide-open veld, and he remembered from his walk that earlier afternoon the sight of that little band of people around the open grave, while the sky had darkened with the approaching storm. The hill was too steep.

The clergyman had remained standing at his church with its steeply raked roof, and the parsonage with its hollyhocks in the garden. 'I don't know,' he said, 'you want to walk and I shouldn't like to delay you – but if you should wish to come in, just for a moment. . . .'

The eagerness with which he accepted the invitation surprised even Versluis, and it appeared that the clergyman did not quite expect this acceptance, but after a barely noticeable moment's hesitation he turned and with his long strides walked quickly and definitely in the direction of the parsonage without pausing to see whether Versluis was following. Only when he reached the stoep did he stop to hold the door open for his visitor. 'I wonder,' he began undecidedly, but a door off the hallway opened and they could hear the crying of a baby.

'August?' a woman said and stopped when she saw the stranger.

'Mathilde,' said the clergyman, 'this is Mr Versluis, our visitor from the Netherlands. Mr Versluis, my wife.' A young woman with large eyes, her hair tied in a tight plait on her head and with a whimpering baby in her arms, nodded to him. 'And Friederike,' Scheffler added in a lowered voice, 'our daughter.'

Mrs Scheffler shyly held the baby out to Versluis, and involuntarily he took a step backwards. Babies disconcerted him, they were strange creatures that he was unable to deal with, and he felt ill at ease with this pale, complaining creature with its sour smell of vomit.

'I don't know,' Scheffler repeated with the same hesitation; 'Mathilde, perhaps the study would be. . . .'

'Adèle is in the living room, August,' she said softly. 'I'm just going to put Friederike to bed.' With a slight curtsey towards Versluis she disappeared once more.

'You have met my sister, haven't you, Mr Versluis?' the clergyman asked. 'Shall we go and sit with her?' He did not wait for an answer,

116

however, and with one of his characteristically abrupt gestures he turned to Versluis to relieve him of his hat and gloves.

The room into which Versluis was now led was a gloomy chamber behind the verandah. Mrs Scheffler moved quickly around it with the baby on her arm, collecting scattered napkins and pieces of clothing, and her sister-in-law reclined on a settee near the window. The room was furnished with the same degree of sparseness and lack of comfort that Versluis had observed in the clergyman's study – a dining room table covered with a red plush cloth was the major piece of furniture, together with a couple of horsehair armchairs which were thinly spread out at some distance from each other; the odd side-table containing ornaments and framed family portraits, a few prints on the wall and the bit of carpet on the wooden floor were not enough to temper an impression of austerity or even poverty.

Versluis was given hardly any opportunity to take in the room, however, for the moment he entered Miss Scheffler raised herself with a cry of surprise from the settee on which she was reclining and offered her hand to him without a sign of any reticence. 'August has been promising for such a long time that he was going to invite you around, Mr Versluis,' she called gaily. 'I'm pleased that he has finally done so.' Her sister-in-law disappeared with the napkins, bits of clothing and the baby, closing the door silently behind her.

'One has so many good intentions, but little ever comes of them,' her brother said, drawing a chair closer. 'Or perhaps I should be honest and add that one seldom has the courage of one's convictions,' he continued, without noticing that a sewing-basket had been left on one of the chairs. Reels of cotton, tape and pins became scattered across the floor, and his sister burst out laughing.

'You'll have to excuse us, Mr Versluis,' she said. 'We are unfortunately not very accustomed to visitors, at least not a family visit like this. People coming to see the pastor officially are a different matter, but even then I have to confess it can be difficult for us.'

'I'm afraid I have to agree with my sister, Mr Versluis,' her brother said from where he was kneeling on the floor, picking up pins. 'We come from a mission station, not a parsonage, and we are accustomed to a relatively free and improvised lifestyle, so we tend to shock other people a little. My wife's father was a clergyman, in Germany in fact, and I fear that we still tend to shock her with our casualness.' His sister laughed once more, and he was forced to smile too. 'But I had forgotten, Mr Versluis, you must excuse me, these things are presumably strange to you and you wouldn't understand. We grew up in the

117

country among the black people, simply, even in poverty, one could say; in any case we were hardly affluent. . . .'

'But we were happy,' his sister added quickly.

'Oh yes, we were happy. We had a very happy childhood.'

Versluis had sat down on a chair that had been placed for him and looked from the laughing young woman on the bench to the priest who knelt in front of him, the pins and cotton completely forgotten, and he was unsure of how he should respond to their unconstrained geniality. In his own home and in the midst of his family Scheffler had entirely lost his characteristic absent-mindedness and nervousness; he and his sister treated Versluis as if they had known him for a long time and felt totally at ease with him.

'We used to walk barefoot as children,' the clergyman said, and as he knelt there, grinning and with his tousled hair, he looked more than ever like a schoolboy, playing with a toy on the carpet. 'It's good to walk barefoot, Mr Versluis, it gives one a wonderful feeling of freedom. But I suppose that you didn't get much of a chance to do it in Europe – as a child, I mean.'

'I do not believe that I have ever in my life walked barefoot,' Versluis replied carefully. Was this young man perhaps joking with him? he wondered for a moment, but this suspicion disappeared as soon as it arose. The friendliness, the honesty, the sincerity were unfeigned.

And Miss Scheffler? he thought, and turned towards her. As she sat there, supported by the back of the settee, a light rug thrown across her legs, her deformity was still plain, but she appeared unconcerned about it, and without the slightest degree of self-consciousness she laughed with, and at, her brother who was crawling about the floor searching for the pins. They must have grown up in a happy family Versluis reflected; they had shared their childhood and were able to laugh together in this carefree way because they knew and understood each other. Had she also run around barefoot as a child? he wondered. Had she ever run? He quickly turned his eyes from the rug that covered her knees.

'But what do you mean by saying that Mr Versluis wouldn't understand, August?' Miss Scheffler asked, suddenly serious. 'Why should you not understand something of our lives, Mr Versluis?'

The greyish-blue eyes looked directly at him in honest curiosity. 'What your brother meant, Miss Scheffler,' Versluis said at last when the clergyman remained silent, 'is that I am not a church-goer, indeed not even a believer, so that I know very little of clergymen or missionaries.'

118

The greyish-blue eyes remained fixed upon his face. 'Not a believer – but does that mean that you believe in nothing?' She looked quickly at her brother for some clarification. 'It must be a very lonely existence, I should have thought. Is it at all possible to believe in nothing?' she asked, and leant slightly towards Versluis from her recumbent position on the bench, as if she did not want to miss a gesture or word of his reply.

'I am not a believer in the sense of the word as you appear to understand it,' he said just as the clergyman also began to say something. 'I do not belong to any Church. I am not a Christian, nor do I adhere to any other doctrine.'

She considered these words in silence and then nodded deliberately. 'Not to go to church and not be a Christian is one thing. But there must surely be something in which you do believe, entirely separate from conventional doctrines, some or other guiding principle in terms of which you live or some goal towards which you are moving, isn't there?'

He should actually be offended by these personal questions and make an attempt to change the subject, but he found himself unable to do so: as with her brother, her interest was so genuine and open that her questions could hardly be considered impertinent, and any attempt to evade them would appear to be nothing but rudeness.

It was quiet in the room which was already beginning to grow dark behind the wide verandah and the pot plants on the window sills. Miss Scheffler looked at him with her direct, thoughtful gaze; her brother was still kneeling on the tiny patch of carpet in the middle of the floor. What answer could he give? Versluis thought. And he tried to draw up an account of the things in which he believed: order and regularity; dependability; honesty; that debts should be paid and obligations fulfilled; that commands be carried out, orders met and letters answered; that servants should be worth their wage and cabmen be sober; that a fire should be made on winter evenings and wine properly stored. But how could he give these people such an answer? One which in this context could only sound flippant. Trapped, he sat in that dusky room while brother and sister awaited his reply.

'I believe in duty, and in acting in accordance with the dictates of one's conscience,' he said at last, more coldly and deliberately than he had intended; and Miss Scheffler nodded once more, although it was clear that these words neither satisfied her nor answered her question.

'I'm sorry,' her brother said, his head upside-down as he continued to search for the pins, 'I didn't wish to make you feel uncomfortable

119

– I mean, I didn't intend to drag your personal beliefs into the conversation.'

'August is a priest, and yet he never wants to drag anyone's personal beliefs or spiritual life into any conversation,' his sister declared in a lightly reproachful voice.

'Because an ordinary conversation during an afternoon visit is clearly not the best time to discuss such matters, Adèle.'

'But why ever not? These are after all things that touch one's whole being, including one's social life and one's afternoon visits, these are not matters that you discuss only at appointed times with the priest in his study.'

It was clear that she was interested in this discussion and was determined to press the subject further, but her brother seemed uncomfortable, and so it was Versluis who felt compelled to intervene. 'I don't mind discussing these matters,' he said, 'as long as you understand that my opinions differ completely from your own. I do not wish to offend unintentionally or perhaps insult you concerning something that may be important to you.'

But Miss Scheffler did not allow him to finish. 'But that is precisely what is so interesting,' she interrupted him, 'to be able to speak to someone who has opinions that differ from one's own and those of people around one; it encourages one to ask all sorts of questions and to start thinking differently about everything.'

'I'm afraid that my sister sometimes feels a bit confined here in Bloemfontein,' Scheffler said with a smile. 'In our tiny community there is not much room for dissenting opinions or even for penetrating discussions.'

'No, no,' his sister said rapidly, almost too eagerly. 'It's not just a question of Bloemfontein or the people here. . . .' But then she stopped and made an impatient gesture that referred wordlessly to her deformed back, the rug, the settee, and Versluis looked away uncomfortably. 'I go out very seldom,' she said. 'I would not even have been at the poetry reading if Mrs Hirsch had not insisted upon it and come to fetch me herself in the carriage. But one needs to talk to people, to learn something new, to experience challenges – small challenges, perhaps, but they are also significant. And August doesn't always understand entirely. He has been away, he lived abroad all those years, and he doesn't always understand what it is like to be trapped in a single room, in a single house, not even to have had the possibility of any of the opportunities that he's had.' For a moment they were silent in the dusky room: the clergyman had sat down near his sister, the sewing-basket, into which he had untidily bundled everything, still on his knees. 'But no,' she continued more softly, 'what I am saying is not true. You do understand, August, you too feel the limitations of life here, of our life here; and it is precisely because you have been away that they are even more difficult to accept than for me who has known nothing else.' Her tone was confiding and there was a fondness in her smile, as if they had forgotten the presence of the stranger, or perhaps they no longer regarded him as a stranger.

Scheffler returned his sister's smile, then he noticed the sewing-basket on his lap and put it down impatiently.

'My sister knows me only too well, Mr Versluis,' he said, 'and she is more honest, or in any case more outspoken than I am – I would still hesitate to say all these things, but they are completely true. It's not Bloemfontein or my congregation here, I wouldn't complain about those – that is to say, I don't wish to complain at all, that's not my intention. It's just that sometimes, it's that my situation. . . .' His voice died away: frowning he stared at the ground as if he were searching for words, and then the three of them were startled in their seats by the sound of Mrs Scheffler's hand on the door knob. Conscious of having interrupted their conversation, she remained outside the circle.

'Friederike is in bed,' she began, but left the sentence unfinished as she looked enquiringly at her husband. Her hand rested on the back of his chair, the small wedding ring glinting in the half-light, but she refrained from touching him as she waited for him to speak. Versluis suddenly realised the significance of her unspoken question, and he stood up rapidly.

'I must go,' he said. 'I was not aware that it was so late.'

'But wouldn't you like to stay for something to eat?' the clergyman asked.

'I'm sorry, but Mrs Van der Vliet is expecting me for dinner, and I fear that it is almost time to eat already.'

The clergyman laughed, his sister laughed, and even young Mrs Scheffler, who clearly stood wondering whether there would be enough food for an unexpected guest, was forced to smile. It was Scheffler who spoke: 'Yes of course, the insuperable Mrs Van der Vliet, she would find it difficult to forgive such an insult to her table. But you must come again, Mr Versluis, you must come and have a meal with us one evening, we'll arrange something.'

'Yes, you must come again,' his sister said with the same sober, unfeminine directness that had struck him previously, although he found it less disturbing now than at first.

121

'You would be very welcome,' her sister-in-law added more quietly.

He took leave of the women and left them in the dusky living room: on the threshold he looked back and saw that Mrs Scheffler had lit the lamp and was bending over the gleaming white shade as she replaced it over the glass of the lamp. The translucent porcelain glowed between her hands, its soft light caught her face and hair and touched her sister-in-law on the settee where she had turned around, half-erect against its back, to watch the departing guest. He glimpsed this scene for an instant over Scheffler's shoulder as he turned, the two women together in the halo of lamplight, and then the clergyman drew the door behind them.

His place at the table was the only one still vacant, but Mrs Van der Vliet greeted his appearance with smiling benevolence, without any sign of disapproval or reproach, and accepted his apologies gracefully. 'He is a very fine young man,' she said, reaching for the knife in order to cut him a slice of bread. 'One could perhaps say something about his style of preaching and about some of the doctrines that he expounds, but no-one can deny that he is a good human being. Although it does not help to be too good, Mr Versluis, as you will no doubt agree,' she added with a sigh.

'How is Miss Scheffler? And the baby?' asked Miss Pronk from across the table, and he improvised some trivial answer to satisfy her. 'What did you talk about?' she enquired further, and he stalled. About nothing that could possibly interest her, he realised; indeed, about nothing that would sound like proper conversation if he were to relate it at this table. But Miss Pronk was not interested in any response. 'Did you enjoy being there?' she asked in a tone of almost scornful surprise, and leant across the table to tease Du Toit about the impression he had made on the Bloem girls. She was in a continuous state of loud excitability, and Versluis found it difficult to adapt himself to the boisterous conversation at the table after the gloomy room and the intense, serious discussion at the parsonage. Fortunately the young people had already forgotten about him, and even Mrs Van der Vliet sat regarding their fun with a smile and did not try to involve him in any conversation. He could see that glowing lampshade as if it had been imprinted on his retina, and he recalled the light-filled room, glimpsed for a moment on his way out as he had turned on the threshold, with the two women together, and he experienced an unexpected pang of grief at the memory.

122

Miss Pronk was to be married in the house, where they were also having the reception, with the result that as the festive day drew nearer, the familiar routine was increasingly disrupted. Additional servants were brought in to assist with cleaning and preparation and all the ladies of the Dutch community banded together to provide support: all day long people darted and chattered up and down the passages and across the verandahs, while Mrs Van der Vliet's heavier tread and deeper voice sounded above the din as she issued orders and dealt firmly with any attempt to challenge her sole authority. Chairs were brought and tables moved, armfuls of tamarind and greenery were placed to decorate the rooms; they took their meals at a table in the corner of the verandah, nor did Mrs Van der Vliet encourage them to linger there, for her mind was on greater matters. Even from his room Versluis could hear the clatter and the noise; the excited cries of women's voices, with Miss Pronk's high, penetrating prattle among them; the noise of shifting furniture and the bustle in the kitchen.

These preparations lasted for only a few days and then the house was taken over by a festival spirit. On the verandah stood long tables covered with white cloths; the rooms were decorated in flowers, greenery and painted devices, and bridesmaids ran across the passage in their white dresses, trailing veils behind them.

The Voigts had sent their carriage to convey Mrs Van der Vliet, who was festively rigged out in deep purple and decorated in a profusion of frills, ribbons and little artificial violets, to the Dutch church, and she had insisted that Versluis accompany her. It was clear that there would be no way for him to avoid the occasion, and so without any enthusiasm he put on the morning coat and top hat that Pompe, despite all his master's reservations, had packed for him. Pompe had been unable to imagine any existence, even in Africa, where such garments would be utterly useless. And Pompe had been right Versluis reflected acidly to himself, as he buttoned his gloves and took his seat beside Mrs Van der Vliet in the carriage, both of them decked out in European gala dress in the scorching heat of the summer afternoon. Soon they were rocking through the dusty streets of this outlandish, half-civilised country in which the dogs lay sleeping in the shade, where black women openly suckled their children and black men relieved themselves under the banks of the spruit. Mrs Van der Vliet paid no attention to the black man squatting at the side of the drift through which they drove, however: she had had the hood of the carriage lowered, and she now sat very erect on the edge of the seat, holding her black umbrella which she had opened out high above their heads, both so that she would be visible to all passers-by, and so that she would not miss anything. The black man got up slowly and pulled up his trousers, showing little interest in the carriage which splashed by through the puddles of the drift and struggled up the incline on the other side on its way to the market square.

The church was already full, but without for a moment considering Versluis's possible wishes, Mrs Van der Vliet leant upon his arm and conveyed the two of them through the crowd, which opened before her like waves before the bow of a ship, shifting and changing seats to make space for the new arrivals. Serene and triumphant she established herself directly in front of the pulpit in the pew intended for members of the bride's family, while the violets on her hat vibrated in satisfaction on their little metal stems. As usual the women and girls of Bloemfontein filled the bare, lofty space with the low buzz of their voices; the colours of their dresses and hats, and the sweetness of eau de Cologne and lavender water seemed to form wide, undulating flowerbeds along the aisles. The front pews were occupied by a number of familiar faces from the Dutch community: Mrs Van der Vliet looked about inquisitively while she wiped her neck and forehead with a small handkerchief, and prodded Versluis's side from time to time to point out acquaintances. 'Mr Peeters, Member of the Volksraad,' she said. 'And there are the Van der Posts from Philippolis – I did not think that they would be able to be here. And Mr Vos, too, of course, from Smithfield,' she added with less enthusiasm, and turned her eyes from him.

Versluis had not been looking forward to this ceremony and would have chosen to avoid it; yet when it materialised it demanded very little of him and he found that he was able to endure it without any exceptional strain. The service was short and the sermon brief, there was a degree of festivity about the whole event: he held one side of the hymnal which Mrs Van der Vliet had generously shared with him, but he was not required to take part in the singing, and the only uncomfortable moment occurred during the prayer when he had to rise with the other men, as was apparently the custom there. This made him an isolated figure among all the seated ladies in the front row of the church; he looked out over the bowed heads in the wings on either side, across the undulating, colourful sea of ribbons, flowers and bows on the hats, past the bridal party marked by the billowing white veils of the bride and bridesmaids and Helmond's palpable self-consciousness, and finally to the bare white wall opposite. From the pulpit above the congregation the voice of the priest rose and fell melodiously in the phrases of the prayer, disturbed only occasionally when an instance of wrong gender, or a faulty construction or accent marred his formal Dutch. Did anyone else notice this? Versluis wondered, casting an inquisitive eye around the church; but the heads remained bowed, the eyes shielded by hands which were fashionably dressed in gloves. Are they following the prayer, he thought to himself, and does it mean anything to them? Do these allusions have some kind of unintelligible significance, does this strange system of values have any real meaning, and were the brightly clad wedding guests really lifting up their hearts in all humility to the Lord? He glanced down at Mrs Van der Vliet beside him with her violets quivering among the velvet bows of her hat. He did not know the answer, nor could he begin to guess it.

He would be riding back with her in the carriage, Mrs Van der Vliet informed Versluis firmly after the bridal couple and their train had been escorted out by a triumphant flourish of organ music, and she would brook no refusal. Would the Voigts not perhaps want to use their carriage themselves? he wondered, but when he offered this as a suggestion she did not think it worthy of any consideration. It went without saying that the Voigts would be walking to her house for the reception she said, it was after all very close by, just across the spruit; and holding her folded umbrella before her like a sceptre, she led him through the crowd which had gathered outside and which filled the paths around the church – greeting, waving, talking, nodding, commanding, smiling until finally, accompanied by a whole entourage, she took her place in the carriage. They could surely take Mrs Van Andel along, she declared. Mrs Bloem hoisted herself with a great deal of effort up the steps, and a couple of excited women were also taken in and introduced as visitors from Fauresmith. Crowded into one corner, Versluis sat engulfed by the pleats and folds of their gowns – threatened by heels, parasols and hatpins as they all laughed and talked together and offered each other peppermints, and the girls clutched one another, screaming in feigned anguish as the vehicle struggled, lurching and pitching, with its load through the drift.

If half of Bloemfontein had filled the church for the marriage ceremony then the whole community had now converged on Mrs Van der Vliet's house and garden for the reception: people milled together in the rooms containing wilted greenery, garlands and paper mottoes; they flowed in and out over the decorated verandahs; children chased each other up and down the paths and between the flowerbeds. Although Versluis recognised familiar faces here and there from the circle of local Netherlanders, most of the people were unfamiliar:

125

English speakers in festive dress, the men in morning or frock coats, the women wearing brightly coloured gowns, their hats loaded with ribbons and flowers pinned to headdresses piled high on their heads. Shoes and boots were dusty, dresses trailed in the dust; light beads of sweat appeared beneath the bright haberdashery and shiny top hats, and the glass of champagne which someone thrust into his hand was lukewarm as usual. He was filled once again with revulsion and loathing for this land, and then he was pushed aside by a group of excited and slightly drunk young men who did not even notice him, and he stepped with the heel of his shiny black shoe into the soft earth of a flowerbed. These people were clerks, accountants and shop assistants; it was a town of civil servants, teachers and grocers parading with their wives in their frippery beneath the fluttering buntings which had been strung between the trees in the garden; and, indeed, how many of the Dutchmen present would he wish to receive in his own home? A high-pitched, nervous laugh familiar to him, but which he was unable to place for a moment, made him look round and he saw, at the edge of a group of young men drinking beer under the trees, the young Dutchman whom he had met at the Hirsches': he was laughing and gesticulating wildly, while none of his companions paid much attention to him. In the Netherlands the man would have been an assistant in a grocer's shop, Versluis thought aloofly, or a clerk in one of the provincial shipping companies, and would never have shared a table with him at the same reception.

'Our young men are a gay lot, aren't they,' a voice beside him remarked, and he recognised Doctor Brill from the College. His father had occupied a chair at Utrecht, Versluis recalled, and his wife was born a Van Beveren; at least he moved on a somewhat higher cultural level, and he greeted the headmaster with some relief. 'Shall we indulge ourselves a little in the festive joys by going to congratulate the fair young Mrs Helmond?' Brill enquired, and they made their way carefully through the rustling trains of the women to the verandah where the guests were now gathering. The bride stood radiant beside her husband, the billowing veil thrown back from her face and shoulders, and she talked and laughed too loudly and excitedly as she accepted their congratulations. Beside her Helmond seemed more sedate, buttoned up stiffly in his frock coat, his face sweating from the heat and the closeness, wearing a smirk of arrogance, satisfaction and possession on his lips. When Versluis offered his hand to congratulate her, the young Mrs Helmond cast herself upon him with a lascivious little squeal and greeted him with a kiss which he found as unpleasant as it had

126

been unexpected. The white veil billowed around him; he smelt the overwhelming scent of the perfume which she had poured over herself and saw the powder which lay across her neck and shoulders, and he would have stumbled if Brill had not put a hand under his elbow.

Others were awaiting their turn; they grew impatient and pushed the two men aside; an unpleasant scuffle started on the stoep. The women suppressed small, anxious cries, top hats were knocked off, and Mrs Helmond's veil was pulled awry for a moment until the bridesmaids were able to rush to her aid. Relieved, Versluis and his companion freed themselves from the crush and found themselves a place with some acquaintances beneath the syringa trees at the edge of the company. People moved tirelessly up and down along the paths; there was a great deal of shouting and calling, and later speeches were made and toasts proposed from the stoep, the words only partly audible at that distance and above the noise. Then a middle-aged woman untied the ribbons of her hat and, seating herself in front of the piano which had been carried out on to the stoep, she began to play polkas and waltzes in a determined, measured way. In the house, where the furniture had been pushed against the walls, they began to dance. Feet pounded across the wooden floors of the stoep, and every so often the white of Mrs Helmond's bridal gown and of her billowing veil was visible among the bright colours and milling people, as she laughed and joked and talked incessantly, surrounded by a group consisting almost entirely of loud young men. In the garden where the afternoon was growing cooler, the music sounded clearly amongst the trees, and in the street in front of the house the servants had gathered to observe the merriment over the garden wall, and ragged children had climbed onto the wall to be able to see better. The little group under the trees talked casually about other weddings from the immediate past, about the weather and gardening, changing from English to their best Dutch to ask Versluis about his impressions of the country. In the late afternoon a hooded cart stopped in front of the house, decorated with white ribbons and feathers on the horses' harness, and groups of people began to draw nearer from all corners of the garden. 'The bride and groom are about to leave,' said Doctor Brill, and they both rose, too, and moved towards the house. There were sudden shouts and cries and a few young men produced some guns and began to fire shots randomly into the air, causing the horses to rear, and through the rice that rained down the bride and groom were visible for a moment. Once they'd got in, the cart left in a cloud of dust with fluttering feathers and streaming ribbons, and some of

127

the young people ran along to throw some old shoes after it; the Dutch contingent had gathered to form the centre of the group around the steps of the verandah and they now remained there, crowded together with Mrs Van der Vliet in their midst, standing arm-in-arm with Polderman and another young man. The celebratory shots became wild and undisciplined. *'Lank zullen ze leven . . .'* someone began to sing and then they were all singing together on the stoep and around the steps, surrounded by flags, buntings, greenery, rice, and the flowers that had been trampled by the horses' hooves. *'Lang zullen ze leven in hun gloria. . . .'*

Versluis had remained with Brill to watch the departure of the bride and groom at some distance: laughing and in high spirits, the women in the group left them to get some rice and join in the send-off of the newly-weds. The carriage finally disappeared down the long, straight street in a cloud of dust which rose high around it, and the young men and boys who had run along with it began to turn back one by one; the guests now also began to take their leave and depart – the women put up their parasols, the men searched for their hats, and they called back and forth to one another. Mrs Hirsch waved to Versluis from a distance, Mrs Prince took leave of him with a friendly smile, and one of the judges to whom he had spoken during the course of the afternoon raised his hat in passing. The party had ended, and some of the braver coloured children had come into the garden to get their hands on some of the left-over food. Only the little band of Netherlanders, both from the local community and those who were visiting from other towns, remained gathered around the steps of the front stoep with Mrs Van der Vliet, in purple, wielding her sceptre above them – some twenty or thirty people singing together as if they did not know that it was all over; *'in hun glo-ri-a. . . .'* A stout young man had begun to direct them with a walking stick and a few of the women were helpless with laughter; even Mrs Van der Vliet was forced to smile.

'Shall we join our countrymen?' Brill remarked drily. 'Or do you feel that you have had enough festivity for one day?'

'I'm afraid that I have always found such gatherings rather wearisome,' Versluis replied evasively, for he did not find the noisy display of brotherhood among the Dutchmen at all appealing. More departing guests came by and bowed to them, but they were all strangers to Versluis until he recognised Doctor Krause some distance away. Square in his black frock coat, Krause was looking back as he walked away and lifting his cane to attract the attention of someone in the crowd.

Versluis had not noticed the doctor among the guests earlier on, and the sight of that small dark figure brought the memories of his first few weeks in that country to his mind with disturbing clarity, so that he forgot for an instant both what he had been saying and the figure beside him.

'I was about to suggest that we take a stroll up and down the street for a while while I wait for my wife,' said Brill. 'It will probably be some time before she manages to separate herself from all her acquaintances. But of course that is to say, if you have no objection to it. If you feel tired you'll probably want to rest – or perhaps. . . .'

'No,' said Versluis, 'no, I still feel perfectly well. Shall I accompany you then?'

Doctor Krause disappeared among the group of people; his top hat remained visible for a moment, but he was already moving away from them with a woman at his arm and children behind him, surrounded by his family, and it was with relief that Versluis began to stroll up and down the street in front of the house where the dust was gilded by the evening sun and the tracks that had been left by the horses' hooves, and the wheels of the bridal carriage, were filled with a deep shadow. The last of the wedding guests walked by and greeted them, but the little band of Netherlanders remained on the stoep: someone else had sat down in front of the piano to accompany them; they had changed to 'Piet Hein', and were singing, laughing and calling out in the gathering dusk: the dissensions among them, their feuds, rivalry and bitter quarrels forgotten for the moment as they were united by the emotions induced by the wedding and the music.

'Have you made yourself at home amongst us yet, Mr Versluis?' Brill asked after a while.

'I am very comfortable at Mrs Van der Vliet's.'

'I believe that our good Mrs Van der Vliet is taking good care of you. And have you been able to settle down to some extent in Bloemfontein?'

He pondered this for a moment and looked at the straight, dusty street that receded towards the west, at the stone walls of the gardens, at the willows along the spruit. 'I am not sure that it would make any sense for me to try to settle down here,' he said. 'After all I could never become a settler in this town or of this land, to take your question literally. My stay is only temporary.'

They turned and saw Doctor Krause coming through the garden gate with his wife, still looking back to make sure that he was being followed by his whole family. With a hand over his eyes against the evening sun, Krause peered down the street for a moment, then recognised the two men some way away and raised his cane once more, this time in farewell – before the little band made their way in the opposite direction, only his gleaming top hat still visible among the bobbing heads of his children. Brill and Versluis raised their hats in a departing gesture.

Brill laughed softly to himself as he watched the receding Krauses. 'And *echt Deutsch* our good doctor has remained, don't you think?' he asked. 'That could have been a group in any street of any town in Germany – or Pomerania, to be precise. One cannot easily hide one's origins, can one?' They put on their hats again, and resumed their casual stroll along the street. 'And as for our fellow countrymen. . . . Our countrymen hoist the flag just as unmistakably whenever they have the chance to do so.'

The boisterousness on the verandah had turned into rowdiness: everyone was shouting and talking at the same time and a few hardened singers were still trying to render the 'Zilvervloot' above the noise. The last departing guests remained at the gate for a moment to look on smilingly, and in the garden the servants stood amongst the scattered chairs, bottles, and empty glasses, observing their masters' merriment.

They walked past the house, their shadows lengthening at their feet: the Krauses had already reached the corner of the street and turned away, the glimmering black top hat had vanished. Brill gave Versluis a sidelong, enquiring glance for a moment, but then resumed the conversation where it had been interrupted, without any comment. 'Indeed, as you say, your stay here among us is only temporary, and I wouldn't know if you'd be able to show as much understanding for those of us whose stay in Africa is more or less permanent – for whom it is not a visit, but a question of displacement, of transplantation, I should perhaps say with greater accuracy. As a result we have divided loyalties and we are living, as it were, with a foot in both worlds, which gives rise to some tension.' He gestured towards the verandah. 'In one sense we are living here like the inhabitants of a besieged city,' he added with a smile, 'and we can never feel at ease. But you have no doubt noticed this yourself.'

'It can't be very pleasant to live in such a state of tension,' Versluis remarked, and Brill, who was still looking at the jolly group on the verandah, did not respond immediately. But then he turned and smiled at his companion.

'Pleasant?' he asked. 'Oh, our countrymen seem to be enjoying themselves immensely despite everything, don't you think?' They continued on their stroll, leaving the house and its people behind them once more. 'But of course I generalise, each one of our group came to Africa and decided to stay for his own reasons, reasons about which it is best not to enquire in some cases, but so what, what does that matter? For some this country offers an agreeable home, but for others life here is a continuous state of exile – the degree of adaptation differs from one to the other, and so also the amount of satisfaction or not, and the extent of the tension that each one suffers. Finally I can only speak of myself, and as far as I am concerned, I must admit that in the four years that I have been here, Africa has been good to me. It is true that the coach on which we travelled to Bloemfontein overturned, but my wife and I were not hurt, and one could even regard the incident as symbolic of our life in this country – there is plenty of discomfort – nobody can deny that: irritations, frustrations, but no lasting injury or scar. Africa has always seemed to be filled with promise ever since Advocate Hamelberg mentioned the possibility of this appointment to me in the Netherlands, and I must confess that the reality has never disappointed me.'

They were walking more slowly: the gardens to either side lay in shadow, the houses had disappeared behind the trees, and the sounds of merriment were muffled in the distance. In front of them the long, straight street receded towards the east and ended in veld, in space, in sky.

'But I am happy,' Brill said pensively, 'I am in an exceptional position as head of this College. It has been sorely neglected since its inception, it is nothing to be proud of in its present condition, but that in itself is a challenge, and even more of a challenge in my view is the particular task that has been entrusted to me.'

He was beginning to tire Versluis realised with an unpleasant feeling of surprise, for he had assumed that he had left his physical weakness behind. A church service, a wedding reception, a conversation with a few people, and now this restful stroll in the cool of the late afternoon, these things could surely not be too demanding for him? But no, he then realised, it was simply that he was unaccustomed to such large and rowdy gatherings. In the tranquil round of visits to the club, card evenings, music evenings and dining with friends that he had grown used to at home, such demands had never been made of him; and, naturally, he realised with relief, it was impossible for an unacclimatised European such as himself to be resistant to the heat.

Brill had not noticed anything, and his face lit up enthusiastically

131

now that the conversation had moved on to his subject. 'Education is in itself interesting and satisfying for a teacher, but to be given the chance to be responsible for the education of young people here in Africa in particular, that is an extraordinary task – an extraordinary vocation I should say. I hope that I'm not boring you, Mr Versluis, because not everyone is necessarily interested in the demands and problems of education; but I trust that as a visitor and outsider you are able to understand what I am trying to say.'

'No, no, not at all,' Versluis said confusedly. He took off his hat to press his handkerchief against his forehead; he pressed it to his lips. In the course of their walk they had stopped in the middle of the street again. What was keeping Mrs Brill? he wondered with some impatience; why did she not come, so that her husband could leave and he would be free to take refuge in his room while this growing dizziness was still manageable? But there was no sign of her at the house, there was to be no release. He thus remained standing in the centre of the dusty street still briefly gilded by the evening sun, grateful for the support of his cane, and looked at the younger man opposite him, seeing as if across a great distance an enthusiasm which he could neither understand nor share.

'By far the majority of my pupils were born here in Africa,' Brill resumed, 'but they are almost without exception children of foreigners, of immigrants – in other words they are the first-generation citizens of this country which until recently was nothing but an uninhabited wilderness. They thus find themselves in a position which is both difficult and challenging – on the one hand they have no real ties with Europe, it's a distant part of the world about which they have only heard; but on the other hand they have not yet become part of this country. They speak English, but it is an English in which the English-speaking purists of our community take no delight; while their Dutch, as you have no doubt noticed yourself, bears only a superficial resemblance to our mother tongue. They are in the process of creating a new way of speaking for themselves, just as they are creating a new identity for themselves as the inhabitants of a new country, as members of a new nation, and I find it exhilarating to be part of this process. I imagine that this would be not uninteresting even for an outsider like yourself.'

Versluis pressed the handkerchief to his forehead, to his lips once again; but then he forgot his growing feeling of illness for a moment and found Brill's discussion had faded into an unintelligible gush of words. On the verandah of Mrs Van der Vliet's house the mixed voices of the Netherlanders had suddenly taken recognisable shape in the form of the 'Wilhelmus', and a sudden confusion overwhelmed him as he heard that familiar tune. There used to be performances in the park where the music had been played from the bandstand and strolling people had halted under the trees; there had been a time in the Netherlands when the king was surrounded by soldiers and officials, uniforms and bunting and the tricolour on the flagpole, and the national anthem was sung out of a sense of loyalty; but how was he to take it here? The dirt road was gilded in the sunlight; at the end of the straight street the veld stretched away, already grey in the blowing pallor of the dusk. Was it a feeling of alienation that gave rise to this giddiness within him, he wondered, or was it indeed a sign of his physical weakness? He could see Brill's face opposite him, caught in the glow of the setting sun, with hair and beard lit up and gleaming eyes. 'But what really interests me is the question of language,' continued the headmaster, oblivious of the national anthem being sung behind them, 'or of dialect, if you like. In my opinion this local patois has the potential of becoming a full-blown language, and as such it would be central to the development of a sense of their own identity among the whites in this country. It is Dutch that has been adapted to the land and its conditions, it is proof that Europe has been left behind and a new world accepted. Or do you think that my evaluation of this vernacular is excessive?'

He waited eagerly for a reply, and Versluis saw with a feeling of relief that young Mrs Brill was rapidly approaching them with short steps, her dress held up out of the dust, while she laughingly called out an apology for keeping them so long. 'But you must come and visit us,' Brill said, 'then we'll be able to discuss all these matters over a glass of wine.'

'Yes, you must come and visit us,' his wife added. 'It's always agreeable to have visitors from the Netherlands.'

He was released: they said farewell, they left. He was able to flee, his feet unsteady in his weakened state, uncertain whether his cane would be able to support him. At the house the merry band of Netherlanders was still crowded around the piano on the front stoep and they greeted his appearance jovially – glasses were offered to him, bottles raised; but he mumbled his excuses, and they made no attempt to detain him.

His room was cool and dark, an enclave of tranquillity in the chaotic house, and for a moment he leant with his back against the door and closed his eyes. Was that bile burning at the back of his palate; was it saliva, or blood? He tried to swallow it, and remained standing there; he was exhausted when the fit of coughing had passed. The room was silent: he could still hear along the passage the distant sounds of voices and music in which he wanted no part.

The fit of coughing had left him too exhausted to take off his clothes, and when he bent down to try to untie his shoelaces, he was overwhelmed by such dizziness that he gave up: fully clothed he lay down on the bed with his head pressed into the pillows. Reality faded and his thoughts became confused, but for an instant a sudden, clear image emerged from the confusion. In the winter park the trees stood bare and the bandstand was deserted, the lawns and paths from which people had listened to the music in the summer, were deserted. The flag had been lowered and the wind beat the rope violently against the flagpole. The wedding feast was over.

He was feeling better, he had already recovered – a cup of tea, a restful morning on the verandah, and all would be well again. 'You are not looking very well this morning, Mr Versluis,' Mrs Van der Vliet said, however, and eyed him sharply.

'This heat is exhausting,' he said. She merely shook her head and gave no indication that she felt the heat under the ample folds and pleats of her rustling black dress.

The house had already been tidied and an army of barefoot servants had erased almost all signs of the festivity: all that remained as a reminder was a dusty mixture of rice and sand that the gardener was sweeping away at the front of the house.

'You should go and rest,' Mrs Van der Vliet said firmly, and he felt an irritation which was more disturbing than the oppressive morning heat.

'I was thinking rather of trying to get some fresh air before it gets too hot,' he said, and in the face of his determination, Mrs Van der Vliet lost all interest in the subject.

'Will you be going past the German church by any chance?' she asked.

'I was planning to go to the bank,' he improvised, but she paid no attention to this information.

'I thought that you might leave a piece of wedding cake at the parsonage for Miss Scheffler; she wasn't at the wedding, the poor soul. Besides you know them well enough to drop in.' And at the table she busied herself wrapping pieces of cake in silver paper. 'It's customary

134

here,' she explained scornfully, 'it's the way the English do it, and I did promise Miss Pronk, she was set on having it done this way.'

He had not really intended to go out today, nor did he feel like visiting the parsonage, as the solemn carrier of a piece of wedding cake wrapped in silver paper, but he had no choice now but to retire to his room and prepare himself for the outing.

The triple mirrors on the chest of drawers silvered the subdued light that filtered in through the lace curtains and blinds: pure light was reflected in the triple surfaces, it caught no piece of furniture, no familiar pattern from the wallpaper or ceiling. He did not want to go out, Versluis thought, and remained standing where he had begun to put on his gloves; but equally there was nothing that could keep him there that morning. What had he planned to do? he tried to recall; how had he wanted to pass the morning? The bed was made: clothes hung motionless in the wardrobe; he saw the manicure set, the ivory brushes, the crystal vials on the cabinet before him. And the afternoon? he wondered. The day; and all the days that he would be spending in this town? Emptiness flowed from the silver surface of the mirror and filled the room, rising without a sound, until he could feel its chill at his heart, at his lips, and it overwhelmed him in a grim deluge. There is nothing he realised, and stared uncomprehendingly at the glove in his hand, the flasks on the cabinet. There is nothing, just emptiness.

He did not know for how long that moment of wordless panic lasted, but it passed – leaving him as exhausted as the weakness that had descended upon him on the previous evening after the wedding, his hands and forehead cold with sweat. He was not well, he thought for an instant, and then rejected the idea before he had even had a chance to absorb it. A floorboard creaked, a broom knocked against some skirting board, and outside the servant was busy collecting the strewn rice. All around him, beyond the limits of this room, houses were being tidied, gardens watered and paths raked, calls were being made; outside in the bright morning sunlight a carriage moved down the street, people stood talking outside a shop, childrens' voices rang clearly through the open window of a classroom. All around him life was carrying on, and it would sweep him along as it had always done. He would put on his gloves, don his hat, take up his cane; and as soon as he had recovered and had enough strength to face the outside world he would deliver the silver package to the parsonage.

The front door was open, but the servant who shuffled towards him on bare feet when he knocked seemed surprised to see a visitor. He did not understand what the woman mumbled to him, nor could she grasp that he merely wished to deliver his parcel; bewildered, she disappeared in the direction of the living room. How was it possible that in the space of thirty years the whites had been unable to teach their servants to speak Dutch? Versluis wondered impatiently. But then the woman returned and gestured to him to enter. In the living room where he had been received on his previous visit, a man rose as he entered and Miss Scheffler, recumbent as she had been previously, extended her hands to him. 'We must be quiet,' she said softly, even before she had greeted him. 'The baby is asleep.' And he became aware of the cradle that had been set up behind her settee, and at the same time realised with some repugnance that the man who had been sitting on a chair beside her was none other than Gelmers, the young Netherlander whose loud behaviour at the reception had irritated him so much the previous day. 'My brother and his wife had to go out, so they left her with me,' Miss Scheffler continued. 'And Mr Gelmers was kind enough to keep me company.'

He turned his eyes from the disagreeable young man, but he could hardly ignore the hand that was being held out to him; he found it soft and slightly clammy. Was it this fellow's conversation that made Miss Scheffler look so lively today? he wondered. For she was being as cheerful and chirpy as a young girl and, recumbent as she was, propped up uncomfortably on the bench on one elbow, she seemed to be able to leap up at any moment. She now gestured impatiently to the two men to sit down. 'She is usually very good,' she continued in the same subdued voice. 'She hardly ever cries; she is a bit unwell, that's all, but I think that the medicine that the doctor gave her has made her sleepy.' Versluis realised that it was her responsibility for the baby that had provoked such tension and excitement, and that she was maintaining herself in that uncomfortable position, half-recumbent and half-sitting, in order to keep an eye on the infant. 'Do you think that it is wise of my brother and his wife to leave her in my care, Mr Versluis?' she went on to ask with that direct, searching gaze which still seemed immodest to him. Somewhat disconcerted, as he searched for an appropriate reply, he realised that the irony was being directed at herself. Fortunately she did not wait for a reply but continued talking in the same unconstrained manner as her brother when he was at home, apparently completely at her ease in the company of two men who were almost total strangers to her. 'Do you have any experience of small children, Mr Versluis?' she wanted to know. 'You don't have any young nephews or nieces? You didn't have any younger brothers or sisters?'

'Unfortunately my life was rather isolated in that regard,' he said stiffly. 'I have no experience whatever of small children.'

'Mr Gelmers has just been telling me about all his brothers and sisters, it's a consoling thought that at least he has some experience in this area, isn't it? Then he can rush to our aid at once, should aid be required.' Gelmers remained uncomfortably silent, however, and stared at the floor, not allowing himself to be enticed by Miss Scheffler into saying anything. The colour of his suit was wrong and its chequered pattern too loud, Versluis observed as he glanced sidelong at his fellow-visitor, and his boots were too light; he was all too clearly someone of a lower class, from a single living room full of screaming children in which the laundry was hung out to dry and the smell of food was noticeable in the passage outside. Had he come to South Africa with only that one suit?

'But I am not entirely inexperienced myself,' Miss Scheffler continued, oblivious of the two men's silence. 'Unfortunately I hardly knew my own little brothers and sisters, they all died so young, but we grew up amongst the black children at the mission station, and they always had lots of toddlers and babies. I actually have quite a good grounding in child care, even if it is of a rather primitive kind.' She laughed, and then looked around quickly and guiltily, but no sound came from the cradle. She disconcerted him, Versluis thought once more. Then, with the same unexpected clarity with which he had seen Gelmers in a single living room filled with children in some working-class suburb or provincial town, he could see her just as lucidly in an image that was inserted into the words of the conversation like a small slide, like the slide of a magic lantern, without his being in any way prepared for it: a hobbling, bare-foot girl, the daughter of a missionary, amidst her coloured playmates, with the same alert, eager expression on her slender face, and her dark hair falling across it. He could hear the cries of children and he could see her amongst them, and then he looked up and found the young woman stretched out on the settee in front of him. Was that how women dressed to receive morning visits in this country? he wondered. But he could not say, since he had never before made a morning call. It was probable that anything was permissible in this land with its random mixture of formality and neglect. Furthermore her hair, which on previous occasions had been combed back and concealed under a bonnet, had not been tied back today, so that it kept falling over her face and had to be constantly pushed back. And she wore a loose gown that could have been as much a nightgown as a dress, so little did it resemble any known style or fashion. Indeed, he thought to himself, he would hardly be surprised if she were to kick off her shoes and walk barefoot around the living room.

She looked at the cradle once again, listened for a moment, and then turned back to the visitors and looked at them expectantly. Gelmers kept staring at the floor, however, without any sign of his usual boisterousness, for some reason clearly uncomfortable, and so she turned to Versluis, and fixed her grey-blue eyes upon him as if she expected something surprising, even challenging, from him.

'Mrs Van der Vliet sends this to you,' he said, holding out the parcel that he had brought and offering it to her. 'It's a piece of wedding cake,' he explained, 'from the wedding yesterday.'

'Oh yes,' she said, looking at the little square shape in its silver wrapping. 'The wedding . . .' she repeated, and then she shook her head and put the small parcel on the table beside her. 'It was kind of Mrs Van der Vliet to remember me: you must please thank her for me. I seldom go to such functions.'

They were silent for a moment. No-one moved in the house; there was no-one in the street outside. Nothing disturbed the day.

'It was a very gay occasion,' Versluis said. 'That is to say, the reception was exceptionally lively.'

'Mr Gelmers was just telling me about it when you arrived,' she said, and looked at Gelmers once again, as if to encourage him to continue his report, but he merely shuffled his feet and muttered something unintelligible. 'It sounded like a really festive occasion to me.'

'That was my impression too,' said Versluis, and wondered as he was speaking whether there was any sense in continuing this formal exchange of clichés. His visit had no doubt lasted long enough now, and he should be able to start making moves to end it. 'Unfortunately I have no experience of weddings or receptions,' he added, 'so I have no standards by which to judge them for you. I am certain that Mr Gelmers would be a far better reporter than I.'

'Yes, I don't have much experience of these things either. We are often such outsiders aren't we?' she said after a moment's thought. 'We don't know, there is so much that we don't know, even about the most common things in our daily lives. There are so many things that we will never know; is that not true, Mr Versluis?'

138

She looked at him expectantly, as if she were turning to him for confirmation, an admission that his own experience of reality was no different from hers. What did she mean by her question Versluis wondered, offended; why should she, this invalid spinster, this daughter of a missionary, this parsonage woman, why would she want to implicate him? As usual she did not consider it necessary to elucidate her words, her question.

He had stayed long enough Versluis decided. Where had he put his hat? But while he was looking around to find it, they were startled by the sound of a horn outside.

'The mail,' Gelmers said, and looked up.

'It's the mail coach,' Miss Scheffler assented, but she did not move, her thoughts on other things.

Gelmers had taken his own hat and was turning it nervously in his hands. 'I must go,' he said, and stood up while he was speaking. 'I'm expecting letters from home.'

'It'll still be quite some time before the mail is sorted,' said Miss Scheffler, but he paid no attention to what she had said. In contrast to his former silence he now took his leave, thanking her and trying to disguise his eagerness to be gone, in a nervous, confused flood of words. He was very welcome there, she assured him, he should come again when her brother was at home, though it was not clear whether or not he heard her. He had apparently forgotten about Versluis, and only at the door did he hesitate, half turning, and make no more than a clumsy little bow. Versluis bowed in return, relieved that he did not have to shake the young man's hand again.

He was gone. 'Do you know Mr Gelmers well?' Miss Scheffler asked.

'I met him one day at Mr Hirsch's house, that's all.'

'At first he spoke in such a lively way about all sorts of things, his family and his journey here and so on, and then suddenly I couldn't get another word out of him.'

'Perhaps I made him feel uncomfortable,' Versluis said, and she nodded without any attempt to offer a polite denial.

'It could be. Isn't his accent perhaps wrong, or something like that? It's so difficult to know – as a European you know all the unwritten rules and regulations, but for us in this country that's all an unknown territory. We don't have as many rules here in Africa.'

'You probably have other rules that are unfamiliar to visitors to this country,' he said, 'or at least, other customs.'

'Yes, that's probably right. One forgets, doesn't one? one's at home here, life is taken for granted, and one forgets that it's not necessarily the same for others.' Instinctively she looked at the cradle again, and then sighed to herself. 'Poor Mr Gelmers, I hope that he'll come again. He seems to me to be very lonely.'

'He gave me the impression of being a somewhat sociable person,' Versluis said.

'Did he? I'm pleased to hear that, because in his situation he needs friends.'

'I'm afraid I know nothing about the young man,' Versluis said dismissively, and took his hat, ready to leave.

'Oh, Mr Gelmers had given me the impression that he was quite a good friend of yours, or else I would not have discussed him in this way with you. I was concerned for his health.'

'He seems healthy enough to me,' Versluis remarked, preparing to stand up, though he hesitated before moving: just another minute or two before he had to face the growing heat, the dust of the street stretching blindingly before his feet; he wanted to stay for just another moment in the repose of this cool room, with its sleeping baby and the young woman reclining on the settee.

'That's what is called a hectic flush, it's not a healthy colour,' Miss Scheffler said. 'Over the last few years we've become quite expert at diagnosing invalids at every stage of throat and lung disease, Mr Versluis, and in caring for them too: we have been forced by necessity to obtain this knowledge. It is not easy to die in a strange country.'

She added the last words with some reflection, her face turned away from him, as if she were thinking of other things and was not aware of the thought that she had expressed; but he found the words chilling. This was a tactless subject, he thought to himself, it was an entirely unnecessary subject, and he tried to rise from the armchair in which he was sitting back, but found that he could not. The chair is too deep, he thought, and he rested his head for a moment against its back and closed his eyes. Miss Scheffler did not notice anything: her elation at her responsibility for the baby, her lively behaviour towards the visitors and the youthful glow which had briefly suffused her slender face, had all gone. She had become quiet and introspective, pulling absently at the rug over her knees.

'And what about you, Mr Versluis,' she said finally, as if remembering at last her social obligations, 'are you not expecting any mail with the post-cart this morning?'

'My servant, who is taking care of the house, should be letting me know how everything is,' he began; 'and there might be something from my attorney. . . .' But then he realised that she was smiling and that the question had been meant ironically, as a reference to Gelmers's excuse and over-hasty departure. 'I hope at least to get a new consignment of newspapers from the Netherlands.'

'Is that all? It sounds like very dull mail, just newspapers, full of news that's already months old. . . .'

'In the absence of any correspondents to inform me of what is happening in the Netherlands, I have, unfortunately, to be satisfied with newspapers.' Now he must go, he thought, but still he did not move, still overwhelmed by the inexplicable weakness that, insidiously, continued to take hold of him; he remained sitting in the armchair opposite her with his hat on his knees.

'Is there really no-one – apart from your servant and attorney, I mean?'

'I have no brothers or sisters. There are a couple of aged aunts,' he added when she continued to look incredulous. 'I have a few friends from whom I hope to hear something now and again. . . .' But what business was it of hers? he wondered, and left the sentence unfinished. His tongue dragged, and he found that he no longer had the strength to sustain this polite conversation.

'I've always had my brother,' Miss Scheffler said suddenly, as if her words were a continuation and expansion of some train of thought of her own. 'There are only two years between us, and for as long as I can remember he's been there, he and the coloured children of the mission station. But when he turned sixteen he was sent abroad to study, and he stayed away for six years. . . .' She turned away towards the cradle, and he could see only her high shoulders and the outline of her head silhouetted against the lace curtains and the dim light outside. 'At that stage it was no longer possible to make friends among the black people, this land had already begun to come between us with all its arbitrary decrees; the dividing lines are too implacable, even at a mission station. Yes,' she continued with a smile, 'this land must sometimes seem very strange and incomprehensible to you. It's strange even to me sometimes, like something observed from a distance. I bear that distance within me, even though I have never been away.'

She was speaking to herself, her attention apparently fixed upon some distant theme, and Versluis's presence was forgotten, something that happened often in the course of their conversations. Or perhaps all she needed was the presence of a listener, Versluis thought, and so he was not required to reply or respond in any other way. Nor did his lack of response seem to appear strange to her, and for the first time he was grateful for the informality of life in the parsonage and for the

141

fact that it was possible for him as an almost total stranger just to sit there, leaning back in the chair with his eyes shut, overwhelmed by his incredible exhaustion.

'It is as well to learn to be alone,' Miss Scheffler continued in the same meditative way, her hands clasped on the rug. 'I used to read, I used to read a lot. I used to go walking in the veld, for miles, completely alone, without anyone remarking on it or becoming concerned when I stayed away. I wonder if there is anywhere else where one can be as solitary as in the veld.'

It was quiet in the room, quiet outside beyond the lace curtains and the broad shadow of the verandah. He leant back, soothed by the silence, and then started up confused, unsure of where he was. He saw the room, the horsehair chairs in a formal circle, the engravings on the walls. Had he fallen asleep for a second, or briefly lost consciousness? He sat up with some effort; but although it seemed to him that the silence had already extended far beyond the bounds of all politeness, Miss Scheffler gave no sign of being aware of anything. Was she too polite to show that she had noticed anything, or too engrossed in her own thoughts, withdrawn far into another world as she lay on the bench opposite him. Or had that moment of yawning darkness in the regularity of the real world been no more than an hallucination? His heart beat wildly, his mouth was dry. He must get up and leave, he thought once more with greater urgency, and knew that he did not have strength enough for the gesture.

She had been alone he remembered vaguely from the last words that he had caught of the conversation; her brother had gone away. Where to? he wondered in bewilderment, the past and the present confused for a moment, and only then did he know clearly where he was. Across the distance between them, in the silent room in which their voices were still subdued owing to the sleeping baby in the corner, she looked at him once more. 'You must also have been alone as a child,' she said. 'You also know.'

There was no question, no attempt to obtain any further information: it was simply the expression of a thought that had come to her in the course of her meditation and which she now uttered as she looked at him across the distance. What was he meant to know? he thought. The pale right-angle of the window in the dusky gloom of the room, the coldness of the pane against the forehead, and the view of the empty garden below, the gravel paths raked and the trees bare. The servants are in the kitchen or the stableyard, and the child is alone in that dark house, kneeling on the window seat, on the stairs, lingering on the landing to listen to the ticking of the grandfather clock. The clock ticks through the silence of the series of waiting rooms, the heavy drapes fall across the doorway and all sound is excluded. There is just the unstirring silence, the unstirring darkness in which the silver surface of the mirror reflects the daylight outside.

He knew, Miss Scheffler had remarked, with a serenity that rendered any discussion or explanation superfluous, and perhaps she was right; but that knowledge had been acquired in silence and had never been transformed into words, its nature unknown, its extent unexplored.

The visit had now lasted long enough, Versluis reminded himself once more; the conversation had gone far enough. For the last time he forced himself out of the chair, and with an almost superhuman effort he managed to defeat his inertia, his tiredness, his exhaustion; like a swimmer returning from the deep, he burst through the surface and stood up, gasping from the effort.

'I'm afraid I have to go now,' he said. 'I'm sorry to have missed the Pastor and Mrs Scheffler.'

'And I haven't even given you a chance to tell me about the wedding,' she cried; although he knew her well enough by now to suspect that the words were intended ironically. 'But in any case, thank you for giving me the opportunity to talk. It is good to be able to speak to someone in this way: one needs it, sometimes it is necessary to be able to talk. But I have already said that, not so? Excuse me for lapsing into repetition, but that's what happens when you don't see many people, if you spend too much time with your own thoughts. Isn't that true?' She lifted her hand to touch her neck, and then quickly pushed her hair back from her face in a gesture that suggested shyness and uncertainty rather than vanity. 'Possibly it is not very interesting for you, a morning visit to the pastor's sister, here in a remote corner of Africa – ours is a very limited existence, we live in isolation. But it is precisely for that reason that we welcome your visits – that you came, and that you return, in spite of everything that might possibly put you off.'

She spoke so rapidly and indistinctly that it took some time for Versluis to take in what she had said. He was surprised by the obvious sincerity of her words and by the sudden timidity with which she spoke, stammering like her brother at moments of excitement or candidness, although before he was able to say anything in reply, she had carried on. 'For August particularly,' she said more softly, as if it were something she was telling him in confidence, purely for his own information. 'It is difficult for a clergyman – I don't know if you understand what I am trying to say, but it is something that I'd like you to know.'

'I'm afraid that neither my background nor my convictions make me a particularly suitable confidant for a priest,' he began in some confusion, but she shook her head.

'It's not a question of agreement or approval; it is simply that he can talk to you, that he feels free to talk. It is so important to be able to find words, to be able to give expression to everything that you think and feel, and for a priest there are so few opportunities, far fewer than for ordinary people. . . . We live in such silence, Mr Versluis; have you ever noticed that? The silence of this country is so immense, the distances, the isolation so great, even more so for someone like August, for him it is much worse. . . .' But she was talking to herself again, scowling as she considered the idea. Versluis stood before her, leaning on his cane, his hat in his hand, not knowing how to interrupt her so that he could leave. It was only when the servant arrived suddenly and without summons in the doorway that her attention returned to her immediate environment. 'I am pleased that you came,' she said with total artlessness. 'I hope you'll come again soon.'

The servant was asking about tea, but he did not want to stay: he said farewell, he left the gloomy room and from under the verandah he stepped once again into the blinding glare of the dusty road, white in the sunlight.

The post-cart had brought the mail, and the bugle call which had heralded its arrival had roused the town in a way that was matched by not even the passenger coach. The expectation and excitement were tangible; even Versluis was affected each time and wondered if there would be anything for him. But when the sorting had been completed and Van der Vliet, who had been despatched to the post office by his wife, returned late that afternoon, the only thing for Versluis was a bundle of newspapers.

'All of it's from Holland,' Mrs Van der Vliet ascertained with approval, as one by one she looked at the letters for the occupants of the house.

'These letters are all still addressed to Miss Pronk,' her husband said jokingly. 'We should write "unknown" on them and send them back.'

'We shall keep them until they return,' she said firmly, however, and cast one more glance at the stamps containing a portrait of King

Wilhelm before locking them away in the sideboard for the former Miss Pronk.

Versluis's newspapers were delivered to him, but no letters: not from the faithful Pompe, nor from the aunts or the Van Meerdervoorts; not even from old De Bruïne at the club he reflected, although he could hardly expect De Bruïne to write to him. Consequently that evening, after supper, he went to sit in the shade under the verandah with the newspapers that had been in transit, by boat and by post-cart, for so many weeks. Behind the climbing creepers on the stoep of this dreamy, dusty town in the interior of Africa, at the other end of the world, he flattened the creased pages and read the superseded reports from Petersburg, London and Berlin, about the Russian or Austrian Emperor, the King of Italy, the German Chancellor. He then searched the fine print of the columns for news reports from the Netherlands and for names and events that bore more immediate significance for him: he read about the Court, the First Chamber, the Minister President; Scheveningen, he saw in passing, and the Kursaal, The Hague. . . . There the grey of the winter afternoon had long turned to darkness; lights burnt in the shops windows and the wet streets gleamed under the street lamps, the wheels of the carriage ploughed through a dirty mixture of mud and melting snow. The church bell sounded its fine, hesitant peal from beyond the roofs. The curtains were drawn, and Pompe came to find out whether more coal was needed for the fire, revealing his lack of faith in the maids.

Versluis put down the newspaper; he could see the wide dome of the sky, the flaming hues of the sunset with its rose tints already touching the hills in the distance, and the golden haze of smoke and dust that drifted in the air. The Netherlands were far away, he thought absently: a country at the far side of the globe, invisible in the darkness of the winter evening; and the events reported in the newspapers were too far removed to hold his wavering attention, relativised by time and space. He would read further later on; later, he thought impatiently. Or perhaps Brill would be interested in these reports from abroad, or possibly old Mr Bloem; if so, he would rather pass the newspapers on to them. The dusk intensified, and only Van der Vliet's white shirtsleeves still gleamed dimly through the haze as he strolled about in his vegetable garden; the trees stood out darkly against the glowing sky.

With Miss Pronk's departure after the wedding, a sudden quiet descended on the house, which Versluis welcomed. The constant tapping

145

and tripping of her heels; her incessant prattle; the high-pitched laugh that would suddenly echo in the passage or outside on the stoep; the repeated calls to the servants to look for something, pick up something, iron something; the breathless flood of gossip at the table; the coquetry and flirting with the two clerks and inadvertently even with himself and Van der Vliet; the fluttering eyelashes and the sudden chill of her pale blue eyes – no, he thought with a certain degree of satisfaction, as far as he was concerned her departure was no loss. Polderman and Du Toit no longer had any inclination to linger at the table in the evenings after dinner, but were off as soon as possible to prearranged games of cards or billiards, and there was no longer anyone prepared to pay any attention to Van der Vliet who remained, nodding and smiling, at the end of the table. Even Mrs Van der Vliet gazed at the empty place and sighed as if someone had died. 'We will be only too pleased to have the Helmonds with us once again, won't we Mr Versluis?' she asked, and did not wait for a reply since it would not have occurred to her that he might not share her sentiments. 'Such a lively girl, she enlivens the house the moment she walks in here. Now there's a fine couple for you, Mr Versluis, they suit one another so. Such a manly man,' she added, with an intensity that astonished Versluis; but she did not enlarge on the remark.

But the Helmonds finally returned from their honeymoon; a hooded cart from which dusty suitcases were off-loaded stood outside the door, and young Mrs Helmond's high heels sounded through the house once again. The honeymoon was over and Helmond had to remain in Bloemfontein for another week or two to wind up his affairs before they could settle in Aliwal North; his radiant wife tripped through the house in a new emerald-green dress edged in yellow, uttering a cry whenever she encountered a familiar object, as if she hadn't seen it for years. 'Mr Versluis,' she called out in surprise, 'are you still here? Are you all still here, as before? It's almost as if I've never been away,' she added, but she had vanished before he could answer her.

She had changed, although he would not have been able to say precisely in what way. In the more formal dress of a married woman her figure seemed fuller; her face more rounded, the slightly discontented look had softened. Her gestures were more restrained, and although she had retained her exuberance, it was no longer so shrill and uncontrolled, as if she were aware of her new dignity. She kept looking at the broad gold wedding ring on her hand as if to remind herself of all that it implied, and was consciously trying to behave accordingly. Somehow the obstreperous girl was becoming a woman

146

in the context of this new relationship, and this observation caused Versluis to feel even more uncomfortable than he had in the presence of her excessive coquetry and the searching gaze of her pale, protruding eyes.

On their return Helmond had moved in with her, so that from time to time Versluis would hear his voice in the adjoining bedroom, and they would come across each other in the passage or on the stoep, and they sat together at the table. The attorney's lack of courtesy had offended him during their initial meeting in his office, and although they had frequently found themselves in one another's company in Mrs Van der Vliet's house since then, Helmond had shown no signs of friendliness towards him, nor had he made any attempt to acknowledge Versluis's presence. Now, however, the man moved about with a new degree of self-assurance, as if he could boast some sort of knowledge or achievement that inexplicably raised him above his surroundings; with a self-conscious aloofness he would draw on his cigar and puff out his cheeks, his pale red lips drawn into a little smile beneath the drooping moustache. He stood in the garden with Polderman and Du Toit, speaking, as usual, as if he were instructing them and they had no choice but to listen gratefully: Versluis could not catch what he was saying because he was speaking in a low voice, but suddenly the two young men roared with laughter, at once excited and nervous. They turned and saw Versluis under the verandah and immediately looked uneasy, as if they had been caught in some immoral act; they muttered something, Polderman called genially to Versluis that it was almost time for dinner, and they moved back into the house. Only Helmond remained standing where he was, head up and one foot slightly forward in a victorious pose, sucking at his cigar – then he flicked the damp end carelessly on to the raked garden path and leisurely followed them inside. He was the married man who, with smiling, almost haughty nonchalance, was able to look down upon young shop clerks and upon Versluis alone on the stoep in the gathering dusk. He dominated the table as much with his immense figure, his broad shoulders and the smell of his cigars, as with his opinions on local affairs and dogmatic pronouncements on the actions of Brand and Burgers, Barkly and Shepstone – whom he always mentioned disparagingly. As for his wife, she toyed affectedly with the food on her plate, glanced at him every so often from beneath her pale eyelashes, and made trivial remarks to which he paid no attention. With something of her old playfulness she hung about the table when the men decided to play cards after dinner, leaning over her husband's shoulders to see his hand. Versluis realised he was tired, and waited for the end of the game in which he had become involved with Helmond, Van der Vliet and young Polderman before he could go to bed. Mrs Helmond darted about the table with a lace handkerchief in her hand and dispensed the scent of tuberoses; her swelling breast was pressed against her husband's shoulder, her hand brushed his, and as he sucked his cigar through the clouds of smoke he fixed a look of cold, calculating desire upon her.

The table, the company, the room slipped away from Versluis and faded into a haze of cigar smoke; an infinite space dropped away, some areas receded invisibly into the distance; whole worlds that were alien to him and that would always remain unexplored, where people touched and looked at each other without trepidation, embroiled in an intricacy of relationships which he could hardly imagine. 'Three hearts,' said Van der Vliet after intense deliberation, his eyes blinking at his cards, and coughed over his cigar. Through the haze of smoke around the hanging lamp Versluis observed the newlyweds opposite him, suddenly conscious of their contact; their sensuality and desire; of the bodies beneath the heavy folds of the enveloping clothes; of Helmond's broad shoulders tautly covered by his jacket, and his wife's white neck and the fullness of her bosom above the tightly-laced corset. With his hand he tried to clear the smoke before his eyes and concentrate on his cards, unsettled by the feelings that he had begun to sense around him and of the intimacy that they suggested. He did not wish to know of such things, he did not wish to have them thrust upon him in this way; it had nothing to do with him or his life. He was tired, he wished to retire; he longed for the white bed on which the cover would have been turned back for him, for the order and regularity of an existence in which everything was under his control, as measured as the pocket watch that ticked on his bedside cabinet.

The submerged sensuality that he sensed, the chance touching of hands, the glances that he would intercept now and then as an intermediary, disconcerted him, and while the Helmonds remained in the house he chose to withdraw as quickly as possible from the company with the excuse that he was feeling tired, that he had been exhausted by the heat, that he wished to lie down. 'Poor Mr Versluis,' Mrs Helmond would cry with a low, bubbling laugh, and then forget about him even before he had left the room, pressed familiarly against her husband as she showed him something in the album or stretched out beside him on the settee as he sat drawing at his cigar, his knees covered by the wide folds of her dress which she had spread out around

148

her. Even when the members of the town's Dutch community called in the evenings to offer their congratulations and to stay for a visit – the men with cigars and gin, the married women with the bride in her room, engaged in confidential talk behind closed doors – Versluis preferred to withdraw into his own room. It was a relief to him when the newlyweds were invited out for the evening, which happened frequently, and the customary peace was restored. On such evenings Polderman and Du Toit always went to the hotel, and Van der Vliet shuffled inconsolably, restlessly, around the house and up and down the stoep in his slippers. 'How dull the house is when the young people are out,' Mrs Van der Vliet observed over her crocheting, and dropped it to her lap with a sigh. 'We really must arrange a few Dutch evenings before they leave us entirely, then at least we'll have those to think back on; and we should ask a few young people over, that's always jolly. They could dance on the back stoep if they felt like it.' The crochet-work lay forgotten as she became engrossed in this idea.

'Do you know anything about this young Hollander who has apparently come to town?' she then asked with a certain sharpness and looked enquiringly at Versluis.

'I met him at Mr and Mrs Hirsch's house,' he answered carefully, not entirely sure of what she meant by the question.

'That doesn't prove anything, the Hirsches open their doors to everybody; people have scarcely alighted before they're asked over to the Hirsches.' She contemplated such reckless hospitality for a moment, and then returned implacably to the subject that interested her. 'Did he say anything about himself?'

'Not as far as I can remember.'

She waited, but he had no further information to impart. 'Mrs Brill says that she does not think that he's from a very good family,' she then declared ominously.

'I should think that he came from some little place somewhere in the country; possibly from the east of the country, judging from his accent.'

'And Mrs Bloem said that he was particularly rude when she asked him to dinner. He hardly took the trouble to find a proper excuse. He did attend the wedding reception, but I, you will understand, had no say in who was to cross my doorstep on that day. Nor did he, may I add, have the courtesy to come and greet me or introduce himself to me: me, into whose house he had barged without any invitation.' She fell silent once more, muttering, as her feelings of indignation and injustice were aroused. 'Polderman asked if he could bring him over one evening while the Helmonds were still here, but I said no. My house is not a hotel,' she declaimed, emphasising each sentence as if it were a slogan. 'There are three hotels in this town, he's staying in one of them, he can eat there too. My house is not a boarding house. Those who come here are respectable people who have been invited and who know how to behave, not a gallimaufry from passenger coaches and outside rooms. I will not have that young man in my house,' she decided, and took up her crochet-work again as if there were nothing more to be said on the subject. She looked unshakable in the wide folds of her black dress, her chin resting on the brooch with its plaited locks of hair, and the only sound in the dining room where they had remained on their own after supper was the fluttering of the moths against the shade of the lamp hanging above the table. That evening Versluis lingered at the cleared table longer than was customary, the book in his hand half-forgotten as he listened to the furious beating of wings.

But then the newly-weds would be at home again and guests would once more appear after supper, and the peacefulness would be broken; little scenes of married bliss would be enacted for the appreciative audience, marked by a great deal of playfulness which brought tender smiles to the faces of those present. Behind the displays for the visitors with dalliances and little jokes, there remained, however, a deeper sexuality that disconcerted Verluis. He was conscious of every look, every gesture, of the couple's subdued voices in the room next to his, of the shadowy outlines cast on the blind by the lamplight; he was conscious of the scraping of feet in the dark under the verandah, the smothered little cries and suppressed laughter behind the thick screen of creepers. Every fresh revelation of the carnality and sensuality that had been introduced into the house by the newly-wed couple caused him to recoil anew, quickly to avert his eyes and his attention. There were aspects of life that ought to be concealed behind closed doors or properly be performed only in the semi-dark, phenomena that ought to be revealed only in the privacy of a consulting room; there were emotions and actions that were equally unsuitable for display to the world at large, just as the removal of malodorous, soiled linen or the emptying of chamberpots and slop-pails by the servants occurred secretly, without being impressed upon the consciousness.

Contaminated by all this, the house was no longer the haven of order, rest and tranquillity that it used to be, and his comfort was disturbed just as cruelly as it had been before in the hotel. The Helmonds' stay there was but temporary, he reminded himself, and

150

within a week or two they would be on their way and he would be released from their presence; though in the meantime they remained a daily source of irritation and chagrin. Restlessly he walked up and down in the dark along the garden path behind the house, conscious of the large, gliding shadows on the blinds of the room, of voices in another room, and of a feeling of discontent that he was himself unable to explain, but which was interwoven with this uneasiness.

Versluis gave the newspapers that he had looked through to Mrs Van der Vliet. 'Dutch papers,' she observed with approval; but she merely glanced through them and appeared to find nothing of interest in their contents – in the afternoons Mrs Helmond read the local reports in the Bloemfontein weekly papers to her in deplorable English or translated them fluently, though inaccurately, into Dutch and they were able to pass whole afternoons discussing them. 'Polderman will surely want to see them too,' Mrs Van der Vliet remarked about Versluis's Dutch newspapers, and put them aside.

'Holland, oh cripes,' Mrs Helmond cried with an impatient shrug of her shoulders. 'Rain and mist and mud as far as you can see. I feel cold at the very thought of it.' Polderman, too, showed no interest in the newspapers, and it was finally Van der Vliet who appropriated them, frequently shuffling down the garden path to the privy with a months-old Dutch paper under his arm.

Something was wrong, Versluis realised, and wished once again that Helmond would finish his unspecified affairs in the town so that he and his wife could be on their way. Doors banged and he could hear Mrs Helmond's angry voice and her footsteps, and when he joined Mrs Van der Vliet as usual for coffee that afternoon Mrs Helmond was sitting sulking in a corner of the drawing room, clutching her handkerchief in a little bundle in her hand. It did not take long for the cause of her vexation to be imparted to him as well, without his enquiring about it: that evening her husband was going to a billiards tournament at the hotel with some of his old acquaintances from his bachelor days, and for the first time since her wedding she was going to be left alone, despite her loudest protests. Choking over her words in anger and annoyance, she sprang up and clattered out of the room to launch a fresh attack upon her husband's sensibility.

'Oh, these young people, Mr Versluis!' Mrs Van der Vliet said with some sympathy as she passed him his cup. 'But misunderstandings and disappointments are our lot in life, and they must learn that just as each of us learnt it in our day.' The face of her first husband remained immobile behind her chair and showed no sign of the sufferings of earlier years. As she sat drinking her coffee in her formal mourning-dress, there was nothing to give one the impression that Mrs Van der Vliet had ever rushed from any room in tears, nor did her attitude to her present spouse indicate that she was ever likely to find herself in such a predicament.

And what of himself, Versluis thought as he put down his cup, what did he know of such things? He had happily been spared such little performances and outbursts, and even problems with the domestic servants had been dealt with by Pompe. Before him, as he cast a quick glance over his life, he could see only the empty stairway and corridor, the empty rooms in which the clock ticked and mirrors reflected the emptiness. Only occasionally he recalled, as Mrs Van der Vliet sighed once more and shifted into a more comfortable position in her arm-chair, pleasantly lost in her own recollections, only now and then there was a moment – at night when one went up the stairs, alone in the silence of the house, in the lightness of spring or early summer when a blackbird sang outside and the paths in the garden stretched away into that lingering twilight as if, somewhere in that haze of shadow and floating green, they might lead to some unsuspected destination. A girl laughed, a young man called from far beyond the walls, hedges and gardens in the luminous evening, and he lingered for a moment at the window before shutting it and going to bed; he stood there with his hand on the catch as if waiting for something, and expecting that perhaps – now, even now – a voice would call to him from among the flowerbeds and the gathering dusk.

He was not called, of course not; he closed the window, he readied himself for bed. But in the smooth, undisturbed surface of life a tiny crack had appeared – just for a moment. A little tear, a slit so fine that one would not be able to thrust even a visiting card into it, a hairline in the enamelled surface of reality; and in the indivisible second that it remained visible a bottomless chasm had opened and a gulf yawned before him with no guiding sign or beacon. He had already been aware of that desolation as a child, of the hairline cracks in the varnished appearance of things which opened up into infinite space, and from time to time the recollection of this would descend on him unexpect-edly, giving rise to sensations of anguish and threat. Until that day when old Doctor Slingeland and the specialist that he had sent for from The Hague had silently entered his room to inform him of the results of their consultation. The safe layer of varnish had splintered and split off and the fine cracks had grown until the walls had tottered and toppled down; he had then entered that threatening desolation, and nothing remained to keep the fear at a distance. After that life had resumed its course and he had found the means to carry on – remedies, aids, makeshifts against the horror – but he had experienced it, and its reality could never again be denied.

Helmond left for the billiard tournament at the hotel. His wife ignored him at the table that evening and took no notice of his departure, but no matter how affronted her silence might have been, it was at the same time also triumphant. For as compensation she had elicited the promise that they would extend their stay in Bloemfontein for a few days to include the great reception and ball that was to be held on the German Kaiser's birthday. Her husband had scarcely left and the table had hardly been cleared before she commandeered the whole dining room so that she could display for Mrs Van der Vliet's inspection the dress that she was planning to wear, and discuss it with her in the finest detail; metres of crimson silk and netting were draped over the chairs, gleaming in the light, while they deliberated over the possible addition of flowers or trimming.

'You're also coming to the dance aren't you, Mr Versluis?' Mrs Helmond remarked to him. 'It's true that all your friends here in Bloemfontein are Germans.'

His friends, Versluis thought; who were they? Who did he know here apart from the chance Netherlander who dropped in to have a glass of gin; to whom could her remark refer except perhaps the Hirsches or the young German priest and his family? He would hesitate, however, to call any of these people his friends.

'Are you going to bed already?' Mrs Van der Vliet asked, methodically inspecting some seams.

'Mr Versluis always does a disappearing trick when people are about,' Mrs Helmond said. 'If you want company it's best not to rely on him.'

He said goodnight to them as they sat in the lamplight with their heads bowed over the ballgown. 'But you are coming to the dance aren't you, Mr Versluis?' Mrs Helmond called after him. 'I must dance the polka one last time with you before we leave. We might never see each other again.' Versluis was, however, already on his way down the passage and could pretend not to have heard her. Who was there? he wondered. The aunts. De Bruïne at the club? Nobody had written to him yet from the Netherlands.

There was no-one, he thought, and then closed his mind to this realisation. There was no reason for him to go to the German reception and he pulled the door of his room shut behind him; but the next morning Pastor Scheffler arrived, standing as usual in the middle of the hall because he was on his way somewhere else and could not stay, to inform him somewhat coyly that the German community would be holding their customary reception and ball in honour of the birthday of their Kaiser, and to make sure that he would be there. Mrs Hirsch had especially asked him to extend the invitation on behalf of herself and her husband as well, the clergyman continued, and they were also offering the carriage if Versluis wished to use it. He was just able to avoid the landau being thrust upon him to convey him the short distance across the spruit to the German club, but then he had to surrender himself to the arrangements that the excited priest had made to collect him from the house on the appointed day and to accompany him to the club.

The approaching ball had become the focus of Mrs Helmond's life. Discussions at table were almost entirely devoted to this subject, and as it drew closer it provoked in the house a degree of rowdiness, bustle and excitement equal to that which had preceded her wedding a few weeks earlier, life becoming a series of crises over gloves that had been creased and shoes that had changed their colour. From the very beginning Versluis dreaded the occasion: he did not dance, and he had no energy for the noise and the people, the endless conversations with strangers and people whom he scarcely knew; he wanted to be left in peace he thought, he wanted to rest, he wanted to withdraw into this unsurmountable tiredness and be free of all further obligations. But then he pulled himself together. How long had he been there without making any attempt to fulfil his social obligations? He had met virtually no-one apart from the little group of Netherlanders who called on Mrs Van der Vliet; and the attendance of a wedding, a poetry reading, and two meals at the Hirsches hardly made up an acceptable grand total of social outings. He had used his illness, his recuperation and the summer heat as excuses to avoid becoming more involved in this alien community; he had withdrawn into the cool, dusky rooms of the house and found in them a precious refuge; his card holder was still full of the visiting cards that the attentive Pompe had placed in it before his departure from the Netherlands. But he had not been ill for some time now, and would hardly even describe himself as convalescent; he felt tired, the heat was exhausting, and in addition he felt himself always disconcerted by the astonishing ragbag of people that made up the local community; by the unexplained and inexplicable formalities and the sudden and equally inexplicable departures from them; the unassimilated mixture of scrupulousness and carelessness; the diffidence and the lack of refinement of which there were a multitude of instances at every gathering in this country, so that he felt no desire to involve himself more closely in the life of the town by joining the round of calls and receptions. But this had to end, for he had obligations towards the community in which he found himself. He would go to the dance, and after that he would begin to call on the people who had extended invitations to him, and he would leave his visiting card with the President, the State Secretary, the State Attorney, the Chief Justice, and the incumbent of the Dutch church.

He had undertaken to do all this with reluctance, and with some aversion too, he realised as he dressed for the ball. Mrs Van der Vliet had had his evening dress pressed, and his dress shirt had been freshly starched. Nevertheless he fastened his cufflinks and put on his jacket, conscious of the fact that there were already beads of sweat on his forehead and that his hands were burning. The evening was oppressive with a storm in the offing and darkness had not brought its usual relief from the heat: the lamp exuded heat, and beyond the open windows the air quivered in the dark. Everything seemed distant and unreal to him this evening, slightly distorted as if he were seeing it through the hot shivering air above the glass of the lamp, and it seemed to him as he dressed that he was dealing with the body of a stranger. The house was filled with servants scurrying about to help Mrs Helmond, and he could smell something burning down the passage and hear excited voices. In the dining room Mrs Van der Vliet sat talking to the clergyman – his wife, he said, would be coming later, with the Krauses – reminiscing about how the Netherlanders, while they had still constituted a large community, had come together for similar festivities. With a heavy tread and rustling skirts she walked with them as far as the stoep and expressed misgivings about the effects of the night air on Versluis's chest and the approaching weather. 'But wouldn't you like to come along yourself, madam?' Scheffler cried excitedly, and she shook her head as if the mere contemplation of such a thing would be unacceptable in the presence of her black mourning-dress and the twisted locks of her brooch.

Everything that evening was touched with an aura of excitement, each social event sufficient to sweep up the whole little community in its passage. In the dark streets of Bloemfontein, usually disturbed after nightfall only by the barking and sporadic fighting of the dogs, the shouts of young men on their way back from the hotel were heard, or the lament of some drunk. From every direction there now appeared small groups of advancing people, visible from afar by the bobbing lanterns with which they lit their way. Although Scheffler walked more slowly for the sake of Versluis, he failed to notice that he was getting hardly any response to what he was saying, and talked away gaily, once again enlivened by his own characteristic youthful exuberance at the prospect of the approaching festivity. He did not usually go to such feasts he said, but an exception could always be made for the Kaiser's birthday. 'And it's a chance for Mathilde to get out a little; it doesn't often occur in her life, and we all need a bit of gaiety, don't we, even if it does seem vain and worldly in the eyes of some people.' He had brought no lantern himself, and the faint flashes of lightning that lit up the night were not sufficient to illuminate the uneven road, but he stopped talking to help Versluis through the drift, while the swaying lanterns of the people in front of and behind them revealed their path from one stone step to another. When they had climbed up the other bank and Versluis remained standing there, breathless from the effort, Scheffler carried on talking as if he had not been interrupted, although he remained standing too. 'In any case, Friederike is fortunately much better, and that's already a cause for gratitude. And having my sister with her in the house is also a great help and comfort. For both of us,' he went on to add after a moment's thought, with seriousness and conviction. 'For both of us.'

It had been a mistake Versluis realised anew when he saw in the distance the lit-up clubhouse upon which they were all converging, with its flags and strings of Chinese lanterns across the verandah and a buzz of voices that reached them even at that distance. It had been a mistake he knew as he paused in the doorway and glanced quickly at the rooms which were already cramped and over-peopled, filled with the glow of candles and the fumes of paraffin lamps in the heat of the summer evening. But the clergyman was introducing him to the Consul who was waiting to welcome the guests at the door, and he was forced to attend to the formalities of the introduction and conversation.

'It's a pleasure, a pleasure indeed,' the man assured him with a smile as he shook his hand. 'We have of course been aware of your presence in our midst, we have heard of the visitor from the Netherlands who speaks German so well, and my wife was at your interesting reading,' – in dove-grey satin she stood beside her husband, smiling like him – 'and it therefore goes without saying that I have been eager to meet you. Although within the circumstances I thought it better not to impose myself: too many doctors are not a good thing, they create the impression of a consultation over a sick-bed, don't you think?' Laughingly he leant over towards Versluis while he retained his grip on his hand, his words indistinct above the noise of footsteps and voices that echoed through the rooms of the little clubhouse. Scheffler had introduced the man as Doctor Kellner, Versluis recalled, and realised that he must be a physician.

'Fortunately I have recovered completely,' he replied politely. 'A call from a doctor could be nothing more than a social visit as far as I'm concerned.'

For a moment the eyes behind the silver-framed spectacles looked at him more sharply; almost involuntarily they settled on his face, took it in, and drew their own conclusions. 'I am overjoyed to hear that,' the doctor nonetheless continued. 'The fine climate of the highveld is indeed the best physician you could wish for, it is a fact that is becoming well-known throughout the world. We have always been a somewhat mixed bunch of people here in Bloemfontein – tonight you'll be able to see for yourself how large our German community is – but I believe that with the influx of visitors from abroad we are becoming truly cosmopolitan. I am sure that you will find your stay here interesting.'

Smilingly he peered at Versluis through his spectacles. Versluis felt less than comfortable before those grey eyes: he uttered a few platitudes about the town and the climate, half expecting the doctor's fingers to close about his wrist and take his pulse. But then a large German party with adolescent children appeared, and he was able to get away in the tumult of their arrival.

Scheffler had vanished, lost in the animated mill of people, and Versluis wandered into a side room in which covered tables containing refreshments had been erected and people were unpacking crates of beer. In the dim light of a couple of lamps he saw Schröder from the hotel, assisted by the barman Gustav, almost unrecognisable for a moment in a dark suit, and then Frau Schröder appeared before him with the half curtsey with which she always greeted him and looked obligingly up at him. How was he? she asked. Had he recovered? she had so often wondered. He found the unfeigned pleasure that this thin, colourless woman displayed on meeting him surprising and even

157

touching; trapped in the corner behind the door, he exchanged a few platitudes with her until her husband called peremptorily from where he was working and she whirled around to join him. 'But it's so nice, all of us Germans being together, isn't it?' she managed to say with a radiant expression before she left Versluis. 'Almost as if one were at home again.'

'As if one were at home again', he thought to himself, and moved with difficulty through the gay people – women changing into their dancing shoes in the hall, men talking together in a dense cloud of pipe and cigar smoke. He heard bits of conversation in German and English, and from time to time saw one of the Netherlanders that he had met at Mrs Van der Vliet's house, to whom he would bow in a courteous pantomime of recognition. In the large hall at the back of the clubhouse where the piano stood, the floor was covered with chalk for the dancers, and the older women were now taking their places on the chairs along the walls, where they kept leaning over to talk past each other and waved their fans enthusiastically. He noticed Mrs Hirsch in burgundy and black lace, and then Hirsch himself was touching his elbow and stood beaming before him, a diamond pin glinting in his tie.

'At last!' he called above the roar of voices, the clatter of footsteps. 'We were wondering where you have been, we were wondering how you are. Your young friend visits us regularly; we were asking him only yesterday about you, but he couldn't tell us anything.' A number of women pressed past them with a rustle of evening gowns and the swish of trains; the scent of gardenia from the girls' swept-up hair, and the smell of the roses that they had pinned to their bodices, wafted past. With his arm half around Versluis's shoulders Hirsch pulled him aside. 'I must admit that I am partly to blame. I could have got in touch, but only last week no fewer than three wagonloads of supplies arrived from Algoa Bay: just imagine, three in one day, and when something like that happens one just has to leave everything and start unpacking and checking. They're our lifeline, those wagons, they're our blood supply, without which we couldn't exist – this isn't Amsterdam or The Hague, it's not Hamburg or Berlin, even if it may look like it tonight! It takes effort to get all these pretty dresses that you see here, and the lamps and the piano, the wine and the beer and the glasses – even the floorboards and the planks for the ceilings. It's all been transported across four hundred miles in ox-wagons, laboriously and at great expense!'

Sweat glistened on his flushed face: he spoke too loudly and too elatedly, as if he had already had a few glasses of wine, but in the general hubbub no-one noticed. 'Come,' he continued, 'you haven't met the President yet, have you? Let me introduce you – he has already been enquiring about you.' Still with his arm around Versluis's shoulders he conveyed him through the rustling, creased evening gowns and trains, the small groups of conversing people, the chairs, to a little podium where the guests of honour were gathered beneath a portrait of the Kaiser wreathed in drooping flowers, and the flags of the Empire and the Republic.

The President rose to greet him, a large man with a silvery beard, the orange sash of office across his chest, and smilingly held out his hand. Versluis's attempted apology for the fact that he had not yet paid his respects at the Presidency was politely brushed aside. 'Not at all, I should long ago have sent a message myself to welcome you here among us, but we delayed as a result of the reports that we received about your health. Be that as it may, you are very welcome – may I introduce you to my wife, so that she may add her assurance to mine?' From where she sat beside him, Mrs Brand offered her hand too, smiling like her husband. 'I wanted to send you a basket of fruit,' she said. 'Usually we have such fine grapes, but this year there was virtually nothing in the garden; both the starlings and the children saw to that.'

Hirsch was already engaged in a conversation with someone else, his attention distracted, and it was the President who took Versluis by the arm to introduce him to the officials and their wives on the podium. 'But come and sit with us for a moment, Mr Versluis, so that we can talk. You come from Delft, I believe. I studied at Leiden myself, quite a few years ago, of course – in fact, I graduated in '45 – but I have retained the most pleasant memories of the city.'

The room was filling up, the drone of voices increased. Would he be able to get away, would he be able to get out? Versluis wondered for a moment. The President was talking about his tutors at Leiden and about new developments in education in the Netherlands, and it took an effort for Versluis, who had no great knowledge of the subject, to keep his attention fixed on the discussion. He was conscious of the tightness of his starched collar and of the sweating of his hands in the calfskin gloves. But then Doctor Kellner approached them to announce that the ceremony was about to begin, and the short audience was over. 'We will be seeing each other again,' said the President. 'If you are still here when our Volksraad convenes you should attend a few sittings. I'm sure you'll find them interesting. You will in any case be a very welcome visitor.'

159

'You must come and have dinner with us one night,' his wife added and leant forward to look up at Versluis. 'I'll invite you when the house is not so full of children, then you and my husband will be able to talk in peace.'

He thanked them, bid them farewell, stumbled over the trains of the women who had taken up their positions around the dance floor, then they yielded and made a place for him among their rustling gowns on one of the chairs against the wall, between the podium and the door. He would have preferred to have been nearer the door and the fresh air outside, with the possibility of escape if the heat and stuffiness were to overwhelm him, but for the present he was trapped there. He pressed his handkerchief to his face; he unbuttoned his gloves.

Doctor Kellner had taken up his position next to the podium to welcome the guests, and he explained the purpose of their gathering, shifting from German to Dutch and English. People coughed and shoes scuffed across the floorboards, chairs creaked, and the women's dresses rustled as they shifted restlessly; the flutter of their fans sounded as a light whirr throughout the room, causing a hardly discernible cooling of the stuffiness of the hall.

'Some of us, members of the older generation in particular, come from elsewhere, while others were born here,' Kellner began his speech, a smiling, good-natured master of ceremonies with his silver-rimmed spectacles and grey beard. 'But notwithstanding the nature of our links with South Africa where we were either born or have settled, each one of us has retained some bond with the fatherland: bonds of birth and remembrance, or else bonds of piety which have been passed down to us by the previous generation, and so it is significant that we should come together on occasions like tonight to do homage to our country of origin or to show our allegiance to the fatherland.' The motion of the women's fans rippled like a wave along the rows of chairs where they sat crowded together: the men were crowded near the door in a phalanx of black evening dress, and Versluis noticed the bobbing of Frau Schröder's coiffure, with its large hairpins, above their shoulders for a moment. They listened amiably to the doctor, but the young people were eager to dance: the girls with drooping flowers in coiffure or décolletage; the young men with heavily oiled hair. They shuffled about in a subdued way while he spoke, although they had clearly resigned themselves to the fact that his speech was still going to take a long time.

'And those of us who, either through birth or descent, feel a special bond with Germany will be particularly moved tonight at the thought

160

that it is our beloved Kaiser's birthday.' With these words he turned towards the framed portrait, the wilting wreath. 'Not only because of the glorious achievements of the immediate past, by which we can ourselves bear witness to the final unification of our so-beloved fatherland. . . .' He switched to German again: he surrendered himself lovingly to the construction of the undulating phrases, the unbroken surge of sentences and clauses, following them successfully through every whirl and eddy to the coast where they would rise, topple and break. His audience was forgotten while he lost himself in the sombre euphony of his mother tongue. '. . . But also arising out of those more intimate, more profoundly heartfelt bonds,' he continued, radiant, impassioned, his eyes raised high above the portrait on the wall to one side of him. His hand on his forehead, face in shadow, the President sat listening attentively, or asleep: beside him his wife sat very erect in a vault of satin and lace, her fan folded to create an impression of concentration. 'I do not need to attempt to express these emotions, for all such attempts are doomed to failure from the start. Each one of you who is of German descent will know what I mean and will, from your own memories or such precious remembrances as have been passed down by parents or grandparents, be able to call up your own series of images which will remind us, as we have gathered tonight on this special occasion, of the way in which our own destinies are inextricably bound up with that of the mighty German nation. Isolated we may be, thinly spread across a part of the world that stands at the very threshold of its development and growth; but even in our isolation there is the consolation that we are not completely cut off from that greater civilisation, that fuller and richer life elsewhere – that we have maintained our bonds with it, and, in a sense, that we are part of as we gather here to pledge our allegiance to our beloved Kaiser Wilhelm.'

Everyone applauded: that had merely been a word of welcome Versluis realised with relief; the toasts and speeches would come later, so that he was now free to try to escape from this crowded room in which chairs were now being pushed back and people were getting ready to dance. He was trapped among the couples that were moving out on to the dance floor, and was unable to make his way to the door. The oldest of the Hirsch girls glided past in white and greeted him with a smile, and at the other side of the room he noticed Polderman, oblivious of everyone around him as he stood talking to a girl with yellow ribbons in her hair. She was much shorter than him, so that he had to bend double over her, uncomfortable but entirely happy. Then the dancers moved aside to let him through and he nearly walked into the Dutchman Gelmers who was standing on the edge of the dance floor, looking out over the heads of the people. How restricted his circle of acquaintances was in this town, Versluis reflected irritably as he turned away in an attempt to avoid the disagreeable young man. Nevertheless it was impossible for him to go anywhere without coming up against some or other familiar face.

The pianist began to play, the openers took the floor, and the floorboards droned under the rhythmical onslaught of the dancers. Versluis reached the door and felt a hand on his arm, but the noise in the little hall was so great that he could not hear what was being said to him; he was merely aware of Doctor Krause's broad, bearded face next to his and the movement of his lips. 'And so,' he shouted more loudly, 'how are you? Not too bad it would appear, eh, if you're up to all of this. Will we be seeing you on the dance floor this evening?'

He led Versluis out with him into the hallway: Versluis saw the powerful, hairy hand on his sleeve and hoped that he had not allowed his aversion to show. It was ridiculous to keep avoiding the doctor like a child and to feel threatened by his mere presence, fearful of his touch, as if his approach could be nothing but professional and his interest merely medical. He took a deep breath, adjusted his cufflinks, and followed the doctor into a room leading off the hall which had been appointed as a smoking room for the evening. German hunting scenes and engravings of Bismarck and Van Moltke adorned the walls, and a group of older men had installed themselves here in armchairs, the light of the single hanging lamp dimmed by a thick cloud of cigar smoke. Hirsch rose immediately from among them to draw up a chair for Versluis. 'In one fell swoop you are now seeing gathered together all the older members of Bloemfontein's German community, and in a single breath I can introduce you to all of the pioneers,' he called. 'Mr Baumann, Mr Fichardt – our honoured visitor from the Netherlands about whom you have heard so much.'

'We are pleased to be able to welcome you here, Mr Versluis,' said Baumann. 'And we are doubly pleased to have a visitor who can speak such excellent German as, according to our friend Hirsch, you can. Our little group is small, and we can always use reinforcements.'

'Then there is also the fact that myself and our friend Fichardt here both come from Prussia and our German is not good enough for the gentlemen from Hesse,' Krause growled. 'No, don't worry, you needn't deny it; we know very well that we are are not quite acceptable in your eyes.'

'We could go on for a long time on that subject,' Baumann said

162

with a laugh, 'but for the sake of our guest we will not pursue the conversation tonight; rather, as representatives of the German community in the Free State we will present a united front to the world.'

'As far as I'm concerned, nowadays, I'm only too pleased to hear German spoken,' said Krause, cutting off the end of his cigar. 'And whether it's from Hanover or Schleswig, it's all the same to me – particularly where our children are concerned. It's hard enough to give them a good basic knowledge of German here in Africa, let alone all sorts of nuances which don't mean anything to them. As long they manage to get together sufficient knowledge of the language to enable them to get along when they go and study abroad later on, the honing can be done over there.'

'Indeed, Pastor Scheffler did come back from Berlin speaking an excellent German, even if he was raised on a mission station amongst the natives,' said Fichardt. 'But as far as our younger generation is concerned, if they are going to remain in this country, the language that they are going to need for the future is English – we have to be practical about these things.'

'You have probably noticed that Bloemfontein is overwhelmingly English-speaking, haven't you, Mr Versluis?' Baumann said politely, to include the visitor in their conversation.

'To tell the truth, up to now I have come across mainly Netherlanders and Germans.'

'Indeed, we have had a German community here since the establishment of the city,' Fichardt said, 'and since you are lodging with Mrs Van der Vliet, as I understand, you would naturally have met most of the Netherlanders.'

'Even if, unfortunately for you, there are not as many of them as before, Mr Versluis,' Hirsch remarked. 'Do you recall how many Netherlanders there were here in Bloemfontein when you began practising in the town, Krause?'

'One was always stepping on a Hollander,' Krause said. 'Nothing personal, Mr Versluis, don't misunderstand me, but the town was full of them – and I must say in all honesty that the majority of them did not make themselves very popular.'

The other men in the group smiled. 'As our friend Doctor Krause said, Mr Versluis, nothing personal,' Baumann added drily. 'But I'm afraid that in most cases it was not the best of your countrymen that were shipped out here in the earlier days.'

'Landdros Van Soelen,' Hirsch said and grinned broadly.

163

'Postmaster Heijermans,' said Fichardt.

'The late first husband of our good Mrs Van der Vliet, and his friend Van Iddekinge who carries on in our midst to survive and deprive,' said the doctor, although even he had lowered his voice slightly.

'You see, Mr Versluis, in the early days of the Republic most of our officials were Dutch,' Baumann explained. 'But I take it that you have already been informed by Mrs Van der Vliet of the vanished glory of those years.'

'She mentioned that her husband had been Secretary of the Volksraad,' Versluis said, and the portrait in the drawing room flashed like a sudden hallucination before his eyes, with its drooping moustache and the pale, staring eyes. Even this was becoming too much for him, the voices, the heat of the lamp and the smoke from their pipes and cigars. In the room next door the piano boomed on in a polka, and the feet of the dancers trod in time across the wooden floor. Everything was becoming too much for him Versluis thought in a sudden fury at his body's reluctance, and at the tiredness, weakness and dizziness that he was once again experiencing as he sat in his evening suit and starched dress shirt, drawn into the circle of chatting Germans.

Laughing, Krause leant over towards him: once again Versluis marked the broad, bearded face and glinting pair of spectacles before him and smelt the cigar smoke that clung to his clothes and hair, mingled with the faint scent of medicine, and he recoiled involuntarily. 'He came to Bloemfontein as a teacher and ended up as clerk of the Volksraad, with a few thousand pounds to his name – in gold, mark you, not bluebacks. Mrs Van der Vliet has reason to continue mourning such a husband, for there are not many like him. To turn a bent penny into gold, in those difficult years, that takes some doing!'

Baumann was also smiling, leaning back comfortably in the blue haze of his cigar smoke. 'We do not wish to cast aspersions on anyone, Mr Versluis,' he gave a formal assurance, 'we're just chatting about the old days and about the former inhabitants of Bloemfontein.'

'We're not accusing him of anything, you understand,' the little Fichardt remarked drily. 'The gentleman was paid for his labours. He received a salary, and from time to time he would act as clerk of some state department or as magistrate, and accounting was not exactly one of his strong points, nor was it anyone else's in those days, the Auditor-General included.'

'And so he carried on, making the most of his talents, building up his contacts and procuring an erf or two here and a farm there,' Hirsch added. 'And so the miracle of his life was enacted. Nor has the good

164

Mrs Van der Vliet had any reason to sleep unsoundly for a single night since his departure.' He had disappeared for a moment to return with a glass of champagne, and he now roamed restlessly around them, glass in one hand and cigar in the other. The men were all speaking at the same time and through the laughter Versluis could not make out much of what they said. He ought to try to get himself something to drink too, he thought, and pushed his chair back to fetch something, but he was overcome by a sudden bout of coughing. He pressed his handkerchief to his lips and could smell the scent of eau de Cologne with which it had been sprinkled. Out of the corner of his eye he saw Krause, who was sitting next to him, shifting to send his cigar smoke in a different direction, and observed him give the other men a small sign of warning.

'Can I help?' Hirsch asked at once, leaning over the back of his chair. 'A glass of water perhaps?'

'Thank you,' said Versluis, 'I have some lozenges,' and searched for the box of pills in the pocket of his waistcoat, feeling threatened at the realisation that throughout this attack he was being observed and scrutinised; but for the moment he was unable to flee as he sat helplessly hunched in the throes of coughing.

For a moment everyone was silent, and then slowly and carefully, without drawing attention to the gesture, Baumann put out his cigar. They had become aware of his illness Versluis thought, or they had been freshly reminded of it, and the conversation would no longer be able to pursue any normal course. He wiped his lips; he folded his handkerchief and put it back in his pocket.

'Yes,' Baumann said pensively after a while, 'we have been through numerous changes. It's been almost thirty years now since I settled here, Mr Versluis. I lived in a tent: there were hardly three houses in the whole settlement.' This fact was clearly of great importance to him and he regarded his early arrival as some special achievement; the others shook their heads appreciatively.

'I can still remember my wife's face when we first arrived here from Germany,' Krause said animatedly. 'She was prepared for anything, but not for that.'

'And then there were quite a few years of drought, one after the other,' said Baumann.

'Houses with clay floors, when we finally had houses, and with roofs lined in clay that leaked.'

'And the dust storms – why does it seem to me that we don't get such storms today as we did then?'

'I remember finding a wildebeest in our back yard one morning.'

'At night you could hear the wild dogs and hyenas howling. You could see them lying along the ridges here above the town during the day.'

'There were lions just the other side of the mountain – the officers of the garrison often went shooting lions.'

'I remember,' Baumann began solemnly, and waited until everyone had stopped talking to listen to him, 'I remember how the late Doctor Fraser went out one day with a couple of officers. . . .'

Versluis did not listen to the hunting tale that the old man related with a great deal of solemnity and verbosity, sitting straight up in his chair, while the other men listened politely. His distress was increasing, not only on account of his bodily discomfort and weakness, but also owing to the constriction of the evening suit that contracted tightly around his body: the stiffened dress shirt; the knotted tie; the narrow, shiny evening shoes. The room in which they were sitting closed itself around him with its low ceiling, and the reek of paraffin from the lamp that cast dancing shadows on the wall, the rattle and clatter and drone of the dancers next door – together with the shouting of the young people in the passage and under the verandah – rose to engulf him completely. Then, through the glass doors that led to the stoep the young Dutchman Gelmers appeared suddenly and, seeing Versluis he stopped for a moment and a smile of recognition began to form on his lips, but then he became aware of his mistake and both smile and recognition were wiped away. The young man cast a vacant, detached gaze over the small group of men in the room as if he had come to look for somebody else. He was already turning to go back outside when two girls came running in, laughing and breathless, from the stoep, where the voices of some young men were calling teasingly after them. They bumped into Gelmers and drew back; he staggered, his feet caught up in the folds of their dresses, and then grabbed at them to stop himself from falling. His face was distorted in panic; he struggled hopelessly, like a swimmer, in the white pleats and folds of their evening gowns – but then they disentangled themselves. Just as suddenly as it had arisen, the panic was under control once more. The girls' high heels clattered across the wooden floor, the rustling of their gowns disappeared, and Gelmers, in heavy shoes, pounded after them with a loud cry.

The men who had been listening to Baumann's tale had not noticed anything, and only Gelmers's resounding cry caused them to look up, the tale interrupted.

166

'That young man has no breeding,' Baumann said with cool disdain as he sat very erect in his chair with his hands on his knees, the personification of pique and indignation. 'But I assume that he is still very young,' he then added in slight extenuation and with a slight bow in Versluis's direction, as if Versluis might take such criticism of a fellow-countryman to heart.

The whole episode involving Gelmers's arrival and departure had hardly taken more than a few seconds, so quick that Versluis had not been able to interpret the rapid succession of observed reactions and emotions. 'I hardly know him,' he replied in confusion, and noticed that the conversation had reached a point at which he would be able to leave without appearing to be impolite.

'It was of course your daughters who were responsible for all the excitement, Hirsch,' Krause remarked. 'Was it not one of them that has just enticed away our young friend?'

Standing behind their chairs, holding a champagne flute in his hand, Hirsch shrugged his shoulders. 'They are young, let them enjoy life. The suffering is yet to come.'

'What do they know of suffering, what will they ever have to suffer?' Baumann asked rhetorically, still miffed at the interruption of his story. 'We are the ones who suffered so that they could go to boarding school and learn to play the piano and go to dances. My wife and I were the first to possess a piano in Bloemfontein, and for how long did we do without one here? They will never be able to speak of suffering, not one of them.' But he smiled with satisfaction at the thought, his displeasure forgotten.

'We fixed up this country for them,' said Fichardt, and rose to withdraw from the group. 'They are going to have to inherit it and bear the responsibility for what happens to it: that is not an easy lot.'

'They, with their ball gowns and their music lessons, where we lived in tents and where our wives had to wash their own laundry in the spruit,' Baumann grumbled in good-humoured disapproval.

'Come now, my friend, don't be so hard on our young people,' Krause rebuked him, however. 'My sons will in any case all be going to Germany for a proper education to prepare them thoroughly for the future, whatever that may be.'

'I heard just this week that Marthinus Steyn has also decided to send one of his sons to Holland so that he can continue his studies and read law,' said Fichardt. 'And I'll send mine over too, when they they are old enough. Other things will be demanded of them than was the case with us, and they will need a different kind of preparation, but I doubt whether they will be less successful in their journey through life than we were in our day.'

'By the way, speaking of lively young daughters, Baumann,' said Krause, 'when is the beautiful Miss Sophie to be married?'

The company was beginning to show signs of dispersing Versluis saw, and he stood up too, but this passed Baumann by, who began to expand upon the financial prospects of his future son-in-law.

'I assume that you are just as disinclined as I am to step on to the dance floor to-night,' Hirsch said gaily.

'I think I'll be satisfied with getting myself something to drink.'

'A very good idea,' he assented, and hooked his arm through Versluis's to walk along with him. 'I wonder,' he then continued in a more confiding tone, 'if you might get a chance to say a few words to your young countryman – it's a difficult issue of course, but perhaps he doesn't quite understand the nature of our informality here in the Free State. It's a young country and we do not have as many rules and proscriptions as exist in Europe; but on the other hand, we are not entirely uncivilised and we still try to maintain certain standards.'

'I don't know what you mean,' said Versluis and stopped in the doorway while people pushed past and the dance blared on.

'I'm talking about young Gelmers,' Hirsch said, and he lowered his voice so that he would not be overheard by the people walking by, with the result that it was only with difficulty that Versluis was able to hear him above the din of the music. 'My wife, who is the personification of kindness and hospitality, does not want him in our house any longer; she says that he is too unrefined and too wild with the girls. Well, perhaps her judgement is a trifle harsh, and in any case we do not wish to accuse him of anything, but the young man is – what should we say – a little too exuberant; his gaiety and humour are perhaps well-intended, but the family is not the proper place for them. I had thought that a few words from you would not have been out of place, coming from an older man and, as I said, a fellow-countryman out here in the unknown. If he carries on in this way, I fear that there will no longer be very many houses here in Bloemfontein where he will be welcome, and that he will have to look for company in the billiard rooms and bars of the hotels.'

'I am afraid that you are mistaken,' Versluis said, conscious of the fact that this was the umpteenth time that he had had to refuse responsibility for Gelmers's actions and deny any close bond with the young man. 'I have met the man on only that one occasion at your house; there is no call for me to engage him in such a conversation.'

Hirsch raised his eyebrows, his face distorted by the lamp that hung directly above them. 'Is that so?' he asked. 'I had indeed formed the impression that he was avoiding the Dutch community – or perhaps it's the other way round, who knows? I'm sorry to have bothered you about this.'

He turned around, his hand resting on Versluis's arm, but then a horse-cart drew up outside the door, and in the light of the Chinese lanterns that fell across the verandah they saw laughing faces peering out from under the hood – women with shawls and scarves over their heads and wrapped around their shoulders, and men in evening dress. Versluis had been forgotten, and with a glad cry of welcome Hirsch went out to the arrivals, his champagne glass still in his hand.

Versluis took refuge from the fresh wave of guests in the room across the lobby where drinks and refreshments had been set out, where he found only Gustav who was busy polishing glasses in obvious dissatisfaction, and who looked at him without any signs of recognition or interest. Versluis hesitated as he faced him, the table with its white cloth between them: he did not feel like any wine or champagne, nor did he want any beer. All he wanted was to get away from there: away from the people and the noise, the brooding, uneasy summer evening, and the heat of the lamps. In the room next door they had switched to a waltz, and the feet of the dancers were muffled, a dragging and scuffing sound across the floor. 'A glass of water, please,' he said finally.

But where could he flee? he wondered as he stood there drinking the water. Back through the night with its restless flashes of lightning to Mrs Van der Vliet's house; to the rented room; the strange bed? The water was lukewarm and cloudy, and he put down the glass and propped himself up on the table. No, he thought, further than that, to the end of a journey that would take many days, a sea voyage of weeks, to the house that stood empty at the other end of the world, irrevocably beyond his reach.

He was beginning to attract attention as he stood there leaning on the table he thought with some agitation – although Gustav did not think him worthy of a second glance as he stood watching the dancers in the hall, seen through the slit as mere flashes of colour and motion in triple time. The new arrivals were still exchanging greetings and talking in the lobby and a group of young people burbled in looking for punch; they poured some for themselves while they stood gaily laughing and talking about the events of the evening, mixing German and English, and not one of them listened to what the others were saying. From behind the table where he was passing the glasses across,

Gustav's eyes moved deliberately over the bare arms and shoulders of the girls, without their being aware of his gaze, and he stared down their décolletages as they bent laughingly over the punch bowl. A girl in a simple cotton dress who stood out among the evening gowns of the others gaily made her way through them and brushed past Versluis on her way to get some beer from Gustav, and it struck Versluis that he was in the way there. He was always in the way, he thought, and saw the girl's gleaming dark hair into which she had stuck some flowers, and the provocative look with which Gustav held her eyes as he passed her the cans of beer, the sudden flickering of his tongue between his lips.

He turned away, he pushed the door open and entered the hall where the women still sat talking along the wall and fluttered their fans; the President and his party still occupied their place of honour beneath the German flag and the Republican one with its four colours, and the waltzing couples continued to turn around the dance floor. Fichardt came by with a woman on his arm who smiled and bowed to Versluis, and he said something that Versluis was unable to catch at once. It was *'An der schönen, blauen Donau'* he realised a moment later, and it took a while before it penetrated that this was the name of the waltz, a Viennese waltz in this place where the collars of the men were beginning to droop and their faces glowed from the heat, where the faces and bosoms of the girls on the dance floor gleamed with perspiration. Sweat and dust, the powdered chalk with which the floor had been coated and the smell of the paraffin lamps, the oppressive darkness of the night beyond the glass doors were beginning to oppress him. Where could he go? he wondered, and began to move carefully around the edge of the dance floor in order to avoid the slipperiness of the floor, the turning couples, and the spread-out trains of the women's evening gowns. Polderman spun by with a plump girl in yellow, his face fixed in a smile of rapture; Mrs Hirsch nodded politely from across the room and waved at him with her fan. His efforts to avoid the dancers had, however, landed him in the corner next to the piano, and he stood trapped there for a moment while he waited for a gap to appear among the dancers. The pianist was the same one that had played at the Helmonds' wedding reception, a middle-aged woman in black with sturdy forearms: she sat squarely on the piano stool and struck the keys with an unerring thump that made the jet ornaments on her bonnet quiver. Why was she wearing a hat in the ballroom? Versluis wondered idly as he stood waiting beside her. She turned out the waltz as mechanically as a barrel-organ operator, and the dancers

170

revolved with faces that were radiant with pleasure. They became entangled and then moved apart again, so that Versluis was able to see for a moment, at the other side of the room, a young woman in a simple brown dress, although by the time he had realised that she was the young Mrs Scheffler the spinning couples between them had obscured her from him once more.

With a few determined strokes of her fingers on the keys, the pianist ended the waltz and swung around on her stool to look at the company and decide when she could begin the next dance. Out of breath the dancers remained standing on the dance floor; the young men were combing back their hair, the girls pressing their handkerchiefs to their flushed necks and faces, when they all turned around in response to a commotion at the entrance.

It was the late arrival of the Helmonds realised Versluis as he saw the flash of crimson among the dark suits and the lighter dresses. They had chosen that particular moment for their entrance into the hall, assured and even a trifle provocative as they stood in the doorway and looked about them without any indication that they knew that they were drawing any attention. That brilliant colour was too garish for this little community Versluis thought as he took this opportunity to make his way through the people on the dance floor. The cut was too daring and the cleavage too low. Even in the Netherlands, in a much more sophisticated community, he would have found her décolletage unseemly, and although it never ceased to amaze him by what indirect and crooked ways the boundaries of acceptability ran in this country, it was clear to him from the combination of suppressed shock, dismay and excitement that he marked around him that it was not considered acceptable here either. The girls giggled and whispered among themselves, some of the older women smiled behind their fans, and a hardly suppressed thrill of excitement broke out among the younger men.

He had no desire to prolong his exposure to this display of the Helmonds nor to involve himself in the reactions that they were provoking in those around him. In fact, it was probably an appropriate time to leave, since he had seen and greeted all of his acquaintances, and his presence had been marked by everyone.

'Here you are, Mr Versluis,' a girl then said to him in English and thrust a bowl into his hands, 'here is some ice cream for you.'

It was one of the Hirsch girls. 'Have you seen Pastor Scheffler anywhere?' he asked in German.

'Across there, with Mrs Krause,' she answered in the same language. 'You must eat it quickly, before it melts,' she called back laughingly as she hurried away. 'We packed it in ice, they brought us some ice from Kimberley!'

In the corner of the room he saw the clergyman bending over the chairs of a number of older women to whom he was handing ice cream, his face flushed with pleasure and the heat, his hair dishevelled. He could not leave without saying goodnight to Scheffler he thought, and if he did that the clergyman would feel obliged to walk back home with him; but on the other hand he could not see himself finding his way back to Mrs Van der Vliet's house on his own on such a dark night, along uneven streets and through the spruit. He would have to stay.

The music had stopped for a while; people stood talking in small groups; they ate ice cream, moved about, and the crimson of Mrs Helmond's gown kept flashing among the more restrained colours as she and her husband made their way through the crowds, surrounded by a small swell of people and accompanied by a group of excited young men. More people had gathered around the President to pay their respects and to congratulate the Consul on the occasion. The pianist waited motionless on her stool, the ribbons of her bonnet unfastened, her hands on her lap.

Versluis looked down at the bowl in his hand in which the ice cream had already melted to an unappealing white mush, and without anyone noticing he went out through one of the glass doors that led to the verandah at the back of the building. It looked out over a garden that sloped down to the spruit; there were only a few people there who had gone out to cool off, the rest were crushed together either in the room where the refreshments were being served or on the front stoep with its Chinese lanterns. He put the ice cream down on the windowsill and leant over the balustrade of the verandah to get some fresh air, but he soon realised that this was a vain hope. In the hall behind him people moved about in the hazy glow of the lamps, and through the open doors and windows he could hear the drone of their voices together with a few tentative chords on the piano, as if the pianist were practising the next dance or wanted to hurry the dancers up.

In the light of the single lantern hanging from a pole at the steps of the verandah to light the way to the privy, he saw the starched shirtfront of a man approaching through the dark, and then recognised Doctor Krause coming along the path. 'Yes,' he said out of the blue, 'as one gets older, one's bladder is no longer what it used to be, eh?' He grunted a little as he climbed the stairs. 'I belong at the bedside, not in ballrooms; it's my wife who insists on being here because she's

172

afraid she might miss something. And for the women it's also a difficult sort of life, this, you die. . . .' Versluis made no reply, uncomfortable as usual in the doctor's presence, but Krause was apparently unaware of this. 'And you,' he asked gruffly, but not without a certain friendliness. 'You oughtn't to be hanging around in the night air after coming out of that stuffy ballroom drenched in sweat; you should know your body better than that by now and also respect it a bit more.'

'I'm feeling fine,' Versluis said. 'I'm much better now. It's just a bit too close for me in there.'

Krause stood looking at him searchingly for a while in the dim light of the lantern and then shrugged his shoulders. 'Then you haven't chosen the best place to revive yourself, our spruit stinks to high heaven again this evening. But that's a good sign,' he added cheerfully on his way indoors, 'it's a sign that we'll get some rain – perhaps even tonight. The weather's coming up nicely.'

He disappeared into the hall where the music had resumed; the dance had begun once again, and the last of the loiterers on the verandah had also gone back inside. Versluis went down the steps and strolled slowly through the garden until the light of the single lantern hardly illuminated the bordered pathway for him any more and the music had faded behind him. Krause was right, he realised, for in the brooding heat of the night a heavy stench was discernible among the fruit trees and vegetable gardens on either side of the spruit where the nocturnal creatures now called, from the cattle and horse stables of the town, from the outhouses, and from the malodorous spruit itself with its slime, mud, duckweed and stagnant pools.

He hesitated and could no longer see where he was going; trees rose darkly in front of him and beyond them, on the other side of the low stone wall, came the croaking of frogs along the meanderings of the sluit. There was no moon, and above him the sky was dark except when it was filled for an instant by a blue flash of lightning. He stood there with his head raised and could hear the noises of the nocturnal creatures and the barking of dogs far away, as well as the distant dance music; he heard a rustling behind the quince and fig trees that grew in speed and intensity. He looked around, startled by the sudden closeness of the sound, and then heard people talking – the insistent, whispering voice of a man and the quieter, demurring voice of a woman; a suppressed groan; a cry; sounds that he could hardly distinguish among the rustling of the leaves and branches, the music, and the noise of the nocturnal animals. He shouldn't be here he thought anxiously, and turned around quickly but almost fell over the

173

stones that lined the pathway; then he stood quite still in the shadows as a dark figure appeared from amongst the trees and walked rapidly towards the clubhouse, a woman who was buttoning up the bodice of her dress as she walked. A while later a man followed her, walking slowly and casually with his hands in his pockets and whistling softly to himself, and as this man stood aside for a moment under the lantern for someone who was coming down the steps of the verandah, Versluis recognised the sturdy figure of the waiter Gustav. To Versluis that packed hall, its noise, and the resounding music all seemed unreal from where he was standing as he looked back at it from the dark garden. The streets of the town were deserted, the orchards and gardens empty between the stone walls, the lamps in the house had already been put out and their inhabitants were asleep: only the music continued to sound through the emptiness, through the dark, becoming weaker and weaker until it died away in the desolation of the surrounding veld.

He would go now, Versluis decided, and he would go alone, without the clergyman's careful guidance. Why had he ever allowed Scheffler to inveigle him into coming on this outing in the first place? It was a mistake to allow control of one's life out of one's hands even for a moment, for if one did, chaos came flooding through the unguarded fissures and tiny cracks, to engulf everything. There was too much that one did not wish to hear or see, that one did not want to know, far too great a menace lurked just beyond that regulated and guarded terrain which ought to be kept at bay, which must at all costs be kept at bay.

He walked back to the lamplight where in the uncertain light he could see someone standing at the railing, and he was already quite close before he once again recognised, with the same displeasure as always, the figure of Gelmers. He could walk around the building before being noticed he thought quickly, for the young man was leaning against one of the posts of the verandah, his head turned away, and he had not seen him yet, but Versluis realised at once how absurd this notion was. Why should he, a middle-aged man in evening dress, have to slink around the building, stumbling and staggering about in the dark, in fear of someone so much younger than himself? And *fear*? he reflected half-indignantly as he moved forward; fear was surely much too strong a word, even for the irrationally powerful aversion that this young man evoked in him.

Gelmers did not look up, his face was turned away and his head bowed. His shoulders were shaking, and then Versluis perceived that he was coughing, the sound inaudible above the booming of the polka

174

in the hall, the drumming of feet on the wooden floor and the raucous voices. He was caught in an uncontrollable fit of coughing with his handkerchief pressed against his mouth. Panic gripped Versluis as he hesitated on the steps. He could go and ask someone for a glass of water or call one of the doctors he thought, but still he wavered, unwilling to push past the young man. There was too much that one did not wish to know, too much knowledge from which one should be spared, and he groped with trembling fingers in his waistcoat pocket for the little pillbox containing lozenges. 'Mr Gelmers,' he said, but the young man did not hear him, and Versluis was unable to bring himself to touch him in order to attract his attention. But then the shaking of Gelmers's shoulders ceased and he remained standing there for a moment, still holding the verandah post. When he looked up it was with a glassy stare, without seeing Versluis who was standing in front of him proffering his abalone-shell pillbox, and upon his lips and on the crumpled handkerchief that he was clutching there were dark stains that even in the dim light of the lantern one could recognise as blood.

The pillbox fell from Versluis's hand and the cough lozenges rolled out across the boards of the stoep, he slid across them and could feel them crunching beneath his feet as he tried to reach the glass door to the ballroom. The heat and glow, the colours, the fumes from the lamps, the whirl of people and noise rose up in front of him: like the unreal reflected world of a mirror, he found them before him and he remained standing in the doorway without knowing how to enter, until the weight of his body took over and he toppled forward, heavily and without a sound, through the splintering glass of the mirror.

'I slipped,' he said. 'I stumbled.'

'You fainted,' said Doctor Krause calmly, sitting beside him with his pocket watch in his hand.

Why had everything gone blank? Versluis wondered. And then he noticed that he was no longer in the ballroom, but in the smaller room in which he had sat earlier that evening talking to the other men in the light of the single hanging lamp. The music had stopped.

'Here, drink a little of this,' said Krause, and held out a glass of brandy to him. He wanted to refuse, but the two doctors lifted him up on the bench on which he lay prostrated, and talked to each other with lowered voices.

'Are you feeling better?' Kellner asked. 'Can you walk as far as the door?'

'I don't need any help,' he said, but they took no notice. Possibly they were not even listening.

175

'My carriage is outside,' said Hirsch, who had just entered. 'Come, my friend, let us take you home.'

He was not the one who needed help, Versluis wanted to say, there was nothing wrong with him. Gelmers was the one they should be attending on the verandah where he stood with bloodstained lips; although as soon as that image came to Versluis he wiped it out again. The men around the settee helped him up, and he allowed himself to be led, for although he found that he could move without any difficulty, he was feeling faint and unsteady and so welcomed the support that they offered him. He was only dimly aware of what was happening around him: the men in evening dress, the lamplight, the people crowded around the entrance of the ballroom, curious, sympathetic, shocked.

Hirsch's landau was waiting outside and they helped him into it and covered him with a fur cloak, for which he was grateful, for he realised that he felt very cold. After a short discussion Krause and Pastor Scheffler took their places on the bench opposite him, while Hirsch climbed up on to the box with the coachman. Versluis saw a faint flash of lightning in the heavens above him, so distant and unreal that he made no attempt to comprehend it. On the box the Malay coachman sat straight and motionless, and made the horses move very slowly, so that even the rocking of the carriage on its suspension was barely noticeable.

During the night the storm broke, and the crash of thunder and the force of the rain on the roof were so heavy that he was woken briefly from his drugged sleep. By the time he woke again, however, the storm had passed: water gushed from the gutters and dripped from the eaves, and the first light of dawn appeared through the blinds.

'I'll come and see how you are feeling in the morning,' Krause had said as he gave him the sleeping draught.

'That won't be necessary,' was all he had managed to reply before he lost consciousness. 'I'll let you know if I need you.' As a result no-one disturbed him until he was woken later that morning by creaking floorboards and the rustling of a dress which betrayed the presence of Mrs Van der Vliet. The Helmonds had set off that very morning with all their luggage for Aliwal North, after dancing almost until dawn, and so her complete attention could now be devoted to the fresh crisis that had arisen in such a timely way in her life: silently, calmly and competently she took over once again, arranging for clean pillowcases and a jug of water beside the bed, and offered him tea, milk flavoured with aniseed, and beef boullion. With an unhurried proficiency she shook pillows into shape, drew up the bedclothes and set curtains and blinds so that they diffused the sunlight; and for a moment, still half-befuddled by the sleeping draught, Versluis could see those tiny, deft hands also laying out all the corpses that she had already told him about in the same thorough, the same unhurried way.

'Is the light too bright?' she asked. 'The sun is declining, before we know it, it'll be autumn again. Perhaps that was the last rain we'll get before the winter.' She moved slowly around the room, putting a chair right here, an ornament there, and looked around for any task that the servants might have left undone. 'But it rained heavily,' she said. 'If it's not dust, it'll be mud. If there's one thing you can't do in this country, it's keep your house clean, even if the servants sweep and polish all day long.' She moved the towels on the towel-rail by millimetres, she merely touched the ewer on the washstand, intent on establishing her control over the room and its contents. 'Nor will the Helmonds have an easy ride,' she added with a certain degree of satisfaction. 'The roads will be a mudbath of course, and all the rivers and streams will presumably be full, all because they wanted to stay a few more days for the dance.'

He lay there in a half-drugged haze; he drank the tea that she sent him and dropped off to sleep again, grateful also that the din had ended – that clangorous piano and the drumming feet, the ceaseless whirl of faces and voices.

It must have been afternoon when he woke up again, for the sun had disappeared from the room and the light had softened; and he saw that Pastor Scheffler was standing beside the bed. The sudden appearance of the clergyman did not surprise him, nor did he feel any discomfort about his own position, propped helplessly against the pillows in his nightshirt as hardly anyone except Pompe and his doctor had ever seen him. He had thus already reached this point, he thought bitterly, and turned his head on the pillow. Was it progression or regression? He did not know.

'I did not want to wake you,' the clergyman said. 'But Adèle and Mathilde were concerned about you, they insisted that I come and see how you are.'

He could barely find the strength to reply: he nodded, and for the clergyman that was enough. 'Mrs Van der Vliet says that you do not want the doctor to come,' he said with some concern as he stood bending over the bed.

'It's not necessary, in a few days I'll be entirely well again. This is

177

not the first time,' he added when it appeared that the clergyman was not going to be convinced by this assurance. 'It is not the first time that such a thing has happened to me – a sudden weakness, that's all it is, and it passes.'

Scheffler was, however, still looking at him; his young face serious, as if there were more that he wanted to say, but was unable to find the right words, and Versluis quickly shut his eyes to end the conversation.

Scheffler understood the signal. 'I won't tire you any longer now, but I'll come again, in a few days when you are feeling stronger.' But then he began to fumble around in his pockets. 'Oh yes,' he said. 'I had forgotten completely, but I brought this for you, you must have dropped it last night.' Versluis did not comprehend at once what it was that was being held out to him. 'I'm afraid that it is broken,' said the clergyman. 'Someone must have stood on it. But perhaps a jeweller will be able to repair it for you.'

'It doesn't matter,' said Versluis. It was his abalone-shell pillbox; its little lid dented and almost torn off its hinges; but it was indeed not important. 'How is Mr Gelmers?' he asked.

Surprised by the question, the clergyman stood still, on the point of leaving. 'Mr Gelmers?' he repeated unsurely. 'Oh, he came to the dance last night, but I don't think that he stayed for long. I didn't see him again later on. Is there perhaps a message that I can give him?'

'No,' he said rapidly, 'I was just asking,' and then the clergyman said farewell and left.

So, Versluis thought to himself after he had been lying on his own for two days, so he had reached this point, and he was surprised by his equanimity. He had lost consciousness and toppled over in front of the Presidential couple and two-thirds of the inhabitants of Bloemfontein, prostrate on the dance floor in his evening dress. Bearing the bruise on his forehead where he had hurt himself in the fall and heedless of the disgrace, he lay there in bed, waiting – yes, for what? The Bloems, the Brills, the Voigts all enquired after him; Mrs Prince, whom he had met only once, sent a bowl of figs, and Mrs Brand, the President's wife, a basket of grapes with a kindly note, which were delivered by one of her sons. Mrs Van der Vliet brought him all these messages along with the tea, the boullion, the eggnog, but they had no effect on him, and these people were as removed from him as the aunts, the

178

Van Meerdervoorts and De Bruïne had become when he had left them behind at the other end of the earth.

Tired from lying in bed, he finally got up and moved carefully to the armchair, clutching bits of furniture, and collapsed exhausted into it. Each time he was weaker, he thought, and each time the return to reality required more effort; he could not carry on like this he thought with a surge of anxiety, and turned his face away from the bright window.

Later on he asked Mrs Van der Vliet to send for Doctor Kellner, and he appeared with unexpected promptness, careful and precise, wearing a black frock coat and silver-rimmed spectacles.

'My brother-in-law, Doctor Krause, has been attending you up to now,' he remarked.

'They sent for him when I was brought here when I was ill; he was not my choice. I would prefer you to treat me.'

Kellner put his bag down on a chair and did not pursue the matter. 'And what would you like me to do for you?' he asked.

He did not know himself what answer to give to this, and finally there was probably no answer to the question. 'That evening at the club I . . .' he began, and then hesitated over the precise wording. 'I fainted. I am already feeling better, but I thought that it might be desirable for me to be examined.'

'Apart from that, you're in good health?'

'I came here for the sake of my health.'

The conversation was formal and aloof, and the doctor hardly looked at him as he stood beside the bed, erect in his black frock coat.

'Was your physician in the Netherlands not able to treat you over there?'

'They advised me to go to a clinic in Switzerland, where I would get more specialised treatment – both my own doctor and the specialist that he called in.'

'But still you chose the exhaustion and discomfort of a voyage to Africa?'

He did not answer at once: seeing a poem by chance in a newspaper, a sudden intuition – how could he make that comprehensible to this methodical, careful man? 'They could offer me no certainty of a cure, not even in Switzerland,' he said, and looked at the spotless white cover on his bed.

'And Africa. . . .'

'I had heard of the wholesome effect that the inland climate had had in certain cases and hoped that I would also be able to benefit from it.'

179

'And have you had any benefit in the time you've been here?'

It was quiet in the room. 'I do not know what would have happened if I had gone to Switzerland or remained in the Netherlands,' he said at last. 'Here. . . .' He reflected for a moment and saw the ride in the carriage with the Hirsches, the walks in the late afternoon, the fall in the mud when the storm had overwhelmed him. 'The night before last at the club was the first time since my arrival that something of that sort has happened to me.'

'And the other signs of illness? Fever, coughing, spitting blood. . . .'

How did this man know what was ailing him without his having been informed of it? Versluis wondered, but was pleased that the need for explanations had been avoided. 'Fever, sometimes,' he said, and looked at the white cover. 'Coughing, sometimes; shortness of breath and tiredness – more often. Or perhaps I should say, almost continuously.' He could see Gelmers in the dim lamplight under the verandah. 'Blood – yes, now and then there is blood.'

'Perhaps it would be best if I examined you first,' Kellner said.

By now Versluis had grown accustomed to undressing before strangers and being touched by strange hands, and Kellner's examination was so impersonal that the doctor appeared to be hardly involved in it, his thoughts elsewhere. His carefully manicured hands were as cold as the touch of his stethoscope and other instruments. 'May I?' he asked and gestured towards the washstand, washed his hands very thoroughly and for a long time, and hung the towel back on the stand after he had used it as precisely as Mrs Van der Vliet would have done, before returning to the bed.

'What do you wish me to do for you?'

'What is there that you can do?'

He made a small dismissive gesture with the well-manicured hands – his cuffs were spotlessly white and starched, his cufflinks flashed in the light. 'I can give you something to alleviate the cough a little, a drug that might help if you are in pain, a sleeping-draught – that is to say, if your doctor from the Netherlands has not already provided you with these things.'

'That will be fine.'

'This is first-aid – these are palliatives that I am offering you, not a cure.'

'They also help,' Versluis said in a subdued voice.

'A cure. . . .' The doctor looked away through the large windows to the garden and the fruit trees. 'A cure,' he finally said, 'is as far as I can see no longer in my power.'

180

He waited for a long while before he spoke, struggling to formulate the thought, and to an even greater extent, the words. 'I am thus in the process of dying, you mean?' he asked, and once the question had been uttered it sounded to him as cold and clinical as the gleaming silver instruments in the doctor's case.

Kellner smiled slightly behind his beard. 'We are all in the process of dying, if you consider it carefully, Mr Versluis; but there are various steps in the process, and you have presumably lived for long enough and seen enough of the real world to know that yourself. There are stages of surrender and acceptance, and not one of them is reached without a struggle. To accept the appearance of death; to accept the principle that you, too, have to die; to accept your own personal death as it draws gradually nearer – each of these stages constitutes a fresh crisis, and when the time finally arrives to die, then the crisis of dying is perhaps the easiest of all. To die is actually not that difficult,' he added thoughtfully as he closed his case. 'But to accept the idea of dying, that involves a struggle, sometimes even a life-long struggle.'

There was nothing more Versluis thought: the silence between them, the white cover over the bed, the room in which the shadows of the late afternoon were growing in the corners behind the furniture and the curtains. That is all he thought; that is all. It was actually very simple.

The doctor took up his case, he picked up his hat where he had put it down. 'I will tell Mrs Van der Vliet to send the garden-boy over to fetch the medicine. And if there should be anything for which you might need me, do call me. I live just a little way down the road, opposite the College.'

He bowed; he left; with virtually no sound he drew the door shut behind him. It was so simple, so obvious, Versluis thought to himself, to tell someone that he was dying. And it was so simple to hear the news.

3

H E GOT up; he shaved and dressed himself, more slowly and
deliberately than usual; he occupied his place at the dining
table once more, where the Helmonds' departure had left a
clear gap. Mrs Van der Vliet presided majestically over the head of the
table while at the foot her husband nodded and smiled and no-one so
much as looked in his direction. Polderman stared at the water jug in
front of him and did not always hear when somebody addressed him,
and Du Toit looked tensely from one person to another, eagerly
looking out for and anticipating unspoken demands or desires, so
that he was always passing things that were not wanted and enthusiastically replying to remarks before he had comprehended them
properly.

'He has a girlfriend,' said Mrs Van der Vliet and shook her head
meaningfully when Polderman left them as soon as dinner had ended,
wearing a flamboyant tie and more pomade than usual worked into
his frizzy red hair, and Versluis recalled his dancing partner with the
yellow ribbons at the ball.

'Mr Du Toit will be missing his company,' he said.

'Du Toit can find company enough at the hotel,' she said unconcern-
edly. 'There are enough people with nothing to do hanging about in
the bar.' How would she know? Versluis wondered as he drank his
weak, milky coffee. 'He is sending far too many collars to be washed
these days,' she said, her thoughts turning once again to the more
interesting subject of Polderman. 'I'll have to speak to him – how
much does he think one pays for starch? This is not a boarding house.'
Her spirits visibly rose at the mere prospect of the encounter.

Versluis instructed one of the servants to remove the remaining
Dutch newspapers from his room, knowing that he would not read
them again, and after a moment's consideration he locked his little
writing desk and put it away in the wardrobe. He used it so seldom,

182

and he could see no reason for needing it again in the immediate future.

He paced around in his room, he walked down the passage; he took his cane, hat and gloves and set off into the street on a little expedition to the shops or the bank that would not be too demanding on him. How long had he been there? he wondered, and when he stopped to ponder the question he discovered to his surprise that it had only been a few months. His new environment had already begun to grow familiar to him – yes, he realised, even this land with its severity and heat, even this town with its dusty streets and outhouses, its cows in back yards and its dead dogs in the streets. All its indolence, indifference and outlandish narrow-mindedness, he was growing accustomed even to these things, not to the point of acceptance, but at least to the point of forbearance. As he contemplated the thought he was not sure whether it pleased him or not.

He dropped in at the parsonage to thank the women for the messages and good wishes that Scheffler had gone to convey to him, and he was greeted in the hallway with disarming delight by Scheffler himself even before the servant had put in an appearance. 'It's wonderful that you've come now,' he cried. 'My parents are here. In fact, they have come over from Bethany. You must come in and meet them.' In his enthusiasm he had grabbed Versluis by the arm and was pulling him unceremoniously into the living room, even as Versluis was still trying to say politely that he did not wish to impose, and that he would rather come back on a later occasion.

They were still embroiled in this undecided contest when Mrs Scheffler appeared behind her husband to discover who the visitor might be. 'Good morning, madam,' Versluis said in confusion; but she would not listen either. 'You must come in,' she said softly but firmly, and before he could raise any further objections her husband had already propelled him inside.

'It's Mr Versluis!' Miss Scheffler cried from where she was lying propped up on the settee with her loose hair falling over her face. And it was as if he had been expected, such was his welcome into the circle where she was sitting with the two old people, the white-haired old man holding the baby on his lap and the elderly woman in black wearing a lace bonnet. He was introduced to them and greetings were exchanged while Miss Scheffler took over the baby and her sister-in-law silently set out the teacups.

183

'Sit down, sit down, Mr Versluis,' Scheffler said elatedly while he drew a chair closer for the visitor. 'My parents arrived only this morning, and I had been wondering whether I shouldn't drop in at Mrs Van der Vliet's tomorrow to invite you over to meet them. They will be staying in Bloemfontein for two nights; we are fortunate this time. They don't usually grant us such a long break.'

'It is not easy to get away from a mission station,' said his father. 'There is always work to do, and never enough time or people for everything. But my wife had to come to see Doctor Krause and I also had business to do here in Bloemfontein, which I had been putting off for much too long, so we had the hooded cart harnessed and came.' He nodded encouragingly to his wife who was lying back in her chair as if she had just collapsed there in exhaustion. On her lap she held a crumpled handkerchief, and the black bombazine of her dress was stretched tautly across the arch of her abdomen. She smiled, however, upon being referred to in this way, and for an instant the tired face with its lacklustre eyes lit up.

'I trust that it is nothing serious, madam,' Versluis said, and she shook her head.

'No, no, it's nothing,' she assured him in a voice so low that the words were virtually inaudible, then she cleared her throat and pressed the handkerchief to her lips in a way that suggested that she was feeling uncomfortable at all the attention that was being paid to her.

'Mr Versluis, a cup of coffee?' the young Mrs Scheffler enquired behind him.

'No thank you, I can't,' he began. 'Mrs Van der Vliet. . . .'

'But Mr Versluis must stay for supper tonight,' her husband cried. 'It's almost time for supper, isn't it? You'll agree to stay tonight, at least, won't you? We'll send a note to Mrs Van der Vliet, and tomorrow morning I'll go and explain myself, and ask to be forgiven for disrupting her routine by keeping you here.' In that relaxed family circle he was entirely at ease, so buoyant that it seemed as if nothing could upset him. 'Mathilde, tell Rebecca to lay an extra place this evening.'

'Yes, do stay, Mr Versluis, it'll be very agreeable,' said Miss Scheffler looking at him radiantly with her hair falling across her face, the baby still in her arms. 'It's always so good to have a table full of people, and we really so seldom have it.'

'You will stay, won't you, Mr Versluis?' her sister-in-law enjoined more quietly, and then bent down to pick up the baby, which grabbed at her hair with little searching hands and grasped at her brooch. For a moment Versluis and the new arrangements for supper were

184

forgotten, and she smiled down at the child in her arms, oblivious of the others.

Miss Scheffler pushed the hair from her face. 'And after supper we can make some music. Will you? Father, August, will you play for us?'

'I don't think it's fair to impose that on Mr Versluis after we have already forced him to stay to supper, Adèle,' her brother rebuked her with a smile. 'Do you know when last we had a chance to practise together?'

'But you are still practising yourself, you know that you play every day when you have the chance.'

'A few minutes are all I steal here and there – that's not practising, it's improvising.'

'And besides, Father has brought his viola along, haven't you?'

'Just in case August should have the time and inclination. But do you think I get the time to improvise, let alone practise? And anyway, who is there at home to play for? Your mother laughs at me and says that I'm being absurd when I sit down by myself with my viola.' He smiled at these words and looked at his wife, but she did not hear: the baby had been brought to her so that she could kiss it goodnight, and she stretched out weathered hands to it on which a wedding ring glinted dully; her daughter-in-law bent down to hold out the baby to her, and the two women were unaware of the conversation around them.

'Are you fond of music, Mr Versluis?' the old Reverend Scheffler then asked and turned to him with the same bright, penetrating gaze that marked both his son and daughter.

'In the Netherlands I used to attend the subscription concerts each winter: this winter is in fact the first series that I have missed. I am no connoisseur of music, but I enjoy listening to it.'

'Then I don't believe that we'll be able to give you much joy. Not only do we hardly ever have an opportunity to practise, together or apart, but our climate is anything but beneficial to the instruments.'

'I would still like to hear you,' Versluis said. 'I have heard no music since I left the Netherlands.'

'We'll not count the indefatigable Mrs Hopwood at the dance will we?' Scheffler said with a smile. 'But our musical life in Bloemfontein has fortunately improved since all these girls' schools have appeared in our midst.'

'Do you play too, Mr Versluis?' his father asked.

'Unfortunately not.'

'That is a loss – for yourself, at least. It is hard to have to be

185

dependent on other people for your music; that is to say, if it is something that you want and if it means something to you. I remember how precious my old viola was when I had just arrived here as a young missionary.' He leant forward and patted Versluis paternally on the knee for emphasis. 'The whole voyage from Hamburg, eighty-three days on the ship, and then another six weeks by ox-wagon from the coast – my wife said that I was more concerned about the trunk containing the viola than the one with the household goods and the clothes in it.' Once again he looked smilingly at his wife, but she had lapsed into reverie, her head propped up on her hand, the handkerchief on her lap. 'But chattels and clothes one can replace. Where in this country would I have obtained another viola? Where in this empty wilderness?' He sat very erect and looked brightly at Versluis as if he were daring him to find an answer to this question. He was smaller than his son, but the resemblance between them was clear: he was growing bald, but his white hair stood up untidily about his head and the expression of the blue eyes behind the lenses of the spectacles was bright and candid. He could have been in his sixties already, and his wife looked even older, but he possessed the same youthfulness that in his son gave the impression of boyishness: a certain dignity and alertness, the gestures quick, the gaze penetrating and the face deeply tanned as one would expect of someone who spent a great deal of time outdoors. 'I have had it now for forty years, Mr Versluis!' he said with obvious satisfaction. 'For thirty-five years I have endured the heat and the dryness of this land, to say nothing of our bitter winters – have you ever experienced a Free State winter? And properly tuned only now and then, apart from the odd attempts that I have made myself – the same viola that I played as a student in Germany in the year of the great revolutions and the parliament in Frankfurt; that I still remember well.'

The young clergyman listened with a smile: he knew his father, and clearly he was also acquainted with all his stories, but he was ready to listen to them once again. 'But Rebecca must take a note to Mrs Van der Vliet,' he remembered, and jumped up. Versluis tried to protest once more, but Scheffler paid no attention to his objections, and the old missionary tapped him on the arm again to draw his attention.

'I had a musical education, that was important to my parents, but there was no money to study music properly. And who could blame them? My father was a simple country carpenter, and we were seven children. But he saved up; I have no idea of all the sacrifices that they made, the whole family, and in my final year at the seminary, just before I was ordained, they gave me this viola which I have kept all these years, as a gift.' He spoke completely freely to the stranger who had just been brought into the family circle. 'And when August was still a boy he obtained violin lessons from an itinerant German who worked at the mission station for a few months; and when the man left – overnight, just like that, without any warning – he left his own violin for the child.'

In the meantime some activity had ensued around the dining-table: Scheffler returned with the note that he had written; his wife, with the baby on her arm, was giving the servant instructions; and his sister, who had also been listening to her father with a smile, but only half attending to what he was saying, suddenly cast the rug from her knees, leapt up, and hobbled quickly towards them without the aid of her sticks. The old man paid no attention, however, to the good-humoured wrangling of the women over domestic duties. 'We were able to play duos, August and I,' he said, 'no matter how well or badly it went. There on the veld in the midst of that desolation, when the inhabitants of the station had all gone to their homes, after they had gone to bed, we were able to play the music that I had brought with me from Germany.'

'Or try to play it,' his son, who had rejoined them, corrected him.

'All right then, we tried, at least we had good intentions. And no matter what you might say, it was something to be thankful for, to be able to sit together like that and play music in that emptiness.'

'Yes,' his son said, 'that was fine. I miss our music evenings at Bethany.'

'To win souls for God is a great thing: that was why I left everything behind and came to Africa, both my wife and I. But then the conversion and baptism of people is not everything.' He leant over to Versluis and looked keenly at him with his intense blue eyes, frowning gravely. 'I remember walking away from the wagons where we had outspanned one evening on the journey up from the coast, far away, until I could no longer even see the campfire or hear voices any longer – it was probably dangerous, because there were still plenty of wild animals all over the place then, but what did I know of danger? I was a green newcomer fresh from Germany, and besides I was still young and full of self-confidence. And then I suddenly realised how dark the land around me was, without a flicker of life or civilisation anywhere in the vicinity, and how desolate, and how far I was myself from everything and everyone that I had known up to then. But in that same instant I realised that that was exactly why I had come out to Africa, to light

187

up that immense darkness, or light one lamp – or at least to try. Sometimes –' he still looked frowningly at Versluis, as if he were hoping for some clarification of thoughts that he had not yet managed to formulate in any satisfactory way himself, '– sometimes there comes a brief moment of insight, not so? Something – and I say this in all humility – something like the visions of the saints and the prophets, in which everything is suddenly illuminated as if by a flash of lightning. And so that was my little vision, shortly after my arrival from Germany.'

'You've achieved much more in all these years than merely lighting a little lamp, Father,' Scheffler said quietly.

His father considered the remark, and then shook his head soberly. 'That we cannot judge. I tried, and it is the endeavour that is of value to our Lord, not the visible results.'

'But just think of what Bethany looked like when you began to work there all those years ago. . . .'

'There were other helpers too, we are not the only ones responsible for that.' He rejected the idea with similar conviction. 'Those are not the things that we ought to be looking at, even if they are the most obvious things and we, in our human weakness, tend to attach too much value to them; it is not merely the souls that were baptised and the numbers of people who came to church on Sunday to hear the Word – all that is indeed important; it is not merely all the people whom we taught in schools to read and write, or the houses that we built, the gardens, the water-furrows, the trees that we planted in the wilderness – those are all important, those too, but there is something more. That little trunk with Goethe and Schiller and Shakespeare that I brought along, the whole way on the ship and the ox-wagon, that is also important. And my old viola – that I could sit by candlelight in the wilderness at night when the natives had wrapped themselves in their skins and lay sleeping in their huts, and the jackals and the wild dogs were howling along the ridges, and that I could play Mozart . . . that is also important, even if one cannot measure its value. I felt that I was sending that music out into the land; it spread, like the rings on a pond, out into the silence and the loneliness just like the Word of God that I had come to disseminate. We came to light lamps, tiny lamps in an immense darkness.'

He sat there very erect, almost defiant, with his hands on his knees: a small man in a worn black suit, the jacket of which hung slightly too loosely across his shoulders: his eyes gleamed, his spectacles flashed.

Scheffler listened to his father with a smile, but it was a smile of love and understanding. 'The only problem is that the country did not prove to be particularly receptive to Mozart,' he remarked drily.

'What does that matter? The country is still developing, and it must decide for itself what it can use, what it needs – it takes or it rejects, and all we can do is contribute what we can. It does not matter.' Impatiently he looked about the room as if he were completely bewildered by all the thoughts that had come to him, as if he wanted to leap up and rush out and carry on with the great task that awaited him beyond the family circle. Then he looked at Versluis once again with the same disconcerting sharpness. 'I have also dug ditches and built stone walls myself,' he informed him soberly, as a matter of fact, not as an achievement to be flaunted. 'I planed planks to make doors and door frames, and coffins too. My father was a carpenter, as I have said.' He spread out his hands in front of him and looked at them, powerful workman's hands. 'One does what one can,' he said. 'The Lord makes use of you wherever he needs you.'

His daughter-in-law had withdrawn with the baby; his wife's head nodded forward where she had dozed off. His daughter had begun to set the table with a deftness and agility that spoke of much practice while she supported herself from chair to chair to maintain her balance.

'You belong to the Reformed Church?' the old missionary suddenly asked Versluis. It was an entirely natural question, not at all obtrusive, but it caught him unawares, unsure of the way in which he ought to formulate a reply and of how it would be received.

'Mr Versluis is a freethinker, Father,' Scheffler said when Versluis did not reply immediately.

'Do you believe in God?'

The direction that the conversation had taken without any warning made Versluis feel uncomfortable, as had happened a number of times with the Schefflers, but there was no avoiding it. The old man looked at him enquiringly, and his daughter had stopped at the table, leaning on the back of a chair. She looked expectantly at them in the lamplight, her attention distracted from her work.

'No,' he said at last.

'Is there nothing as far as you are concerned?'

'No.'

The old man considered the answer in silence without passing any judgement, and shook his head, but in incomprehension rather than disapproval.

'It's something that my son will be able to understand better than I can,' he said. 'He returned from Germany a few years ago, and in Germany this sort of view of life is common now, I believe. It was

189

different in my day.' He pondered this for a moment, but then he shook his head once more and, having lost interest, moved away from the subject. 'Naturally I view life from a different perspective; it is possible that we learnt an outdated theology, but I cannot see how anyone can live without some kind of framework into which it all fits, all the joys and all the disappointments, everything that seems in our eyes to be meaningless or futile.'

His son leant forward in the lamplight as if the conversation had only just begun to interest him. 'But if you believe in nothing, Father, then emptiness itself may provide a framework for your life. Like yourself sitting playing your viola in the candlelight, with nothing but the dark and the wilderness around you and the universe stretching away at the other end.'

'But at the other end of that space, at the other end of the wilderness, there is God,' his father said. Scheffler appeared to want to continue the discussion, and he began to reply eagerly, but the old man's interest had waned: his eyes moved impatiently about the room and his fingers felt in his waistcoat pocket for his old-fashioned pocket watch. 'Adèle,' he called, 'when are we eating?'

His daughter had come nearer. Her one hand remained on the back of a chair and she had the cloth with which she had been wiping the plates in the other, as if she also wanted to join their discussion, but when he spoke her attention was fixed entirely on him. 'In five minutes, Father, as soon as Mathilde comes back.' He groaned and closed his watch, and then he rose and went from the room without saying a word. Only as he was passing his wife did he put his hand on her shoulder for a moment, and she looked up and smiled at him; slightly dazed from her sleep, but fully aware of who had touched her in passing.

'Should we put out some beer, August?' Miss Scheffler asked. 'Or do you want to open some wine tonight? You still have a bottle that Mr Fichardt sent you at Christmas.'

'I'm coming,' her brother said pensively; 'I'm coming. I'll see to it,' but it was not clear that he was wholly aware of what he was saying. 'It's a very isolated life that one lives at Bethany,' he said to Versluis. 'There are a few missionaries and their families, all occupied by their own work and duties, and the natives – it is very seldom that my father gets the opportunity to speak to anyone outside his own little world, especially not someone like yourself with whom he can speak German.' This was however not intended as an apology for Scheffler's father, Versluis realised, but rather as an explanation of his disquisitions and

190

monologues, a request to show patience with and understanding for the old man's idiosyncrasies.

'Each of us has to endure his own isolation,' Miss Scheffler said from where she had remained standing with the cloth in her hand, the lamplight behind her. 'But Mr Versluis has presumably come to realise that himself by now.'

'But Father to a far greater extent than us, I think, Adèle. At least we live here in the city, not in total isolation.'

'Yes, but Father has his faith; his loneliness makes sense to him, and so he is no longer lonely.'

'And what about us, Adèle?' her brother asked. Then his wife opened the door and came inside and looked questioningly from one to the other. 'I'll go and open the wine,' he said.

Mrs Scheffler proceeded to the table; the servants brought in bowls of food; Miss Scheffler went across to her mother and bent over her, touched her hands lightly, and said something to her, and the old woman held her by the hand and looked up into her face while she listened. There was something about the collective interaction of these people Versluis thought as he sat watching them, to one side and beyond the circle of lamplight, that to him seemed strange and which he could not describe: a mutual courtesy that bordered on formality; a constant consciousness of and disposition towards one another; a sense of caring and consideration. He did not understand it, nor did he understand them.

'Mr Versluis,' young Mrs Scheffler said beside him, 'will you come and sit down?'

The food was on the table: Scheffler was occupied with the cork-screw, his mother was preparing to take her seat at the table, and a chair was drawn out for Versluis. Miss Scheffler looked up at him with a welcoming smile, without a trace of self-consciousness about the clumsiness of her movements in that relaxed family circle, as if it were entirely natural to be moving about the room in that hobbling, lame way, bobbing from chair to chair. That was why the furniture was scattered so widely throughout the room, Versluis realised as he occupied the place indicated to him at the clergyman's right hand, so that she always had something to hold on to as she moved around awkwardly but rapidly without her sticks.

The old missionary had rejoined them: they all sat down and bowed their heads so that he could say grace for them, and they joined hands in a circle around the table for the prayer. Caught up, whether he liked it or not, in the intimacy of that gathering, holding the priest's hand

191

on one side and the elderly Mrs Scheffler's on the other, Versluis gazed at the brilliance of the tablecloth in the lamplight – with the breadboard and the water jug, the salt and pepper, oil and vinegar all laid out precisely upon it. The table spoke of neatness, sobriety and constant vigilance against indulgence and prodigality: he felt if he were to take only a little too much food, while Scheffler was carving the meat and his wife was removing the lids of the dishes, there would be too little for the others, so exactly had the portions been calculated; but in spite of this the clergyman and his wife insisted that he should take some more and they chose the choicest bits for the two elderly people without concerning themselves about what might be left for them. The wine was French and better than he would have expected in that house: even the women acceded to half a glass being poured for each of them, so that a flush suffused their cheeks and old Mrs Scheffler suddenly grew lively and talkative beside him.

'Do you know Königsberg?' she enquired unexpectedly when Versluis turned to her to pass the bread. Her voice was so soft, almost as if she had no breath left with which to speak, that Versluis had to stoop to hear what she was saying. He could see her gleaming hair combed down and parted exactly in the centre under the frayed bonnet, and her fine, golden earrings. 'Königsberg on the Pregel? That is where I come from.'

'And not once been back again,' said her husband from across the table, 'neither my wife nor I. Thirty-five years we've been in this country, and one day we'll be buried here no doubt.' Thoroughly, mechanically he chewed his meat and wasted no unnecessary emotion over this fact. His wife smiled, however, as if she were caught up in pleasant memories, and merely toyed with the food on her plate.

'You could always go over for a visit again, Father,' Scheffler said, but the idea did not interest the old man.

'What for? It only costs money, and in any case, what do we want to go there for? The people we once knew are dead, there are no longer any points of contact. Our children are here, our friends and colleagues are here, our house and all our earthly possessions. Everything that we have built up together, is in this country.' He methodically cut the food up into fine pieces, conveyed it to his mouth, and chewed. 'I have my music, I have my Mozart, even in Bethany. I have my books, I can read my theological works and collections of sermons, and my poetry. That which is important we brought along and preserved with us.'

Beside him his daughter sat listening to him. Her eyes gleamed in the light, and the soft glow of the lamp – together with the hair that she had not tied back, so that it kept falling across her face – tempered the severity of her features and the lines around her eyes and mouth so that she looked quite young, with a quality that in the soft delicacy of the lamplight was almost beautiful.

'You could at least go to the coast once in a while, Father,' she interjected.

'To the coast? What would we want to do at the coast, we who have had nothing to do with the sea except on the journey out here? Our children want us to retire to Port Elizabeth, Mr Versluis, and we have indeed spoken about it, for the sake of my wife's health, but we do not wish to spend our old age among strangers. We belong in Bethany, and our graves ought to be there, beside those of our children who are buried there.'

His daughter smiled and looked at Versluis across the table, as if she had expected just this answer, and had deliberately provoked it in order to prove something to him. 'We are fond of our desolate tracts of ground, Mr Versluis,' she said softly.

'Do you find that strange, sir?' her father enquired. 'But, yes, it probably is. It is a barren and inhospitable country – lots of stone, lots of sand, lots of dust, nothing to soothe the eye or win the heart.'

'The Netherlands is only a tiny, flat country, and yet there are people who love the Netherlands very dearly.'

'And aren't you one of them?'

'I grew up in the Netherlands; in the circumstances it is the country to which one is accustomed and the one by which one judges other countries.'

'It's like the plants,' Pastor Scheffler said beside him; 'all the succulents and the arid plants that persevere here and survive the drought and the frost.' He stared thoughtfully at the gleaming tablecloth. Opposite him his wife ate in silence, with an eye on the guests' plates, and leant over to her mother-in-law to ask if there was anything she needed.

The Reverend Scheffler frowned and then put down his knife and fork. 'What is all this about?' he asked peevishly. 'What are you going on about again, August?'

'About us, Father,' came the reply from his daughter, however, 'about our love for this land.'

He considered the explanation in silence for a while. 'Love . . .' he repeated at last. 'I don't know, perhaps I would be inclined to agree with Mr Versluis rather, that it's a matter of habit – at least as far as your mother and I are concerned. You were born here, you have a 'certain claim to the land, you have different feelings towards it, no doubt.'

'And what about you and Mother?' his son asked. 'Have the last thirty-five years given you no claim to the land?'

'Perhaps, but in so far as we belong to some earthly thing, it has always been to the country from which we come; we will never be able to loosen our bonds with it, no matter how much we have grown away from it through all the years. To us the unification of Germany and the establishment of the Empire and the Kaiser's birthday will bear a totally different significance from what it does to you, it will always mean something more to us. But to you – yes, it is possible for you to devote yourselves entirely to this country and to belong to it.'

'We who have been sitting here speaking German all these years,' Miss Scheffler remarked ironically.

'But Adèle, how could we possibly not want to speak our own language?' her sister-in-law cried out in horror. This was the first time that she had involved herself in the conversation in this way, and it was obvious that only her dismay at the remark had led to such an intervention.

'And what would you want us to speak, Adèle?' her brother asked with a smile.

'Not German or Dutch or English, not a foreign language, but one which belongs to this country, like those of the black people or the farmers. But don't worry, Mathilde,' she added quickly, 'I was only joking.' The young Mrs Scheffler, however, merely shook her head.

'At Bethany we celebrated the Kaiser's birthday too,' the old woman added suddenly. 'There was a special service in the church, and we raised the flag; and in the evening all the mission families came across to our house and we made music and sang. And your father made a speech. It was fine,' she said, and reflected somewhat melancholically on the gathering. 'All the old German songs. And some of the children recited.' She had finished eating, and had left half of her food untouched on her plate: a tiny woman in black who had aged prematurely and was coming to the end of her life, recollecting in her thin, virtually inaudible voice one of the highlights of her existence.

'It is good to be able to speak German in Africa and to hear German spoken in homes,' her daughter-in-law continued in the same indignant tone. 'We are going to speak German to Friederike when she gets older.' It was apparently a matter about which she had strong feelings, even though she spoke in a subdued way and did not look up from the table.

194

'My wife was born in Germany,' Scheffler said to Versluis, 'and she also went to school there. German culture is something much closer to her than it might be to any one of us.'

There was a moment's silence, as if the conversation was on the point of changing and being continued with greater vigour along lines about which there were diverging opinions. Young Mrs Scheffler, however, was reluctant to express any further judgement, and in that moment of hesitation the danger of any disagreement or conflict passed.

'Thank you, Mathilde,' her father-in-law then said, contented. 'We have eaten well.'

'August?' she asked, holding the dishing-up spoon, and it struck her husband that he had forgotten about the food which had grown cold in front of him. 'No thank you, no more,' he said, and hurriedly began to finish his food.

'We had another German poetry afternoon at the school,' Miss Scheffler proffered in order to help edge the conversation back along a more general tack. 'Mrs Baumann arranged it for us. Mr Versluis read us some Hölderlin, Father.'

'Are you fond of poetry, Mr Versluis?' asked the old Reverend Scheffler.

'I often read it, although I must confess that I am unaccustomed to performing in public.'

'Poetry and music have always been a great source of comfort and encouragement in all the tribulations of my life as a missionary.' He sat there with his hands clasped before him on the table. He had finished eating and had pushed the plate aside: he looked old and tired, his former buoyancy, curiosity, and provocativeness suddenly gone. He had spent thirty-five years in that country, he had stacked walls and dug foundations, and at night he had played music or read from the books that had accompanied him from Germany. The silence of the land had become a part of his existence, woven out of its threads. And now, as he sat at the table, at the end of his life, only that silence, that loneliness, remained. It showed for only a moment as they sat in silence around the gleaming white tablecloth, in an instant of unguarded revelation to which he had abandoned himself, and then Mrs Scheffler began to collect the plates and her father-in-law looked up again with something of the old challenge in his eyes.

'Did you also go to the reading, Adèle?' he asked.

'Mrs Hirsch sent the carriage for me, she fetched me and brought me back – she invited Mathilde too, but it was when Friederike was so ill, so she didn't want to go.'

'And did you enjoy it?' He was not listening to her reply, having withdrawn into some distant world of his own, but he asked the questions lovingly and attentively. His wife had dropped off again and nodded beside Versluis at the table.

'I had expected more, of course I was disappointed. Or perhaps I had expected too much, and so I was punished for my presumption.'

'I have to admit that my choice of poems was not very exciting,' Versluis said.

'Oh, no,' she replied quickly, 'that was not what I meant, Hölderlin was the only thing that I found worthwhile. Perhaps I have simply read too much poetry and have become fastidious, but I am really unable to appreciate *Du bist wie eine Blume* or *Die Glocke* any longer.'

'The other women appreciated them,' her brother remarked neutrally.

'Yes,' she agreed, 'the other women appreciated them.'

Mrs Scheffler had rung the bell to summon the servant and had stood up. 'We ought to have poetry readings here at home,' said Miss Scheffler. 'We never do any longer.'

The servant could not understand Mrs Scheffler's Dutch with its heavy German accent. For an instant the young woman's voice sounded sharp and impatient, and her husband looked up in displeasure, his attention distracted. 'Yes,' he then said, 'but there is never enough time any more. There are sermons to be written or meetings or gatherings to be attended, house calls. . . . And Friederike has been ill.'

'One of these days it will be autumn, and then we'll have long evenings again; then we must have poetry readings. Perhaps Mr Versluis will come and read to us. Mr Versluis. . . .' She looked at him across the table, still with those sparkling eyes and the slight flush across her cheeks, softened by a moment of abandonment and the lustre of the lamplight. 'And if our winter evenings are not too severe for you, perhaps you will come then.'

'Thank you very much,' Versluis began politely, and suddenly broke off. *If I am still here then*, he had wanted to say, but he suppressed the words in time: in the end nothing was arranged, he was not committed to anything. 'I still cannot imagine how I will find your winters.'

'Oh, they are severe,' Scheffler said thoughtfully as he rose from the table. 'Fine, sunny winters, but bitterly cold. Mathilde, are we having coffee?'

196

'Severe, but fine,' said Mrs Scheffler.

'Adèle,' her sister-in-law said. 'Will you put out the cups? I just want to look into the kitchen quickly.' Miss Scheffler leapt up immediately, roused from her reverie, and began to move about the table with her usual laborious dexterity, one hand clutching the back rests of the chairs. Versluis was left alone at the table with the slumbering old woman and the missionary, who seemed to feel himself obliged to pay some attention to the guest.

'Did you come to South Africa for your health, Mr Versluis?' he asked.

Versluis recoiled a little from the topic that had been so tactlessly broached. 'Yes,' he admitted, however, when he could no longer withhold an answer.

'We get a great many foreigners nowadays coming to seek a cure here amongst us – or a miracle, perhaps. Do you find that you have benefitted from the change?'

The blue eyes were sharp again, as probing as those of Krause or Kellner, although without the impersonality of their appraisal. In the end, what did it matter? Versluis thought tiredly. 'I am unfortunately still somewhat weak,' he said.

'Our climate frequently does work miracles. And one can also work miracles with the judicious use of medication.'

'Coffee, Father?' his daughter asked. 'Mr Versluis?'

'Aconite, and bryonia, or drosera – these are old, tried remedies that I have always recommended myself, and they have brought relief to a great many people.'

'Father, do you feel like some music tonight?' asked Scheffler, who had again joined them. 'Mr Versluis, would it bore you, or be too tiring? You must be honest.' He had gone to fetch a violin-case which he placed in front of him on the table while he waited for the replies to his questions.

'I would love to listen to your playing,' said Versluis. 'Provided you will excuse me if I do not stay very late.'

'We won't be staying up very late ourselves,' Scheffler said laughing. 'For years my father has grown accustomed to going to bed early and getting up at five.'

'August,' his sister called, 'will you be having your coffee here, or at the table?'

'The early morning air is particularly good for the respiratory system,' the old man informed Versluis as they rose from the table. 'And I myself believe that the dew also contains a healing power. I get up early and I go to bed early, and it has never done me any harm, I have lived for nearly sixty years without any serious illness, my eyes are still good. . . .' He stood stiffly before them, a proud little man in a threadbare suit, the tufts of his hair standing up wildly about his skull. 'Hard work and a simple life, those are the best ways to stay healthy.'

'And if you have ever been ill during the course of your life I do not believe that you gave yourself enough time to realise it, Father,' his daughter said with a smile as she stood waiting for them behind the coffee table.

'Yes indeed,' he agreed seriously, 'there really was no time to fall ill, there was always much too much work. Even now, too much to do and too little time, and too few people.' He looked impatiently around the room, although all that he saw in the lamplight was a shadowy chamber and the cleared table at which his wife had dozed off. 'August,' he said, 'you people want me to play, you want to make music; I must fetch my viola.'

'I have brought it for you, Father, it's there in the corner next to the sideboard.'

'First come and have your coffee, Father,' said his daughter, but he did not hear her. 'Mother?' she enquired. 'A cup of coffee?'

'She's asleep,' the old man said, lowering his voice. 'Let her sleep, she's lain awake for many nights. I'll take her to bed in a while.' He tiptoed carefully past the table, across the creaking wooden floors uncovered by any carpet.

'We could play just one duo,' Scheffler said, removing his own violin from its case.

'Papa would really like to play,' his sister said softly to Scheffler, 'otherwise he wouldn't have brought his viola along. We'll be late again tonight, even if he talks about going to bed early.' Occupied with the adjustment of the tuning-pegs her brother did not hear her. With her head lifted Miss Scheffler listened to him playing the first uncertain chords, and then remembered her obligations. 'Mr Versluis,' she said, and passed him a cup of coffee.

While the two men were preoccupied with their instruments, Versluis seated himself in an armchair beside Miss Scheffler.

'Friederike is asleep,' her sister-in-law informed Adèle in satisfaction as she sat down with them, and the two women smiled at each other. 'August,' she then added with concern, 'your coffee will get cold,' and he swallowed it hurriedly and returned to his violin.

The coffee was not strong enough and the cups were tiny, but the coffee beans had been freshly roasted and ground, and it was welcome after the coffee that Versluis had learnt to suffer at Mrs Van der Vliet's. He leant back and looked at the room with its framed engravings, its arrangements of dry grass, its family portraits on the side tables, at the men tuning their instruments and the sleeping old woman. Young Mrs Scheffler sat down at the end of the settee on which her sister-in-law was reclining, and with lowered voices the two women discussed domestic matters while they drank their coffee. This was how other people lived, he thought to himself – they sat together in the lamplight drinking coffee, they made music together, talked together, and they did not need many words because they shared so much knowledge and they were each familiar with such a large communal field of reference. Later, in the dark, moribund town in which he bid Mrs Van der Vliet goodnight and withdrew into his room, in the deep night where the nocturnal creatures called and the dogs barked at each other, he would recall that other people were living their lives, glancing at the clock, listening for a moment to see if they heard a baby crying, before turning smilingly back to their companions. In bed he would adjust the wick of the lamp that had been brought in by the servant, pick up his book, and continue reading.

Mrs Scheffler took her sister-in-law's empty cup. With his viola and bow in his hand the Reverend Scheffler stood for a moment beside his wife's chair and bent over her to listen to her breathing. The two women on the settee next to Versluis were so close that he could have touched them, and in that modest room a couple of paces would have carried him to the other people, enabling him to touch a hand·or a shoulder. Yet they were infinitely far from him and forever unreachable in their fellowship, wrapped up in the swathes of their own little pursuits, diverted in the course of a life of their own in which he had no share and which he was able only to observe from the desolation that extended out from its boundaries, as if he were looking at the room and its people through a window and they were separated from him by the cold transparency of glass.

Scheffler looked up from his violin. He had finished tuning it and appeared to have found the sound satisfactory; he looked up and smiled across the room at Versluis, as if he wanted to convey his satisfaction to him, knowing that it would be understood and shared. Mrs Scheffler lifted the lid of the coffee pot to see how much was left. 'Another cup, Mr Versluis?' she asked rather hesitantly, but nobody wanted more, and it was finally her husband who got the last half a cup.

'Do you like Mozart, Mr Versluis?' he asked as he stood drinking it. 'We usually play Mozart; there are only a few pieces that we know well enough to perform, and we never get a chance to learn anything new. Father, Mozart again tonight? Which one would you like?'

'Mozart in Bloemfontein,' Miss Scheffler said thoughtfully. 'Do you find that strange, Mr Versluis?'

'In this country I am surprised every day, Miss Scheffler.'

'Pleasantly or unpleasantly? I mean, by the presence of things that you don't expect to find here, or from a lack of things that you do expect?'

'Both, actually.'

She laughed. 'We are still such an outlandish, half-hearted sort of a country, not so? We have still not decided what we want to be or where we want to go. We still cling to what we have and are too afraid to abandon it, even when it has been redundant for ages.'

He had already grown accustomed to these people Versluis thought; the process had taken a very short time. Her familiarity, her flighty thoughts, her unexpected impulses no longer seemed strange to him and he had begun to learn how to conduct a conversation with her. 'Is Mozart one of the things that you would like to abandon?' he now asked.

She looked at her father and brother, both standing bowed over the score, and considered the question. Her sister-in-law had removed the coffee cups and had gone to sit nearer the lamp with a basket of darning. The two of them were alone. 'No,' she said slowly, 'not Mozart, not Goethe, not Hölderlin, they mean too much to me, the little that I know of them. And yet, Mozart at the end of the last century in Vienna, and we eighty, ninety years later in a far corner of the world, in this new land – what bridge is there, what connection can there be between the two worlds that would make the music meaningful for us?'

'Is a great work of art not valid for all time and in all places?'

'Yes, certainly; but finally it is also a product of a particular time and place.' She shook her head, dissatisfied with the way in which she was expressing her ideas. 'I should like, from this place, from my own environment and my own time, to be able to produce something for the whole world and for all time,' she announced with some passion, but then she reconsidered at once. 'Oh well, what could I do? But I'd like to see it done. I should like to see this silence given a voice.'

The two men had begun to shift their chairs into the correct position: Scheffler propped his score up against a framed portrait on the little table. 'August, be careful with Aunt Sieglinde!' his wife cautioned.

Miss Scheffler turned away from Versluis and their brief, intimate discussion. 'I would like to help Mathilde with her darning,' she remarked, 'but according to her I don't do it neatly enough. And she's actually completely right. I have no domestic skills.'

The two performers shifted their chairs once again, adjusted the tuning-pegs slightly, and shifted the scores to catch the light from the lamp on the dining-table behind them: they were ready, and Miss Scheffler's last words were hurriedly whispered. In the room there was a feeling of tension and expectation about the music that was about to begin, and it was the focus of everyone's attention, even of the young Mrs Scheffler with the darning on her lap. They raised the bows to the strings; they looked at each other, and they began.

The instruments, violin and viola, were indeed not in a particularly good condition, and it went without saying that it was the playing of amateurs without any technical proficiency or the necessary fluency of performance. The duet that he knew from the concert halls of Europe came to Versluis in that living room in the interior of Africa, performed by an aged missionary and his son, as something strangely transformed, like a landscape seen through panes of slightly irregular glass or an image slightly distorted by its reflection in an antique mirror. A mixture of doubt and recognition was evoked in its perception, so that there was a tenuous moment of uncertainty in which one asked oneself, is it or is it not?

The initial shock of uncertainty passed, however, and the shape of the melody began to emerge recognisably – Versluis relaxed. It was not as bad as he had begun to fear for a while: he would be able to stay without feeling compelled to do so out of politeness. He would be able to listen and even enjoy the performance, in spite of all its limitations, after the long period in which he had not been able to listen to music. Beside him Miss Scheffler sat bent forward a little, listening as if she were eager to reach out to the music lest she miss a single chord, her elbow resting on the back of the settee, her hand raised to shade her face from the glare of the lamp. But then her mother moved restlessly and woke up, and her attention returned at once to the room and she wanted to leap up, but her sister-in-law was quicker and went over to the old woman and led her by the hand to where they were sitting. She seated her in a chair, spoke softly to her, placed a cushion behind her back and a shawl around her shoulders. Only when the old woman had settled did Miss Scheffler herself relax, lifting her hand once more against the glare of the lamp, and shift her attention back to the music. Still groggy and half-asleep the old woman sat with them, smiling and nodding, comforted by the playing and the presence of her children. The two players, however, had hardly looked up from the score, and they did not even notice when Mrs Scheffler cried out softly as she bent to pick up her darning, and moved quickly to the window.

'What's the matter, Mathilde?' her sister-in-law asked, looking around.

She was standing with her hand pressed against the windowpane, looking out into the dark. 'There was someone on the stoep,' she said. 'I saw a face at the window, but now there is nobody.'

'It's someone who heard the music and wanted to see who was playing. Or perhaps visitors who did not want to disturb us.' But she was not interested, her concentration broken.

'Perhaps it was someone who came to call August. Old Mr Hecker is ill.'

'If it had been an emergency they would have knocked.' She turned away with some impatience, but her sister-in-law remained standing for a while in front of the window, where the panes mirrored the illuminated room against the darkness. She was not reassured, even when she sat down and took up her darning once again.

The muttered discussion between the two women had also distracted Versluis and he found it difficult to attend to the music again. Only the two performers remained oblivious of what was going on around them and carried on, completely caught up in their playing, frowning and preoccupied, for nothing could be taken for granted as both the music and the demands of playing together required their sustained effort and concentration. But then the performance came to an abrupt end, and it took a moment for Versluis to recover from his surprise and realise that it was the first movement that had been brought to such an unpractised and violent conclusion.

For a few minutes there was silence. Young Mrs Scheffler looked up and listened, but there was only the fluttering of moths, the creaking of chairs, the barking of dogs far away in the dark, and although she had left the door which led to the passage ajar, the house itself was also silent. Miss Scheffler did not stir as she reclined on the settee, as if a single word, a movement on her part, might have disturbed or broken something that had been laboriously built up, and could be maintained only with great care. The two men leant across to each other, exchanged a few words, and took up their instruments again for the second movement. Something may still happen Versluis thought, still disturbed by the interruptions that had accompanied the first movement and the abrupt manner in which it had been closed. This had apparently passed Miss Scheffler by, but presumably this was the only form of her acquaintance with the composition – as a piece of music poorly performed in rooms where people moved about and whispered to one another, and so this simply constituted both her notion of the duet and how Mozart ought to sound. This realisation disconcerted him, as if it were only at that moment, in that fleeting moment of insight, that he was able to measure the real distance between this country and the world from which he came – so that he became fully aware of the boundaries that separated him from these people, the infinite differences in their respective worlds of experience, values and associations.

Scheffler looked at his father, and they began to play again. Versluis realised he felt tired, as he so often felt of late; the weariness came so easily and so quickly. After this movement he would leave he thought, and looked at the two men, their brows furrowed in concentration as they were again absorbed by the music; at Miss Scheffler leaning forward on the settee beside him; at her sister occupied with her darning; at the slumbering old woman: that small family bound by mutual ties of familiarity and love which also served to exclude him, the visitor from another world, whom they had benevolently invited in on that particular evening.

He put his hand over his eyes. The playing was not good – it was obviously not good – yet the piece was being lovingly performed, and furthermore he marked, now that he was able to listen to it without distraction, it was being played with a degree of insight and under-standing. The two amateurs with their lack of training and practice, with instruments that were no longer in particularly good condition; the two clergymen there in the interior of Africa, who were bowed with such intensity over the score in search of the secret of the music that they were trying to interpret, had nonetheless grasped something of it, no matter how insecure and incomplete; and gradually in the lamplight of that room there transpired something which transcended their technical limitations. Briefly, while the playing continued, any consciousness of alienation was suspended. Nor was there any feeling of strangeness: the perfect totality of the music enveloped them as they listened to it and bound them together, the circle completed. Moved by this unexpected experience, Versluis leant back and shut his eyes. Time and space had ceased to exist; the deserted streets of the town; the expansive loneliness of the veld in the starlight; the house waiting with its furniture enshrouded in dust covers: all of these were obliterated in the darkness beyond the circle of lamplight and the music that embraced them, both him and the others together.

Mrs Van der Vliet said not a word about his sudden treachery, she accepted his apologies with a forgiving smile and devoted her attention to the matter that was of palpable importance to her, namely the cause of the Schefflers' unannounced visit to Bloemfontein. In silence she considered why it should have been necessary for Mrs Scheffler to consult a physician, and in the end she decided that it was worth the effort to try to obtain further information from Mrs Krause. Thus, after the breakfast table had been cleared and the necessary instructions for the morning had been given, she took to the streets wearing a little hat decorated with porcupine quills and a shawl edged in jet. She was trailed at a distance by her husband bearing a large black umbrella, and a basket of figs which was to serve as a pretext for the visit. Such information as she obtained from the doctor's wife was not, however, of the sort that she felt free to disclose to others, and so she merely shook her head gravely during lunch. 'They are going back to Bethany early tomorrow morning,' she said. 'Indeed, I doubt whether we'll be seeing old Mrs Scheffler back in Bloemfontein again.'

That afternoon some of her Dutch friends came to visit, bubbling with excitement around the coffee table about all the news that needed to be shared and complaints about market prices, shops and servants. Versluis sat reading on the verandah behind the creepers, thankful to be left in peace that afternoon. He had not realised that he had missed hearing music that much, nor had he known how much its relative availability had meant to him. Things that he had continued to take for granted had become rare, he thought, lowering the book from time to time to stare out from behind the screen of climbers on which the dusty leaves were already being touched by the first marks of colour. An echo of the previous night's playing continued to occupy his memory and filled the day's expanse; it floated more and more thinly out across the garden where Van der Vliet was shuffling pensively past the beds; over the willows along the spruit and the roofs and chimneys of Bloemfontein, becoming confused with the noises of the town, the cocks crowing and dogs barking; and it filled the dismal, hazy, blowy day with joy and hope. He took up his book again to continue reading. Sometimes there were moments of repose he thought; there always had been; somewhere there was rest.

He had left soon after the end of the duet, and they had not spoken much as he said farewell: he had allowed Scheffler to accompany him only as far as the garden gate and had insisted on continuing on his way alone. It was close enough, and besides the moon had already come up – nor had Scheffler protested. 'I have to ride out to Brandkop on Friday,' he had said suddenly, with the gate between them, 'I have to visit some of the black people there. If you would like to come along – it's not far, it won't be tiring for you, and I'd appreciate the company.'

With the music still in his ears, his eyes blinded by the shimmer of dirt roads and corrugated iron roofs in the moonlight, Versluis had agreed, without considering what he was doing, and only later did he have doubts. He did not wish to be joggled over bad roads, on a call to farm workers who did not interest him in the slightest, and his reluctance was confirmed on Friday afternoon when Scheffler drew up in front of the door with a cart and horse, neither of which was any longer in its prime. But it was too late to withdraw: Versluis was ready on the front stoep, with the coat and scarf which at Mrs Van der Vliet's insistence was draped over one arm, while she too had come out to greet the clergyman, followed by a servant with a basket of food and a travelling-rug. Scheffler had barely had the chance to greet Versluis with a quick wave of his hand before she had collared him and was enquiring about his parents and family, her inquisitive questions punctuated with incidental, submerged allusions to her mother's health. The clergyman tried his best to answer while he attended to the horse, issued instructions to the servant about the loading of the basket, and helped Versluis in. He became entangled in his replies, dropped first his hat and then his whip, and disentangled himself with palpable relief from the onslaught as soon as he saw an opportunity to get away. They should not stay out too late, Mrs Van der Vliet enjoined him as he climbed in next to Versluis: Mr Versluis should be careful of the night air, as she was always telling him, and especially of dewfall – dew was a deadly thing, she impressed upon them. She had packed coffee for them, and rolls, and there were dried peaches wrapped in a napkin. Scheffler nodded and thanked her and waved his whip in a departing gesture, and at last they were free to leave, while Mrs Van der Vliet remained in front of the house staring after them, her hands folded across her front.

'Mathilde packed some food for us for the journey,' Scheffler said with a laugh. 'But of course one couldn't possibly tell Mrs Van der Vliet that, she would take it as a personal insult.'

He was in a cheerful mood at the prospect of the outing that lay ahead, oblivious of the creaky old cart or the tardy horse: they drove across the square in front of the Presidency and up against the hill past the girls' school and the Roman Catholic convent, and soon they had left the town behind, past the dam where the shadows of the willows were already beginning to lengthen in the afternoon sun and the grooms were busy brushing down the horses, and out on to the veld. The chimneys and treetops and the languid sounds of the town fell away beyond the ridge, and Scheffler thrust his hat to the back of his head and made encouraging noises to the horse, which showed few signs of any response.

'It's always like a holiday for me to be able get away from the city a little,' he said by way of explanation, and then he was forced to laugh at his own words. 'Yes, I know, Bloemfontein probably doesn't seem much like a city to you with its cows and chickens and fruit trees, but I find even that handful of houses becomes claustrophobic after a while. I am not used to seeing such constant reminders of civilisation about me.'

Versluis felt compelled to smile in his corner of the vehicle at the spontaneity of these remarks as he leant against the cushion that had been placed there at Mrs Van der Vliet's insistence. 'In that case your years in Europe must have been very hard for you,' he remarked.

Scheffler reflected. 'The years in Europe were temporary, I was there with a firm goal before me; and it was also an exciting time for me, full of new experiences and discoveries. But still. . . .' For a moment he was silent; he looked away; he lowered the whip. 'Yes,' he said, 'the grey streets and the rows of houses, and then in winter the sky that was so low and the darkness that seemed as if it would never end. And there is nowhere in Europe where you can get away, you can never really breathe, even the countryside is densely inhabited, built-up, hemmed-in. Not like here.'

He gestured with the whip towards the drab veld around them where the late afternoon sun had begun to cast a lustre over the grass. In front of them, to the west, lay the low hill towards which they driving, while further along towards the horizon more hills receded in the hazy light, the undulations of the landscape hardly discernible across that immense distance.

'It's not far,' Scheffler said. 'About three or four miles, no more. You are not tired?'

'Not yet,' it was Versluis's first unthinking impulse to say, but he suppressed this reply. 'No,' he said, 'I am not tired.'

'This is actually not my work; we have a black missionary's assistant, but I like going out to one of the farms now and then when I have the chance. I am used to this kind of work, I grew up among these people, not among whites. And in any case it serves as a good excuse to get away from the town for an hour or two, I have to admit that. I'm afraid my motives are not entirely pure.'

'Can one's motives ever be entirely pure?' Versluis asked.

'Probably not, since human beings are imperfect creatures. And that's precisely what makes them interesting, don't you think – that's what makes life interesting.' He turned to Versluis, his face lit up in another wave of enthusiasm. 'As a priest I should probably not be saying this, but I can say it to you without shocking you – their traps and divisions, the whole mixture of reticence and uncertainty, their half-heartedness, the give and take and deliberation, these are the things that make human beings interesting, aren't they?'

'Unfortunately I do not have as wide a knowledge of human beings as you do, Pastor. I fear that I shall have to remain in your debt regarding the answer to your question.'

'I believe that when you say such things you are mocking me. You are older than I am, and you must have had quite a lot of experience of people during your life.'

'But you are after all a priest and you have had the opportunity of getting to know people more intimately.'

'Perhaps, but I am not a particularly good priest, alas.' He looked at the horse and the white road ahead of them, at the low mountain against the sky. 'Even my calling is a half-hearted affair, full of uncertainty and doubt, even something that ought to have been a matter of conviction and commitment. I wanted to be a missionary like my father, that is the example that I know, the work that I know, the people that I love; but I was told that I could use my talents to a better purpose, that I should regard the education that I possess as an sign – my own father helped to convince me that I should rather become a priest, almost as if he regarded his own position as inferior.' He gave Versluis a quick sidelong glance, as if he wished to ascertain whether his companion understood what he was trying to say, and then he looked back at the horse and the white road in front of them. 'I am not a very good priest,' he reiterated quickly. It was a confession: the words tumbled out and he fell over them in his haste. 'I don't manage at all well with the parish work that I have to do – I'm probably not sufficiently interested in it, or I don't try hard enough. I have no patience with the tea gatherings and choir practices and church fêtes, I did not want to be ordained for these things. Do I shock you?' he asked. 'Do you think it improper for a priest to be talking about his calling in this way?'

'I make no demands of priests,' Versluis said when Scheffler waited for an answer; 'I expect nothing from them. I am not shocked.'

'I don't even preach very well, and that's really the most important thing, spreading the Word of God. There are so many things that I should like to say, so much that I should like to share and discuss with others, but preferably in a discussion such as this one where we're together; not solemnly from the pulpit, with a few dutiful verses from the Bible and a couple of moral precepts thrown in. When I give a sermon people complain that my ideas are too elevated and that they can't follow me; they sit there in the pews and I can sense their uncomprehension, or I can see their heads beginning to nod. And when I do make an effort to preach so that they'll understand, I upset them with the points I make.'

The short-lived cheerfulness of their departure had gone; it made Versluis feel vaguely uneasy and he tried to recall whether it had been he who, with an ill-considered question or remark, had given rise to such sudden seriousness and set the conversation on this course. He looked at the flatness of the veld through which they were driving, where the undulating stems of grass scintillated in the light of the sun, and searched for some way of changing the subject without appearing to be offhand. Although, before he could say anything, Scheffler had turned to him once again.

'Do you mind my telling you all these things?' he asked intensely and, as usual with him, the question was not merely a polite one – he really wanted to know, so that the direction of the conversation depended upon Versluis's reply.

'No,' Versluis said, although he had hardly uttered the word before Scheffler had set off again.

'I can't say these things to the others: these are matters that I clearly could discuss only with other clergyman, but I fear that they would understand even less.'

'If you . . .' Versluis began, and then stopped: if you want to complain, he wanted to say, but realised that that would not be the best way of putting it. But what could he say then? If you wish to pour out your heart; if you wish to bewail your fate – these expressions were all too dramatic to be used here. And yet, he thought, the young man *was* pouring out his heart; it was indeed fate that was being bewailed in this instance; and he felt a vague sense of discomfort at the realisation that he was the one who had solicited a confession which he could neither avoid nor manage as they rode alone together in the swaying vehicle, on an interminable road through the veld with the late afternoon sun in their eyes. Would he be able to find some meaningless remark to steer the conversation in a different direction? he wondered. Leaning back into the corner, he studied the profile of the young man beside him. He had never in his life felt as isolated with another person as he did now on this lonely road he thought in astonishment. His life had been protected, his isolation at all times safeguarded and carefully maintained through the services of others, and at the realisation of what was now happening he experienced a sense of unexpected faintness, of elation perhaps, as if doors were opening one after the other in front of him and infinite vistas were unfolding before him in successive rooms, down a long series of corridors, and out over the expansive land through which they rode.

Scheffler was unaware of the thoughts that were passing through his companion's mind. 'I can talk to my sister,' he said, 'to Adèle.' His voice softened; there was both tenderness and pride in the way that he said her name. 'Adèle is an exceptional woman, do you know, Mr Versluis. She is really the one who should have had all the opportunities that came my way because I happened to be a boy; she is the one who should have gone to study abroad, if such a thing had been possible for a woman. She has so much intelligence and insight, so much talent – she writes poetry, although she would never talk about that herself, and Doctor Brill has tried to encourage her to submit it to a literary journal. Sometimes I feel guilty about Adèle – but that's another matter. I can talk to her, and sometimes I am surprised to find how much she is able to understand, how far ahead of mine her ideas are; but it is not right to burden her with all of these things, all these questions to which there are in any case no answers. Besides, it is not right for me to burden you with them either; I have no right to do this to you at all.'

'You need not apologise,' said Versluis. 'I merely fear that I am not able to contribute much to the discussion.'

Scheffler smiled. 'But I am telling you, I am aware that there are no answers, Mr Versluis. I do not expect you to give me any advice – you needn't feel uneasy.'

'I fear that I may not even be able to provide you with the right sort of understanding,' he said carefully. 'As I have already said to you, these are matters about which I know little – issues such as your position or your calling are things of which my understanding is incomplete or even entirely faulty.'

209

'Perhaps that is why I appreciate talking to you, because you are a total outsider, a stranger from abroad who has temporarily come to live amongst us; somebody who has no connection whatsoever with our little world, whether by blood or birth or personal interest. Someone who does not even share our spiritual world, but who stands entirely aloof from it all, passing through it without being touched by it. I envy you such freedom.'

For a moment they were silent: the creaking of the vehicle, the clinking of the harness, the thud of the horse's hooves on the road were the only sounds in the stillness. 'Is it freedom?' Versluis finally asked. 'And is it something to be envied? I had not been aware of that. It has simply been the way in which I have always lived.'

'You are able to look and take in and carry on,' Scheffler said. 'One can no longer do that once one has become part of things. It's not that I want to abandon the things that I have, my house and my family and my own place here in the community, but I am aware of the limitations of my life. I am all too aware of them. I should like to break away, I should like to excel, but the limitations are there and they keep me back. I am continually being checked. I suppose that there is a price that one has to pay, whatever one's lot in life. It has to be purchased, one has to pay, for everything worthwhile that you possess; and then there is so much more that is beyond one's grasp.'

He was talking indistinctly to himself, sitting forward with his elbows on his knees, the reins held loosely in his hands; they were silent again for a while and there was only the creaking of the little cart, the clink of the harness, the thud of horses' hooves. The hill towards which they were driving had drawn nearer, silhouetted in a haze against the brightness of the western sky, and its growing shadow was waiting to receive them.

'But the country is beautiful,' Scheffler said suddenly, roused from a chain of thought along which Versluis had been unable to follow him. 'The land is beautiful, is it not, Mr Versluis?' He was cheerful once again, his face radiated enthusiasm, and the question was like a challenge which permitted no contradiction. The town had long since disappeared behind them, only the low outline of its mountain was still visible in the distance beyond the ridge, and around them the veld ranged widely, the crested grass scintillating in the light.

'Yes,' said Versluis, 'it is beautiful,' and Scheffler smiled at him as if this were a token by which they had become companions in a shared secret. Through the light of the afternoon, across the scintillating land, they carried on riding in silence towards the hill ahead and the first shadows of evening.

Beyond the hill they discovered a gum plantation, ploughed fields and a stone house with locked shutters. 'It's the Fichardts' farm,' Scheffler said for Versluis's information as they rode past. 'They come out for holidays.' He had sat up purposefully once again and had drawn the reins more tautly, and the horse had broken into a sudden trot that carried them around the plantation towards the spot where drifting smoke and the sound of voices indicated the presence of the settlement, and where mud houses and decrepit grass huts were scattered along the ridge. Their arrival was greeted by barking dogs, but then they were recognised: children ran closer, people appeared in doorways, and a laughing black man rushed forward to grab the horse. It was clear that the priest was welcome here and that they were overjoyed to see him Versluis saw as he alighted from the cart, a bit stiff from the long journey, and some time passed before an older man from the group of blacks came forward to shake his hand and welcome him in formal Dutch. This was the first time he had ever greeted a black man he reflected while the man's hand lay politely but listlessly in his for a moment, almost as if it contained no bone; and then a few members of the group disengaged themselves from the clergyman to welcome him with the same formal courtesy.

Scheffler stood in the midst of these people, laughing elatedly and speaking to them in their own language with a fluency that Versluis would up till then hardly have expected from him, his companion forgotten beside the cart. The men who had come to greet Versluis remained standing in his vicinity, but their attention was riveted to the priest and what he was saying, and they took no real interest in Versluis nor did they require his presence – unlike the servants in the hotel or Mrs Van der Vliet's house, whose existence was justified solely by their serviceability – and Versluis did not find this perception particularly pleasing. The foul-smelling and impoverished farm labourers; the boisterous conversation in an unknown language; the shouts of the barefoot children; the growling of the emaciated dogs that slunk around the group and the smoke swirling from the fires – he found all of these bothersome, and with a quick, impatient gesture he turned away from the people.

His movement suddenly recalled his presence to Scheffler who quickly made his way towards Versluis. 'I'm sorry,' he said, still laughing from the interrupted conversation, 'but it's been such a long time since they last saw me: there is so much to say. There are just a few matters that I need to discuss with them, then we can have some coffee. Shall I ask them to bring a chair for you?'

But Versluis felt no desire to remain at this gathering. 'No thank you,' he said, 'I'd rather take a short walk. I'd like a little exercise.'

'Are you sure?' Scheffler asked, but he was eager to return to the people who were waiting for him, and he was already looking back over his shoulder to indicate to them that he was coming. 'You don't mind? I'll be finished here in quarter of an hour. Or let's rather say a half an hour,' he called as he walked back. 'These things always take longer than one expects.'

Then he was gone, surrounded by a group who accompanied him as he walked, and he disappeared through the haze of the smoke into the dark interior of a shack, bending under the low lintel. Versluis turned away with a sense of relief now that there was nobody to take any further notice of him, with the exception of a few half-naked children who gazed curiously at him from a distance. Without choosing any particular direction he walked past the dilapidated grass huts that stood sagging against the ridge, and beyond them he found the homestead that they had seen on their arrival and made his way towards it. Behind him the labourers' shacks and their inhabitants had disappeared from view, and only the children were still visible on the hill, wrapped in skins or blankets; but the moment he saw them they turned and fled without a sound.

The small stone house bore no signs of habitation, but it had been well maintained: the stoep was swept and the garden paths had been raked, and it was clear that someone was tending it. As he raised the latch of the garden gate a sudden calm descended upon him among the beds filled with English flowers, so unexpected here in Africa and, at the end of summer, they were in full bloom: he could hear the buzzing of bees and saw a few butterflies fluttering by and gradually, as he strolled beside the beds and the greenhouse with its neat rows of plants, their tranquillity possessed him.

After a while he sat down on a bench in the shade of the verandah and gazed out over the garden in the late afternoon sun. Seldom since his arrival in Africa had he felt such peace he reflected; it was as if the drive out to this place had freed him of all cares and obligations and had instead delivered him into an unaccustomed state of freedom. Birds called and the wind rustled through the leaves of the bluegums beyond the garden wall: he sat alone on the stoep of an empty farm house without a single person in the vicinity and felt only that infinite peace. It was enough just to sit there he thought; and only when he noticed the lengthening of the shadows did he leap up at the thought that Sheffler was probably waiting for him, and had possibly even began to look for him. Far away he heard a chatter of voices like chirruping birds and saw beyond the trees, among the shrubs along the ridge, a flutter of blankets where the children had been startled by his sudden movement. He had thus not been alone, he realised as he brushed down his clothes, and then he hurried out of the garden to return to the clergyman; he fastened the latch of the gate, and chose a shortcut through the gum plantation to the labourers' shacks.

How much labour it must have taken, he thought to himself as he hurried on, to have laboriously established that garden through the course of the years: to have broken open the ground and rendered it receptive, to have cherished the seedlings and carried the water. What faith it must have taken to have planted these trees in the empty veld, to have worked for a goal that lay so many years ahead that it seemed to be scarcely attainable, and already to have seen its shade and refreshment in one's imagination. Close to the house the trees were fully grown, the bark flaking in strips from their stems, but further along they became younger and younger, until whole rows and lines of slender, silvery tree stems extended away from him in all directions. The regularity of the planting disoriented him and the gleaming silver stems rose up before him like the spokes of a fence; light and shade fell in long, straight strips across the ground like traps to ensnare his feet. He stopped in the middle of the plantation, blinded by the setting sun that was now shining directly through the slender stems. For a moment he did not even know where he was, caught in that maze of light and shade, struggling in that network of patterns from which he was unable to free himself; and from far away out of the immense silence that enveloped him he heard a high-pitched, mocking sound, the call of a strange bird or the laughter of children darting away amongst the trees. Fearful and distressed he groped for a way out, felt the smooth silver stem of a tree beneath his fingers, stumbled over a root, and fell. He was often falling, he thought dully to himself as he kneeled in the dust; he was always falling. He ought not to go out unaccompanied any longer he added, admonishing himself, but without fully grasping the implications of the warning.

He was in the bluegum plantation on the Fichardts' farm, to which he had come with Pastor Scheffler; the sun was already low in the sky, and there was no sound around him except the dry rustling of the bluegum leaves in the wind. The moment of panic had passed and he again felt the same sense of tranquillity that he had experienced in the

213

garden. To have come so far, to have had to travel for such a long time in order to find such peace, he thought ruefully, and he saw beneath his hand the stem of the tree, glistening in the light. He saw the roots, the red dust of the earth across which large ants darted to and fro. He was dying, he thought with the same sense of resignation. He was dying, not in the sense that everyone was approaching some vague, undetermined end, but as a purposeful action the end of was which already in sight: his death was implacable, as much of a fact as the stem and the roots of the tree, the ants and the dust, that he was now seeing. For him there was no prospect of watching the seed germinate and grow into a tree. It was all over.

All around him the landscape had come to rest: the bird was silent, the children had disappeared. The clergyman was waiting for him he thought, and very slowly he carried on walking along the narrow lanes of the gum plantation, through the network of knotted light and shade. He hesitated for another instant and then broke through the entanglement of the net to where the smoke from dung fires was suspended along the ridge above the decrepit farm labourers' houses.

Scheffler was coming towards him with long strides from the bank of smoke. 'I thought that you might have got lost,' he said. 'Is everything in order? Your clothes are covered in dust.'

'I went for a walk,' Versluis replied evasively, and found himself shrinking slightly before Sheffler's solicitude and his quick, searching gaze. The young man was already kneeling before him in an attempt to brush the dust from the knees of his trousers. 'I went to look at the flowers in the garden,' he added quickly, as if by changing the subject in this way he might avoid any further uncomfortable questions.

'Mr Fichardt is a very keen gardener. Have you ever seen his garden in town? It's really a small paradise.' Scheffler leapt up. 'Shall we have some coffee and unpack our food baskets?' he asked, again with an air of a schoolboy rejoicing in some treat. 'We could perhaps find a place for ourselves up against the hill, then we'll have a fine view, and we'll be less likely to be disturbed by the people.'

The afternoon sun was already quite low and the sky had lost its usual blue intensity: only the surface of the veld – waving crests of grass and scattered rocks and bushes along the hillside – was still touched by the light as the shadows lengthened. 'It's not becoming too chilly for you?' Scheffler asked. 'Are you sure?' He stopped and turned around to look back at Versluis who was following more slowly across the uneven ground. He had burdened himself with both baskets of refreshments, having refused to let Versluis help carry them, but even with that load he was quite far ahead, as if he were hardly able to contain his eagerness sufficiently to maintain the pace of his companion. 'Is it not too far for you?' he again asked a while later. 'You're not getting tired?'

'No,' said Versluis, 'no, not at all,' even though it was becoming increasingly difficult for him to follow the clergyman along the route that he was forging so recklessly across the uneven ground, stones and eroded gullies. But then Scheffler seemed to become aware of this himself, and he stopped. 'I'm sorry,' he said. 'There is a spot that I always go to when I come here, a sheltered place with a view across the whole plain, but it is thoughtless of me to want to drag you there at all costs.' He stood apologetically in the long grass with the baskets, the rug, the cushion, hesitating between going on and turning back.

Versluis wiped his forehead. He was becoming short of breath, his shoes were dusty and scratched and strange thorns and burrs clung to his trouser legs. The setting sun was in his eyes, but when he held up his hand to screen the light, he saw before him only the colourless expanse of the veld without any recognisable destination for their expedition. 'No,' he said with sudden determination, 'let's carry on, I would like to see the spot myself,' and it seemed to him that he could perceive a sense of relief and a fleeting look of gratitude on Scheffler's face.

'It's not far,' the clergyman said, 'just over here. Come – look out, be careful. . . .' He waited a while to make sure that Versluis would manage. 'Put your hand on my shoulder, then you'll have something to hold on to.'

Scheffler remained where he was, burdened by the paraphernalia of their little expedition, so that Versluis could put his hand on his shoulder as he clambered over the rocks that lay in their path, and Versluis, out of breath and with the sun in his eyes, was gratefully aware for a moment of the support that the younger man provided him. 'Here we are,' Scheffler said, and began to arrange things so that Versluis would be comfortable. 'Come and sit here, with the cushion at your back. Something to eat, a cup of coffee. . . .' He had already begun to unpack the baskets on to a flat rock – first the bottle of coffee and rusks that he had brought from his own home and then, with a surprised smile, the basket that Mrs Van der Vliet had provisioned with characteristic thoroughness to provide refreshments for four or five people – cake and sandwiches and fruit, and cups and saucers packed in straw. 'We'll have enough food left over to give some to the children as well,' he said. 'We could not possibly allow Mrs Van der Vliet to feel slighted by taking any of this back to her.'

He was setting everything on a tablecloth that had also appeared from Mrs Van der Vliet's basket, and Versluis let him do it while he leant back against a rock to look out across the falling expanse of bare veld and the cupola of the sky from which the colour had already begun to drain. There was nothing; there was no longer anything.

'That's Spitskop,' Scheffler remarked beside him. 'And those over there are the Stutkraal Mount and Bloemfontein Mountain, that's all one can still see of the town from here. And that there against the sky in the distance is Thaba Nchu. That's a beautiful mountain; it's always beautiful, at any time of the day.' Leaning back, his eyes half-closed, Versluis looked at that opalescent mountain on the horizon, hardly discernible any longer against the milky whiteness of the sky.

'I like coming out here to the farm whenever I . . .' Scheffler said, and then broke off as he searched for the right words and grinned apologetically. 'Whenever I simply want to get away. It's near, and yet very far. The Fichardts have let me spend a night or two here on occasion, whenever I have felt the need to be alone.' Slowly, pensively, he set cups out on the unfolded white cloth. 'I like coming to this spot in particular, as I have said, my vantage point over the veld. This is where I most love to withdraw, among the rocks on this koppie.'

'You should rather have come on your own,' Versluis said, once again conscious of his weakness and exhaustion as he leant back against the rock.

'That's not what I meant,' came Scheffler's quick reply, however. 'Sometimes one also wants to share something with someone else, even if it is only a view over the veld, otherwise I would not have asked you along this afternoon. Otherwise I would not have dragged you here.' He looked absently at the teaspoon in his hand and then grinned. 'But I have to admit that I have never sat here in as much style as I do this afternoon. May I pour you some coffee?'

'Actually, I don't feel like anything at all.'

'No, nor do I really.' He looked at the tablecloth, the cups, the saucers, the food. 'What are we to do with it all then?'

'We could give it to the children as you suggested.'

'Yes, let's give it all to the children – Mrs Van der Vliet needn't know anything about it. I must just remember to thank her for all her effort when I take you back.' Quickly he began to thrust it all back into the basket from which it had only just been taken, as if he were in a hurry to get it out of the way, and bundled the tablecloth untidily on top before he slammed the lid. 'It was really very good of her to take so much trouble,' he declared as if he were replying to some kind of reproach or criticism. And then he put the refreshments and their aborted meal out of his mind, like the basket that he had pushed impatiently to one side, and stretched himself out on the ground beside Versluis. He propped himself casually on one elbow in the dust and the dry grass without a thought for his clothes. There was only the sound of the wind, the rustle of grass, the call of a single bird: it rose out of the silence, grew louder, tipped and spilt out. Then they could hear nothing more, drifting on that wide expanse of silence.

'I can still hear the duet that my father and I played together,' Scheffler said, half to himself, looking up at the sky. 'I can't rid myself of the melody.'

'I find, too, that it keeps coming back to me,' said Versluis.

'Adèle said that night . . .' the priest began, and then broke off again. 'I don't think she is right, even though I don't like disagreeing with her – she has far greater insight and far better judgement than I, and she is right most of the time. But I cannot agree for instance that Mozart has no significance for us here in Africa simply because he is European. She sometimes expresses such opinions, she is given to pronouncements that cast doubt upon matters that are accepted entirely as a matter of course by other people – for example, she upset Mathilde the other evening with a chance remark about the fact that we speak German, even though she had naturally not intended to.'

'And Mozart?' asked Versluis. The sky was losing its colour, the far-off mountains gleamed; the melody that the two men had played together in the lamplight murmured through the long grass and across the plain. He felt tired, as usual, but it did not matter.

'She posed the same question after the poetry afternoon. We listen to Mozart or Schubert, we read Goethe or Schiller, and then we look up and see this hard, barren land and we are struck by the distance between what we have heard and what we see around us – as if there were two entirely separate realities existing here, side by side, a spiritual world and that of our daily existence. It is exactly this that Adèle regards as our weakness, the fact that we are torn between two worlds and so can be completely loyal to neither of them.'

'But surely it's not simply a matter of free choice. Not everyone who finds himself in this position has chosen freely.'

'Most of us have – my parents came here voluntarily and decided to stay. I myself chose to return to Europe, I even came back quite eagerly. . . . Is it right that we should keep looking back and long to

217

return and refuse to make the most of what we have? It is different only for you, because you will eventually go back to Europe, and so for you these few months in Africa are no more than a break. They impose no demands on you.'

'Perhaps,' said Versluis. 'But perhaps precisely for that reason I should withhold judgement on those who find themselves in such a totally different position from my own.'

'Visitors sometimes see things more clearly and make better observations – people who are passing through with travel guides and binoculars, without being really involved in anything that they perceive, who carry on and forget. They could perhaps indicate things to us that we ourselves do not know.'

Versluis looked at the young man stretched out on the ground at his feet, his clothes dusty from the sand, preoccupied with nothing other than the wide, colourless landscape before them and the questions that worried him. What is it that you want to know? What questions do you wish to ask? he would have liked to ask in this moment of intimacy; for what kind of knowledge are you searching, what kind of freedom do you desire? But he did not ask these questions.

'It's becoming increasingly clear to me that I don't belong anywhere myself,' the clergyman continued. 'That's why I am not as conscious as Adèle is of such dichotomies. I grew up with vague visions of Europe, because at home Europe was always present in the background. I went abroad and discovered when I was there that I am really from Africa, and then I returned to find that I had been away for too long to be able to adapt myself here, and that there was nothing left for me. Or almost nothing,' he added more quietly. 'But it is different for Adèle, because she has never been away. And besides, she is also much more wholehearted and convinced about everything that she believes and does – women are often like that, aren't they?' He looked up at Versluis with a slight smile. 'Her love for this land is entirely undivided, and I believe that it is more deeply felt than anything that I have ever experienced; much more intense even – yes, I could even say more passionate. There is no denying that Adèle is an intense and passionate person, and that she can also be uncomfortable sometimes, even for those of us who know her.' The smile was still on his lips: he spoke tenderly, as he did whenever he spoke of his sister. 'She really knows this country, this land in which we grew up; she understands it.'

This land of stone and rock and sand Versluis thought to himself, propped up against the pillow: how did one understand this land, and what did it mean to know it? He looked at the undulating plain before him, at the toneless sky. In that moment of shared intimacy he would have been able to pose the question to Scheffler, and in the context of their conversation it would have evoked no surprise.

'Sometimes I believe that we have failed,' Scheffler said thoughtfully, his head turned away towards the gradual change of colour in the west, so that his words were indistinct. 'We brought civilisation to this place; our houses and churches; our furniture and books and fashions from Europe: unasked we brought it all here and dumped it as if Africa were some kind of a trash-heap, and we came to live our lives here in accordance with patterns that we or our parents brought from elsewhere. We live off memories and surround ourselves with phantoms, and as for Africa itself, we see it only at a distance from behind the lace curtains that we have hung in front of the windows of our living rooms. The pioneering farmers who began by carving out an existence for themselves in this country, we violently drove back – today the farmers are buying pianos and sending their daughters to boarding school, and the children try to appear smart by speaking English. And as for the black people, what haven't we done to them? Given them the dubious gifts of European houses and churches, of money and alcohol and diseases that were totally unknown to them. With one hand we attempted to uplift them, as we say, without their ever having asked for upliftment, and with the other we push them away whenever they come too close and we feel threatened. What have we done in this country? And by what right?'

Why did the clergymen feel this need to pour out his heart to him, Versluis wondered, and why to him exactly? These were clearly things that mattered to the young man, things that he had been bottling up for months, even years, so that they now burst forth almost violently. He was suddenly aware of the peculiarity of his situation, alone in the veld with this intense young man, listening to a monologue full of fire and fury which he was himself unable to share; and then he was struck once again by the thought that he had never before been so alone with another person as he was now. In the narrow, tall house in Delft there had always been servants in the basement or in their rooms in the attic, ready to be summoned whenever he required their presence; there had been neighbours in the house on either side, separated from him by the mere width of a wall, and passers-by within calling distance on the canal outside his windows. In that small and densely inhabited country there had always been people everywhere, and even on his travels he had never been physically alone: porters, stewards, couriers and the

219

hotel staff had always been at his beck and call, and there had always been people at the next table, in the adjoining room or coupé, pedestrians in the parks or streets.

He had lived alone in that vast house, gone to the club on his own and returned on his own by cab; he had travelled to Spa, Como or Lausanne on his own, sat unaccompanied in a hotel lounge or on the terrace with his book and his Baedeker, but he was always surrounded by people. He had never been as isolated as he was now. If he were to cry out, who would hear him? But never before, he realised at the same time, had anyone poured out his heart to him or spoken to him as openly and without inhibition. Never before had such intimacy arisen between himself and anyone else as that which had now been created, unsolicited and one-sided, between himself and the young clergyman. Never before had anyone made a confidant of him.

He looked at the young man beside him, at the determined profile and the untidy hair. At the same time Scheffler turned his head and looked at him with the intense gaze of his bright blue eyes, his brow gravely furrowed with effort, and his last question still hung unanswered between them.

What had he asked? Versluis tried to remember, and began to search confusedly for some sort of comment or reply, because one was clearly expected of him. He had been under the impression that Scheffler was pouring out his bottled-up thoughts and feelings in a unilateral, monological flood of words, but this had been a mistake. How was he supposed to have known that? he thought in rising panic, with those penetrating eyes, that expectant gaze, fixed upon him. What sort of experience did he have of the intimacy of human beings or of the way in which it ought to be managed? What was the answer?

Scheffler had been speaking about emptiness, he remembered, and he saw before him the veld in the evening light, the slight undulation of the grass, the hills on the horizon and that single, far-off mountain in the east, nearly lost in the haze. 'What else is there?' he then said softly. 'What else could you want? Is it not understandable that the people who find themselves in this country should chose to surround themselves with lace curtains and grand pianos and anthologies of poetry?'

Scheffler smiled and suddenly relaxed, as if these words had been vital to him. Versluis had spoken: the monologue had become a discussion, its declamatory vehemence had been diluted.

'When I came back from Germany after the completion of my studies . . .' the pastor began pensively, and considered for a moment before continuing. 'When I came back, Mr and Mrs Hirsch had also been there to visit their family; they had gone by ship as far as Cape Town and then travelled overland in their new landau with the coachman whom they had hired in the Cape. And I travelled with them, apparently for the company, but really to save money – it was always the most important consideration for me. And I can still recall the feeling of identification that I felt once we had gone through the last of the mountain passes and reached the plateaux of the interior. That journey lasted for almost a month, and for most of it the route passed through the Karoo, through semi-desert where from day to day we hardly saw a farm house or a tree. In the morning we would wake up with days of that arid landscape behind us, we drove through it all day, and when we came to outspan in the evenings we knew that days of it still lay ahead of us. After a while it began to feel as if the journey had taken an eternity and would still continue forever, as if that ashen landscape with its ridges had no beginning and could have no end. The others complained, and after a while they stopped complaining, they simply suffered it without a word. They couldn't press on fast enough to get that part of the journey behind them, but for me it couldn't have lasted long enough, and after all those years that I spent abroad, it seemed to me that I should never tire of looking at that landscape.'

They were silent: the wind murmured through the grass, a bird called. In the sky the sudden splendour of the sunset vanished as quickly as it had appeared, and as they watched they saw it spill and drain away. Only the distant mountain still flamed out and blazed like a beacon against the horizon.

'We did not travel on Sundays,' Scheffler slowly continued: 'the Hirsches wished to honour my feelings as a Christian, and because of their thoughtfulness I in turn did not want to say that it really didn't matter to me and that we might just as well carry on. On Sundays we thus made camp and spent the day on the veld, and for them this was a delay which would lengthen the journey by yet another day, but for me it was always one more day of reprieve that I had been granted, and I accepted it with gratitude. The Hirsches stayed at the campsite and waited for the day to pass, and I remember how I went walking on that first Sunday, just like that in my shirtsleeves, without a jacket or a hat, because I had already forgotten how the sun can burn one in summer. I walked away blindly into the veld, away from the route that we had been following, up over the rises, among the stones and little bushes, across that dry ground where the lizards vanish so quickly into

221

the crevices that one hardly sees them. I was back again; I was on my way home, to Bethany, to the Free State; every stone told me this, the sun on my face, the wind blowing ever more strongly against me as I climbed higher. After a while I could hardly see our camp below me, the tent was just a mark on the veld, lost in that expanse. It was already late, time to go back to eat, but I pressed on up the rise to get to the top of the hill and see still more, and when I reached the top where the wind blew hardest, the landscape merely extended still further before me, great ashen hills that turned into greyish-blue mountains against the horizon. I had returned – that, for me, was the true moment of homecoming.'

He broke off and glanced quickly at Versluis. 'You must excuse me,' he said, 'you are probably wondering why I am relating all this, and I don't exactly know myself, I know only that the journey and that walk and seeing Africa again were important to me, that they form a kind of pivot at the centre of my life around which everything revolves, before and after. I believe that it was only then, on my return after so many years, that I realised that this part of the world has a identity of its own; it was at that moment that I made my choice, that I turned my back forever on Europe and accepted this country.'

'I cannot understand it,' Versluis said; 'that is to say, I could never experience it as you do. But yet I believe that I can guess what you mean.'

'People react so differently to Africa,' Scheffler said. 'Some feel threatened, they try to deny the reality of this, they try to recreate and maintain Europe as best they can around them. Others adapt themselves to a greater or lesser degree, but it remains a compromise. Who is prepared to abandon himself totally and give himself up to this land? And can one blame them for it? They draw back; they are scared: the land threatens them with its emptiness and silence. It takes no notice of them, it takes no interest in what they are trying to achieve. I can understand that. In the first days of that journey I felt the same fear whenever we made camp and that desolation came upon us. But you have to persevere with what has been given to you, then anguish will gradually subside. The land will remain aloof, it has no need of us and takes no interest in is; but precisely for that reason it will do us no harm. We will be able to continue living here, in this silence, like the plants of the desert that grow in the rocky crevices, thrusting their roots down in order to stay alive, their little flowers so tiny that one can scarcely see them against the gravel and sand in which they grow. There is nothing, absolutely nothing; but one can live like that.'

He spoke softly but with complete conviction: he was announcing a firm observation, the result of ideas that he had spent years contemplating on his own. 'In other countries there are gods and spirits in the woods and ravines and streams, but here there is nothing. No spirits have ever possessed this land, no gods have ever been born here, nothing has ever happened here. There is only this empty space, this silence. It waits, but actually it expects nothing.' He was playing thoughtfully with the earth as he spoke, his head still half-averted, breaking up the dry clods between his fingers. 'Heaps of stones,' he said dreamily to himself; 'layers of rock stacked one upon the other beneath the earth, slate and ironstone and dolomite, fissures that break open, ravines that crumble away through the centuries. Ridges where the rock-rabbits hide, heights in which the eagle makes its nest. Bleached bones, scattered as the body decays. Bright little stones that glitter in the sun. The empty river beds, the rocky courses of streams.' With his head upside down he continued to speak, muttering to himself as though he could hardly share these incoherent thoughts with Versluis.

Emptiness, Versluis thought, a low horizon at the very edge of the landscape, beyond which one discovered only the low line of another horizon. He would never return to the Netherlands, he knew with unsettling clarity. He would never again see the coastline of a trusted land or the roofs and chimneys of a familiar city rising above the horizon.

'I once read somewhere,' said Scheffler, and he was forced to laugh at the thought, 'I read in a book on Eastern religion that with death the soul leaves the body through the mouth, and at that point there is an instant of terror and anguish when it has to pass through the constriction of the throat – like sand in an hourglass I imagined. And perhaps that's how it is, how do we know? One second of unthinkable fear that we have to endure alone, in which no-one can stand by us, and then we are released into infinity. . . .' He laughed aloud, enchanted by the idea; his hair stood up more confusedly than ever on his head, and his black suit was covered in dust. 'It's that constriction that terrifies us, from which we recoil, the death that every one of us has to die. That is perhaps also what we recoil from in this country, giving ourselves up to an uncharted emptiness.' Then he fell silent. 'The sun has set,' he said, as if he had only just become aware of it.

The sun had set. Drained of all colour the cupola of the sky arched across the wide arc of the earth, emptiness reflecting emptiness, emptiness balanced against emptiness, vacant surface joined to vacant surface like the two wings of a shell as if, for a fraction of a second, everything had suddenly been consummated. It would pass Versluis thought; even before he could take it in entirely it had passed, and he was left with only a memory. He would never be granted another such moment of insight he realised, tired and somewhat sad. Through the narrow mouth of the hourglass the sand continued to spill.

'It's getting chilly,' Scheffler said, and leapt up quickly. 'I'm sorry, Mr Versluis, I've just been sitting nattering on and you did not even stop me. You should never have remained out here in the evening. . . .' He looked about in confusion for the baskets, his hat, as he spoke.

Leaning against a rock, Versluis made no move to get up himself. 'What would you like to do then?' he asked. The clergyman looked at him without understanding. 'What would you chose to do with your life?'

Scheffler did not answer at once. 'What can I do?' he asked. 'I am married; I am an ordained priest; I have obligations towards my family, my sister, my parents, the members of my congregation – what can I do but what I'm doing now?' He stood there without moving, with Mrs Van der Vliet's basket of food in his hand. 'I am afraid,' he then said with disarming simplicity. 'I talk about surrender, but I keep drawing back from that moment of constriction and keep making excuses for myself. Besides, I don't have the courage to give it all up.'

He was right Versluis thought, they should go now – for the grey shadow of evening had already fallen and darkness came so quickly: the night air had grown chilly. He drew himself up with difficulty, for he was stiff from sitting for so long, and Scheffler automatically bent down to help him and to try to brush the dust from his clothes once again. He spoke as he did so, 'To abandon everything,' he said pensively, 'everything that we have brought from elsewhere, and to advance into that emptiness with empty hands, that is what I should like to do. It sounds very brave and impractical, but it would not be very poetic. To abandon everything that you can and then gradually to lose all that has remained, that would not be easy. To possess nothing and to be nothing any more, to live in poverty like these people in those huts against the ridges; to observe and listen and become part of this land and its silence; to live in God, nameless and unknown; to die and be buried here, and to leave your body to the land so that the bequest may be consummated. All that sounds high-flown, doesn't it?' But then his boyish grin flashed suddenly through his seriousness. 'To become one with this land in the way that the gods and spirits in other countries are one with them, and also in the process to allow it to become one with you, in the dark among the stones and roots and gravel.' He bent down to pick up the pillow, to fold the rug. 'We must go,' he said dutifully, but without any urgency.

The land was grey and shadows lay along the ridges. Oblivious of the load that he was carrying, Scheffler was already walking ahead and once again he did not want Versluis to take anything from him. 'It will be a long while before I'll be able to prise away some time to come to Brandkop again,' he remarked. 'It's already almost Easter, and there are so many additional obligations that demand my attention.'

Versluis followed more slowly, leaning on his cane. 'Can you see?' Scheffler asked, and stopped to wait for him. 'Put your hand on my shoulder: I'm pretty firm on my feet, and I know the way.'

Gratefully he made use of the offer once again, and supported by the clergyman he made his way onward like a blind man being led through the dark.

'Would you mind taking pity on Mr Gelmers a little?' Scheffler then asked suddenly as they walked further, and so totally unexpected was this question that Versluis stopped in his tracks for an instant.

'Why do you ask that?' he said, hoping that he had not betrayed the extent to which the question had struck him with its unpleasant suddenness.

'Because I suddenly thought of him as I began to look over all of my obligations – he comes to visit us at home quite often nowadays, and I think that he needs help.'

'Financially, you mean?'

'Perhaps, I don't know. He is not very well, and he needs medical care, but that is not what I was thinking of either. I think that he is lonely.'

'I was under the impression that he had quite a number of acquaintances among the younger people.'

'No, I'm sure not. I had thought that you, as a Netherlander also living as a stranger amongst us, in many ways in similar circumstances – but it was just a thought, nothing more.'

He did not pursue the matter, nor did Versluis try to take it any further. The outing with its lengthy discussion and its intimacy had developed into something more than he had expected, and he had no desire to allow it to end on this note or to accept responsibility for the unsavoury young Dutchman about whom Scheffler seemed to be concerned. But fortunately he appeared to have dropped the idea.

Nightfall was deepening from grey to indigo, and from the gathering

225

shadows in the distance they were greeted by the calling of voices and barking of dogs. All along the ridge the fires of the farm labourers were points of light in the darkness, and on their return they were once again immediately surrounded by people, so that it was impossible to get away at once. The darkness and the dancing firelight, the faces of the black people and the alien language excluded Versluis like walls rising up before him. He was enclosed by strangeness. There was nothing Scheffler had said, he recalled as he climbed laboriously into the cart. A rented room in a strange house awaited him, he would never be at home in this country. Passively he let the clergyman spread the rug over his knees, as submissive as a child.

They did not speak on the way back; the amiable silence between them was broken only by the jingling of the horse's harness, the creaking of the cart, and the thud of the horse's hooves. They were already close to the town when they encountered the servant who had been sent out with a lantern by Mrs Van der Vliet, to determine what had kept them and whether anything had happened to them.

The morning sun was already beginning to reveal the first signs of gold among the leaves of the fruit trees in the orchard behind the house; it fell obliquely on the creepers that screened the verandah, showing the first yellow leaves amongst the foliage. The year had progressed further than he had thought, Versluis observed as he left the house and noticed a chill in the air.

'One of these days there will be dead leaves all over,' Mrs Van der Vliet said with a grave sense of satisfaction as she stood on the front stoep watching the servant sweeping in front of the house. 'First the leaves and then the dust storms – in this country there is always some form of affliction.' This morning she had cast a crocheted shawl around her shoulders which she drew about herself with a shiver as she spoke. He would have his trunks brought from the back room and unpack his winter gear Versluis thought, for there was no Pompe to perform such tasks and so, reluctant and unsure, he would have to accept responsibility for his life.

The servant at the parsonage knew him by now and let him in with a shy smile, but when he entered the gloom of the living room he found, not the two women as he had expected. Instead it was once again Gelmers in his yellow checks who first caught his eye.

'Another visitor!' Miss Scheffler cried from where she was sitting at the dining room table. 'First Mr Gelmers and now you. I am always

226

so pleased to have visitors in the morning to keep me company, especially when Mathilde is out. People in Bloemfontein don't often call in the morning, and sometimes it is difficult for me to get through it without any distraction.'

Versluis bent over her hand and bowed coolly in the direction of the other man in the hope that, as on the previous occasion, he would decide to leave. But Gelmers remained standing obstinately in the centre of the room as if he had not the slightest intention of going.

'I'm afraid that I am disturbing you,' Versluis said to Miss Scheffler.

'Oh no, not at all. I was engaged in a rather dismal task, but it is not at all urgent. Come and sit down, Mr Versluis, and talk to us.' She was already gathering the things that lay on the table in front of her into a bundle, and he had sat down opposite her before he noticed that his hand had come to rest for a moment on a design of Scottish tartan.

'What are you doing?' he asked.

Taken aback by the sharpness of his question, she looked up, but she was too polite to show any further signs of surprise. 'These are the belongings of the Scottish woman who passed away a while ago – do you remember her, or was that before you arrived in Bloemfontein? Mr Gelmers, did you know her?'

'I don't know,' the young man said from where he had remained standing on the piece of carpet in the centre of the room.

'She was a young visitor who came here from abroad for her health, but she did not live long. I never saw her myself, but both my brother and the Wesleyan minister visited her.'

'I don't know anything about these things,' said Gelmers. 'I take no interest in such people.' He walked slowly away to the window and his thick-soled boots thudded across the floorboards, but Miss Scheffler took no notice of his brusque rudeness as she carefully, almost lovingly, folded the tartan dress.

'She stayed here in the hotel, and by the time we found out about her she was too ill to be transferred – too ill even to know that there were people who took an interest and wanted to help her. She was entirely alone; she had no-one in this country.'

Versluis looked at the woman's few belongings on the table before him: the hairbrush; the little sewing kit; the hymnal; coloured ribbons; a few handkerchiefs. The possessions of others – dog-eared, worn – had always repelled him, and the smell of illness and death clung to these remains.

'But you must have known her, Mr Versluis,' Miss Scheffler said. 'I remember now, it was shortly after my brother went to visit you in

227

the hotel that Mrs Schröder told him about the young woman who had just arrived and who was ill. You must have known of her while you were staying at the hotel.'

'I don't remember,' he said. 'I was ill myself, I do not know who the other guests were.'

'I do not like all this talk of illness,' Gelmers remarked emphatically from his position in front of the window. 'Why do we speak only about illness? None of us is ill.'

There was a short, uncomfortable silence, but just as Versluis was about to respond to this discourteous reproach, Miss Scheffler spoke. 'You are quite right, Mr Gelmers,' she said calmly. 'She is dead and rests in peace, why must we continue talking about it? They determined that there were no relations, not even in Scotland, that there is no-one interested in her, and so we have these few things to dispose of. But that is no problem, there are enough poor people who would be happy to have them.' As she spoke she began to put the objects on the table back into the worn little case that was lying beside her on a chair. 'Mr Versluis,' she asked with an enquiring tone, and he suddenly realised that she was asking him to pass her the ribbons and handkerchiefs in front of him. Quickly he picked them up and thrust them into her hand, the handkerchiefs containing a name in marking ink in the corners, together with the bundle of multi-coloured ribbons for attaching to a hat or tying in someone's hair. She shut the lid of the case, and for a moment the three of them were silent.

'The sun began to shine in here again this morning,' Miss Scheffler remarked. 'Look, it's already catching the window-seat.'

Together they all looked at the narrow strip of sunlight which fell across the stoep to touch the window-seat, a single gleam of brilliance in the dark room.

'I must go,' Gelmers said.

'Don't you want to stay until my sister-in-law comes back? Then we can all have a cup of tea –'

He paid no attention to the invitation. 'I must go,' he repeated without even allowing her to finish speaking. 'There are still all kinds of things that I have to do, I am very busy this morning.' He had already taken leave of her automatically and made a half-bow to Versluis without looking at him, his hat pressed with both hands to his chest. His heavy boots thumped across the floorboards and he kicked clumsily against the door as he opened it, and then he was gone.

'I hope that I haven't driven your visitor away,' said Versluis.

228

'Oh no, he simply drops in from time to time. When you have grown up in a parsonage you become accustomed to the fact that there are always people coming along who need some sort of help.'

'It must be a nuisance for those living in the parsonage.'

'In some ways, perhaps, but on the other hand one is grateful for the opportunity to do something for others, or at least to be able to try. Mostly it's so little,' she added, and paused as if unsure of whether to continue, but she finally decided against it.

'I don't wish to keep you myself – I came merely to thank your sister-in-law for the refreshments that she so kindly sent along when I went out with your brother yesterday.'

'Did you enjoy the outing with August, Mr Versluis? I know that he did, I could see it when he arrived home last night; I was very happy. Mathilde was a bit disturbed because it was so late; naturally she was concerned about you, and she had to keep his supper warm – but then Mathilde likes to live according to a fixed routine, she sometimes has a hard time with us. But August has so few opportunities to get away, and it means a great deal to him.' Again she paused for an instant, she pondered once more. 'He is very lonely you know,' she then added.

She looked at him across the plush cover of the table with that open, confiding gaze, but he avoided it; he lowered his eyes and stared at the burgundy plush. 'I feel guilty about taking up his afternoon,' he said. 'There are others who have more of a right to his time than I do.'

She too lowered her eyes and stared at the cover between them. 'To have a family, to have obligations, these don't imply a life without loneliness, Mr Versluis. But you probably know that, just as well as I do. People who are often alone have ample opportunity to observe and see these things, isn't that so? And to think about them too.' But she continued more quickly, as if she felt that her last words had been too personal. 'I see so much loneliness around me and it saddens me; for days I was unhappy about this girl who came here to die on her own in a hotel room. I should have liked to go to her and hold her hand, to put my arms around her and tell her that I loved her and that I wanted to stay with her in the last dreadful moments. But now it is too late.'

'If she were still alive,' Versluis said before he was properly aware of what he was doing, 'would you really have gone to her?'

She considered his question for a moment, and then smiled and shook her head. 'I should have been too embarrassed, I should have been afraid of what she may have thought, and I should probably have

229

done nothing. One is usually too afraid, isn't one? Too afraid of making the gesture, of offering one's hand, of saying the right words; you keep to yourself until it is too late, and then all you have left are remorse and reproof.'

He ought to go now Versluis thought, and bent down to pick up his hat, and on the floor he saw a crumpled, little red ribbon that had fallen out of the bundle on the table. 'I'm sorry that I have not found Mrs Scheffler at home,' he said. 'Would you be so kind as to convey my thanks to her?' But she was not listening to what he saying, nor did she appear to have noticed that he had stood up, his hat in his hand.

'Mr Hirsch's coachman,' she began – 'you know him, don't you? He is very isolated, because there are only one or two other Malays here. There is nobody who speaks his language or who shares his religion, and the black people are afraid of him, because they say that he has knowledge of witchcraft. They believe that he casts spells and controls an immense power. I so often think of that man, even though I hardly know him. But what could I do for him in his loneliness, no matter how much I should like to?'

'Mr Hirsch appears to be a good employer,' Versluis said. 'And if he really does possess supernatural powers, that must be a source of some comfort to him,' he added in a lighter vein in order to depart, but Miss Scheffler did not smile.

'No,' she said firmly, 'it is not good to know, or to see or to feel too much, or to have too much power. Perhaps that is a special gift, but it could never be easy or pleasant. It is better, I sometimes think, simply to go through life accepting everything without asking questions or having to bear the burden of your knowledge around with you.'

Versluis waited another moment, and then he took his leave. He could see that she was not in the mood for company or a visit today, even though she had greeted his arrival cheerfully enough. She might have cleared the clothes and the personal belongings from the table, but they stayed between them, and she did not try to persuade him to wait for the return of her sister-in-law. So he said farewell and left, pausing for a moment on the stoep as he stepped outside, his eyes blinded as usual by the white light reflected from the street. When he saw the figure of a man outlined before him against the glare he thought for a moment that it was Scheffler, but then he recognised Gelmers.

'Is there something wrong?' Versluis asked.

'I'm just feeling a bit dizzy,' the young man said evasively. 'I walked too fast coming here, and it's so hot today. . . .' But the words died away incoherently and his hand groped towards the pole of the verandah for support.

'Can I do something for you?' Versluis enquired uncertainly. 'Rather come back into the house and sit down for a while.'

'No,' the young man said firmly, however, and his feet were already feeling for the verandah steps. Instinctively Versluis put his hand under his elbow to support him, and he became aware of the ashen face and the sweat covering Gelmers's forehead under the brim of his hat, together with the unsavoury odour of illness. But when he tried to remove his hand, Gelmers stumbled over the garden path as if he were about to fall, and Versluis was unable to let go of him.

'Shall I walk with you?' Versluis asked, even though under the circumstances he had hardly any choice. 'Where do you live?'

'In the hotel. The Bloemfontein Hotel.'

It was the hotel beyond the market square, at the other end of the town. 'Is that not too far for you to walk?' he asked, but Gelmers did not answer. 'Wouldn't you perhaps like to come and rest at Mrs Van der Vliet's?' he continued with a rising sense of desperation. What was he to do? They could not stagger through the town in that way, with him supporting this ashen man through the streets, affording a general spectacle to the shopping housewives and servants. Should he go back and risk upsetting Miss Scheffler? Should he call the servant at the parsonage, or have Doctor Kellner, who had mentioned that he lived somewhere in the vicinity, summoned? At the corner in front of the church Gelmers stopped at the intersection, however, and shook Versluis from his arm. 'Thanks,' he said abruptly, 'that's enough, I can carry on myself.'

'But you cannot possibly walk to the hotel on your own,' said Versluis, but the other man took no notice of him.

'They wanted to tidy my room,' he said. 'That was why I went out, but it was stupid of me. It's not good to go out in the heat of the day.' It was clear, however, that he hardly knew what he was saying: the heat of summer had passed, and where they were waiting on the corner of the street the morning air was cool. 'But my room will be ready now, I must go. There are still many things that I have to do,' he said, and turned away without uttering a word or raising his hat.

Versluis remained, staring after him uncertainly as Gelmers walked slowly but with determination down the rise towards the drift and the market square. The man was surely in no condition to reach his hotel unaided, he thought; but on the other hand he had let it be known

231

clearly enough that he wished to be left alone, and Versluis could hardly have forced himself upon him. Besides it was not really that far to the hotel he thought to himself, and there would always be someone in the vicinity to assist him should Gelmers become ill. He found that he was shaking, and was unpleasantly reminded of the way in which their earlier encounter on the verandah of the German club had ended in his own collapse on to the dance floor before the assembled population of Bloemfontein. Such a public disgrace surely could not happen to him a second time, at the intersection of two streets in front of the German church! He would surely not lose consciousness suddenly at this point, toppling into the dust in his pearl-grey suit, to be picked up by some chance passers-by and carried back to Mrs Van der Vliet's house.

He groped hurriedly for a handkerchief in his pocket, only then to discover that he was still clutching the crumpled little red ribbon that he had picked up to return to Miss Scheffler in the living room. What was he to do with it now? He looked around impatiently. He could not really knock at the parsonage and hand it to the servant, but then nor could he simply abandon it here in the white dust where anyone could see him from behind the curtains of the nearby houses.

Somebody might see him standing in the middle of the road, he realised, and he thrust the ribbon into his pocket. Meanwhile he did not seem to have attracted any noticeable attention. A dog lay sleeping in the street, and in the distance he could see an ox-wagon moving across the market square. Gelmers, erect in his check suit, had already reached the pedestrian bridge across the spruit, and was passing the domestic servants who were returning from the well with buckets of water balanced on their heads. The moment of dizziness had passed and, without any further reflection, Versluis carried on, leaning on his cane. How well he already knew these houses, these gardens, these orchards and dry-stone walls, he thought to himself, and how well he would get to know them in the short time that he had left. A servant was shaking out a tablecloth in front of one of the houses, and a group of women were busy in front of the Anglican cathedral. At the end of every street there was the expanse of the veld, grim and waiting. Had it really been only yesterday that he had ridden out with Scheffler to Brandkop? he thought wearily. It felt that so much had happened to him in the interim that weeks or months might have passed.

He had already passed the cathedral when he realised that he was being called, and he turned round in some confusion to see a woman in a striped dress standing on the stony verge above the street. 'Excuse

232

me,' she said hurriedly, with one hand shielding her eyes against the sun, 'excuse me for calling after you in the street in this way, but I recognised you as you passed by, and I so wanted to know how you are.'

Versluis saw that it was the teacher from the English convent school. 'Oh, well, very well thank you,' he said, conscious while giving this assurance of its inaccuracy, and confused by the sudden confrontation.

'Really?' she asked obtrusively while she continued to peer at him from beneath the shelter of her hand. 'Really?'

No, of course not, he thought, suddenly exhausted. The woman was surely able to see for herself what he looked like and could draw her own conclusions without his having to bellow out a report on his health to her in that way in the street. She stood elevated above him in her brilliant but unflattering yellow dress. Did the woman have no taste whatsoever? he wondered, and wished that he could free himself with as little ceremony from her as Gelmers had just done with him.

'I came with some of the other teachers and sisters to begin the preparations,' she informed him as if the information might signify something to him. 'For Easter.'

'Oh yes, for Easter. I hadn't been aware that it was already Easter.'

'It's only on Sunday – it's Passion Week now. But I forgot, your own Church is probably not as liturgical as ours, perhaps you don't pay so much attention to Easter.'

'I do not belong to any Church,' he said, leaning heavily on his cane. Now he had shocked her he reflected too late, but she showed no sign of shock as she stood gazing down at him – it was rather something like concern or sympathy.

She looked around, but her companions had already entered the church, and she hesitated for a moment, as if she were considering whether she ought to be conversing alone with a virtually unknown man, even if she was standing on the ridge upon which the cathedral had been built. 'I must go,' she said. 'There is still much that we need to do. But if – I don't know – I don't want to make you feel obliged to do anything, but if you were perhaps to feel like . . . on Good Friday or Easter Sunday. . . . The services are particularly moving, even if you aren't Anglican or even a regular churchgoer. If you wish to come, you would always be extremely welcome.'

'Thank you,' said Versluis, 'that's very kind of you,' and he raised his hat in parting. He had turned away and was already walking off when he heard her call and saw her hurrying towards him, holding the hem of her dress out of the dusty street.

233

'You must excuse me,' she said out of breath, 'but I should like you to know this, that is to say, I should like to tell you myself, in case you should hear it from someone else, or even perhaps not at all. . . .' What was this woman talking about? Versluis wondered in astonishment as he observed her timidity. 'I am going to join the sisterhood,' she said then. 'I am to be accepted as a postulant after Easter.'

It was not clear to him what precisely this signified, and so he had difficulty in finding an appropriate response, but the teacher's thin, freckled face was radiant with joy at the prospect. 'I hope that you will be very happy in your new life,' he said without understanding.

'Oh, I shall, I know I shall. To know what you want to do with your life, to put everything that you have at the service of the Lord – how could one be anything but happy?' Then she turned away quickly and walked with quick steps, almost ran, up the rise in front of the cathedral, with her dress lifted out of the dust. In the darkness of the cathedral porch her dress flashed once more, and then she had vanished and Versluis was free to continue slowly down the empty street, leaning on his cane.

'I have received a letter from Mrs Helmond from Aliwal North,' Mrs Van der Vliet announced as she took her place for lunch amid a great deal of rustling at the head of the table.

'I hope that they are well,' Versluis remarked.

'Oh yes, she sounds very cheerful,' she said, smoothing down her dress. Her husband, as always, had already occupied his place, as if meals provided an eagerly awaited break in his monotonous existence, and Polderman was just positioning himself at the table, but as yet there was no sign of Du Toit, and she clasped her hands while she waited. 'And did you have a pleasant morning, Mr Versluis?'

'I dropped in at the parsonage, but Miss Scheffler was the only one at home, so I did not stay long.' It was perhaps better not to say anything about Gelmers's presence, he decided, for Mrs Van der Vliet had let it be known on a number of occasions that she wished to hear nothing of him. While if he were to mention his encounter with the English teacher he knew that the whole meal would become a diatribe on the creeping extension of Anglican or Popish influence in the town, with particular reference to the convent schools. She showed a complete willingness, however, to occupy herself with the question of why Mrs Scheffler herself had not been at home and whether she had taken the baby with her; but even this subject did not enjoy her full attention while she kept glancing at the empty place at the table. 'Polderman, go and see what is keeping Du Toit,' she directed, and Polderman leapt up obediently.

They sat at the table in silence, and Van der Vliet nodded and smiled while he waited for his food. 'The Helmonds are busy furnishing a house for themselves,' Mrs Van der Vliet informed Versluis in the interim. 'Five bedrooms, although I do not know what they want with so much space. And they are just as busy as they were when they were here – two dances and a picnic in the short time that they have been there, she writes. But they are indeed an extremely lively couple, everyone likes them.'

'They are young,' came her husband's unsolicited contribution from the bottom of the table.

'When one is young, one believes that one has a great deal of time,' Mrs Van der Vliet said, without any obvious sign that she had heard him, 'one believes that one's life will never end. It is only when one grows older that one realises how little time one has.'

Surprised by the manner in which she had responded to what her husband had said, Versluis looked at her. Who would have expected a pronouncement of this sort from this calm, phlegmatic woman or suspected that she occupied herself with such thoughts while she sat, day after day, in the living room with clasped hands watching over the portrait of the deceased? He added nothing, however, nor did the conversation continue, for at that very moment Polderman appeared with Du Toit, who took his place with a muttered apology which Mrs Van der Vliet ignored. She rang the bell and the servants brought the food, Van der Vliet said grace, the water-jug was passed and water poured, and Mrs Van der Vliet enquired solicitously about Versluis's appetite. Then they ate in silence which was disturbed only by the clatter of cutlery, and it took a while for Du Toit to be allowed to announce the news that he was suppressing with such obvious difficulty.

'The Dutchman who is staying at the Bloemfontein Hotel collapsed this morning in the middle of the square,' he announced. 'Right next to the well, right in the mud where all the blacks gather.'

The report did not, however, elicit the response that he expected, and Mrs Van der Vliet merely raised her eyebrows. 'People who are ill ought to stay in bed where they can be looked after and not gad about in the streets,' she declared.

'What's the matter with him?' her husband enquired with some interest.

235

'I don't know. They say it was convulsions, but others maintain that it was a stroke.' He looked hopefully from face to face in the expectation that he might be interrogated further, but Mrs Van der Vliet maintained a stony silence and refused to show any further sign of interest: he had been late for lunch this afternoon, and no small sensation of which he knew could possibly excuse him from such a trespass.

It was only after the meal that Versluis was able to corner Du Toit in the passage to ask him about further details. 'The Netherlander about whom you were speaking,' he began, 'the man who became ill this morning, Gelmers. . . . Do you know anything about that?'

'I couldn't get away from the shop, sir, I merely saw people running across the square.'

'Was there someone to help him?'

'Oh yes, all the blacks at the well, and people also came out of the shops when they saw that something was wrong.' Confused by Versluis's sudden interest, he was trying to speak formal Dutch, and he became almost unintelligibly entangled in cases and tenses.

'And how is he?'

'I heard nothing more, sir. But I did see Doctor Krause walking in the direction of the hotel, so I suppose that he was on his way there.'

Versluis nodded, and Du Toit slipped away, in a hurry to get back to his work. So it had turned out well Versluis thought with relief, and the young man had been taken care of. What more would he have been able to do if he had accompanied him that morning? Except perhaps to catch him as he stopped and began to totter, staggering with the body of the unconscious young man in his arms, to the general amusement of the servants at the well.

On the stoep at the back of the house Van der Vliet was standing screwing his eyes up in the mild afternoon sun. 'I wonder if we'll still get any rain, or whether we've seen our last little shower,' he remarked. 'It wouldn't surprise me if we got some frost within the next week or two.'

'Does the winter come so quickly in Africa?' Versluis asked.

'Oh, here everything is sudden, this land knows no mercy. You haven't experienced one of our winters yet, have you now? But you'll learn. The winter here destroys everything, not like in the Netherlands where the rain still nourishes the earth. Whatever survives the drought here is killed by frost. There is no mercy.'

He looked pensively at the neat beds of his vegetable garden, at the rows of trees in the orchard, and then cast a quick glance at Versluis, as if he wished to apologise for such unusual verbosity, and with a muttered farewell he shuffled away in his slippers.

Versluis sat on the back stoep where the sun was softened by the creepers; the late afternoon light and the colouring leaves were compounded into a hazy screen of gold behind which he sheltered and basked in the heat. He had slept and rested, he had given his dusty shoes to the servant to clean and had drunk coffee with Mrs Van der Vliet in the drawing room, he had forgotten or come to terms with all the fatigue and afflictions of the previous week or two, or whatever the case may be: all that had been left behind. Smoke was already beginning to waft through the pale blue sky above the chimneys of the town, and beyond the trees and the orchards came the distant sounds of late afternoon: cocks crowing to each other, a dog barking, and a man's voice, so far away that one could not make out his words. This afternoon he had taken up the *Aeneid* once more, after a long period during which he had not looked at it because he had felt too tired for the concentration that it demanded and the feelings that it evoked. But now behind the golden screen of creepers he was reading the fourth book, the story of Dido's love for Aeneas and her suicide after his departure, its passion and despair carried on the mighty waves of verse.

He lowered the book for a moment, at the point at which Dido lay with bleeding wounds upon the pyre, waiting for the release that death would bring. All was well, he thought to himself, consoled. For there were always times in which the anguish and uncertainty abated, when the horror passed and the pain was suspended for a while; moments in which meaninglessness and confusion were exorcised, and when reality, however briefly, appeared to be perfect – even in this forsaken town, even in this foreign land of exile at the edge of civilisation. It had been a good thing not to have read Virgil for a while, to discover him anew this day in the cosy warmth of a late summer afternoon, in the shelter of the glowing golden screen of climbers.

Nobody came to interrupt his train of thought; in the house all was still. Slowly he raised the book and read further. '*Tum Iuno omnipotens longum miserata dolum.* . . .'

'Then the almighty Juno took pity on her lingering pain and anguished death, and sent Iris down from Olympus to release the wrestling spirit from the knotted limbs. . . .' Slowly he savoured the words upon his tongue and lingered over the syllables. Around him the day had become still: the gathering swell paused, imbued with gold it towered in the air, and the crest was petrified at the very moment when it should have tilted, toppled and broken. 'And so Iris descended on saffron wings, glittering as the dew, trailing a thousand colours as she caught the sun, and came to rest over Dido's head. "I take this lock of hair as an offering to Pluto according to my command, and from this body I release you," she said, and with her right hand she cut the lock. And all warmth flowed from Dido's body, and her life vanished upon the wind.'

With the book on his lap Versluis remained sitting there, not reading any further, nor did he make any move to go indoors, even though it was growing cold. The wave raised itself and caught the golden light, its crest fixed in a vitrified swell. It is good he thought, it is good.

4

T HE DAYS of sitting on the verandah had passed: the air was too changeable, Mrs Van der Vliet determined in a manner which brooked no opposition, and she announced that she would have a fire made in Versluis's room each morning and evening against the cold. 'You must take care,' she warned him, 'the winter here is severe, and one should not expose oneself unnecessarily to danger, Mr Versluis.' His polite protests made not the slightest impression. 'I'll have an eiderdown put out for you,' she added adamantly.

He thus gave up opposing her, and an eiderdown was indeed spread out over his bed and wood brought in and carefully stacked by the servant to provide a small fire which tempered the growing chill of the early mornings and late afternoons. The sun was now touching the windowsill of his room in the course of its long decline to the north and it fell obliquely across the floor, so that it was good to be able to remain there with his books. He felt less and less inclined to leave his room, even for meals or afternoon coffee in the living room with Mrs Van der Vliet.

Thus it was in his room that Scheffler found him on his next call. 'Still Virgil?' he asked with a smile.

'Among others. I've begun to read French again, but it is to Virgil that I keep returning.'

'I never learnt French,' the clergyman said as he began to page through the books on the table. 'It's one of the things that I've always been meaning to do, and since I have never got around to doing it, I probably never will.'

'You could always still start.'

'There is no time, there is never any time. What's more, what use would it be to me here in Africa?'

'You would be able to read Montaigne, or La Rochefoucauld or Pascal, like me.'

'I should be able to do so much,' Scheffler said and lingered over the *Pensées*. 'How are you?'

'Well, as you can see. I stay in my room, and I'm finally reading all the books that I brought with me. Doctor Brill was also kind enough to lend me a whole pile from his own library.'

'That's the best thing to do, the weather has suddenly turned cold; the farmers are expecting an early frost this year. It's best to stay indoors and –' he looked at the title on the spine of the book he was holding, 'and read Pascal.' He paged through the unintelligible text as if he hoped nevertheless to decipher something of it, but then he shook his head and reluctantly put the book down. 'You came to visit us the other morning,' he said, 'and both Mathilde and I were out. Adèle told us that you had been there. I wanted to come over myself, but there was absolutely no chance – first it was Easter, and then there were other things, I also had to preach and conduct the services for the black people. . . .' He was pacing up and down in front of the hearth, in which the glow of the fire was hardly visible in the bright sunlight that fell across the floor. 'Did you hear that Mr Gelmers has been very ill?'

'I had heard something of the sort – someone mentioned it, Mr Du Toit. . . .'

'That he *is* very ill, I should have said. He has had a number of bad haemorrhages, so bad that Doctor Krause was concerned and let me know.'

Versluis put the book-holder that had been moved by Scheffler back in its place and tidied the books in the pile beside him. 'Is Mr Gelmers a Lutheran?'

'I don't know what he is,' said Scheffler, dismissing the question with an impatient gesture. 'He did not ever try to make contact with Dominee Radloff, and it appears that he never went to services in the Dutch church, but that is beside the point. And he is very ill, as I said.' He forgot about the books and walked across to the window: with his hands behind his back he stood staring into the garden where the first leaves on the peach and pear trees were beginning to change colour. 'He is dying,' he said in a low voice. 'The doctor says that it's a matter of weeks, perhaps not even as long as that.'

They were silent. It was too hot in that room with the sun shining in over the floorboards Versluis thought, the fire had made it stuffy; the dressing gown that he was wearing was too heavy, its weight oppressive.

'I have almost no experience of dying,' Scheffler said in the same tone without looking around. 'I am a priest, I am intimately involved with life and death, but I have never been that close to death. We have taken him in and he will die in our house, we are closest to him in this strange place. I will find out what it means to die.'

'Would you mind passing me the water-jug?' Versluis asked, and Scheffler automatically turned round and passed him a glass and the jug.

'Death is really so close,' he said, smiling at the thought. 'One thinks that it is far off, even though one should know better, but then you suddenly discover that it has been carried into your home.'

The wide sleeves of the dressing gown were in the way: he knocked over the little pile of books and the glass of water fell off the table, shattering on the floor. Upset, he stared at the shards, the jug still in his hand, but Scheffler had been roused from his reverie and was already on his knees, sweeping the pieces together. 'Don't worry,' he said in agitation, 'there is no permanent damage. Broken glass brings good luck. I will ask the servant to come and sweep it up for you.'

'Wouldn't you like to stay and have some coffee?' Versluis asked.

'I must be going, I just dropped by in passing, as usual. But actually – what I came to ask, if you would like to, when you feel well enough again, was whether you might not come across to us again.' Versluis put the jug down. 'Of course we are always happy to see you, all of us, but it is particularly for the sake of Mr Gelmers that I am asking.'

With his handkerchief Versluis wiped off the water that he had spilt on his dressing gown. 'If he is that ill . . .' he began.

'He is weak, but is still entirely conscious of all that is happening around him, and since he has not made many friends in Bloemfontein, particularly amongst the Dutch people. . . . I had thought of asking Doctor Brill to visit him, but he has so many responsibilities, and so I wondered whether you wouldn't be kind enough to come over occasionally.'

'I did not ever have any contact with Mr Gelmers,' Versluis said rapidly. 'We hardly know one another.'

'I am asking you only because I know that you have the time, you have no other responsibilities, and if you would perhaps like to come and read to him, or simply just sit by him. . . . I am certain that the mere thought that someone was taking an interest would mean something to him in itself. I do not wish to burden you in any way, I know that you are not in good health yourself. . . .' He stood there like a schoolboy, so uncomfortable at the favour he was asking that Versluis began to feel uneasy himself at his own reluctance.

241

'I'll come,' he said to end the conversation as quickly as possible. 'I'll come and visit you and your family again one afternoon. But wouldn't you like to sit down?'

'No, no thanks,' came the clergyman's hurried reply. 'I only hope that you come soon, and that we'll then have a chance to talk properly; I have to be on my way now.' He picked up his hat and said farewell. 'Mathilde and Adèle send their best wishes,' he added. 'They'll be just as pleased to see you again as I shall. And thank you very much,' he said, 'thank you for being prepared to help.' With these words he disappeared.

The sun fell in across the windowsill, the fire was wasting among the glowing logs in the grate. But Versluis did not take up his book to continue reading. On the floor the shards of the broken glass remained where Scheffler had swept them.

'Pastor Scheffler tells me that they have taken Gelmers in with them,' Versluis tried in the silence that had fallen around the dining table. 'He's the young Dutchman that Mr Du Toit told us about.'

With ponderous dignity Mrs Van der Vliet cut the small piece of meat on her plate into still finer pieces and then with her fork she carried the fragments to her mouth without showing any sign that she had heard.

'I heard that the people at the hotel said that they would not have him there any longer,' Polderman ventured.

'Pastor Scheffler has far too kind a heart,' Mrs Van der Vliet declared. 'I have always said that.'

'They would probably have turfed him on to the street if he hadn't found anywhere else to stay, they're not particularly interested in anything other than money. I heard that they told him that they were running a hotel, not a hospital.'

'Too much kindness turns to folly,' Mrs Van der Vliet pronounced, carefully wiping her mouth. 'People simply take advantage of his kindness and lack of experience.'

'But surely there was no-one else prepared to take him in. I don't think that he made any friends in this town.'

'What are these people doing in Bloemfontein?' she asked. 'If they don't know anybody here, they should stay where they come from.'

'He came out for his health.'

'People who are ill should stay with their friends and family rather than heap trouble and inconvenience upon strangers. Where are the

242

Schefflers meant to find room for guests in that house? And what about poor Mrs Scheffler? With only one servant for the whole household, and she some raw woman that they brought in from the mission station, and a man to look after the horse and the garden. What about all the extra laundry? All the sheets?'

'I did not get the impression that the Schefflers considered it a burden,' Versluis remarked, but she was unstoppable, carried away on a sudden wave of meddling concern.

'And what about all the extra heating? What does wood cost nowadays? As much as four pounds a load at the market.' Her voice grew shrill, for this was clearly a matter about which she harboured strong feelings: she rang the bell fiercely to summon the servants. 'And who, may I ask, is going to pay for the doctor and the medicine?' Polderman and Du Toit stared at their plates, while her husband shrank at the end of the table, as was his custom whenever she was overcome by one of her fits of rage. 'And what about the meals? People who are ill require special diets that have to be specially prepared, nobody knows that better than I. Where is Mrs Scheffler to find the time, with a baby and a lame sister-in-law? What is the price of milk now? That is, if one can get it with winter coming. What do eggs cost? Three shillings a dozen I had to pay last week, not a penny less.'

It was no concern of Mrs Van der Vliet Versluis thought, disgusted by this performance, but he knew from experience that it was useless to try to reason with her when she was in such a mood. 'No doubt Mr Gelmers will reimburse the Schefflers for any expenses that they may have to incur,' he remarked reassuringly, but Mrs Van der Vliet had no desire to be reassured.

'Reimburse them? The fellow is as poor as a church mouse. Mrs Krause told me herself that his luggage consists of a suitcase – one solitary suitcase, Mr Versluis, imagine that! The gentleman landed here with two collars and a shirt, and there is no point in Doctor Krause's expecting to be paid, let alone the Schefflers. He arrived here without any winter clothing – how do you think he left Holland? Not that he'll ever need any winter clothing now.' Her lower chin trembled in indignation as she passed the plates to the servants. 'And then he'll finally have to be buried by charity and at the expense of others,' she added in a rising voice. 'No, such people ought to remain where they belong. Whatever are they doing here?' On that rhetorical question the subject was closed, and they ate their compote in an uncomfortable silence.

After the meal Versluis came across Polderman on the stoep where he was smoking a cigar before going to visit his girlfriend.

'Do you perhaps feel like going to visit Gelmers?' he asked, and the young man took the cigar from his mouth and stared at him with an expression of astonishment on his pleasant round face.

'I don't think that he'll want to see me, Mr Versluis,' he then replied. 'He never really showed any desire to have anything to do with us Hollanders.'

'Perhaps he'll feel a greater need for some contact now that he is ill?'

'I don't know,' Polderman said doubtfully. 'If he is as ill as they say he is, I don't believe he'll be in need of any kind of visit.' He stared uncomfortably at the cigar in his hand, wavering between generosity and reluctance, and Versluis did not pursue the matter.

In the large house life carried on. Miss Pronk's old room was turned out, scrubbed and aired, and her presence had already almost been forgotten; the faint scent of talcum powder and tuberoses that had clung to the curtains had vanished. Mrs Van der Vliet moved tirelessly up and down the house after the servants, inaudible save for the rustle of her dress in the gloom or the telltale creaking of floorboards. In the living room, into which she would withdraw in the afternoons, she had had a foot-warmer installed over which she would spread out her skirts with great satisfaction while she drank coffee beneath the portrait of her deceased husband. In the garden Van der Vliet shuffled about amongst the beds, picking the last of the fruit and supervising the sweeping of the leaves that were beginning to fall. The bells of the Anglican cathedral and the little Catholic church further along the ridge routinely marked the passing of the days. Sometimes, when the wind blew from the west, they could hear a tinny peal from the English convent on the outskirts of the town; and all these bells, which had initially annoyed Versluis, had now grown as familiar and reassuring to him as the routine of that well-ordered house, something on which he could depend, knowing that they would carry him forward in safety.

One day the gardener brought him his trunks from the outside room, and he took out his winter clothes and packed those for summer away in the tissue paper which had enfolded them in the Netherlands. Would moths get into them while they were packed away? he wondered, and considered whether he should ask Mrs Van der Vliet for some naphthaline. But did it matter? he then thought, and sat down on the edge of the bed, fatigued by the effort, and unable to find an answer to the question. Neatly folded, with tissue paper between each layer and bundles of tissue paper thrust into the sleeves, the light summer suits lay in the trunk together with the panama hat and the linen underwear, and he shut the lid and locked it, and gave instructions for the trunks to be taken back to the outside room.

A sense of apathy and fatigue which he was unable to dispel had taken possession of him, nor did he even feel inclined to shake it off any longer. To be left alone was enough for him: to read or just to sit upright in a chair with his eyes open and a book in his hand, without a thought passing through his head, as if he sat waiting – but for what? He looked at the door, but no handle was turned; no footsteps sounded in the passage outside. Silently the sun shifted across the windowsill.

He ought to go to the Schefflers again he thought, but he hesitated and drew back. He was too tired for the walk and the company; he did not feel strong enough; the mornings and late afternoons were already too chilly for him. Moreover, he did not want to disturb them while they had a sick man in the house who was presumably enough trouble himself: he did not wish to force himself upon Gelmers, nor was he willing to have the young Dutchman forced upon him in that way. At the same time he realised that he could not put off going there forever, after all the hospitality that he had already enjoyed at the parsonage and the repeated, sincere invitations that he had received from the Schefflers. Uncomfortably he weighed up the alternatives, and then realised with some surprise that he was thinking of the parsonage and its inhabitants with a feeling that he could scarcely place, but which he was almost inclined to call longing, were it not that this word was entirely inappropriate in the context of his calm, ordered existence. What was there in the parsonage that could attract him? he asked himself soberly. An impulsive, sincere young priest who was experiencing problems with his office; his unconventional sister; a bare, formal living room and conversation that was unpredictable from one sentence to the next, concerning both the direction it might take and the heights or depths that it might reach – all these things surely meant nothing to him. Had he developed such a need for company here in Africa; he who had moved so undisturbed and self-possessed between his house and the club with a regularity that was as regularly broken by an evening with the aunts or dinner at the Van Meerdervoorts, a visit to the concert or a vacation? No, it then struck him with a sudden, unwelcome clarity: it was simply that, wrenched free from his familiar way of life with its reassuring routine, he had suddenly been made aware of things that previously had hardly penetrated to him, and together with this had come the consciousness

245

of an incompleteness in his own existence which he had scarcely suspected till then. For an instant he remembered the room in the lamplight, the women occupied in it together, the two men bowed with eyes closed over their instruments, and then he violently terminated this train of thought and focused his attention elsewhere. He postponed the visit to the parsonage for the moment.

The country was changing, and day by day Versluis discovered ways in which it was transforming itself around him. That grey, disconsolate land under its cloak of dust and driving sand, monotonous in its expansiveness and desolation, with its endless, unmarked distances and low horizons that promised nothing – each day it was refined further and the lines of the landscape stood out with greater clarity. The trees changed colour in the orchards, along with the willows along the spruit and around the dam, and the falling leaves were blown away by the wind; dust was whirled past his window. The severity of the sun had been tempered and the white sky retained hardly any heat. Motionless, the land lay stretched out, the wide, empty streets of the town, the houses in their cleanly stripped gardens. And the veld that surrounded them, bleached as white as bone beneath a lofty sky, sparse and cold as it grew towards winter: without motion, without sound, it lay waiting and increasingly he too found himself lowering his book to listen, with his head raised, even though he would not have been able to say what he was listening for. A footfall in the passage or a voice calling in the garden, the peal of a bell, or a bugle in the distance which announced the arrival of the post-cart? Any one of these perhaps, and perhaps none of them. Sometimes a visitor arrived, one of the members of the little Dutch community would come and sit with him and talk, and once or twice Hirsch looked in, lively and full of invitations to come and eat with them once again when he felt like it – during the school holidays the girls were going to stay with friends in Fauresmith and the boys were going on a hunting expedition, then it would be quieter in the house and his wife had said that they should ask Mr Versluis over. Once, to his surprise, a short letter arrived from old De Bruïne at the club, which he read and put aside, and intermittently the mail continued to bring his newspapers from the Netherlands. He left them unopened for days, until Van der Vliet came to ask shyly if he might borrow them and carried them away with him to some unknown sanctuary.

Day by day during the course of that autumn Versluis also marked the changes in his own condition, steady and implacable since that evening when he had slipped on the dance floor and fallen amongst the dancers in their gay attire. He observed the attacks of fever, the fits of coughing, the moments of weakness and dizziness and the occasional haemorrhage, registered them, and then brushed this awareness aside: he would drink a glass of water, take a cough lozenge or drink some laudanum or the medicine which Doctor Kellner had prescribed, stay in bed later in the mornings or lie down during the day. Mrs Van der Vliet asked no questions, and neither of the physicians imposed himself upon him.

The brilliant light-drenched days were filled with a peacefulness that, being unexpected, came as a kind of deliverance, while the nights on the other hand were times of sudden and irrational anxiety. He would nod off quite soon, but then sleep restlessly; and his dreams were feverish and confused, filled with images that evoked memories and associations which he was unable to place, dreams of parting and departure, in the narrow grey streets of a familiar city that he was nevertheless unable to identify. He wandered over the cobbles knowing that he was doing so for the last time and that time was running out, conscious, with a sense of growing anxiety, that he could not remember the address to which he was going. Squares, canals and vistas succeeded one another like a pack of cards being shuffled before his eyes, and he became entangled in the folds of his flapping cloak. There was no more time he realised despairingly while he searched in vain in his waistcoat pocket for his watch, he would now have to look for a cab; but the streets slid away beneath his feet and he could not find one. The lacquered black trunks, spattered with rain, were being carried from the house and he could no longer stop the porters, even though the ship was already anchored far out, and no matter how hard he tried, it was already irretrievably late and he had been abandoned there forever with the trunks lying in glistening piles in the rain – unclaimed baggage in the middle of an empty square.

But then there were also other, more astounding dreams in which the journey had almost come to an end and the destination was in view, with the coach continuing to rock across the endless sweep of the veld, rising and falling like a ship over the undulations of ridges, ravines and streams while dust rose in lazy clouds behind it. Prostrate in that narrow, swaying carriage he waited for the journey to end and saw the English teacher opposite him smile and lean forward towards him in her yellow dress. 'I am Christ's bride,' she said rapturously and a white veil enshrouded her. She was dressed like a bride he noticed, but no, he then realised, it was the heavy, powdery white dust from the journey that had whitened her hair and clothes, as pale as the hand that she now held out to him. The touch of her fingers was icy: he recoiled from it with a cry of terror and heard Hirsch's laugh.

But then he had escaped the constriction of the coach: silently and as effortlessly as a shadow he glided along the streets of Bloemfontein which had grown so wide that the houses and trees hardly remained visible above the horizon to either side. He roamed from one unrecognisable street to another, in search of some familiar landmark, and with relief he noticed someone in the distance. It was a woman, he saw as he hurried towards her, and then he recognised the cheap red-and-green tartan dress and realised that it must be the young Scottish woman who had died in the hotel; but when he reached her he discovered that she was a stranger who passed him by without recognition. Of course, he remembered with relief, Miss Scheffler had said that she would be giving the leftover clothes to the poor, and he continued across the wide plain, carried forward like a phantom, swept onward like paper whirling from the town's rubbish heaps. Until, once again, in the light of an invisible sun, he perceived someone in the distance and hurried forward. It was a man in a white summer suit he noted as they approached one another; it was a middle-aged man who supported himself on his cane as he moved forward: he saw that it was himself approaching him from afar, and his heart was gripped by fear and horror. But when the man drew close to him he could see that this lonely figure, too, was a stranger who passed him without any sign of recognition. Even the clothes that he had packed away so carefully in tissue paper had been handed out to the needy inhabitants of the town he realised, and he woke up in an awe-filled panic. Through his windows with their raised blinds the moonlight fell across the table, the chair, the floorboards, and in that chill light the room was as bright as day. Outside in the cold the dogs of the town were barking and howling from one garden to another, and then they fell silent. In the hearth the glow had died.

He would now be startled from his sleep in the dead of night, that most chill and silent hour, to lie immobile and with a beating heart. He had no wish to light the candle beside his bed and read, he did not want to drink any water or take laudanum to calm himself; all he wanted was to be able to sleep until dawn, when the sunlight would bring both life and sound back into the world, but he already knew that after that first, restless sleep he would not easily or quickly settle down again.

It had rained on the day that he had left Delft he remembered as he lay without moving on the pile of pillows, blinded by the moonlight. Pompe had fussed around him, a travelling-rug over her arm, and had accompanied him from the front door to the cab with an umbrella; in that light the raindrops had fallen like pearls on the trunks which the servant had carried out. Then Pompe had shut the door and the carriage had begun to move, clattering over the cobblestones: he saw the rows of narrow houses, the bare trees along the canals and their surfaces rippling in the rain, and in his winter coat he was shivering with cold, but he did not look back. In the deserted house, Pompe had begun to draw the blinds, enshroud the lamps in dust covers, and cover the furniture.

How far away that winter afternoon was already, both in time and space, and yet how close as he lay in bed, immobile in the cold.

He could see the dull brown light and the low sky above the gables; the passing houses; groups of workers; a woman walking by with rapid steps, her head bowed under her glistening umbrella; the pools of water and mud through which the carriage was being drawn. He was rocking on the springs, deeply wrapped in his coat; a child on a street corner shouted something; a man peered from the darkness of a newspaper kiosk; and in the cigar store a light was already burning against the darkness of the day. The Netherlands was so close, the day of his departure had not yet passed nor had his parting been completed: he was separated from it by an invisible screen of gauze, a tiny layer as thin as glass interposed between reflection and reality – touch it, and fingertips would touch fingertips. With the merest effort a hand could be held out to grasp another hand, a gateway thrust through the separating layer of glass and the world of mirrors entered, its ground as firm as that of the reality that had been left behind. But it was not possible to check the course of events, to beat with his cane against the roof of the carriage and command the coachman to turn back. Without a sound the glass closed behind you and sealed you within the hermetic mirror-world in which your feet made no sound and the cab carried on, silently swaying on its way to the harbour.

Back past the cigar store and the newspaper kiosk, past the servant-girls with their baskets and the labourers with bags over their heads in the rain, past the pump, the trees and the tall houses. Pay the coachman and have the trunks untied and off-loaded, piled up in the rain on the pavement of that deserted street; retrace your path up the steps and through the narrow door into the house that has just been left behind, the house in which the blinds are now drawn, the

249

lamps wrapped up and the furniture covered with dustcloths. Without a sound move through the chilly, darkened rooms and up the stairs to the room where the bed has been stripped, the bedside curtains removed, the grate empty. Above the mantelpiece the silver vacancy of the mirror reflects the vacancy of the room.

Raise the blinds and stand for a long time in front of the window, looking out across the garden at the back of the house with its vacant flowerbeds and dripping trees. No, there can be no going back: with each instant time grows irrevocable, and life continues on its implacable course.

Go back through the cold, deserted house and draw the door shut behind you without looking back; have the trunks loaded once more; climb in and give the coachman his instructions. Back through the muddy streets, beneath the lowered sky; distant steeples beyond the polder and the ditches that catch the daylight; move past the last memories of the Netherlands; and then there is the harbour with its clutter of ships' funnels and masts, and the sea voyage, surging up and down over the surf with marine birds that announce the land. Accept the low coastline that is now looming up above you against the sky, accept the long journey by coach in the swirling dust and the hotel room, and town with its empty streets and the vacancy that surrounds it: accept this vacancy, accept the loneliness; accept death. Accept; accept.

The moonlight slid over the edge of the table, fell across the floor and then withdrew back over the windowsill: propped up against the pillows he followed that silent movement. Far off a flurry of barking and howling rose up again beyond the houses and then grew still. The moon had set, and in that immense darkness nothing moved.

Versluis fell asleep again and was woken by the servant kneeling to light the fire. His coffee was brought, and after that the water for washing, the ewer wrapped in towels to keep it hot. It was already light, and the first rays of the sun were falling obliquely across the garden, glinting on the bare branches of the trees and the vine; the night and its terrors had been left behind.

The young Baumanns and Hirsches had arranged a picnic to which half of the town's young people had been invited: it would take place on a Wednesday, when the shops were shut for the afternoon, and Polderman and Du Toit were also asked. They were going to go out to Tempe, Polderman, ebullient and excited, informed them at the table, and Mrs Baumann and Hirsch were to go along as chaperones.

'Some people are unable to do anything in any ordinary way,' Mrs Van der Vliet declared with a voice in which she had extraordinarily managed to blend a degree of envy and admiration with her disapproval. 'Once they feel like a picnic fifty people have to be invited at once, as if money were no object.'

'It's really not that many, madam,' Polderman said propitiatingly. 'Only young people will be going.'

'Whatever induced them to think of a picnic when it is already almost winter? It gets dark just after five, and to want to gad about after that in the night air . . . .'

'But it's only to Tempe, madam,' Polderman persisted, and she was finally won over to the cause by a personal request from Mrs Hirsch. Versluis noticed the landau in front of the house with Amien sitting motionless on the box, he heard Mrs Hirsch's cheerful chatter and carefree laugh in the living room, and then her quick, trippling steps and the rustle of her dress came down the passage. She tapped at the door and her smiling face appeared around the corner almost before he was able to answer.

'Mr Versluis,' she said – 'no, don't get up, don't let me disturb you. I can't stay, I just dropped in for a moment to see dear Mrs Van der Vliet, and I can't leave without coming to greet you, nor without bringing you something to show that you are still in our thoughts.' She held out a bunch of violets to him: he could see her tiny hand in a black kid glove and smelt the sweetness of the flowers. 'A few late violets from our garden – probably the last ones before the frost. No, no,' she quickly added, 'don't see me out. It's entirely unnecessary. But if there is something that we can do for you, just send us a note. And as soon as we have a bit of peace in the house you must come and have Sunday lunch with us, my husband has already told you.' Then she was gone and left only the sweetness of the violets behind: he heard her light, quick footsteps along the passage, the sound of her voice in the hall, and when he reached the stoep on which Mrs Van der Vliet was staring after her, she had already entered the carriage and Amien was touching the horses with his whip. She looked round to wave at them, but the carriage was already on its way: above the garden walls and hedges they could see only Amien sitting high up on the box in his funnel-shaped hat with the whip in his hand.

Mrs Hirsch had come to ask Mrs Van der Vliet to contribute a chicken pie to the picnic and, aware of the implicit compliment to her baking skills, Mrs Van der Vliet began to look upon the undertaking with a more kindly eye. She withdrew in silent dignity into the kitchen where she spent the best part of the following day, assisted by both servants, and by late afternoon two large dishes encrusted with the lightest of golden pastries were placed on the dining room table, both to cool down and to call forth the necessary guilty admiration as they filled the house with their aroma. A tin of cinnamon biscuits was added as an unsolicited bonus, and even Polderman and Du Toit's illicit requests for flannels to be pressed and shoes to be polished were met with an unusual degree of indulgence.

Mrs Hirsch's brief visit had involved them all in the outing, filling the whole house with a feeling of gay expectation, and on Wednesday afternoon they all gathered on the front stoep to watch the two young men, brightly clad in flannels and sports jackets, being fetched by their friends in a spring-wagon. Colourful ribbons had been tied to the horses' harness and the hood of the carriage, and the cheerful young people in their gay clothes looked as if were part of a wedding-party. Mrs Van der Vliet was still issuing final instructions regarding the pies which, swathed in napkins and packed carefully into a basket, were now being lifted by the servants into the wagon, but Polderman and Du Toit were both far too excited to listen, and in fact nothing was audible above the laughter and the cries of the picnickers. She was still issuing unheeded warnings about the night air when the wagon began to move. The ribbons fluttered, there was a waving of hands, handkerchiefs and parasols and the confused fragments of thank-yous and goodbyes drifted back to them as the vehicle moved down the street in a cloud of fine dust. It was followed by the Hirsches' landau, filled with the billowing dresses of Mrs Hirsch and Baumann and another group of girls, and finally by a fully loaded buggy driven by Hirsch himself with two of his little boys balanced upon, and clutching a pile of baskets and rugs. With a sweeping gesture he doffed his hat in passing to Mrs Van der Vliet. 'Don't you wish to come along?' he laughingly called to Versluis when he saw him on the stoep, but the question was not meant seriously and no response was expected.

The singing of the young people died away in the distance at the end of the street where they had gone to fetch the last of the picnickers at the Presidency, and the eddying cloud of dust had subsided. Those who had gone out to the stoep to watch returned indoors again, including Mrs Van der Vliet, who experienced some difficulty getting up the stairs in her black dress which she held up above her feet with both hands. 'Those young people,' she remarked, half to herself, thoughtfully and without any disapproval, and she gave a slight smile as if there were things that she too could remember, picnics and outings and carriages filled with singing boys and girls.

'Yes, indeed,' said her husband; and then he shuffled away to his obscure refuge in the garden, while she went back into the house.

The dust had settled, the street was empty; the servants had finished their work, and in the house all was still. Afternoons were always a time of tranquillity and rest, but this was more true than ever on the town's weekly half-day when the shops and offices were closed, and with the departure of the band of laughing, singing picnickers a sense of desolation had descended. The sky was without colour: the sunlight fell white upon the empty street, and nothing moved except for the occasional gust of wind that rustled through the dry leaves and whirled a cloud of dust through the garden.

This was the afternoon for the long-delayed visit to the Schefflers Verluis realised, and so, slowly but with determination, he gathered his strength and began to get himself ready. He would take along his latest Dutch newspapers, even though they were months old, and perhaps a few books as well, which he could leave there in case Gelmers should be interested in them. He dressed, knotted his tie, gathered his hat, his gloves and his cane; he picked up his little parcel of newspapers, and walked through the chilly wind and whirling dust of the afternoon to the parsonage.

There were a few carriages in front of the little Lutheran church on the corner, and a plump woman in mauve was struggling up the steps carrying a vase of crysanthemums, while two girls stared inquisitively at Versluis from the church lobby as he made his way along the garden path of the parsonage next door. The house was still, the windows shut, but the servant came to let him in as usual, and in the living room he found Miss Scheffler on her own, reclining on her settee with a book on her lap to which she was paying no attention.

'Am I disturbing you?' he asked in the doorway, and with a slow gesture, as if her thoughts were returning from some distant realm, she lifted her head and smiled at him.

'Mr Versluis,' she said, half in thought. 'We haven't seen you for some time.'

'I believe that the last time I was here was just before Easter.'

'Yes, you came around one morning, the morning. . . .' She did not complete the sentence. 'Yes, indeed, it was the week before Easter, and it seems so long ago. We have often talked about you and wondered when we would be seeing you again.'

'But perhaps this is an even less appropriate time to call,' he said, sitting down beside her. 'It looks as if some sort of service is being held in the church.'

'Oh, there is a wedding this afternoon,' she said without any interest. 'But I'm not going to it. August won't be long, he's coming back to have some tea before he leaves, so you've come just in time to see him.'

'Is your brother going somewhere?' he asked, suddenly conscious of his own disappointment.

'But of course, you don't know – I'm sorry. A messenger arrived from Bethany with a letter from my father – my mother is again not very well, and there are further problems with one of the farmers in the area. They have never been particularly well-disposed towards us at the mission station, so father has asked August to go out, because he is getting old himself and is no longer able to cope very well with such difficulties. It's only the wedding this afternoon that has delayed him, because he couldn't postpone it any longer.' She closed the book and put it on the table beside her, her face turned away. 'I'm afraid that the occasion – how shall I put it – is not as happy as one might have expected. Marriage is not always in practice what it ought to be in theory, is it, Mr Versluis? Sometimes one is grateful for one's own solitariness.'

This was not a topic that either of them could discuss with any kind of authority or expertise, and to Versluis it seemed better to change the subject. 'How are you?' he asked in a neutral way.

She made a dismissive gesture. 'Sometimes better, sometimes worse, as always. It still comes as a surprise to me that after all these years I have still not grown accustomed to bad times.'

'This cold weather is probably not very good for you.'

'I am actually very fond of our winters, Mr Versluis – you cannot guess how beautiful the winters are here. It is as if the days were lit up from within by a brilliant white light. A white light and a white sky and a white veld that has been bleached clean, and in the mornings by the frost that glistens on the grass, and at night the brilliant moon and stars. And everything is so still in winter, everything is waiting.' Her face suddenly lit up, the tired expression that he had marked on his entrance dispelled: in her enthusiasm she had not heard exactly what he had said.

'Waiting for what?' Versluis asked, and too late he wondered whether she might interpret this banal question as a form of mockery, although it was clear that this possibility did not even occur to her.

'Yes,' she said, 'for what? When I was a child every winter seemed to me to be a time when we were being prepared for some kind of a miracle, and each year all that followed was the same old spring. The miracle has never come, not yet, in any case – or perhaps the miracle is spring itself. Who knows?' Then she shook her head slowly and forced herself out of her reverie. 'But as you say, winter is, alas, not a good time for me. I clench my fists and grind my teeth and endure it. Perhaps in the hope that the miracle will still come,' she added and laughed brightly and freely as a young girl, mocking her own dreams, her own troubles. 'August will be back in half an hour. Will you keep me company until then if I promise not to talk any more about my health? And if I try very hard not to shock you?'

'To shock me?' Versluis repeated.

'Mathilde is always concerned that I might shock people with my rash remarks – but then Mathilde has in many ways remained very German, much more so than August or myself, and she has not grown used to the fact that everything is freer in Africa and that I am just using that freedom in my own way. But perhaps she is right about you – you are clearly not used to Africa yet, nor have you had much time to become accustomed to me. Do I really sometimes shock you, Mr Versluis?'

The question could not be avoided: those greyish-blue eyes were fixed upon him. 'Sometimes you do surprise me,' he said, choosing his words with care; and then the two of them laughed and something in their relationship had changed, nothing that he would have been able to describe in any detail, but a greater sense of easiness had in some way been engendered between them.

'But no,' she then said, suddenly serious again, 'no, I must not be selfish, Mr Gelmers is lying all alone in his room and he'd like some company too. You wouldn't mind giving half an hour of your time, would you, Mr Versluis, just until August gets back from the wedding?' He wanted to say something, but she had already thrown aside the rug that covered her knees and was sitting up on the edge of the settee; she pushed the little table of books beside her away, and looked around for her sticks. 'We have rearranged the study for him, it's the most pleasant room as it gets the sun all day, and it's also convenient if he should need anything during the night. August is using the bedroom as a study now and Mathilde and Friederike have moved in with me,' she told him gaily as she swung herself out in front of him, leaning on her sticks. 'It's only when someone wants to see him officially that there's a problem, but then they go to the consistory.'

She carried on talking, oblivious of the grotesque figure she cut, hobbling down the passage, and as he was forced to follow her,

255

Versluis tried to avert his eyes from the deformity that was being flaunted with such lack of concern. 'I do not wish to disturb Mr Gelmers,' he tried to protest when he was able to say something. 'Perhaps he's sleeping.'

'Oh, no,' came her implacable assurance, 'August was with him just before he went across to the church, and he was awake then; and even if he is asleep, I'm sure he'll be delighted to have a visitor, especially one of his own countrymen. He gets no visitors, just the doctor, he lies by himself all day when August doesn't go in to keep him company, and I know only too well myself how long a day like that can be.'

She led him outside through the hallway and he put out his hand to open the front door for her, but withdrew it again, not wanting to press past her and wary of perhaps touching her. But Miss Scheffler noticed nothing: with a dexterity that was born of years of practice she opened the door herself, leaning on her sticks, and swung out in front of him across the stoep. 'And when August comes back, come and have a cup of tea with us before he goes,' she said. 'That will be nice. Mathilde is just making him some food for the trip, really as an excuse not to go to the wedding,' she informed him with a smile, 'because she feels quite strongly about these things; and perhaps you will keep the two of us company for half an hour or so after he has left.'

All Versluis was able to do was give a slight bow and let himself be carried reluctantly forward, with the little parcel of newspapers that he had brought along under his arm, for he could think of no excuse to extricate himself from this dreaded obligation. Miss Scheffler seemed also to remain totally unaware of his reluctance as she tapped on the glass door of the study and then opened it, supported on her sticks, and led him into the sickroom.

'Mr Gelmers, I have brought you a visitor,' she said softly, and then, before Versluis could say anything himself, she had swung out again and closed the door behind her. He could hear her lame, hobbling passage across the wooden floor of the stoep.

The study in which Scheffler had received him on his first visit had indeed been arranged for the patient: the settee and the chairs had been shifted to one side and a bed had been placed next to the little cast-iron stove with a screen around it for the draught, along with a toilet-table containing a swing-mirror and, in the corner, a piece of furniture which Versluis assumed to be a commode, so that he automatically averted his eyes from it. One of the panels of the screen was folded out in such a way that it obscured the man who was lying in the bed from him, and when he stepped forward the fleeting look of expectation in Gelmers's eyes clouded over and he turned his head away on the pillow. 'Oh,' he said in disappointment, 'it's you.'

'Were you expecting someone else?' Versluis enquired, but he did not answer. 'Are you expecting a visitor?' he asked again, more loudly.

'No, no,' came Gelmers's sharp reply. 'Who would want to visit me, who do I know in this hole?' He leant back against the crumpled pillows: the bed was dishevelled and the room, hot and stuffy from the fire in the little stove, stank of illness and sweat and urine. Would it be possible to open a window a little? Versluis wondered. But that would not be necessary, for he would not have to stay for long. Gelmers lay there, listless and bored, and he clearly had no desire for Versluis's company. Out of politeness he could try to maintain some sort of conversation for five minutes, and then he'd be free to return to Miss Scheffler in the living room.

'I have brought you a few Dutch newspapers,' he tried. 'Perhaps you'd be interested in looking at them, even if the news is rather old.'

'I'm not interested in the Netherlands,' Gelmers whinged, moving his head to and fro on the pillow. 'I've been away too long, it's got nothing more to do with me. What am I supposed to do with them?'

'I'll nevertheless leave them here with you, I have finished with them.'

'I can't read newspapers,' he carried on in the same whining, aggrieved tone. 'They make me tired.'

'Would you like me to read to you for a while?' Versluis asked, and the young man nodded reluctantly, almost as if he were doing Versluis a favour. Versluis still hesitated, repelled by Gelmers's rudeness, by the stuffy room with its stench of illness, and the rumpled bed. He averted his eyes from the small basins on the bedside cabinet, the slop-pail in the corner, the commode, and drew out a chair for himself between the bed and the window where he would be able to get some air and hold up the open paper between himself and the sickroom. He would read for a while, he thought, and then leave, or perhaps Scheffler would return sooner than expected and so release him.

He sat down and opened the newspaper. Gelmers lay back against the pillows with his head turned away, sulking like a child over some private grievance, restless in the rumpled bed with feverish red patches on his cheeks. Versluis felt a rising sense of repugnance, and he quickly raised the newspaper and began to read. But in the brilliant winter light the once-familiar names were strange, and the reports – about the Court and its ministers, a speech delivered to a learned society, a

257

canal – were so uninteresting that he could hardly force himself to the read to the end: his voice disappeared, and he had to clear his throat and begin again. Yes, he thought, yes indeed, what were they meant to do with all of this? Two fugitives together in a sickroom that had been improvised from the study of the Lutheran pastor in Bloemfontein. They found themselves together in a situation that neither of them would have been able to imagine a year previously; they, who probably would never – he turned the page, he searched down the columns for some trivial report that he could read just to pass the time – never again see the Netherlands.

He looked up and saw the garden outside in which the last of the flowers stood shrivelled in the beds, the dead hollyhocks in a dismal row; he saw the dust of the street, white in the afternoon sun, and the few carriages waiting in front of the church, the horses with their heads slung low. Gelmers was not even aware of the interruption.

'Should I read you the serial?' Versluis asked, and then he cleared his throat and repeated the question more loudly; but he got no response. The service could not last much longer, he thought, and he opened the newspaper at the appropriate page and began to read the serial out loud. It was not the first instalment, he saw, but that hardly mattered, because he would probably not have a chance to finish it, and besides, it was doubtful whether Gelmers was listening. So he just carried on reading while the late autumn sunlight fell upon the white dust and the blown beds and the motionless horses stood waiting with lowered heads beside the church wall: a meaningless, incoherent tale about barges on inland waterways, about locks and polders and country roads on which farmers moved about on clogs, an irretrievable world, distant and petrified as the engravings behind glass in the room in which he was sitting.

From time to time Versluis glanced outside to see whether there were any signs of life in front of the church, but all he saw were the carriages and the bored coachman watching over them. Gelmers was still lying motionless against the pillows with his face averted, and for an instant he thought that the young man had fallen asleep and that he would be able to get away; but then he realised that he was still awake, and that tears were running down his cheeks.

The silence in the room had lasted too long: Gelmers became aware of it and passed a hand across his face.

'Should I carry on reading?' Versluis asked uncomfortably.

'It makes no difference,' the young man said peevishly, almost dismissively, and the silence remained between them. He must say

258

something Versluis thought. There was still no sign of Scheffler: there was to be no release.

'Do you come from the country?' he asked.

'No,' Gelmers replied, and then added with some reluctance, 'from Meppel,' as if he were trying to make up for his unresponsiveness.

'I have never been to Groningen.'

'Drente,' the young man corrected him.

'Yes, of course, Drente. I am not well acquainted with the Eastern provinces of the Netherlands. But it is a small city, isn't it?'

'Small enough.'

'Do your family also live there?' he continued, and noticed from the way that Gelmers hesitated that this was an unwelcome question. 'Did you live in the city itself, or outside it?'

Gelmers's face was once again turned away from the pillows, away from the window and the light. 'I grew up on a farm,' he said at last. 'But then I went to work in Assen, in a shop.'

'That's quite a large city,' Versluis said without involving himself in this stilted little conversation, but Gelmers did not hear him.

'Until I got ill,' he added while Versluis was still speaking.

They fell silent again, and Versluis did not know how to continue in the face of this unexpected show of reconciliation and openness. 'It must be a beautiful part of the country, Drente and Groningen and Overijssel,' he said at last. 'But as I said, I have never been there myself.'

'It's spring now, and everyone will be looking out for the first plover's egg. And in the winter we always went skating, not like here.' As he lay against the pillows, tears began to run down his cheeks once again, and he made no further attempt to wipe them away or to avert his face. He lay there weeping silently with the sheet clenched in both hands, and Versluis found himself overcome with discomfort and dismay. He ought to do something, make some gesture, say something, but he did not know how to; he wanted to flee from that close sickroom, away from the weeping young man in the rumpled bed, but he remained sitting in front of the window with the newspaper on his knee, and then he saw with an almost physical sense of relief that people were beginning to come out of the church.

'I believe that the wedding is over,' he remarked, and went to look out of the window, his back turned to the room and the bed.

'It's German people who're getting married,' Gelmers said dully. 'I don't know who they are, I don't know them.'

He could see the plump woman in mauve, wiping her eyes with a tiny handkerchief, the young girls whispering to one another, and a number of men who were uncomfortable in their church apparel, shopkeepers or tradesmen with broad, peasant faces. The bride was wearing an ordinary dress, so that he did not recognise her at once among all the others, nor was she showing any particular signs of happiness, her face swollen beneath the veil that had been thrown back over her hat. She stood morosely beside the hooded cart while the other people milled around her, and then she held out her hand and a young man left the group and approached her to help her up. Versluis saw that it was the waiter, Gustav, from the hotel; his wavy hair plastered down with pomade across the low forehead and the little moustache twirled up; the broadcloth jacket that he was wearing was too small for him, so that it was drawn stiffly across his shoulders and exposed too much of his cuffs. It was a cheerless occasion, as sober as a business deal, cash counted out on to the counter, the amount entered in the cash-book and the account balanced. They stood talking amongst themselves for a while as if discussing what they should do next, and then they climbed into the waiting vehicles which slowly struggled away.

When was Scheffler going to appear, Versluis wondered to himself, so that he could flee from this room? He could think of nothing more to say to Gelmers. A farmer's boy from the country, he thought dully, who had gone to work as a shop-assistant in a provincial city and had bought himself a yellow checked suit because it had seemed to him to be fashionable and elegant; from a careful peasant family who counted every cent, who had deliberated and scraped and saved until they had had enough to send him, in the final stages of his illness, to Africa. But then Scheffler's footsteps sounded on the stoep, his hand was on the door knob, and he broke into a grin on finding Versluis in the sickroom. 'Mr Versluis, we have been wondering when we would see you again!' he cried. 'We've all been missing you.' But as he spoke he was already looking past Versluis towards the bed, his attention was fixed upon Gelmers, and without waiting for an answer from Versluis he moved towards the bed. 'Your sheets are rumpled,' he said. 'Wait, I'll fetch you a clean pillowcase.'

'No,' Gelmers said plaintively, 'it's not necessary.' Scheffler bent over him and straightened out the bedclothes quickly and with unexpected dexterity, and then he supported Gelmers with one arm while, attentively and carefully, he shook out the pillows behind him. Versluis stood waiting at the window, forgotten. 'I'll bring you a cup of tea shortly,' the clergyman said.

'I don't want anything.'

'Some lemonade? A glass of soda water?'

'Nothing, I want to sleep. I'm tired.'

Scheffler remained standing there and looked around the room as if he were searching for something else to do, but he could find nothing. 'I'll have to leave in about half an hour or so,' he said. 'If you're still awake I'll come and say goodbye to you.' But Gelmers had closed his eyes. They were able to leave.

Freed from that sickroom, Versluis lingered for a moment on the stoep, and breathed in deep, grateful draughts of fresh air. Scheffler drew the door shut without a sound.

'I'm sorry that I had to be in church this afternoon, of all times, when you came around,' he said, 'and that now I am on my way again. But on the other hand, if it hadn't been for the wedding I should never have seen you, I should have left this morning already.'

'I am sorry to hear that your mother is not well.'

'Possibly it's nothing, one doesn't know – I don't know what I'll find when I get there tonight. But the wedding this afternoon could not be postponed.' They stood on the stoep looking out over the garden where the dead hollyhocks were swaying to and fro in the wind and the leaves were being whirled along the paths. 'Our passion passes so quickly,' he said pensively; 'and what is left, what do we have then?' Versluis looked up at him in surprise, but Scheffler stood gazing out over the town with its windy haze of dust and smoke across the roofs in the afternoon sun and did not elaborate on the thought.

'August,' his wife called from the hall, 'are you coming to have tea?'

In the living room the tea things had been put out on the table, and Mrs Scheffler stood ready to welcome Versluis. 'August,' she said as a reminder, and looked at her husband.

'Yes, yes, I know, I should have left ages ago. But I still want to have a cup of tea with you and talk to Mr Versluis a little. Where is Friederike – is she awake yet? Pour for me, I'm just going to fetch my things.' And then he had gone again, cheerful now amongst his family.

'August is always pleased to be able to go back home,' his sister said with a smile. 'To Bethany,' she quickly corrected herself. 'Even under these circumstances. But Mother's condition does not seem to be as serious as we had feared.'

'Then he ought to wait until tomorrow morning instead of wanting to go at this time of the day,' Mrs Scheffler said sharply.

'It's better not to put things off unnecessarily, one never knows what might happen.'

'Then he should have refused the wedding and left this morning.' But her sister-in-law made no reply. 'I'm just going to fetch Friederike,' she said, and quickly left the room.

Where she had sat down at the table Miss Scheffler stared pensively at the cups and the flame of the burner in front of her. 'Even if one is going because someone has died, or for a funeral,' she said softly, 'it is good even then. After all, one is going home.'

'Aren't you going with your brother?' Versluis asked.

'I have to stay with Mathilde – that is to say, I want to stay with Mathilde. What's more, how could I possible tackle such a long journey?' she added soberly. 'Not in our little horse-cart. I have to travel in a coach, so that I can recline fully on a bench, or in an ox-wagon, so that they can put up a bed.'

He realised how tactless the question had been and felt uncomfortable, although as usual she showed no sign of self-consciousness as she sat distractedly toying with the teaspoons. But then fortunately her brother returned with a valise and a loose bundle under his arm which he dropped on to the table. 'Adèle,' he called, 'where is the sermon that I was working on this morning? Perhaps I'll still be able to finish it.'

'Mathilde was tidying up here and put it away,' his sister said and had already leapt up to fetch it, swinging from chair to chair as if she were totally oblivious of her hobbling gait. 'Our house looks like a campful of gypsies,' she called cheerfully, 'everything is in a mess. Or like a Koranna kraal. We need only take up our poles and pots and mats to move further on.'

'Mathilde unfortunately finds it less pleasing,' Scheffler said sympathetically, thrusting his possessions into the valise. 'She likes order in her house.'

Versluis looked at the books lying in front of him on the table: a little New Testament, a few German works of theology, and Dante. 'Do you always read Dante?' he asked.

'Always Dante,' Scheffler declared with a smile. 'The more I read the harder it is for me to disengage myself, even if I understand only half of it, and even that not properly. Perhaps I'll be able to get a little further today while I'm on the road – the road to Bethany is fortunately quite straight and even.'

'August!' his sister admonished him as she brought him the manuscript, 'you must take care!'

'But wouldn't that be a wonderful way to break a leg – or even your neck? With Dante in your hand and your thoughts on eternity. *"Per correr miglior acqua alza le vele . . ."*' he declaimed, and then his sister joined him and they completed the verse together, laughingly absorbed in a common pursuit, but without excluding Versluis from their pleasure. '*"Omai navicella del mio ingegno, Che lascia dietro a sè mar sìcrudele . . . ."*'

'What are you laughing at?' asked Mrs Scheffler, who had just entered with the baby. The child was overjoyed to see her father and he had to pick her up and kiss her, so that no-one heard the question. Although Mrs Scheffler did recognise the book that Scheffler was still holding. 'Oh, your Italian,' she said, and lost interest as she turned to pour the tea.

'Do you also know Italian?' Versluis asked Miss Scheffler, and she blushed and shook her head.

'Oh no, not at all, you mustn't be taken in – I was just showing off. Those are the opening lines of the *Purgatorio*, it's pure coincidence that I happen to know them by heart, simply because they come at the beginning of the text and August has quoted them so often.'

'Sugar, Mr Versluis?' her sister-in-law asked. 'August, here is your tea.' But her husband remained oblivious of her as he let the baby pull his hair.

'That is to say,' Miss Scheffler added, 'I do try occasionally – because August quotes from the poem so often and is always talking about it, I do sometimes take the book and a dictionary and work word by word through a few verses.'

'And do you find it rewarding?' he asked, and she nodded slowly.

'Yes,' she said, 'oh yes, it is rewarding.'

Mrs Scheffler sat beside them in silence, waiting for them to finish their conversation. 'August will be getting away from here very late,' she said with a frown.

'He won't be able to get there before dark in any case,' her sister-in-law replied absently. 'It doesn't really make much difference whether he arrives there at ten o'clock or midnight.'

'But all alone, at that time of night . . . .'

'Oh, what does it matter, Mathilde? There are no longer any wild animals along the way as there used to be.'

'August, your tea is ready,' Mrs Scheffler then said firmly, and got up to take the child from him.

'"So that it might ride upon fairer waters, the ship of my imagination now hoists its sails, and leaves the cruel sea behind it. . . ."' Miss

263

Scheffler said, deep in thought, and stared at the teaspoon in her hand. She was still thinking of the poem, Versluis realised, and had given only half a thought to the discussion with her sister-in-law. Then she raised her head and looked directly at him. 'It's beautiful, don't you think so?' she said. 'There is hope.'

Mrs Scheffler had taken the baby into her arms. Breathless and with his tie askew, Scheffler joined them to drink his tea and ask about Versluis's health, how the cold was affecting him, what books he was reading at the moment. . . . 'The annexation of the Transvaal looks bad,' he began; but his wife remained standing at the table with the baby in her arms as an implacable reminder and admonition that he must leave, and in the face of that gaze even his palpable desire for a political discussion could not be sustained. He sighed and drank up the tea. 'I must go now,' he said.

Versluis rose with him. 'So must I,' he said, but the clergyman spontaneously held him by both arms.

'No, no, you must stay, you have been here for much too short a time to be wanting to leave already. I am leaving Mathilde and Adèle behind on their own, and you could keep them company for a while longer if you don't mind.'

'Mr Wocke said that he'll be coming just after supper,' his wife said.

'Yes, Mr Wocke is coming tonight to sit up with our friend, and in the meantime Jacob is here if he should need anything.' He picked up his case and was still looking around the room as if searching for something, but his wife was already approaching with his hat and coat in one hand while she held the baby in the other. The departure could not be postponed any longer.

'You will stay and chat for a while longer?' Mrs Scheffler asked Versluis, and she gave a reassured smile when he agreed. But they had all risen and were moving towards the door to accompany Scheffler: behind the house the buggy was ready and the servant was holding the horse.

'Where has August disappeared to now?' Mrs Scheffler asked.

'Don't worry, Mathilde,' her sister-in-law said, 'he's just gone to say goodbye to Mr Gelmers.'

Tense as she had been the entire afternoon, she shrugged her shoulders impatiently; but then her husband came out and she tried to smile and said nothing. He said farewell to everyone and remained for a few more minutes to talk to the black man holding the horse; his wife was standing beside the buggy with the baby in her arms, and he bent down to kiss them both and then leapt in and picked up the

264

reins. Versluis remained in the doorway of the kitchen with Miss Scheffler to wave him goodbye.

'It's turning cold already,' Mrs Scheffler said and turned back to the house. 'I oughtn't to be standing out here with Friederike.' But she remained standing on the kitchen steps for a moment to look back. 'If only he had taken Jacob along, I would have felt more reassured,' she said.

'You know that we need Jacob here, Mathilde,' Miss Scheffler said with the same patient detachment with which she had been responding to her sister-in-law's anxieties all afternoon, and with the same impatient shrug of her shoulders Mrs Scheffler entered the house. 'And besides, it's almost full moon.'

'Will the moon be rising early this evening?' Versluis asked.

'Yes, it'll be up shortly, I know its movements, I follow them every night when I can't sleep.' She walked, hobbling through the house ahead of him, back to the living room. 'If all goes well, August ought to reach Bethany by ten o'clock at least. He'll be able to ride the whole way by moonlight, with the stars above him and the moonlit road white before him.'

The afternoon was already growing chilly and it was dark in the house. It wouldn't be long before he would also have to leave and return for dinner. After the bustle of Scheffler's departure it was now very quiet and peaceful, however, so that he felt no urgency and Miss Scheffler, too, was moving unhurriedly around the table, gathering the cups, as if it were an entirely automatic activity requiring no thought.

'You should also go to Bethany some day,' she said, 'we should take you, or perhaps you'll be able to go with other people. But, no, perhaps not; perhaps it would be better if you did not see it. You would only be disappointed, and say that I had misled you with all my enthusiastic accounts of it.'

'But you have hardly told me anything about it,' he said, sitting down at the table once again.

'But there's really nothing to tell an outsider, nothing that one would be able to convey to someone else. There is a church and a little school and a little shop, a handful of houses and some native huts. They've made gardens, and there are a couple of stone koppies between which a dam has been built. Other than that, there's nothing.' She stood opposite him, leaning with both hands on the table, and stared past him. 'Very flat, very bare and open – endless distances, lands, rocky ravines which contain water only when it rains; stones, sand, dust. Nothing, utterly nothing. You would certainly not find it beautiful at all, you who have brought other standards along with you.'

'Perhaps I have begun to learn during my stay here to see the beauty of these landscapes,' he said.

'Perhaps. Have you really? Is it possible that you can understand something of what we are trying to say.'

'Something,' said Versluis. 'I believe that I am gradually coming to see that there is something lurking behind this emptiness.'

'No,' she said softly then, smiling, 'then you are still seeing it wrongly. There is nothing behind it, there is just emptiness. It's the emptiness itself that is beautiful.'

'Then I'm afraid that you will just have to be patient with me until I finally come to that insight. There is no lack of desire.'

Mrs Scheffler had disappeared somewhere into the house with the baby, and the two of them were left alone in the living room in which the flame of the burner burnt with a growing light in the gathering dusk. He had begun to feel totally at ease with this passionate, unpredictable young woman Versluis thought, just as with her brother, and the half-teasing, almost coquettish talk that had developed between them did not surprise him, nor was he uncomfortably uncertain, as he had been before, about how to deal with it.

Miss Scheffler laughed: her hair fell loosely across her face once again, but this did not appear to bother her. She stood there smiling, leaning with both hands on the table, and for a moment, in the soft glow of the burner, she looked very young again, untouched by trouble or pain.

'I'm just going to bath Friederike and put her to bed,' said Mrs Scheffler, who had just come into the room. 'Mr Versluis, will you excuse me?' She looked at him uncertainly, as if she felt guilty about the way in which she was neglecting her duty as a hostess, but her attention was immediately distracted by more important matters. 'Oh, I had forgotten completely about the tea things, I'll just take them along with me – no, don't bother, leave them, Adèle, I will. Rather stay and talk to Mr Versluis.'

Her sister-in-law had turned away from the table and was swinging from chair to chair back to her usual place on the settee in front of the window. 'Leave the burner here, Mathilde, if you don't mind; I like it in the dark before Rebecca brings in the lamp. I also like to have a little light during the night when I can't sleep,' she said to Versluis, 'that is, when there's no moon.' Laboriously she stretched herself out on the settee and spread the rug across her knees once more. Mrs

Scheffler had withdrawn with the tea things, and they were alone once more, with the table and the brilliance of that tiny wick floating in the chafing dish between them.

'Poor Mathilde,' she said, 'she worries so easily, and now on top of everything she's concerned about the fact that it may be dangerous for the baby with Mr Gelmers here in the house. But what else could August do? We could surely not have left him lying in that hotel. We can't put him in the outside room.'

'Is he really that seriously ill?'

'When I lie awake at night I can often hear him coughing,' she said after a while, almost as if she had not heard the question; 'a hideous fit of coughing that just goes on and on, so that one doesn't know how his body can stand it any longer. I don't mind. It is worse for August, he sleeps right next door and he is woken up every time and gets up to see to him. But if I wake up and hear nothing; if the whole house is still, the whole town, just the dogs barking now and then; then it's worse, for then I don't know what might have happened, and I am unable to get up to go to see how he is.' She shuddered slightly, as if she found this thought frightful, and drew the rug further up. 'But forgive me, I have still not answered your question. He is very seriously ill: that is why it is important for August, in these last few weeks – these last few days perhaps – to do all that he can for him, even if that means some temporary trouble and inconvenience.'

'What . . .' Versluis began, but she had begun talking again, in such a low voice that he was unable to hear her words. 'Excuse me,' he said.

'No, I just wanted to say that he'll be with us for only a short while. It is no matter, the trouble and the inconvenience.'

'Have you made any contact with his family?'

'So far we've not been able to discover anything, he doesn't want to talk about them himself, and there were absolutely no clues amongst his possessions – August had to pack them for him when he went to fetch him at the hotel. No pictures, no letters, no address book – not even an old envelope with an address on it. We could of course try through the consul, but what is the sense of that if he himself wants no contact with his people?'

'Why would he want to cut himself off from his family?'

'You could put the question the other way and ask why they allowed him to come here, or why they sent him here. According to Doctor Krause, he was already very ill when he arrived, and he should never have attempted the journey.'

'But why?' he asked again, and it struck him that his questions

267

were too intrusive, the interrogation too intense: the discussion was beginning to move entirely beyond the bounds of politeness and good breeding. But Miss Scheffler gave no sign of being aware of this.

'One sees too much, one hears too much,' she said slowly. 'It is better simply not to look or to listen – what does one do with all the useless knowledge that one gathers? What does one do about the suffering of others?' She turned to him as if she expected an answer, but there was no answer: he leant on the table that stood between them with the burner glowing peacefully in the gathering gloom of that late afternoon. 'During the past few years, since Bloemfontein suddenly became known as a place of healing, people have been arriving here on every coach, people from abroad with a single ticket and nothing else, people who turn up here in winter without even a coat or a scarf – they flee in such despair that they do not stop to think for a moment before embarking on their journey. And sometimes, frequently even, they are people who have simply been sent out by their families on a single ticket to come and die here in Africa rather than at home.'

'For what reason?' Versluis asked.

'People are scared of death, Mr Versluis. They are frightened of dying, and they are frightened of being reminded of death. The relative is shipped out to Africa to get him out of the way, and he ends his life among strangers.'

They stopped talking. Outside, beyond the verandah, the last of the sunlight was falling along the unbroken street, and the lowing cows were being herded home from their pasture. After a short while Versluis rose and stood in front of the window to look outside. The cows bellowed, the cowherds shouted, and a clatter of pails came from the nearby stables where the milking was now being done. Here in the house they could hear noises in the kitchen, the crying of a baby and the sound of footsteps over the bare floorboards of the adjoining room.

'When I lie awake at night I have so much time to think about things,' Miss Scheffler said, 'and then I think of all these people and of their loneliness and fear. Of that girl who died all alone in the hotel room where no-one came near her; or of Mr Gelmers, sent here to die, who sometimes lies coughing all night long in the study of a stranger in which a bed has been made up for him. But the fear of death must be the worst, worse even than choking in your own blood.'

The street had fallen silent; the last rays of the sun had vanished from the dust. Versluis turned from the window, to see that she had hidden her face in her hands.

'I'm sorry,' he said. 'I should not have raised this subject.'

'I raised the subject myself. Death is something that I ponder a great deal – how could I not? I should like to go to that man, there in the study, and help him. I should like to do what I can for him, or at least to try, I am not afraid. But what is there that I could do for him? I am a woman, an unmarried woman, a stranger: I may not. What do you do about another person's suffering?' she cried out with sudden passion. 'What do you do about your own inability to help?' She looked at him searchingly, but he gave no answer, and then she slowly wiped her hands across her face. 'I'm sorry,' she said in a low voice.

'Are you really not afraid?' Versluis asked.

'What do you mean?'

'Of death.'

'I've seen and heard too much, I have been thinking too much in my own isolation, especially in these last few weeks. I was still afraid at first, but not any more, there is nothing to fear. Only sometimes, for an instant, you draw back, like wrenching your hand from a burning candle; but then. . . .' She pondered his question, and suddenly her serious face was illuminated by one of those transformations that so characterised her and her brother, making her appear fleetingly young and carefree with her hair falling loosely about her face. 'Like Dante,' she said. 'We return to Dante, Mr Versluis; I find that I so often come back to Dante. On the highest peak of the Mountain of Purification, where the flaming angel stands singing on the shore and he recoils from the the the fire through which he has to pass, so that Virgil has to speak words of encouragement to him . . . *"Pon giù omai, pon giù ogni temenza . . ."* And then he passes between his two companions, through those terrible flames, and on the other side he attains the holy wood in which the young woman is singing and picking flowers beside the water. Isn't that beautiful? I carried those words with me for days, even before I could understand them properly. There is nothing to fear, you just have to pass through that wall of flames, that's all.'

Slowly Versluis walked back to his place at the table. He was tired he realised, overcome by a weariness that was far deeper than the one which usually came over him; he was overwhelmed by an infinite exhaustion which robbed him of all strength and will, too tired to attempt to speak any more or even to listen to Miss Scheffler's words.

'*"Pon giù omai, pon giù temenza. Volgiti in qua, e vieni oltre sicuro . . ."*' But she was repeating the words for herself, without

269

making any attempt to translate them or explain them to him. Then she put her head back on the settee upon which she reclined, as if she were just as tired as he was, and said no more. Earlier in the afternoon he had been surprised by the playfulness of the conversation that had become possible between them; but it was also possible just to sit together, as they did now, without talking and without any longer feeling the need for words. They sat together in silence until the servant brought the lamp and put it down in front of him on the table.

'Adèle,' said Mrs Scheffler in an enquiring tone. 'Mr Versluis – are you still here? It was so quiet, I thought that you had left already.'

'I should indeed have been on my way a long time ago,' Versluis said, and tried to gather his scattered thoughts and attend to the necessary courtesies. 'I have stayed much too long – I fear that I have tired your sister-in-law.'

'I have hardly seen you – you must excuse me, but there is so much that needs to be done in the house, you know what it is like . . .' He bowed politely, but he did not know what it was like nor could he begin to guess the obligations to which she referred.

'Can't you stay for a little while longer?' Miss Scheffler asked from where she was lying on the settee. 'Wouldn't you like to stay for supper? Mathilde, couldn't Mr Versluis stay and eat with us tonight?'

She hesitated, doubtful. 'It's very simple tonight, it's just a meal of bread, but if you wish – of course, you're very welcome.'

'And I am not at all tired,' Miss Scheffler corrected him. 'And Mathilde and I are alone tonight, at least until Mr Wocke comes – it would be nice if you could stay.'

At Mrs Van der Vliet's tonight the table would be overwhelmed by the exuberance of Polderman and Du Toit, back from the picnic and full of tales about their fun and amusement: better to stay here he thought, in this room in the parsonage, with the two women in the light of the lamp. 'Thank you,' he said, 'thank you very much, it is kind of you both.'

Mrs Scheffler remained standing there as if she had not expected him to accede to the invitation and was thus caught off-guard by his acceptance: he read on her face a quick consideration of the amount of food they had, a rapid calculation regarding coffee and bread. 'I'll just go and tell Rebecca that you'll be staying,' she then said and disappeared once more.

'Has she taken Mr Gelmers's lamp to his room yet?' Miss Scheffler called after her, but she did not hear.

He was tired Versluis thought to himself once more, with a weariness that drained him of all volition: too tired for the walk back to Mrs Van der Vliet's house two blocks away, too tired for the conversation around the table, for his empty room in which the fire would have been lit for him.

'I'll just have to inform Mrs Van der Vliet,' he said.

'We'll send Jacob with a note, he stayed here this afternoon in case Mr Gelmers should need any help before Mr Wocke arrives.'

It was growing cold, and Miss Scheffler threw a knitted white shawl across her shoulders, but the grate was empty and there was no sign that a fire was usually made. 'It's getting dark,' she said, and stretched in the direction of the window to look out, but one could make out almost nothing outside: all that the windowpane revealed was the reflection of their own images, thin and transparent against the grey of evening. 'August is not even halfway, not even close to it. And the farmhouses are so far apart, the distances so great, one wouldn't even be able to see a light any more. Only the stars. But he knows the road,' she said quietly to herself, 'every stream and drift and lonely tree. And as for me, I know it too, I can follow him along that entire road, from the moment he goes over the hill at the cemetery to the point at which he can see the koppies of Bethany in the distance. I am pleased that you decided to keep us company tonight, Mr Versluis,' she then said with a sudden soberness. 'If we had been left on our own, Mathilde and I, I would have been thinking all night of August moving further and further away from us along that road.' Her sister-in-law's quick footsteps were approaching along the passage, but she did not hear them. 'It's like the times I lie awake at night and hear Mr Gelmers coughing and coughing, coughing his life away. Sometimes one is aware only of the things that you are losing, of life streaming away like the sands of an hourglass.'

'We'll have to send Jacob with a note to Mrs Van der Vliet,' said Mrs Scheffler. 'Will you let her know, Mr Versluis?' Deftly she began to remove the lamp and the tablecloth while Versluis wrote a few lines on a sheet torn from his notebook.

'"*Pon giù ogni temenza,*"' Miss Scheffler murmured pensively to herself.

'What did you say, Adèle?' Mrs Scheffler looked up, but received no answer, and she was clearly accustomed to her sister-in-law's absent moods, for she gave it no further thought. 'What time did Mr Wocke say that he was coming?'

'After supper, I don't know. I don't think that he arranged any definite time.'

271

'In any case we ought to eat meanwhile, then we will have finished when he arrives and he won't have to sit watching us while we are still at the table.'

'He can always go and sit in the room with Mr Gelmers. Perhaps he won't come until eight o'clock.'

'In any case we will have finished by then, and if we're finished early we'll have more time to talk to Mr Versluis. Perhaps he would even read something to us after supper,' she suggested, and looked up as she spread the cloth over the table. She smiled at the thought and lost her anxious expression: the white cloth in her hands reflected the light up on to her face and imparted a degree of gaiety to that modest room.

'Yes,' Miss Scheffler said, 'we can have a reading tonight. Hurry up, Mathilde, so that we can eat quickly.'

Mrs Scheffler turned up the lamp and dispelled the shadowy gloom of the room; with quick, deft movements she spread the white cloth over the table and smoothed it down. The note was taken; Jacob was summoned and sent away; the servant was called to help set the table and under Mrs Scheffler's watchful eye, plates and napkins, bread and cheese, were put out on the luminous cloth; she disappeared for a moment, and then returned to supplement this sober meal with some jam in a little glass dish. Miss Scheffler sat on the settee with the rug across her knees and paid no attention to the activity in the room as she gazed at the reflection of the lamp in the windowpanes behind which the evening was continuing to darken. She was humming a half-audible refrain softly to herself, like some magical formula or incantation reiterated without volition while her thoughts were fixed elsewhere. '"*Pon giù omai, pon giù ogni temenza. Volgiti in qua, e vieni oltre sicuro . . .*"'

As an initiate Versluis was able to discern and recognise the words, but he could see the slightly irritable glance that Mrs Scheffler gave her sister-in-law as she disappeared once more into the kitchen.

'Mr Gelmers is entirely on his own,' Miss Scheffler then remarked.

'Perhaps he's sleeping,' Versluis said, but these words sounded unconvincing even to him. 'He told your brother this afternoon that he wanted to sleep.'

'Perhaps, and then perhaps not. Perhaps he is waiting.' Did she mean that he ought to go and see? Versluis reflected uncomfortably, but her voice was neither commanding nor reproachful. 'I hope that Mr Wocke comes soon, then there will at least be somebody with him.'

272

'Do you think we ought to remind him?' her sister-in-law, who had just entered with a tray, enquired.

'No, of course not, Mathilde, they are probably still having supper.'

'I have Mr Gelmers's food,' said Mrs Scheffler, who had remained standing there with the tray in her hand, and she looked uncertainly at Versluis. He ought to take it from her he knew, but he made no move to do so; then Miss Scheffler spoke.

'Mr Versluis will take it to him,' she said casually. 'You don't mind, do you, Mr Versluis? August usually does it.'

'No,' Versluis said reluctantly, 'that's fine,' and he had taken the tray from Mrs Scheffler and was already going out into the dark passage when she called him back. 'Wait,' she said, 'the lamp, we haven't taken him his lamp yet. Just a moment, Mr Versluis, I'll call Rebecca.'

The servant lit the way outside and across the stoep and pushed open the glass door of the study; she put the lamp down on a cabinet, and the whirling shadows came to rest, so that Versluis was able to make out the details of the room, and then she went and left him alone holding the tray at the foot of the bed. Gelmers lay propped up against the pillows as he had been that afternoon, with his head back and his blond hair falling across his forehead, and in the lamplight the flush upon his cheeks seemed to be a healthy glow: lying there he looked like a farming lad, tired after a day's work. Should he wake him Versluis thought, should he touch him? But then the young man moved and slowly awoke, smiled expectantly and turned his head towards Versluis, opened his eyes, and suddenly became conscious of where he was. The smile died on his lips and for a moment his face was entirely vacant: a sick man lay in a crumpled bed, and for a moment they stared at each other in silence.

'I have brought your supper,' Versluis said, and then, when there was no response: 'Pastor Scheffler is away, I remained to eat here at the parsonage this evening.'

'Yes,' said Gelmers apathetically. 'Just put it down somewhere.'

Versluis tried to find room on the bedside cabinet nearest the bed, clumsy and irritable – angered by his own clumsiness and the young man's dismissive attitude, as well as the unreasonable demands that were being made of him. Should he help the man to sit up in the bed, should he pour some tea for him, should he even feed him? He suspected that such assistance was indeed required, but nonetheless recoiled at the prospect. He was not accustomed to carrying trays and serving other people, he was not accustomed to close contact with anybody, let alone a total stranger. Should he offer, should he try? he

273

wondered, and remained next to the bed until Gelmers grew impatient. 'That's fine,' he said, 'leave it, I'll manage.'

He had allowed the man to walk away on his own, Versluis thought; at the intersection of the streets in front of the church he had stared after him and watched him walk towards the spruit and the market square. What was there to do? What words were there, and where did one find them, and where did one learn the gestures? He stood helplessly next to the bed.

'Should I draw the blind?' he asked.

'No,' Gelmers said in sudden fear, 'no, leave it open. I want to be able to see out, I want to see the light when I wake up.'

There was nothing more for him to do there. 'I must go and eat,' Versluis said, and turned back to the door, but Gelmers did not hear him.

'There's moonlight again tonight,' he continued. 'The moon will shine here into the room.'

Versluis shut the door behind him. The moon had risen: it drifted out above the last houses and lit up the empty street, the garden with its withered flowerbeds; it lit up the long white road that Scheffler was following. For a few minutes Versluis remained standing there, leaning against the balustrade of the verandah, and looked out over the town in the brilliant moonlight. Was that what had happened? he wondered. Had they, after careful consideration and discussion amongst the family, counted out the amount required to get rid of him, and then shipped him to South Africa on a single ticket with a few hundred guilders to cover his expenses, out of sight and out of mind? Was that what had happened? One saw too much, one heard too much, he reflected to himself, more than one could process or could bear; not because you looked for it or desired it but because it was forced upon you by circumstances, on your own in the corner of the coupé, at a table for one in the dining room of the hotel or on the park bench beside the pond with your newspaper. It was best not to look or listen, to avert your eyes and study the passing landscape, to hide yourself behind your newspaper or lose yourself in the wine list, to examine the cutlery. What did you do about the suffering of other people which you were unable to change in any way, and how did you come to terms with the desolation and fear which you could only observe from afar, without any power to mitigate it, beyond dizzying chasms that you would never be called upon yourself to cross?

274

The women were already sitting at the laid table: they looked questioningly at him as he apologised and sat down, and then there was a moment of silence.

'Shall we . . .' Mrs Scheffler began uncertainly.

'Would you say grace for us, Mathilde?' her sister-in-law asked firmly, holding out her hands to them. Fingers touching, they formed a circle in the lamplight around the table while Mrs Scheffler bowed her head to say grace, and then Versluis was once again faced with the women's interrogating gaze.

'Is there something wrong, Mr Versluis?' Mrs Scheffler finally asked.

'No, nothing; why?'

'I had thought – I'm sorry, but when you came in, it seemed as if something had upset you, and I wondered if perhaps Mr Gelmers. . . .' But she did not finish her sentence.

'Mr Gelmers was asleep, but he woke up when I took his food to him. I remained on the stoep for a while to watch the moon coming up, and perhaps the night air was a little too chilly for me, that's all.'

'Did he eat anything?' Miss Scheffler enquired.

'I left the tray with him, I don't know.'

'He eats hardly anything. August is so patient, he sits by his side and keeps talking to him until he has persuaded him to have a few spoons of soup. He's just as patient as he is with Friederike.'

'At least Friederike isn't as difficult at meal times,' Mrs Scheffler remarked rather sharply. 'Only when she's ill.'

'But Mr Gelmers is ill.'

A flush passed across Mrs Scheffler's face, but she stared at the table and made no answer. The bread was thinly cut and thinly spread, the cheese pared carefully and placed on the slices: she poured tea for them, and the cups were not filled to the brim; except that after a moment's hesitation a little was added to Versluis's cup before she passed it to him. He could see her eyes passing over the plates, calculating how long the bread would last, how long they would be able to manage on half a pound of butter, a pound of tea, and how much the meat from which a stock had been made for Gelmers's soup had cost. How many worlds there were that he did not know, he thought as he lowered his eyes again and scraped some butter on to his bread; how many journeys that he had never undertaken and roads along which he would never pass: the careful thrift of the parsonage, the country lad who was dying in a stranger's study, and the long white road in the moonlight along which Scheffler was at that moment riding into the night, further and further away from them. All that surrounded him was unfamiliar: in this strange land he was entirely alone.

They did not talk much, but ate their bread and drank their tea in silence, and they had almost finished when the servant came to summon Mrs Scheffler.

'Mr Wocke can't come,' she informed them when she returned, with a flush of agitation and alarm upon her cheeks once more. 'The children have whooping cough.'

'Yes, it is the time for children's illnesses again,' her sister-in-law said. 'It's fortunate that they discovered it in time, before he came to spend the night with us.'

'He might have infected Friederike,' Mrs Scheffler said indignantly, her attention distracted. 'But why has he let us know only now, why wait until the last moment? It's extremely inconsiderate.'

'Don't worry, Mathilde, there's still enough time; it's not even seven o'clock yet. Send a note to Mr Picus and ask him if he can come tonight.'

Clearly upset, Mrs Scheffler left to make the necessary arrangements and her sister-in-law, whose thoughts had been half-fixed upon other, distant matters all evening, forced herself to attend to her immediate situation. 'More tea, Mr Versluis?' she asked. 'Shall I ask Rebecca to make some fresh tea for you?'

'No thank you, I have had enough,' he assured her. Nor did she insist, but had already begun to gather the plates, as if she were pleased that the unwelcome formality of the meal was over. Versluis passed his cup and plate to her: at home, he thought, the maid had cleared the table, and he found himself forced to smile at this recollection and the realisation of the way in which his circumstances had changed, so that Miss Scheffler gave him a questioning look. 'I'm sorry, I was reminded of something, something in the past.'

'Oh, have you finished?' asked Mrs Scheffler, who had come back. 'Mr Versluis, have you had enough? I'm sorry,' she added while she produced a table brush and pan and began to sweep the crumbs away. 'I know that you have missed a better meal at Mrs Van der Vliet's than we could have provided.'

'You needn't make excuses, Mathilde,' said her sister-in-law. 'Mr Versluis decided to stay here of his own accord, and I'm not accustomed to anything grander, so neither of us has any cause to complain. You are the only one who is feeling uncomfortable about our simple meal.'

'I can't help the fact that I am accustomed to better things,' she began, but then she suddenly broke off and restrained herself while she brushed the table more fiercely.

Miss Scheffler rose and moved laboriously back to her settee. 'Would you select a book for us, Mr Versluis? The books from which we usually read are on the little shelf behind the door. Or would you like to go and look for something more interesting in the study?'

'No,' he said, 'that won't be necessary, I'm sure that I'll be able to find something here.' It was a collection of well-read, slightly worn books that had clearly been in use for a long time: Andersen, Grimm and Hauff; collections of Goethe, Schiller and Herder; poetry, tales and novels. He paged through them and saw the names in a round, childish hand inscribed on the fly-leaves: 'August Scheffler, Bethanie, Oranje-Freistaat'; 'Adèle Scheffler, von Ihren liebenden Eltern, Weinacht 1866'. He had gone to sit down close to Miss Scheffler with his selection of books, and when she saw this inscription she stretched out her hand to take the book from him, and smiled at it for a moment. 'I still remember that Christmas,' she said. 'I was sixteen. It was in the time of the wars with the Basotho, when the Boers drove all the French missionaries off their stations, and only we were allowed to remain.' Versluis waited for her to continue, but she just closed the book and handed it back to him.

The servant had come to help clear the table, the white cloth was taken off, the plush cover spread over it once again; Mrs Scheffler went to the kitchen to see to the baby and rejoined them. 'Shall we read now?' she asked.

'Yes, come and sit with us, Mathilde, we're waiting for you.'

'I only wish that Mr Picus would come, he'll interrupt us just as we have started otherwise.'

'That's not the worst. How many times hasn't August been called away while he's been reading to us? Come, what would you like tonight? Poetry?'

She considered the question while she went to sit with her sewing-basket in her usual chair near the lamp. 'No,' she said firmly, 'not poetry. Would you read us a fairy tale, Mr Versluis? Something out of Grimm; that always appeals to me, it's so German.'

She made herself comfortable with her darning and for the first time she began to relax a little at the prospect of the evening's diversion. Miss Scheffler reclined on the settee once again with the rug over her knees.

Versluis picked up the old edition of Grimm that had been read so frequently that it was beginning to fall apart at the spine. 'What would you like to hear?' he asked.

'It doesn't matter,' said Mrs Scheffler.

'Read the *Märchen von einem, der auszog, das Fürchten zu lernen*,' said Miss Scheffler.

'But that's so long, Adèle!'

'That doesn't matter, it's still early, even if it is dark. Or are you in a hurry to go home, Mr Versluis?'

'No,' he said, 'I'm in no hurry.'

'No, that's not a nice tale,' Mrs Scheffler determined, however.

'I've always found the title so beautiful, so full of the promise of adventure.'

'Read *Rötkappchen* or *Hänsel und Gretel*, Mr Versluis,' Mrs Scheffler said, 'or *Rumpelstilzschen*,' and they settled down to listen. 'I only hope that Mr Picus comes soon,' she sighed to herself as she bit off some cotton and threaded it through the needle; but then he was free to begin reading about witches and princesses, and magic castles and dark woods, ancient tales filled with folklore and superstition, in the lamplight of the parsonage living room in a far-off corner of Africa. There was no heating in the room: the women had both donned shawls and he could feel himself gradually being possessed by the cold. But the entrance of the servant interrupted the reading, and Mrs Scheffler put down her darning and hurried out of the room.

'It's always like this,' said Miss Scheffler, lying back on the settee, wrapped up in the broad folds of her white shawl, 'there is always some sort of interruption. Let's wait a little while for Mathilde.'

Mathilde returned, wearing the same anxious expression that had for a short while disappeared from her face. 'Mr Picus is also unable to come,' she said. 'His sister says that he has gone to Winburg.'

'Then we must get someone else. Surely there are enough people in Bloemfontein to help.'

'But like this, at the last minute!'

'All we are asking is that they come to sleep on a settee in the study for tonight, Mathilde, and that's not such a terrible request. What about Mr Van Iddekinge, they live nearby. But no,' she reconsidered, 'perhaps not, one never knows what condition he may be in. What about Mr Mathey? Write a quick note to him, Mathilde.' Mrs Scheffler turned away with palpable reluctance to carry out this instruction. 'Have you been to see Mr Gelmers yet?' her sister-in-law added. 'Does he need anything?'

'I have sent Jacob to fetch the tray.'

'Shouldn't Jacob stay with him in the meantime, then Rebecca can take the note. Did he eat anything?' she called, but Mrs Scheffler had already gone, and they heard her rapid footsteps down the passage. They remained sitting there, Versluis with the book still in his hand, his finger between the pages marking the place at which he had been interrupted. Miss Scheffler sighed. 'It is not easy to be dependent on the charity of others,' she remarked. 'I actually meant Mr Gelmers, even if it is just as applicable to ourselves as missionary children or a priest's family. But it's as I've already said, Mr Versluis. I would be just as capable of sitting up with him through the night and doing whatever was required for him, it would be little enough; but I cannot, I may not, it's completely inconceivable. I have to remain lying on this settee thinking of people to whom Mathilde could write a note asking them if they would be kind enough to come and watch over a stranger who is ill for the night. The Bishop talks about founding a hospital here in which the Anglican sisters would be able to care for the sick, and sometimes in my daydreams I wonder whether that might not be a calling for me. But of course they would not take me; in any case they wouldn't accept a Lutheran.'

'I should imagine that such a life would require a great deal of courage.'

'Do you think so? I've never viewed it in that way. I have always rather seen it in the opposite way, as a kind of obsession – you are driven by the love that you feel.'

Mrs Scheffler had returned with her lips pursed as if an unpleasant task had just been completed. 'I have written to Mr Mathey,' she said.

'I'm sure he'll come,' Miss Scheffler said. 'He's always prepared to help. Come and sit down again, Mathilde, and try to calm down a little.'

But Mrs Scheffler remained standing pensively beside her chair, her darning in her hand once more. She said, 'It's nearly full moon. I wonder where August is now.'

'Just beyond Kaffer River,' Miss Scheffler said; 'he's still far from home – from Bethany,' she corrected herself. 'He'll only get there at ten o'clock.'

'Friederike is asleep,' Mrs Scheffler said, and her face softened. 'She is sleeping so peacefully tonight, Adèle. She has been looking much better in the last few days, have you also noticed?' Smiling, she sat down with her darning, and Versluis, who had been waiting, opened the book again and continued reading. The arrival of the servant had disrupted the initial intimacy of their gathering, however, and Mrs Scheffler was concerned about other things, her attention was no longer fully on the reading or even the darning with which she had automatically occupied herself.

It was cold in the room, and the glow which came from the lamp did no more than emphasise the chill: it came in from outside through the dark windowpanes, across which no curtains had been drawn, and rose up through the floor. Could he go and fetch his coat from where he had hung it up in the hallway, or would that seem impolite? Versluis wondered. He had grown stiff in the position in which he was sitting, holding the book up into the light, and his fingers could hardly feel the page as he turned the last leaf. He could of course leave, he thought, but he rejected this notion. He did not want to go away.

The fairy tale had been carried to its inevitable conclusion; the story had ended. Miss Scheffler gave no sign that she was aware of either this or of the sudden silence in the room, but her sister-in-law looked up from her work.

'And what if Mr Mathey can't come?' she asked.

Miss Scheffler did not even turn around. 'Wait, Mathilde,' she finally said in a weary voice. 'Let us first wait and see.'

'Shall I read some more?' Versluis asked.

'Aren't you tired? Then read us another fairy tale; you choose one for us.'

Why did he want to stay there with the two women in that icy, parsonage living room? Versluis wondered. At Mrs Van der Vliet's, the fire would already be burning in the grate and the bedclothes would have been turned back: there would be the glisten of copper, the gleam of floors and furniture, the linen would have been starched and ironed; the vacant room was waiting for him. He let his eyes pass across the book's table of contents and realised that he felt a kind of fear at the prospect of his return, alone in the moonlight through the deserted streets of the town, to the room that awaited him, to the restless night and the long periods of sleeplessness.

A floorboard creaked; there was a rustling in the shadows, and he saw that the servant had appeared again. 'Mr Mathey can't come,' Mrs Scheffler remarked to herself as if she were confirming a well-known fact, and then she got up once more and hurried out to the kitchen, followed by the servant. They waited in silence for her to return.

'We could try Mr Rasch or Mr Leviseur,' said Miss Scheffler. 'Or Mr Borckenhagen perhaps. There are still many other people whom we could ask.'

'Is it really necessary for someone to be with him?' Versluis asked.

'I don't know. August gets up during the night whenever he has one of his bouts of coughing: he gives him some medicine and sits with him when he can't sleep – whether this is necessary, I don't know. It would probably do just as well for Jacob to sleep in his room tonight on the floor. But that was the only reason that August was willing to go, even if Mother is ill and Father needs him, because arrangements had been made for someone to stay with Mr Gelmers on the few nights that he would be away. We promised him that there would be someone to sit up with him during the night.'

'Why is it so important to him?'

'I don't know? Why is anything finally important? One lives by the values that make one's existence meaningful, and for August that is what is meaningful – to give himself, to live for others, to do whatever he can and even more than he can.' She smiled to herself, softening. 'August has never known any holding back, or deliberation, or weighing up; it's always all-out, all or nothing. And sometimes,' she added after a moment, 'sometimes. . . .'

She went no further. It was quiet where they sat together in the living room, absolutely still in the cold, she on the settee, he with book still in his hand, his finger between the pages, and it was quiet in the house: no sound came from the kitchen where Mrs Scheffler was speaking to the servant who had taken the message. Nor was there any sound outside. Earlier than ever, the town had settled down in the cold: somewhere in the distance dogs barked, and then fell silent again.

'There are things about which August does not speak,' Miss Scheffler continued after a pause, 'not even to me, despite the intimacy that there has always been between us; things that I can only assume, or guess; things about which I am forced to draw my own conclusions – one cannot ask, one cannot barge in uninvited. Perhaps he has spoken to you, a stranger. He trusts you. He likes you.'

'I do not know why you should think so,' Versluis said, confused by her words.

'Because it is so. Perhaps you know what I am talking about, even if you can't understand it yourself because you have such a totally different view of life. Perhaps you know what is bothering him; while I, who can only guess, nevertheless could understand it.'

'What?' he asked.

'I don't know how to put it, all the names that one can think of sound so dramatic, melodramatic even. "Despair" is not a word that one uses in conversation. But in practice it's not entirely dramatic, is it? There is just an emptiness, and one goes on.'

Astonished, Versluis looked at her: the lamp shone upon the plush covering that had been spread over the table and she sat at the edge of the circle of light that radiated from it, quite still in the folds of the white shawl which he could see only dimly, talking as if she were merely maintaining a conversation with a chance visitor, out of politeness, until her sister-in-law returned, without a trace of involvement or emotion in her voice.

'I assume that that's the situation in which August finds himself – I assume, nothing more, that everything by which we were brought up and everything in which he has been trained has deserted him, and that now he is merely carrying on, doing what is expected of him without there being anything except the emptiness. You carry on, you sit up with a dying stranger, you ride all alone at night along that long road to Bethany. . . .'

Mrs Scheffler's quick footsteps sounded in the passage once more, and she appeared, clearly upset. 'Friederike is awake,' she said. 'It's all Jacob's coming and going in and out of the kitchen door, it wakes her up every time. I'm going to stay with her for a while.' She had already turned away when she remembered the other thing that she had come to tell them. 'Mr Mathey is in bed with influenza,' she said. 'He can't come.'

'Yes, that's fine,' Miss Scheffler said, deep in thought; and her sister-in-law returned to the baby, without concerning herself any further about the arrangements that needed to be made for the night.

'I can understand,' Miss Scheffler continued, as if there had been no break in their conversation. 'I should be able to go to him and tell him that with me it is no different, no matter how it appears. The pastor's sister, the cripple spinster who keeps herself occupied with acts of charity in the congregation and who helps her sister-in-law so beautifully with everything, she is also living through the same emptiness. But there are things that one cannot say, Mr Versluis, and the closer one is to someone, the further away are the words. Don't you think so too?'

Her voice remained flat and emotionless, without any bitterness or reproach: she could have been talking about the garden, about a Sunday school class, about a church fête.

'Yes,' he said at last after a long period of silence. 'Yes, that's true.'

'And what does one do? Do you perhaps know?'

'I don't know. Why should you think that I might know? Presumably one just carries on, one lives one's life.'

'Does that make the emptiness meaningful? Will the desert bloom and will Aaron's staff suddenly bud in your hand?' He then saw that she was smiling as she spoke, mocking herself. He closed the book and put it on the table, stiff from the cold, so that his movements were slow and difficult. They would not be reading any more that evening.

'I should be thinking of Mr Gelmers, not sitting around here dreaming,' Miss Scheffler then said in a more business-like manner. 'We shall simply have to send poor old Jacob out again with another note. We will finally get somebody, but Mathilde always becomes so agitated about everything.'

He got up slowly, as if he were striving against some resisting force, and began to walk up and down the room to get the blood flowing through his body again, moving laboriously through the gloom and the cold like currents through which he had to pass. He ought to fetch his coat now and prepare to leave, he thought. It was still early, but the day came to an early end in this town, and when there were no visitors Mrs Van der Vliet would also start preparing for bed now; window by window the dim light would vanish, and by nine o'clock the whole house had settled down. He did not want to go, however: he remained in the centre of the room and gazed at the simple chamber with the lamp on the table.

'If I were to stay,' he then began. Miss Scheffler did not reply: he had spoken too softly. 'If I were to stay . . .' he began again.

Still she said nothing. She turned to him and fixed her bright, probing gaze upon him, without any surprise, with neither approval nor reproach, and waited for him to continue; but he did not know himself what more he should say.

'Would that perhaps solve your problem?' he added unsurely.

'We'll find another solution, it is not necessary for you to make a sacrifice of yourself.'

'To spend the night on the settee in the study is surely not that much of a sacrifice, as you said yourself.' But she was still silent, pensive. 'Or do you not consider it a good idea?'

'I did not expect you to offer,' she then said simply. 'It had not even occurred to me to ask you.'

'Why not?' Versluis asked, and sat in a chair next to the settee. She continued to look at him with that bright gaze, without any reserve or false embarrassment, as if she were on the point of answering his question, but then she merely smiled and shook her head. Somewhere in the house a door opened and they could hear Mrs Scheffler talking to one of the servants: that instant of intimacy, the fleeting possibility

283

of a still greater degree of candidness between them had passed, so quickly that he had hardly been able to take it in. Mrs Scheffler's footsteps sounded along the passage once again.

'Do you want to stay?' Miss Scheffler asked in a low voice.

'Yes,' he said in the same low, urgent tone, as if they were engaged in a conspiracy which needed to be arranged before someone caught them at it. Astonishment flashed through his mind. What was he letting himself in for, he wondered, and what would Mrs Scheffler think when she found them like that, whispering with their heads together?

'I think that she is teething again,' she said, deep in thought, oblivious of all else. 'Once something has woken her, it is almost impossible to get her to sleep again.' But then her thoughts were forced back to other, less pressing problems. 'Adèle, what are we to do about Mr Gelmers?'

'Mr Versluis will stay with him,' her sister-in-law said. 'He has just offered.'

Mrs Scheffler looked at him in surprise as he got up, still stiff from the cold. 'I'll stay,' he slowly said. 'Provided that you have no objections, of course.'

She considered this with some calculation, and for a moment he could see apprehension on her face.

'We shall have to inform Mrs Van der Vliet,' Miss Scheffler then interjected firmly. 'Mr Versluis, do you need anything for the night? Jacob can fetch it for you at the same time.'

Before this accomplished fact her sister-in-law's apprehension vanished. 'That's kind of you,' she said, and smiled at him a bit shyly. 'That is very kind of you, Mr Versluis.'

What had he let himself in for? Versluis wondered dully while Mrs Scheffler went to fetch him a pen and some paper so that he could write a note. But it did not matter, it was fine.

Miss Scheffler had cast aside the rug which covered her knees and hobbled through the room to help her sister-in-law, the white shawl wrapped about her shoulders. Why all this sudden activity, Versluis wondered, and what was there to be arranged? But it did not matter. It was nearly eight o'clock and the long day had come to an end, and it would be good finally to get some rest, for he was tired. How long ago it had been when he had arrived there in the afternoon with the bundle of newspapers under his arm: the street had extended emptily in the white autumn sun, and in front of the church the carriages of the wedding guests had waited. It was as if he were gazing across the

284

days and miles of an endless journey, back towards the distant shore from which he had set out, finally to have landed here, weary where he had come to sit at the table with his hands spread on the plush cover in the lamplight.

They would make up a bed for him on the settee, said Mrs Scheffler, eager to be considerate; besides, they let the little stove burn all night, August insisted upon it, so he would not feel the cold and she would send Jacob to put more wood on the fire. It was extremely kind of him to help them out in this way, she assured him once more, blushing self-consciously. They heard her quick steps up and down the passage, muffled lest she wake the baby.

After a while she appeared again, in some distress. 'Mrs Van der Vliet has sent her servant over with your pillows and blankets,' she said uncomprehendingly to Versluis. 'Why are you laughing, Adèle? Why would she do such a thing? Does she think that we don't have enough bedding in the house?'

'It's just that Mrs Van der Vliet doubts whether anyone could make Mr Versluis as comfortable as she can, Mathilde, and she is probably right. Her pillows and blankets are doubtless better than anything that we could provide.'

Mrs Scheffler went to instruct the servant to make up a bed for him in the study and then came back once again, her rapid steps in the passage forming an unceasing refrain that had come and gone throughout the evening. Could she make him some more tea before he went to bed? Or perhaps a cup of hot chocolate? she insisted when he declined, and it was clear from her tone that such a luxury was not often provided in their house. But he wished only to be left alone so that he could rest.

There was nothing more that Mrs Scheffler could do for him: she remained standing there and drew her shawl more closely about her shoulders, raising her head to listen, but there was no sound. Miss Scheffler had vanished without saying a word, and the house was still again.

'I hope that August has arrived safely,' she then said. 'I am always anxious – one never knows, in this country. . . .' She did not finish the sentence, nor did she appear to find it necessary to do so, as if he, a foreigner like herself, would grasp equally well the dangers to which she was alluding: the sudden darkness, a gulf, every threat that might conceal itself in that alien night, or lurk in the narrow shadows at the edge of the moonlight. 'But it is wrong to be afraid,' she then said suddenly, taking courage.

He looked at her as she stood opposite him, a tiny figure, very upright in the lamplight, without a trace of concern or doubt on her face. She drew the shawl about her shoulders and raised her head; there was a smile on her lips.

There was nothing that he could say to her. 'If you will excuse me,' he began – 'I am very tired. . . .' He half stood up, supported by his hand on the table, and she started.

'Yes,' she said, 'yes of course, it's very late, we must go to bed. I'll get Rebecca to get you a light.'

She left once again, but he did not wait for her to return. Groping his way through the dark of the passage, he moved towards the hallway to fetch his hat and coat from the hatstand on which he had hung them.

'Mr Versluis,' he then heard Miss Scheffler's voice and saw her behind him in the passage in the narrow strip of light from the door that she had left open. 'Excuse me for vanishing so suddenly, but I just wanted to go and write this out for you. I wanted to do it at once, because if one waits one always has second thoughts and then one draws back and never does anything – it's wrong to hesitate in that way, isn't it? Here, take this, it's for you; take it and read it later. You need not say anything about it, we need not talk about it, but after our conversation this afternoon I would like to give it to you.'

She spoke in a low, urgent voice, as she had earlier that evening, and, without comprehending, Versluis took the folded piece of paper that she held out to him.

'I am pleased that you are the one who is going to stay with him. Perhaps you'll be able to help him.'

'In what way, do you mean?'

'You come from the same country, you speak the same language; perhaps you will be able to find the right words for him, or the right gestures. Perhaps you will understand what we cannot understand, in spite of all our good intentions – I don't know.' Then she had disappeared, drawing the door shut behind her, and along the passage the servant appeared to light his path outside.

In the study the lamp was still burning on the bedside cabinet and Gelmers sat propped against the pillows as if he were waiting for someone. Versluis stopped in the doorway. What had he let himself in for? he wondered once again, but it was too late now. The servant had withdrawn; the front door slammed shut.

'Close the door, it's cold,' Gelmers whined. 'What's keeping the priest so long tonight?'

'Pastor Scheffler has gone to Bethany, to his parents,' Versluis said and the young man scowled.

'But he said that he wouldn't be away for long.'

'He left only this afternoon after tea, and it's a long way. He hasn't even arrived yet.'

Disappointed, the young man sank back against the pillows. 'Are you also leaving now?' he asked without any interest.

He was indicating Versluis's coat, hat and cane. 'No,' said Versluis, 'no, I am going to stay here with you tonight.' But there was no response to this piece of information, the silence as much of a rejection as any words might have been.

On the settee against the wall Versluis saw that a bed had been improvised for him out of the large white pillows and blankets that Mrs Van der Vliet had sent over, and he looked for a place to put down his coat and other things. The commode caught his eye, then the little flasks of medicine, the glass and the spittoon beside the bed. There had been some mistake, he thought, a misunderstanding, and he ought to knock on the front door and inform the women, so that they could get someone else to perform this act of charity; but as the thought crossed his mind he knew that it was too late and that he was doomed to pass the night with this man in that humid room with its stench of sweat, urine and illness about which he had forgotten.

'Shall I draw the blind now?' he asked, and in the bed Gelmers turned around quickly.

'No,' he said, as upset as he had been earlier, 'no, I don't want to lie in the dark.'

'Is there anything else that I can do for you?' Versluis asked, but Gelmers's alarmed reaction had given rise to a fit of coughing: he lay doubled-over in the bed, his shoulders shaking, and then sank back exhausted against the pillows.

'Give me some water,' he said when he could speak again, and Versluis passed him a glass of water. 'I'm going to sleep,' he then said, 'I'm tired,' and he turned his face away from the light. Scheffler would have known what to do, Versluis thought, he would have been able to shake out the pillows or straighten the blankets, but there was nothing for him to do here. The handkerchief that Gelmers had been holding had fallen out of his hand he saw and, disgusted, he bent to pick it up without looking at it, and put it next to him on the bed.

But Gelmers did not respond: only when Versluis moved away from the bed did he speak again. 'Light the night-light before you put out the lamp,' he said, 'don't darken the room.'

There was no need to get undressed for the night, Versluis thought, and he finally removed only his jacket and shoes. He moved one section of the screen so that he would not have to see the bed from where he lay, and put the lamp down beside the settee, so that the rest of the room lay in shadow. He was tired, but not sleepy; he would read until he fell asleep he thought, and he lay down on the narrow, uncomfortable settee, grateful for the bedding that Mrs Van der Vliet had sent over and for the fact that when he had left that afternoon he had as usual put a book into his coat pocket. It was the *Aeneid* and as soon as he had pulled the blankets over himself, his hand went out to the book, the worn cover resting as familiarly in his hand as it had on so many other sleepless nights and journeys into the unknown. It was also good to have it once more in that room, in which he had landed so unexpectedly, and to recall anew the much-loved lines; to be reassured once again by words which no longer demanded any conscious attention, but which carried him forward on their glorious music. It is good, he thought, and forgot about the strange room, the narrow settee. The lamplight fell across the page; the little stove emitted a friendly glow. It is good.

Finally it was the silence that brought him back. In the house there was no further movement and outside there was not even the sound of dogs barking. He lay without moving with the book in his hand and listened, but there was no sound from the bed behind the screen: there was just the beating of his own heart, the creaking of the settee whenever he moved, the rustle of pages, and when he rose and moved towards the bed, silently in his socks, he heard nothing. Only when he bent down over the sleeping figure did he become aware of the warmth of Gelmers's body, the smell of sweat and illness, and his heavy, regular breathing.

It was time for him to go to sleep too he thought, and remembering the night-light, he found it and lit it. It was late and the town had been long asleep, the streets empty, the houses dark.

It was ten o'clock he saw by his pocket watch just before he put out the lamp: Scheffler had reached his destination. The moonlight fell obliquely in through the uncovered window, and in that brilliance the flicker of the night-light was hardly visible.

Sleep came quickly, even in that strange room with its close stench of illness, in spite of the uncomfortable settee and the presence of a stranger just beyond the screen; a heavy, dreamless sleep from which he awoke with difficulty. He knew that he was lying on the narrow settee in Scheffler's study, not quite fully awake, and that the long night had passed; dawn would bring relief and he would be released from his watch, more quickly and easily than he had feared when it had begun. But then it came to him as he lay there that it was Gelmers's relentless coughing that had forced him back from the silent depths.

He lay on the settee without moving, stiff from the uncomfortable position in which he had been compelled to sleep, and did not open his eyes. This was when Scheffler got up during the night and went to Gelmers to – what had his sister said? To give him water or medicine, to talk to him and sit with him? He would also have to get up, he knew, and he forced himself to sit up. The night was not over yet and the moon had merely changed its position, so that its light still fell obliquely in a broad swath across the foot of the bed.

Gelmers was not even conscious of his presence, caught in a paroxysm that gripped his entire body; bent awkwardly, folded double he lay obscured beneath the blankets, so that Versluis was able to see only the shocked, jerky movements that made it appear as if the whole bed was being jolted, and to hear that unremitting cough which sounded as if it was being wrenched from him. In the room which she shared with her sister-in-law, Miss Scheffler would now also be lying listening to this terrible choking he realised. To lie awake in the dark, listening, he remembered; and forced the memory aside. He must do something, he thought to himself, and looked at the bedside cabinet – the medicine, the glass, the spittoon – but then suddenly Gelmers fell silent.

Versluis did not move. The moonlight caught the foot of the bed; the white bedspread shimmered in its gleam; the light fell in through the high, uncovered window and also on the garden, the street, the sleeping town, its roofs, trees and distant hills, as clearly illuminated in this cold brilliance as daylight. Nothing moved; no night creature called in the silence of the winter night, no floorboard creaked in the house.

Then without looking round Gelmers held out his hand, as if he was aware of Versluis's presence without being able to see him. Should he take it? Versluis wondered dully, but Gelmers gestured impatiently towards the bedside cabinet. He was looking for the spittoon Versluis guessed, and he passed it without looking at it, and turned his head away while Gelmers used it. Then his hand moved searchingly across the bed. The handkerchief had gone again Versluis thought, but he was unwilling to look for it amongst the tangled sheets or under the bed in the dark. There were some clean handkerchiefs on the bedside cabinet and he passed one of those to him.

Neither of the two men had said anything, and it was some time before Gelmers turned around and then fell back in utter exhaustion against the pillows. 'Would you like some water?' Versluis asked, but he did not answer. 'Should I give you some medicine?' he asked and looked at the little flasks on the cabinet, but Gelmers merely shook his head after a while.

'It doesn't help,' he said in a whisper.

'Perhaps it will give you a bit of relief. Or is there something that might help you to sleep?'

'Nothing helps any more.' He lay there with his eyes closed, and his voice was hardly audible.

Versluis realised he was cold, despite the fire in the little iron stove, and he was shivering; Gelmers's fit of coughing had upset him more than he had known and, feeling for the back of the chair next to the bed, he sank into it. His mouth was dry and his heart was beating wildly and irregularly. He was the one who needed a sleeping-draught or tranquilliser he thought acidly, rather than this young man who, with the resignation of total exhaustion, had submitted to his fate and no longer wanted any relief. What rash presumption had ever led him to believe that he was able to undertake this watch, whatever recklessness or thoughtlessness on the part of the two women had caused them to accept his offer?

Where had the journey brought him, where had the road carried him? he reflected once more. Without speaking, without moving, they faced each other in that room, illuminated by the reflection of the moonlight off the bed and the floor; neither of them any longer in any condition to speak or even to move, and gradually the silence was informed almost by a kind of intimacy, as if they had finally reached a point where they understood one another, and where there was no longer any need for words of explanation.

The glint of the moonlight was blinding him, so that he turned his head away, and then he saw that Gelmers had opened his eyes and was lying staring at him, nor did the young man make any effort to avert his gaze.

'Why did you stay here with me tonight?' he asked drowsily, as if the question was one that he had been considering for some time.

'Because the pastor is away and they didn't want to leave you on your own.'

'But why you? The pastor told me that he had already made arrangements with other people, people from his congregation. You don't belong to his congregation, do you?'

'The person who was to have come could not come, he was prevented by illness.'

'And so they asked you?'

'I had supper here tonight, I offered to stay. Does that seem particularly strange to you?' he added when Gelmers pondered his statements in silence without any further response.

'You don't like me,' the young man then said. He was finding it difficult to speak, his voice was low and sometimes inaudible, but it held no emotion: he was stating a fact, without any bitterness or reproach, and before Versluis could formulate some kind of polite denial, the flat voice had continued. 'I could see it on the very first day already, at those Jewish people's who invited me to eat with them. You were the guest of honour, the fine gentleman who spoke beautiful Dutch and who could speak German and talk about all the right things, and nobody took any notice of me.'

Versluis sat listening to the measured voice, leaning back in the chair. He did not have to sit and listen to these unsolicited remarks, he thought to himself; but what could he say, what could he do? It was the middle of the night, time to sleep, not to sit confronting each other in this way in the moonlight.

'Mr and Mrs Hirsch are extremely kind and hospitable people,' he objected. 'I am certain that you were as welcome there as anybody else.'

'They asked me only because I was a stranger and they always ask strangers. But they invited you because they wanted to have you there, because you can speak German and talk about wine.' Had they talked about wine on that day? Versluis tried to remember. Probably – and why not? The conversation had, however, made no impression on him.

What was this sick, confused young man actually trying to prove? he wondered. 'You had best try to get to sleep now,' he began, but Gelmers was not listening.

'Here too,' he said dully, 'they took me into their home because there was nowhere else for me, but I'm in the way here, I don't belong here.' He moved his head restlessly to and fro on the pillow and looked out at the night, at the moonlight. 'One night,' he said, 'one night before I was as ill as this, I went for a walk, when I didn't feel like sitting around at the hotel any more, in my own room or in the bar.

291

When I came past here I heard music. I stood listening in the street outside, and then I came to the house; I looked in at the window, I thought I would knock, and they would let me in; but when I looked inside I saw you sitting there, and I knew that I couldn't go in. You were invited, you belonged in there with them, but I would just be imposing myself.'

'No,' Versluis said, 'no, it wasn't like that at all,' but his voice was too low. Gelmers did not hear him, the words made no impression.

'And you too,' Gelmers quickly added, 'you've come to sit with me, you look down upon me, you have from the very beginning. I have never been good enough for you, I don't talk properly, I don't know how to behave. . . .'

His voice was becoming shriller. 'Quiet,' said Versluis softly, 'quiet. The others will hear you.'

'What are you doing here with me?' Gelmers continued passionately, although he had lowered his voice. 'You needn't bother yourself about me.' Versluis could see that he was becoming increasingly upset: as he spoke he wiped the tears from his eyes with a rapid gesture.

'Go to sleep now,' Versluis said, helpless in the face of this sudden diatribe and display of emotion. It was true, and there was no reply that he could make. What was he doing there?

'Fine, I'm just a peasant, I come from the country, I am ignorant. But I also want to live, do you understand? I also want to live!'

He had raised his voice, the words came like a smothered cry; he lifted himself half up against the cushions and then fell back again, powerless. The handkerchief that Versluis had given him fell from his hand, and in the moonlight Versluis could see the dark stains on it, black against the white of the counterpane. He sat staring at it without moving.

'You'd better give me some laudanum,' Gelmers said at last. 'Perhaps I'll be able to sleep for a while.'

He automatically poured the liquid and mixed it and gave the glass to Gelmers who grabbed it so eagerly that his hand touched Versluis's for a moment, burning with fever.

'Put something in front of the mirror,' he then said, like a spoilt child. 'The light is shining in my eyes, it's keeping me awake.'

The moonlight that was falling in through the window was reflected from the mirror on to the cabinet beside the bed, and Versluis moved towards it to look for something, found a towel and covered the mirror with it. Behind the screen Gelmers lay motionless, as if the sleeping-draught had already taken effect. Only *he* would be unable to

292

sleep now Versluis knew, and he shivered slightly with cold. How much longer, he thought to himself, how much longer would the night last?

'But you will also die,' Gelmers's voice came to him through the dark, muffled by the pillows against which he had pressed his face. 'You will also die just like me, it won't be any different.'

Versluis made no movement as he stood beside the enshrouded mirror, hardly breathing: no floorboard creaked beneath his weight and only the thumping of his heart sounded loudly in his own ears. Was that meant as a threat? he wondered. There had been no sneer in Gelmers's voice; although perhaps he was too exhausted to show any emotion any longer. Was it a warning; or had he merely been stating a fact, as impassive as the ticking of a clock, the fine, alert ticking of a travelling alarm, the almost soundless trickle of sand through an hourglass? In the room, in the house, in the night itself there was no further sound.

Now he would not go to sleep again, no matter how weary he felt, for the hours of inexorable wakefulness had dawned for him. Gelmers appeared to have fallen asleep, his attack over and forgotten, and after a while Versluis could hear his heavy, regular breathing on the other side of the screen. He could light the lamp and read further, he thought, but yet he did not: he lay down and drew the blankets around himself and turned his head away from the brilliant moonlight and faced the dark wall, still confused by his weariness and the unexpected events of the night, and disturbed by both the intensity of Gelmers's fit of coughing and the words that had followed it. Voices and images streamed through his memory, he half fell asleep and then started upright with a pounding heart, roused by some phantasm that he could no longer even recall, listening anxiously in the silence to catch the sound of Gelmers's breathing. But all that he heard was the rapid pounding of his own heart, the creaking of the settee, and far away in the chill of the night the howling of a dog. Each time he awoke he saw the moonlight shift further across the floor as the moon began its descent and sank towards the west. The night was passing he thought with relief; morning approached.

He drifted onwards in a restless, pitching state that could hardly be called sleep, started up, half slumbered once again, recalled vague images when he awoke, and could no longer tell whether they were the spectres of dream or his own confused thoughts. The moonlight slid away across the floor, shifted up the wall and receded in a last, dim afterglow against the ceiling and as its brilliance waned, the

293

flickering night-light on the bedside cabinet began to gleam with a gathering lucency to form a firmer core of light in the darkness. Waking from his restless sleep Versluis saw that gleam, saw the enshrouded looking glass and the outlines of the screen and, reassured, he drifted into a deeper and dreamless sleep.

Something woke him but he could not say what it was: the far-off dogs had quietened down, no sound came from behind the screen. It was the silence that had woken him, Versluis then thought, and he lay waiting, motionless and without drawing a breath, for it to be broken by something, and at last he heard from the bed where Gelmers lay a hardly audible sound, like a smothered cough, a sob or a sigh, a sound like that of someone pressing his face into his pillow in order not to be heard, or like the rattle of somebody choking.

He leapt up and picked up the night-light; he moved slowly towards the bed in his socks in the circle of the light that he held up before him and which, step by step, revealed the room to him, the familiar objects strange as they rose up out of the dark: the screen that he pushed aside, the bed. Gelmers had slid down the bed and was hardly visible where he was lying in a tangle of the bedclothes: he lay on his back with his eyes wide open and one hand extended over the edge of the bed as if he were reaching out or searching for something. He did not notice the light of the little lamp that Versluis held up over him, but with blindly staring eyes he turned his head towards Versluis, and blood gushed from his lips; in the shadows that the flickering lamp cast across the bed there were dark stains on his nightshirt and sheets.

'Wait,' said Versluis, 'wait, I'll go and call somebody, I'll call the doctor,' but while he hurriedly and clumsily tried to clear some space on the bedside cabinet in which to put the little light, Gelmers's hand was clamped about his wrist.

'No,' the young man said slowly and with great difficulty, his voice hardly audible, while something rattled in his throat as he spoke; he gripped Versluis so violently that it hurt, and Versluis, unable to get free, lost his balance, toppled over and was pulled down on to the bed, as if they were engaged in some sort of wordless wrestling match, struggling laboriously amongst the confusion of bedclothes.

'Let me go,' Versluis said, out of breath, 'I must go and get some help,' but Gelmers did not slacken his grip.

'No,' he said again, gasping like Versluis. 'I'm scared. Stay with me.' He threw his arm around Versluis's shoulders and tried to lift himself on the bed, and Versluis put both his arms around the man to support himself and stop himself from falling, conscious of the heat and the weight of the other's body and freshly and unpleasantly aware of the stench of illness and sweat and blood, of the stench of death. For an instant it flashed through his mind that his shirt would also be soiled with blood as he felt the despairing grasp of the young man's hands: Gelmers's head was on his shoulders, his hair, his mouth against his cheek, and the dry rattle sounded once more in the young man's throat; his body contracted and he lifted his head as if he were looking for something, his features distorted by a sudden fear, but then he slackened and his head fell back as if his neck had snapped, his mouth open, a bloody froth upon his lips. The still flame of the night-light lit up the face across which something moved like the alternation of light and dark and a shadow driven quickly across a landscape; and then there was nothing.

He is dead, Versluis realised after the initial alarm had passed, and he was unable to absorb it at once. Is dying as easy as that? he thought, and remained standing there, half kneeling on the edge of the bed, with the body that he was as yet unwilling to disengage from his arms. He was finally startled by a low rustling sound in the darkness beyond the circle of light, like the murmur of a woman's dress in the shadows, and it took a moment before he saw that the towel with which he had covered the mirror had come loose and had slid off. He saw his image reflected in the glow of the night-light, the hair tousled and the shirt creased and stained, and in his clasp, pressed against his breast, the body of the stranger, as if he were trying to nurture or protect the man.

For a long time he gazed at this reflected image without being conscious of its reality, like a far-off figure seen through the frame of a window. And then he looked back at the young man in his arms, at the body from which all motion had vanished, so quickly and totally as to leave nothing behind, the face as peaceful and undisturbed as an empty looking glass. There were journeys which he would never finish, he thought, roads whose ends he would never reach, regions that he would never discover; expeditions along the bodies of other people, voyages of discovery in the hearts and minds of others, long excursions for which a single life was not enough. The familiar shore had been left behind, the destination was not yet in sight; he had stopped halfway in the unmoving silence of a winter morning with the body of this young man in his arms.

He was unable to bear Gelmers's weight any longer, and slowly he lowered him on to the bed. He should go and call someone, he thought dully, and heard far away through the cold the crowing of the first cock. Or he could wait until dawn, he thought, there was no hurry.

He made no move to do anything, but remained motionless beside the bed.

'Rest,' said Kellner and smiled encouragingly as he put the stethoscope back into his case. 'That's always good advice, and finally it's nature's own medicine, isn't it? What could be more pleasant in winter than to stay in bed and be taken care of? We had our first frost last night already, not much, but enough to set our gardens back.' He looked at Versluis encouragingly from behind his small silver-framed spectacles: his whole countenance exuded reassurance and encouragement – the carefully starched shirt, the well-manicured hands, the case in which the instruments were arranged with such neatness and precision.

'Undertaking – in your condition, with all the weakness, the fatigue, the bouts of fever that attend it – a night of watching over an ill person is not to be particularly recommended. It constitutes both a physical and emotional strain and is best left to stronger people – but let us say no more about that. You performed a most charitable act in standing by your countryman in his final hour, and no-one could reproach you for that.' He was ready to leave, case in his hand, but then he remained standing pensively for a moment. 'Our young friend waited too long and arrived too late, it was a waste of money and energy even to have come here. And it is also clear that he received no proper medical care in the Netherlands. What sort of miracles do such people expect from the Free State?'

'When is the funeral?' Versluis asked.

'They are just waiting for Pastor Scheffler to return – he is expected back home tomorrow afternoon.' This particular medical case had now been settled and no longer interested him. He looked around the room with approval, at the white bed in which Versluis was lying against the pile of pillows, at the fire in the hearth, the morning sunshine on the windowsill. 'Rest is what you need,' he said. 'No anxiety, and no cares. But then what have you to worry about? If it is a fine, warm day you could perhaps go and sit in the garden, as long as you take care of the wind. Or else you could go on a little ride if you wish, as long as you don't stay out too long or too late. All that you now need to do is to take care of yourself.' He nodded once more, as reassuringly as to a child, and he smiled behind his beard; there was a flash of spectacles, and then he was gone.

He lay in bed; he fell asleep and woke up again; he drifted between dream and reality, only dimly aware of the movement of the sun across his floor and windowsill. In the passage outside his door he heard the rustling of a dress, the creaking of a floorboard, and he knew that Mrs Van der Vliet had taken control of his life once more, her voice subdued but firm as she gave the servants instructions regarding the services that were to be rendered to him. She also came into his room from time to time, with hands folded across her front, to scrutinise him and to find out if everything was as he wished it to be, and although she did not utter any word of reproach her silence was heavy with an unspoken censure: of those who act irresponsibly and make no attempt to curtail their own folly. Every gesture with which she shifted a chair or pulled a curtain into place was loaded with disapproval, not only regarding the pieces of furniture which she appeared to be wanting to call to order in this way, but also concerning the whole course of events by which Versluis had come to be lying there.

He remained in bed, he fell asleep and woke up; he was tired, he was exhausted, and the doctor had given him a tranquilliser which had made him drowsy. Hours passed, days passed, without his being conscious of their passage, and it was only the regular peal of a church bell that roused him at last. That was not the melodious bell of the cathedral or the tiny one on the Catholic church, he thought drowsily to himself as he lay listening to it, nor was it one of the bells from beyond the spruit which indicated the time: it was the hollow tolling of a funeral bell being rung at the German church.

He was wide awake, alone in his room in that utterly silent house. It was just past lunch-time, with the sun at its zenith, and everything had grown still; that regular peal across the roofs was the only sound to disturb the day. He sat up and pushed the blankets to one side, thrust his legs out of the bed and remained sitting on the edge, spinning like a drunkard under the drugged influence of the tranquilliser. He should have told someone to call him in time he thought, and should have got the servant to lay out his clothes, but it was too late now and he would have to help himself. He grabbed for the backrest of a chair in order to remain upright and put his hand out towards the table for support. Scheffler would first have to conduct the marriage service he thought, with the bride and Gustav, the waiter in that broadcloth jacket that was too small for him. Only when the wedding guests had left, when they had climbed into their carriages and had departed, could the funeral begin: there was still time, even if it was late and he had no-one to help him dress and was unable to find the clothes that he wanted in the depths of the wardrobe.

What did one wear to a wedding? he wondered, searching, groping, unsteady on his legs. What could he wear for a wedding that would also be suitable for the funeral afterwards? Perhaps it would be better to consider this first, because after all he was not expected at the wedding, and there would be no other mourners at the funeral service. So that there would be no-one to take umbrage at his absence: it would be quite sufficient if he were to attend only the service at the graveside. He would thus not go to the church, but rather walk directly up the hill to the cemetery, along the road that made its way, blindingly white, up the incline in the heat of the afternoon sun. And at the top he would find the plains extending before him, bleached bone-white by the harshness of winter, the immeasurable expanse stretching beyond the horizon, its infiniteness to be discovered anew from each new peak in wave upon wave of wide, motionless undulation – so that the days might succeed each other but each new day of the journey offered nothing but the same wide expanse. The coast had been obliterated, and the sea no longer existed. There was only a void.

The bell had stopped ringing. Now something must happen, Versluis thought dimly to himself, but he was no longer capable of any action. The English teacher looked at him in concern and held out her smelling salts to him; he saw her coming towards him in her yellow dress across a vast distance, and her feet flashed in and out from beneath its hem without carrying her any closer.

He was lying on the floor of his room and the glint of the winter sun on the floorboards was blinding him. *Pon giù omai*, he thought absently to himself and wondered where that echo had come from and what the words meant: *pon giù omai*, he repeated, and recalled the refrain that Miss Scheffler had sat murmuring to herself on that last evening at the parsonage.

No-one moved in the house; the tolling bell had fallen silent. It is good, he thought, stretched out on the floor in his nightshirt without the strength to get up. The funeral had ended, and he had fulfilled his obligations.

It was only on the following day, or perhaps even some days later, that something stood out in the dreamy passage of events around him: he opened his eyes to see Pastor Scheffler sitting reading in an armchair in front of the window. The young man did not look up, absorbed as he was in his book and completely oblivious of his surroundings, and Versluis felt no inclination to disturb him. It was therefore some time before Scheffler noticed that he was awake, and when he looked up and saw this he leapt to his feet and went quickly to the bed as if he had been caught out in some form of negligence. It seemed like a reunion after many years, the passage of time since their last meeting like an infinity that had held them apart: Scheffler came towards him with outstretched arms and Versluis lifted his hand to touch him, to embrace him; but he had no strength and his arms dropped listlessly.

'You were sleeping,' Scheffler said apologetically, 'and I did not want to wake you, so I just started reading meanwhile.' He examined Versluis's countenance with concern, and although he clearly wanted to ask him how he was feeling, he suppressed the question. 'I have to ask you to forgive me,' he then said. 'It had not occurred to me for a moment that Adèle and Mathilde would ask you to spend the night at our house, it is completely inexcusable of them to have expected such a thing of you.'

'No-one asked me. I offered to do it myself.'

'But they ought not to have allowed it. Mathilde is very upset about what happened.'

He was not interested in these feelings of guilt or the apologies. 'Tell your wife that there is nothing to be upset about,' he said impatiently. 'I suffered a relapse; it is unfortunate, but entirely coincidental, it has no connection with anything else. She must forget about it.' He had spoken too vehemently, however, he ran out of breath and began to cough. Scheffler automatically looked towards the bedside cabinet to see if there was anything that he could give him, but the light bout of coughing soon passed, and he stood beside the bed with the book in his hands and waited for Versluis to catch breath enough to speak.

'Wouldn't you like to sit down?' Versluis asked.

'I should actually be on my way again . . .' he began, but then he broke off with a grin – 'yes, that's what I always say to you, don't I? But it's the same as always, you know a little of my life by now, always rushing to something else without even catching up. Only now and then is there a tiny moment of peace in the midst of it all.' Then he suddenly recalled something else and his face clouded over. 'That afternoon when we went to Brandkop, I kept you out too long, in the cold and the night air. . . .'

'It did not affect me in any way.'

'Nevertheless, it was not good for you; I should never have been so inconsiderate.'

'If I had wanted to go back I could have said so.'

'You were too polite.'

'If I had another chance to go to Brandkop for an afternoon I would take it; if I were physically up to it, I would want to go again and sit talking on that koppie,' Versluis said with some effort. And then Scheffler slowly smiled to himself as he stood looking away towards the other end of the room, his thoughts elsewhere.

'Yes,' he said, 'so would I.'

They were silent. Versluis lay exhausted against the pillows. 'I must go now,' Scheffler said, 'but next time I'll stay to talk, I'll not start reading.'

'What is it you were reading?' Versluis asked, and the clergyman looked at him half guiltily.

'I sat paging through your Virgil – I finally became curious.'

'And?' asked Versluis.

'I've already forgotten too much of my Latin, there was much that I didn't understand. And yet, I think I know what it is that appeals to you – the way in which it is sustained, its assurance. . . .' He turned and went to the table to put the book back where he had found it.

'You take it,' Versluis said, and then, when the clergyman hesitated, 'take it, I have no further need for it. Perhaps you'd like to read some more of it later on.'

'I'll borrow it from you,' Scheffler agreed at last. 'Until you want it back again.'

'I have read it often enough, that time has passed for me.'

'In exchange I'll come over one afternoon, at least if you feel like it; and if you'll permit me, I'll read you some Dante. Perhaps you'll be converted to him just as you have begun to convert me to Virgil.'

Versluis smiled too. 'It's unfortunately too late for that now,' he said. 'Virgil retains his position at the top. Besides, Dante had to depend on Virgil to guide him on his quest.'

'Only through Hell and on the Mountain of Purification. Even Virgil could go no further than the entrance to Paradise, as one who had not been baptised he had to turn back, and it was Beatrice who took Dante further. Only grace can touch those heights,' Scheffler added in a softer voice. 'Nothing else helps.' Then he thrust the little book into his pocket. 'I'll come again,' he said, 'and stay longer. This time it's a promise.'

'Give my regards to your wife,' Versluis said. 'And to your sister.' Scheffler had already reached the door. 'How is your mother?' he called after him.

'Mother?' He had to think about the question, and then its import struck him. 'Mother was ill, but it was a passing crisis, it wasn't really necessary for me to go out to Bethany for that. I stayed with them for a few days, at home, and then I had to come back.' He remained standing there with one hand on the door knob as if he wished to add something, but then thought better of it. 'They are growing old, both of them,' he said, and looked up and smiled with that sudden grin that lit up his serious face and made him look like a schoolboy. 'Thanks for Virgil,' he said, and then he was gone.

'Thanks,' Versluis repeated. 'Thanks. . . .' He wanted to say something, but it was too late. He forgot what it was, forgot that there had been somebody with him; he lay in a daze against the pile of pillows and gradually drifted into unconsciousness once more.

A new phase of his stay in this country had dawned, and the limits of his world had contracted to the walls of the room in which he lay. No decision was expected of him any longer, he was asked for no opinion. Without a sound the servant came on bare feet to put wood on the fire, without a sound she arrived with his meal and removed the tray as soon as he had pushed it aside. Almost without his being aware of it the more unpleasant tasks of the sickroom were also accomplished: the removal of the slop-pail; the carrying out of the chamber-pot, covered with a white cloth; and the taking out of the commode, which had been placed unobtrusively in a corner behind a screen, to be emptied. The soft shuffle of the servants' feet and the rustle of their starched aprons grew to be the abiding undertone of his life, punctuated, at a distance, by the creaking of a floorboard beneath Mrs Van der Vliet's heavier tread, the rustling of her wide skirts and the sound of her voice – subdued so that he was unable to make out the words.

Discreetly, almost unnoticeably, Mrs Van der Vliet kept watch over the tiniest aspects of his life, showing the same careful attention as she paid to the dusting off and rearrangement of the little ornaments in the drawing room or the washing of her best coffee cups. Like some kind of obscure flower she had blossomed in the folds of her wide crêpe skirts and petticoats, as if this had been what she had sought all her life: the severity of her countenance had softened, the sharpness of her voice had been tempered, and she would even smile uncharacteristically at Versluis from time to time, as if she wished to let it be known that with his final collapse he had endured the test and won her irrevocable approval. There were even times when she swept

301

through the house with a previously unknown rapidity and lightness, and her footsteps rang with a new sense of determination and purpose.

Members of the town's Dutch community came to visit him in his room from time to time, but he found that had no need for such company: he listened to what they had to say and answered their questions; he responded to their comments, and then withdrew unobserved from the conversation – as if he were casting a distant, backward glance on the room in which they found themselves – noticing only the gestures and attitudes without being able to follow the words. Later on he began to sit for shorter or longer periods in the armchair next to the window: sometimes he read, but he was usually too tired to be able to concentrate on the text. From a distance he observed and ascertained his sudden changes of body and spirit, as clinical and unmoved as Doctor Kellner with his stethoscope. One afternoon Hirsch called, and Versluis was able to measure the changes in his own condition as effectively from the way in which Hirsch tried to suppress his natural exuberance as he could from the deliberate circumspection of his Dutch visitors. Despite Hirsch's kindliness and geniality these new circumstances were clearly beyond him. If there was anything that Versluis needed he should simply let him know, came the assurance – anything, anytime. Wouldn't he perhaps like a footstool? Didn't he need a woollen scarf or a warmer dressing gown? And once the worst of the cold was over and he was feeling a bit better again, should he feel the need for a little fresh air, the landau was always at his disposal. On the very same evening half a dozen bottles of Moët were delivered to Mrs Van der Vliet's. Occasionally, on warmer days when there was no wind, Versluis sat on the stoep at the back of the house for an hour or two. In the time that he had been confined to bed – had it been days or weeks? he did not know any longer – a transformation had come over the country and the landscape, and he encountered it again in a barely recognisable form. But was it really the land that had changed? Versluis wondered about it from his armchair in the sheltered corner of the verandah in which he had been ensconced by Mrs Van der Vliet, with its pillows and rugs, a screen before him and the blind half-lowered. Was it the land that had changed, or perhaps only himself, so that on his return he was now looking at it through different eyes, recognising in its already familiar features different elements and other patterns?

The leaves had fallen and only a few still remained to catch the sun, the bare branches glittering in the light. In the garden the paths had been swept, the beds were empty, and down below it the gathered willows glinted wanly along the meanderings of the spruit. Stripped of the shelter of its trees, orchards and gardens, the town lay revealed – gutted in the chill sunlight, a landscape of dust and stone and dry, rustling grass, withered by that immense drought. Between the arches formed by bare trunks and through an interlacing pattern of branches, new vistas were revealed to the observer: of dry-stone walls and leafless orchards and pergolas. Through further bare trunks and interwoven branches could be seen the houses at the far end of the town and the corrugated-iron roofs that dimly reflected the sun. And further still – beyond the last of the houses and chimneys, the last winter trees, the last stone walls and ditches and the final dusty road – the veld stretched outwards. There was no longer anything to obscure his view from that stoep: he could look out over the roofs and chimneys of the town to see the veld extending towards the hills in the north, where they stood out darkly against the colourless sky in the shadow of the afternoon sun.

Van der Vliet shuffled by and stayed for a moment – nodding, smiling, friendly – to make a remark about the weather. Then he moved up and down along the empty footpaths in the garden, stopping to tie a tendril from the vine, or bending down laboriously to pick up a last, lost leaf, but finally he could find nothing to do and shuffled away.

Versluis remained sitting there and thought back to the rattling coach and the cheerless landscape that he had discovered from time to time through the clouds of billowing white dust when he'd been feverish and giddy. He remembered the vulture, hovering on extended wings; he remembered his walks in the evenings to the hill at the cemetery where he had sat down to gaze across the landscape, fearful and at the same time also captivated by the extent and emptiness of this alien, aloof country. Beyond the houses of the town he could see the hills with their rocks and creviced ridges and twisted little bushes etched against the sky, untouched by the life of the community – the barking of dogs or the cries of children at play, the smoke from the chimneys. The landscape no longer evoked any feelings of menace or fear within him: he sat there in an armchair in the sheltered corner of the stoep until Mrs Van der Vliet decided that it was getting too cold, and the servants were summoned to move the screen, the chair, the pillows back indoors.

During this time Mrs Van der Vliet took it upon herself to put his clothes in order: armfuls of clothing were removed from his wardrobes and drawers by the servants, and the days not already taken up with the usual cleaning, washing and ironing were devoted to the unpicking of seams, steaming, beating out and brushing down, hanging out to air, washing, blueing and starching, ironing and pressing – all carried out under her personal supervision. Why? Versluis wondered without any interest. What for? For days the house was filled with a subdued bustle similar to that which had preceded Mrs Helmond's wedding, as if Mrs Van der Vliet, driven by some unexplained and inexplicable obsession, was preparing herself for a new festival, making every effort to be prepared when the day dawned at last. Then the clothes were brought back to be packed into the wardrobes and drawers, waiting and ready.

In the course of this activity she had from time to time brought Versluis things that she had discovered in his pockets, which she had put down on the cabinet beside his bed and about which he had in turn forgotten, so that it was only after a day or two that he took any notice of them: a length of red ribbon which he did not recognise and an envelope of which he remembered nothing at all. He put the ribbon aside and in the envelope he found a poem, written out neatly in a strange hand. Where did it come from? he tried to think. But he knew nothing about it, and it was only when he began to read that recognition dawned. It was the envelope that Miss Scheffler had given to him at the parsonage, on his way to the study, so that he had thrust it into his pocket and not given it another thought. It was the poem that he had sat reading in the club before the specialist from The Hague had come to examine him. Had he mentioned it to her, or else what had possessed her to write it out for him? He was to have met De Bruïne that afternoon for tea, but at the last minute De Bruïne had sent a message that he had to stay at home because or a cold; so Versluis had eaten alone at the club, at his usual table in the corner, and after that he had installed himself in an armchair at the fire. It had been a chilly, drizzly autumn day, outside the traffic had rattled by along the wet street, and there had been no-one else in the reading-room. He had sat there on his own with a few newspapers and magazines which he had happened to take from the table. Without attending fully to what he was reading, ill and feverish, uncomfortable in the clubroom but also reluctant to return to the empty house, feeling restless and irritable as he'd paged through the magazines, his attention had kept wandering to something else before he had even finished the first page.

It was on that afternoon that he had seen the contribution from Africa in some sort of literary journal and had read it with half a mind, a description of a landscape in a Dutch that was slightly too formal, using imagery that had too obviously been taken over from somewhere else; he had read it and paged on, read something else and became bored again, sat staring into the flames for a while, and eventually had asked the porter to call a cab for him. And yet something about that poem had remained with him as he'd allowed himself to be helped on with his coat and had been carried home through the grey, wet streets of the town. Behind the noise of the traffic in the streets; behind Pompe's care; the herb tea; the hot-water-bottle; beyond the cosiness of his study in which he had had the curtains drawn early against the gathering gloom: that expanse had remained as a hardly perceptible presence. Encapsulated as he had been within the safety of his own existence, the consciousness of that greater silence had nonetheless remained with him. It was an amateurish poem, no more: stereotyped words had been yoked together, conventional images had been strung one after the other, and yet it had possessed something which meant that it could not simply be forgotten. The stolid diction and imagery illuminated from within just as an alabaster lamp is irradiated by an invisible flame, so that the stone itself appears to be luminous. Perhaps it could be explained as the lustre of an unassimilated love which could find no expression in the words and thus had to force its way through them to reach him.

It was ridiculous, of course – he'd asked himself why an anonymous poem seen by chance in a magazine should have remained with him in that way. It was perhaps best to read no more poetry for the moment – he was not feeling well, he was feverish, he was too impressionable. It was also shortly afterwards that Doctor Slingeland had suggested the consultation with the specialist from The Hague: that elegant man in grey who had so politely, so urbanely, suggested that he find some relief by moving temporarily to a more suitable climate. 'Switzerland, perhaps, or the South of France,' he had suggested, while Versluis was still trying to come to terms with his verdict. For no matter how courteously and considerately it had been coloured, the finding remained a shock, and the man had carried on talking casually to give him a chance to recover. 'For that matter, it has come to my attention that over the past few years physicians in England have begun to send those suffering from lung complaints to Africa.' He'd added with a little smile, 'That is to say, to South Africa; and, according to reports, with some success too. It appears that they do indeed gain some benefit from the dry air of the "veld", as it is called over there.' He'd pronounced the word with a slight emphasis, as if he thereby wished to place it in quotation marks, signifying a concept that was alien to him. 'If the idea of a long sea journey and a more exotic destination happens to appeal to you . . . .' Then he'd begun to draw on his kid gloves, for the carriage was already waiting to take him back to the station: to him it went without saying that anyone who could afford his services need not hesitate over a journey to Africa. And thus it had happened that in the silence of the sleepless night that had followed, alone in the dark house, in the sleeping city, and to the astonishment no less of himself than of his small circle of acquaintances, Versluis had decided to explore the unknown for the salvation which was unlikely to be gained in more familiar reaches. And so he had eventually found himself in this country, in this town, in this house, reading in amazement the poem that had in the meanwhile passed completely from his mind, and which Miss Scheffler – driven by whatever strange intuition – had written out for him in her neat hand.

During this time, as his life continued to contract more and more – from his room to the stoep, from his bed to the chair – and all his needs and desires, all the stirrings of his spirit moved, day by day, to adapt themselves to a body that was less and less capable of anything – during this time Versluis felt within him a rising longing to escape for one more time, even if it were the last, from the ever-shrinking limits of his little world. The far-off veld, and the stony ridges against the sky which he was able to see from his seat on the stoep, evoked in him a restlessness with their promise of distance and space. The increasingly bleached sky from the other side of his bedroom window recalled memories of more expansive vistas; the phrases of the poem of which he had been reminded in such an unexpected way haunted him with their stolid images suffused with passion: with his face turned to the window he lay against the pillows and listened to the rattle of the sill in the wind and the fine patter of dust and sand being blown against the panes. Why this restlessness, he wondered, particularly now, when he had learned to accept and had cultivated a sense of acquiescence? But the fever withdrew and his pulse abated, so that Doctor Kellner no longer appeared so gravely doubtful on his daily calls. Yet the longing remained, quite apart from the patterns of increasing collapse and more laborious processes of recovery into which his body had been delivered.

One day, while Doctor Kellner sat at his bedside taking his pulse, his wrist still in his hand, Versluis mentioned to him his desire to go out again. 'If you feel like it,' the doctor said slowly, 'if you feel the need to take a short ride, I can think of no objection. As long as it's a fine day and you wrap yourself up well and do not tire yourself too much.' His voice was flat and there was no expression on his face, whether of approval or disapproval. He knew that it would not make much difference any more, Versluis realised when the doctor had left. The end was now so close and so certain that everything had become permissible again, for no prophylactic measures nor any neglect could any longer do anything to affect its inevitability. He lay back against the pillows and stared at the winter sky outside his window while he pondered this latest insight. Step by step one grew in wisdom and was relieved of one's illusions he thought, and finally one found oneself entirely alone, dizzy from this hard-won knowledge.

It was Mrs Van der Vliet who opposed this undertaking with a passion that surprised even Versluis, as if he were not only endangering his own health by the proposed outing, but was also threatening the disruption of her whole world, the undermining of all her authority, and cruelly wrenching from her hands the control that she had gained over her immediate environment. For days a silent battle which was never mentioned directly raged between the two of them over this issue, and only after she had been reassured by Doctor Kellner did she reluctantly agree. *A little fresh air*, he assured her, *a slight change of environment . . . sick people could be extremely unreasonable*, he added as they left the room together, and Versluis could still catch the words; *sometimes one just had to give in to them and not upset them any further. And besides . . .* he continued, but then Versluis was unable to hear what he said.

Mrs Van der Vliet thus let herself be brought round, even though she was not entirely persuaded, stiffly disapproving and with lips pursed at this defiance of her authority. Perhaps Mr Bloem or Doctor Brill would be able to accompany him, she remarked. But Versluis evaded the suggestion, suddenly aware of the fact that he wanted no company to disturb him with any signs of attention, concern or conversation. In a laborious round hand which he himself could hardly recognise, he thus wrote to Hirsch to ask if he could ride out in the landau one afternoon: in order not to cause anybody any trouble, he added, and to save himself any unnecessary fatigue, he would prefer to go out alone, and it no longer even bothered him whether these reasons were convincing or not. Her husband could go with him, Mrs Van der Vliet finally offered, as if she were playing a trump. It was her last desperate attempt to retain some sort of control over the undertaking, but Versluis blocked even this suggestion with an unflinching stubbornness that was part of his weakened, sickly state. He was able to refuse or agree, hold out or concede, without concerning himself about any of the considerations that would earlier have been important to him. Looked at from the mirror-image world, he realised, isolation, loneliness and dying expanded into a dizzying freedom.

Very slowly and hesitantly he began to dress for the trip, supported by a chair or the table, leaning for a moment against the hearth to hold on to the mantelpiece, and sitting down from time to time to recover from his passing weakness. Gradually, however, he felt such strength as he still possessed begin to return, so that when Mrs Van der Vliet came to announce that the landau was waiting, he was ready and could walk to the front door without any help. He leant upon his cane while she fussed about him and lingered beside the landau, disapproving, watchful and concerned. 'You must drive carefully with the master, d'you hear,' she cautioned Amien the driver with the deliberate Dutch that one might adopt to a small child. The coachman's complete impassivity, motionless on the box above her without so much as turning his head in her direction, was clearly a provocation which she could not endure in piqued silence. 'And don't you go too far, d'you hear me? Half an hour the doctor said, no more, and then you must be back. And not in the kloof where the sun has gone already.'

Amien turned around on the box and looked enquiringly at Versluis who had taken his place in the carriage, enveloped in a travelling-rug, supported by pillows. Versluis nodded: the man touched the horses lightly with the reins, the wheels scrunched over the sand, the chassis began to sway with a hardly perceptible motion on its suspension, and the landau began to move. 'Ride out towards Tempe,' Mrs Van der Vliet's voice sounded even more shrilly, 'not up here against the hill. And you drive carefully when you go through the drift, do you hear!' Still Amien gave no sign that he was aware of her existence, his silence more dismissive than any words. 'And you come straight back home, see!' she screeched after them with the last of her breath, and she stepped back with the folds of her black dress drawn about her, out of the way of the horse, the wheels, and the dust.

The horses moved with a careful, tripping gait, kept back by the reins, and the landau seemed to be gliding down the straight street, so careful was its passage; but Versluis found even that tiring after the weeks in his room, and he had to close his eyes from time to time. The houses, stone walls, ditches, the bare trees with the afternoon sunlight on their branches, the stretches of denuded garden passed silently by, and from that distance he looked at them as if he were taking his leave: across the square in front of the Presidency and up the gradual rise past the girls' school and the Catholic convent, for Amien had himself decided upon the route, without asking or paying any attention to Mrs Van der Vliet's instructions. On the shores of the dam the bare branches of the willows were suspended over the pools of water and trampled mud. There was nobody.

Versluis realised to his surprise that for his own inscrutable reasons Amien had chosen for their route the road to Brandkop along which he and Scheffler had driven one afternoon – how many weeks, how many months ago now? Pace by pace, the horses moved along the dusty track across the veld and the landau lurched on its suspension over the uneven patches; Versluis sat up laboriously at the edge of the carriage and looked about him. The houses had been left behind on the far side of the ridge, the town was no more than a hardly perceptible wave of treetops and a smoky haze; the veld was all around them.

Amien sat upright on the box, his attention fixed on the motion of the horses and his strength fully employed in holding them back: Versluis looked up and saw him silhouetted against the sky, with his wide hat and the whip resting across one shoulder, silently carrying his passenger along that empty white road towards a point that they would never attain. Long before they reached that far-off hill it would be time to turn around and go back again.

The carriage stopped. The horses, impatient and uncomprehending, threw their heads back with a jingling of their harness, but then they calmed down and began to nibble at the dry grass beside the road. This was the half-way mark, but Amien made no move to turn around: he remained sitting motionless on the box with his back to Versluis, as if waiting for something to happen. In the stillness a breeze sprung up and sighed through the grass, the rustling died away, and the day was still again.

With difficulty Versluis began to extricate himself from the travelling-rug into which he had been so carefully wrapped under Mrs Van der Vliet's supervision. Amien half turned at the movement behind him, but Versluis reassured him with a gesture. 'I want to take a short walk,' he said, 'just a short way.' And the man did not appear to find this a strange desire, for he offered no resistance: vigilant but without any attempt to help, he watched Versluis lower himself from the carriage.

There had been some degree of recovery, Versluis marked, and although he was weak, he felt that he had enough strength for this final effort – leaning on his cane, stumbling over anthills and meerkat holes, struggling over stones and low bushes where thorns and sticking-grass caught at his clothing and his shoes were scuffed by the stony ground. Just a short way, he thought to himself, keeping his eyes to the ground, as he slowly made his way forward using his cane; for this would be the last time. He considered the thought with detachment; he looked at the shrubs with detachment, at the dry grass, the stones and the sand, and then bent down to touch a greyish, thorny plant. The thorny leaves scratched him and the stem was too tough to be broken off; dizzily his eyes clouded and he had to wait a while, with both hands on his cane, before he recovered. But why did he want to break off a piece and take it back to his room as a token? he asked himself as he turned around. Let it remain where it was growing, clinging to this hostile earth where the grass had already died and the ditches and pools were empty. These tough, thorny plants, as colourless as the veld, the low bushes, the isolated windswept trees, had sent their roots deep into this earth, had anchored themselves amongst the stone, feeling along layers of rock in the dark earth for the last, scant nutrients. In this earth he thought, in this ground, among stones, among the twisted roots of these tough plants, in this country. . . .

He looked up. He had walked further than he had realised, and he was surprised to see that he had left the landau far behind. It formed a black silhouette against the toneless veld and the pale sky of the winter afternoon, the carriage and the horses with Amien on the box, waiting. He knew that he ought to go back, he ought to get back in and be carried back to the town, to his room, to Mrs Van der Vliet who was waiting for them immobile on the stoep in her black dress; yet this realisation evoked no feeling of urgency. There was enough time, he thought, there was now all the time in the world, and so he remained standing there, gazing out pensively and leaning on his cane.

The glimpses of the landscape that he had seen during his illness from his bedroom window had only partially prepared him for the change that had been wrought by the coming of winter. Just as the murkiness of turbid water would sink and settle, so every residual thing in this expanse had subsided to leave only this limpid emptiness. However stark the dusty panoramas of summer had been, they had still offered too much – colour, movement and sound – from which one could withdraw and, one by one, all of those things had been given up: the subtle shades of colour; the glint of the sun on the undulating grass; the murmuring and rustling of the vegetation and the distant, the low, drone of a myriad forms of life nurtured by the heat. All, all had gone, leaving behind a landscape as clear and transparent as glass, the veld bleached white beneath a pallid sky, in which nothing stood out any more except that distant black carriage with its horses and the coachman waiting on the box.

Once, when he had just arrived here; once, in another time when he had still been strange here, alienated from the country in which his stay, as he had thought, was to have been merely temporary – once, his walks in the evenings had taken him to the edge of the town and he had hesitated there, wavering before the landscape that had lain open before him, unknown and unknowable, and an inexplicable fear had filled him at the sight of that emptiness. But there was no cause for fear, he thought as he began to walk slowly and without hurrying back towards the landau, leaning on his cane. The emptiness absorbed you and silence embraced you, no longer as alien wastes to be regarded uncomprehendingly from a distance; the unknown land grew familiar and the person passing through could no longer even remember that he had once intended to travel further. Half-way along the route you discovered with some surprise that the journey had been completed, the destination already reached.